ACE

ODES AND EPODES

WITH INTRODUCTION AND NOTES BY

CHARLES E. BENNETT
PROFESSOR OF LATIN IN CORNELL UNIVERSITY

College Classical Series
ARISTIDE D. CARATZAS, PUBLISHER
NEW ROCHELLE, NEW YORK

Exact reprint of the original edition.
Reprinted 1988 by

Aristide D. Caratzas, Publisher
ORPHEUS PUBLISHING INC.

30 Church Street, P.O. Box 210
New Rochelle, N.Y. 10802
U.S.A.
(914) 632-8487

ISBN (PB) 0-89241-371-9
ISBN (CL) 0-89241-024-8

Dedicated to

PROFESSOR HIRAM CORSON

STAUNCH DEFENDER OF THE IDEAL

PREFACE.

For the text of this edition I have endeavored to make conscientious use of the available critical material. The notes owe much to the standard German commentators. Except in the rarest instances, I have consulted no American edition, valuable and important as some of these are.

To the many kind friends who have helped me with their criticisms I here make my grateful acknowledgments.

CHARLES E. BENNETT.

Ithaca, July, 1901.

INTRODUCTION TO THE ODES AND EPODES.

I.

HORACE'S LIFE.

1. Birth and Early Life. — Quintus Horatius Flaccus was born at the little town of Venusia, on the borders of Apulia and Lucania, December 8, 65 B.C. His father was a freedman, who seems to have been a collector of taxes. In this business he saved some money, and, dissatisfied with the advantages offered by the school at Venusia, took the young Horace to Rome for his early education. This plan evidently involved no little personal and financial sacrifice on the father's part — a sacrifice appreciated to the full by Horace, if not at the time, at least in his later life. In a touching passage almost unique in ancient literature (*Sat.* i. 6. 70 ff.), the poet tells us of the father's devotion at this period. Ambitious only for his son's mental and moral improvement, without a thought of the larger material prizes of life, he not only provided Horace with the best instruction the capital afforded, but watched with anxious care over the boy's moral training as well, even accompanying him to school and back again to his lodgings. One of Horace's teachers at this period was Orbilius, who is referred to in *Epist.* ii. 1. 70 as a severe disciplinarian (*plagosum*). Under Orbilius, Horace apparently pursued the grammatical studies which formed the staple of the literary training of the day. Later, he probably devoted attention to the more advanced rhetorical training; under what teacher is unknown.

2. Athens. — In his nineteenth year or thereabouts (*i.e.* about 46 B.C.), Horace went to Athens to add the finishing touches to his education by the study of philosophy, which still enjoyed a flourishing existence and was represented by several schools, — the Stoic, Epicurean, Peripatetic, and Academic. The Greek poets also engaged his attention largely. Among his friends at this time may be mentioned the young Cicero, son of the orator, and M. Valerius Messalla, who, with many other young Romans, were residing at Athens for the purpose of study.

3. Brutus and Philippi. — After some two years, the 'still air of delightful studies' was rudely agitated for Horace by political events. Caesar had been assassinated in March of 44 B.C., and, in September of that year, Brutus arrived in Athens, burning with the spirit of republicanism. Horace was easily induced to join his standard, and, though without previous military training or experience, received the important position of *tribunus militum* in Brutus's army. The battle of Philippi (November, 42 B.C.) sounded the death-knell of republican hopes, and left Horace in bad case. His excellent father had died, and the scant patrimony which would have descended to the poet had been confiscated by Octavian in consequence of the son's support of Brutus and Cassius.

4. Return to Rome. Beginning of Career as Man of Letters. Maecenas. The Sabine Farm. — Taking advantage of the general amnesty granted by Octavian, Horace returned to Rome in 41 B.C. and there secured a position as quaestor's clerk (*scriba*), devoting his intervals of leisure to composition in verse. He soon formed a warm friendship with Virgil, then just beginning his career as poet, and with

Varius; through their influence he was admitted (39 B.C.) to the intimacy and friendship of Maecenas, the confidential adviser of Octavian, and a generous patron of literature. About six years later (probably 33 B.C.), he received from Maecenas the Sabine Farm, situated some thirty miles to the northeast of Rome, in the valley of the Digentia, a small stream flowing into the Anio. This estate was not merely adequate for his support, enabling him to devote his entire energy to study and poetry, but was an unfailing source of happiness as well; Horace never wearies of singing its praises.

5. Horace's Other Friendships. — Horace's friendship with Maecenas, together with his own admirable social qualities and poetic gifts, won him an easy entrance into the best Roman society. His *Odes* bear eloquent testimony to his friendship with nearly all the eminent Romans of his time. Among these were: Agrippa, Octavian's trusted general, and later his son-in-law; Messalla, the friend of Horace's Athenian student days, and later one of the foremost orators of the age; Pollio, distinguished alike in the fields of letters, oratory, and arms. The poets Virgil and Varius have already been mentioned. Other literary friends were: Quintilius Varus, Valgius, Plotius, Aristius Fuscus, and Tibullus.

6. Relations with Augustus. — With the Emperor, Horace's relations were intimate and cordial. Though he had fought with conviction under Brutus and Cassius at Philippi, yet he possessed too much sense and patriotism to be capable of ignoring the splendid promises of stability and good government held out by the new régime inaugurated by Augustus. In sincere and loyal devotion to his sovereign, he not merely accepted the new order, but lent the best efforts of his verse to glorifying and strengthening it.

In the life of Horace attributed to Suetonius, we learn that Augustus offered the poet the position of private secretary. Horace, with dignified independence, declined the offer, a step that seems to have made no difference, however, in the cordial friendship with which Augustus continued to honor him.

He remained true to the Muse till his death, November 27, 8 B.C., a few days before the completion of his fifty-seventh year, and but a few weeks after the death of his patron and friend, Maecenas.

II.

HORACE'S WORKS.

7. **The Satires.** — Horace's first published work was Book I. of the *Satires*, which appeared in 35 B.C. Five years later, Book II. was published. Though conventionally called 'Satires,' and alluded to by Horace himself as *satirae*, these were entitled by him *Sermones*, as being talks, so to speak, couched in the familiar language of everyday life. They represent a type of literature whose early beginnings are obscure, but which is clearly an indigenous Roman product and not an imitation of Greek models, as is the case with almost every other type of Latin poetry. Horace was not the first representative of this kind of writing among the Romans. Ennius, Lucilius, and Varro had been his predecessors in the same field. Of these three, Lucilius beyond question exercised the greatest influence upon the poet. In Horace's hands, satire consists in the main of urbane comment upon the vices and foibles of the day, coupled with amusing incidents of personal experience and good-natured raillery at the defects of the prevailing philosophical systems, of which he was always an earnest and intelligent student. Besides this we have several pieces dealing directly with

the scope and function of satire as a species of literary composition.

8. **The Epodes.** — These were published in 29 B.C. and mark the transition from the *Satires* to the *Odes*. They resemble the *Satires* in their frequent polemic character, the *Odes* in the lyric form in which they are cast. Though published after the two books of the *Satires*, several of them apparently represent the earliest of Horace's efforts in verse that have been preserved.

9. **The Odes and Carmen Saeculare.** — Books I.–III. of the *Odes* were published in 23 B.C., when Horace was forty-two years old. Many of them had unquestionably been written several years before, some apparently as early as 32 B.C. These *Odes* at once raised Horace to the front rank of Roman poets, and assured his permanent fame. Six years later (17 B.C.), he was the natural choice of Augustus for the composition of the *Carmen Saeculare* to be sung at the saecular celebration held in that year. In 13 B.C. appeared Book IV. of the *Odes*. Though containing some of the poet's best work, this last book nevertheless bears certain traces of perfunctoriness. The Suetonian life of Horace records that it was written at the express request of the Emperor, a statement borne out by the lack of spontaneity characteristic of some of the poems.

10. **The Epistles and Ars Poetica.** — There are two books of *Epistles*. Book I. was published in 20 B.C., Book II. probably in 14 B.C. Of the epistles contained in Book I., some are genuine letters such as friend might write to friend; others are simply disquisitions in verse form on questions of life, letters, or philosophy. Book II. consists of but two epistles, one to Julius Florus, the other to Augustus. Both these pieces deal with questions of literary criticism and poetic composition.

The *Ars Poetica*, as it is conventionally designated, is an essay on the art of poetic composition — chiefly the drama. It is addressed to a certain Piso and his two sons, and Horace probably entitled it simply *Epistula ad Pisones*. The date of this composition is uncertain; but as it is one of the ripest, so it is probably one of the latest, if not the very latest, of all his extant writings. It is often printed as the third epistle of Book II.

11. Chronological Table of Horace's Works: —

35 B.C.	Satires, Book I.
30 B.C.	Satires, Book II.
29 B.C.	The Epodes.
23 B.C.	The Odes, Books I.–III.
20 B.C.	The Epistles, Book I.
17 B.C.	The Carmen Saeculare.
14 B.C.	The Epistles, Book II.
13 B.C.	The Odes, Book IV.
9 B.C. (?)	The Ars Poetica.

III.

MANUSCRIPTS, SCHOLIA, EDITIONS.

12. Manuscripts. — There are some two hundred and fifty manuscripts of Horace's works. No one of these is older than the eighth century, and most belong to the eleventh century and later. Among the most important manuscripts may be mentioned: —

V. Blandinius Vetustissimus. This manuscript, which once belonged to the Abbaye de St. Pierre on Mont Blandin (the modern Blankenberg), is now lost. It was destroyed by fire, together with the abbey, in 1566. But Cruquius (Jacques de Crusque), professor at Bruges, had previously examined it with care, and cites its readings with great frequency in his edition of 1577. Some critics have challenged the very existence of this manuscript, and have charged that Cruquius's citations of its alleged readings are forgeries. But while Cruquius is often guilty of carelessness and gross blunders, it is improbable that he was guilty of dishonesty, and most Horatian critics to-day recognize that *V* was a real manuscript, and that its readings as noted by Cruquius are of value.

B. Bernensis, 363, in the municipal library at Berne, Switzerland. This belongs to the ninth century, and has recently been published in an admirable photographic facsimile.

R. Sueco-Vaticanus, No. 1703, formerly the property of Queen Christina of Sweden, and now in the Vatican. This was written in the eighth century and, according to Keller, is the oldest of our extant manuscripts of Horace.

Keller attaches the greatest weight to these last two manuscripts, *B* and *R*, and holds that in nine cases out of ten their agreement points to the reading of the archetype of all our extant manuscripts.

No convincing classification of Horatian manuscripts has yet been made, and the great difficulties of the problem render extremely doubtful the eventual success of any such attempt.

13. Scholia. — Scholia are explanatory notes on the ancient writers. Sometimes these form separate works of elaborate scope; at other times they consist simply of additions made by copyists to the manuscripts themselves. Our Horatian scholia comprise the following: —

PORPHYRIO, a scholiast who lived probably in the early part of the third century A.D. and has left us an extensive commentary on all of Horace's writings.

PSEUDO-ACRON. This collection bears the name of Helenius Acron, who belonged perhaps in the third century of our era; but these scholia are not the work of Acron. His name apparently became attached to them only in late mediaeval times, as a result of the tradition that Acron was the author of certain scholia on Horace. These scholia of the pseudo-Acron are not even the work of a single hand, but are manifestly gathered from several sources.

Commentator Cruquianus. This is a collective name given to the scholia gathered by the Cruquius already mentioned from several manuscripts. They are relatively unimportant.

14. Editions. — Only a few of the most important editions are here given.

TEXTUAL.

Richard Bentley, 1711, and often reprinted.
Keller and Holder. Editio major. Leipzig. 1864–1870.
Keller and Holder. Editio minor. Leipzig. 1878.
Keller and Holder. Iterum recensuit Otto Keller. Vol. I. (*Odes, Epodes,* and *Carmen Saeculare*). Leipzig. 1899. Vol. II. (*Satires* and *Epistles*) has not yet appeared.
Otto Keller, *Epilegomena zu Horaz,* Leipzig. 1879–1880. An exhaustive presentation of variant readings, with discussion.

EXPLANATORY.

Complete Editions.

Orelli, Editio Quarta Major, Curaverunt Hirschfelder et Mewes. Berlin. 1886, 1892. With complete word index.
A. Kiessling. Berlin. 2d edition. 1890–1898. Vol. I. (*Odes* and *Epodes*) is now in 3d edition. 1898.
H. Schütz. Berlin. 1880–1883. Vol. I. (*Odes* and *Epodes*) is now in 3d edition. 1889.

Wickham. Oxford. Clarendon Press. *Odes* and *Epodes*, 3d edition. 1896. *Satires* and *Epistles*, 1891.
Page, Palmer, and Wilkins. London and New York. 1896.

Editions of Odes and Epodes.

K. K. Küster. Paderborn. 1890.
L. Müller. Leipzig. 1900.

Editions of Satires and Epistles.

G. T. A. Krüger. Leipzig. 14th edition. 1898, 1901.
L. Müller. Leipzig. 1891, 1893.

IV.

THE EPODES.

15. The Name. Sources. — The name *epodus* (Greek ἐπῳδός, lit. 'refrain') was first applied to the short verse following an iambic trimeter. Hence short poems written in similar metres came to be called epodes. The first to employ the epode as a form of literature was the Greek poet Archilochus of Paros (about 700 B.C.). In his hands the iambic epode was mainly a vehicle of invective, so that 'iambics' became synonymous with polemic or abusive poetry. In the *Epodes* Horace consciously followed Archilochus as a model. With a single exception all the *Epodes* have the epodic form (the first ten being iambic), and many of them are characterized also by the bitterness of feeling and expression traditionally connected with this form of composition.

CLASSIFICATION OF THE EPODES.

16. Invectives. — Of the seventeen poems in the *Epodes*, eight breathe the traditional spirit of Archilochus, and thus give the tone to the entire collection. One is directed against a disreputable person who had risen to wealth from slavery, and who now flaunts himself offensively in the eyes of decent people. Another heaps mock imprecations upon Maecenas, who, unluckily, had set before the poet a dish prepared with garlic that caused him a fit of indigestion. Two are directed against the sorceress Canidia. Another invokes the wrath of the elements upon the miserable poetaster Mevius as he sets sail for Greece.

17. Patriotic Poems. — The *Epodes* also give us tokens of the coming patriotic poems that were destined to form so conspicuous and successful a feature in the *Odes*. The seventh epode, written in 38 B.C. at a time of threatened renewal of civil strife, expresses horror at the thought of Rome 'perishing by her own right hand.' The eighth is a jubilant song of triumph at the news of Octavian's victory over Antony at Actium; while the sixteenth, written in the early years of the period following Caesar's assassination, deplores the civil war then threatening, and calls upon patriotic Romans to leave their fatherland, and set sail for the Happy Islands of the West.

18. Love Poems. — Here belong *Epodes* 11 and 15, dealing with the trials of unrequited love and the triumphs of unworthy rivals; also *Epode* 14, in which the tender passion is made responsible for Horace's failure to complete the Book of *Epodes* and send it to Maecenas.

19. Convivial. — Here may be put *Epode* 13, in which the raging tempest without is made to furnish an excuse for convivial enjoyment indoors.

20. Of the two remaining epodes, the first, which also serves as a dedication of the book, is an appeal to Maecenas to be permitted to accompany him to the East in Octavian's campaign against Antony; the second is a graceful idyl descriptive of the delights of country life.

V.

THE ODES.

21. Sources. — Horace's tastes had made him an earnest student of Greek literature, particularly of Greek poetry, and we thus find Greek models exercising the most potent influence over the form and content of his verse. So far as form is concerned, Horace's *Odes* are founded mainly on the measures employed by the Lesbian poets Alcaeus and Sappho (about 600 B.C.). In the content and motives of his *Odes*, as well as in many bits of phrase and epithet, he is also profoundly indebted to the same writers. But while the influence of Alcaeus and Sappho was paramount, as is not merely confessed but proudly boasted by Horace himself, there is scarcely one of the Greek poets to whom he is not indebted in some degree. To Homer and Pindar, Anacreon and Archilochus, Stesichorus and Bacchylides, his obligations are clear and often great, while the influence of the tragic poets, Aeschylus, Sophocles, and Euripides, was likewise considerable.

CLASSIFICATION OF HORACE'S ODES.

22. Gnomic Poems. — These deal with fundamental principles of life and conduct, and form one of the largest and most characteristic classes of Horace's *Odes*. Favorite motives are the uncertainty of life, the wisdom of a rational enjoyment of its pleasures, the cultivation of a spirit of tranquillity and contentment, and the observance of the 'golden mean.' The growing taste for luxurious living, and the spirit of greed that attend it, are also often touched upon. Special themes are the satisfaction of the gods with the spirit of the giver rather than the gift (iii. 23), and the superiority of the righteous man to all the buffetings of Fortune (iii. 29).

23. Patriotic Poems. — Horace's earnest patriotism and keen solicitude for the weal of the state, together with his personal devotion to Augustus and his faith in Augustus's wisdom, led him to devote his gifts to stimulating the national sense and quickening the national conscience. Some of the loftiest and most successful of his poems were the outcome of this purpose. Foremost in this class are to be ranked the six odes at the beginning of Book III., in which the poet emphasizes the cardinal Roman virtues that had made Rome great in the past, and to which, he urges, the rising generation must steadfastly cling in order to insure the perpetuation of that greatness for the future. These virtues are simplicity of living, endurance, fidelity, steadfastness of purpose in a righteous cause, a wise restraint, martial courage, piety, and purity. The horrors of civil war, already repeatedly touched upon in the *Epodes*, are treated again in the fine apostrophe to the ship of state (i. 14), while the song of triumph celebrating the victory of Actium (*Epode* 9) is far surpassed by the brilliant ode (i. 37) on the defeat and suicide of the Egyptian queen and her paramour.

24. In Praise of Augustus. — In the odes classed as patriotic poems, the name and fame of Augustus are also often incidentally alluded to, but there are many odes in which Augustus's glory is the exclusive theme. The fourth book in particular abounds in such, yet they are not lacking in the earlier books, especially Book I. Among the most successful are i. 2, addressed to Augustus as the hope and deliverer of the Roman state; i. 12, in which a review of 'the long glories of majestic Rome' culminates in a lofty tribute to the Emperor; also iv. 5 and 15, both of which recount the blessings of Augustus's sway, under which fertility, peace, honor, uprightness, and chastity reign everywhere.

25. Love Poems. — Love had been the most conspicuous theme in the Aeolic lyric poetry on which Horace's *Odes* are chiefly modelled. The love-poems of Alcaeus and Sappho, so far as we can judge from the scanty remains of their verse that have come down to us, were successful, because they dealt with genuine sentiment and genuine experience. Horace's passion, on the other hand, lacks, as a rule, every token of sincerity; in the case of those love-poems dealing with alleged experiences of his own, the reader with difficulty escapes the conclusion that the experience is fictitious, or else that the poet lacked all depth of feeling. Other poems of this category — and they are by far the more numerous — deal with the experiences of others. Many of these last are more successful, the gem of all being the little three-act drama in twenty-four verses in which estrangement passes to a happy reconciliation (iii. 9).

26. Convivial Poems. — Besides love, the two favorite themes of the Aeolic lyric poets were the praises of wine and of the gods. True to his models, Horace has a number of poems under each of these heads. Of the poems in praise of wine, perhaps the most striking is iii. 21, where its various beneficent effects are enumerated. Yet i. 18 urges that Bacchus's gift is not to be profaned, but is to be used with moderation.

27. Poems in Praise of Gods and Goddesses. — These include odes to Apollo and Diana, to Faunus, to Mercury, to the Muse, to Venus, and two stirring dithyrambics in honor of Bacchus (ii. 19; iii. 25).

28. Personal Poems. — Under this head fall those odes in which Horace gives definite expression to his own ambitions or records some item of personal experience. Thus, in i. 1, he aspires to excel in lyric composition; in i. 31 his prayer to the 'newly enshrined Apollo' is not for lands or gold, but for a contented spirit and an old age of honor and of song; ii. 13 tells of his escape from the falling tree. In ii. 20 and iii. 30 we have lofty prophecies of the poet's eternal fame.

29. **In Honor of Persons and Places.** — Here belong the poems celebrating the rustic beauties of the Sabine Farm (i. 17), the exquisite ode to the fount Bandusia (iii. 13), along with ii. 6, in praise of Tarentum. In ii. 12 we have a description of the personal charms of Terentia, the newly wedded wife of Maecenas. A part of iv. 9 also is devoted to the praise of the integrity of Lollius, a quality to which unfortunately his title is not altogether clear.

30. **The Glory of Poetry.** — Two odes, iv. 8 and the earlier part of iv. 9, are devoted to a glorification of the poet's function. ''Tis the poet that lends glory to the great; 'tis he that consigns heroes to the Happy Isles, and rescues virtue from oblivion.'

31. **Mythological Poems.** — Two poems (i. 15 and iii. 27) are but the elaboration of mythological themes, the *Flight of Paris with Helen* and the *Adventure of Europa*; iii. 11, also, is mainly taken up with an account of the Danaids, particularly of that Hypermnestra who, 'gloriously false to her perjured father,' spared the life of her lover.

32. **Miscellaneous.** — Nearly all of the odes will be felt to fall naturally under one or another of the foregoing classes. The few remaining pieces treat of miscellaneous themes. One is addressed to Pollio, who is venturing the rash experiment of writing a history of the civil wars. Another rallies Iccius on deserting philosophy for schemes of adventure in the East. Two celebrate the return of old comrades. Another is an invocation to the lyre; another a warning to Maecenas that, though welcome if he comes, he must expect plain fare at Horace's home.

33. Characterization of Horace as a Lyric Poet. — As a master of lyric form, Horace is unexcelled among Roman poets. In content, also, many of his odes represent the highest order of poetry. His patriotism was genuine, his devotion to Augustus was profound, his faith in the moral law was deep and clear. Wherever he touches on these themes, he speaks with conviction and sincerity, and rises often to a lofty level. But the very qualities of reason and reflection that made him successful here, naturally limited his success in treating of love and sentiment — the themes most frequently chosen for lyric treatment by other poets. On this account, he has not infrequently been challenged as without title to high poetic rank. But fortunately the question of his eminence is not an academic one. Generation after generation continues to own the spell of Horace's verse. So long as this is true, while recognizing his limitations and defects, we may properly ignore any theoretical discussions concerning the character of his lyric work.

VI.

LANGUAGE.

Forms.

34. *a*) About the time that Horace's *Odes* and *Epodes* were published, certain orthographical changes were being consummated in endings where *v*, *qu*, *u* were originally followed by *o* Horace, however, seems to have clung still to the older spelling in the case of the following endings: —

1) *-vos*, *-vom*, *-vont*, *vontur*, *e.g.* *flavos*, *flavom*, *solvont*, *solvontur*.

2) *-uos*, *-uom*, *-uont*, *-uontur*, *e.g.* *mutuos*, *mutuom*, *metuont*, *metuontur*.

3) *-quos*, *-quom*, *-quont*, *-quontur*, *e.g.* *iniquos*, *iniquom*, *relinquont*, *relinquontur*.

See also Bennett, *Appendix to Latin Grammar*, § 57. 1. *b–d*, for fuller details concerning the orthography of words of these classes.

b) Participles in *-ans* and *-ens* and *i*-stems usually have *-is* in the accusative plural masculine and feminine.

SYNTAX.[1]

THE NOUN.

35. The Accusative.

a) Horace is somewhat fond of employing the perfect passive participle with middle force and of combining with it an accusative of direct object, *e.g. Odes*, ix. 2. 31, **nube candentis umeros amictus**, *having veiled thy shining shoulders with a cloud.*

b) Neuter pronouns and neuter adjectives of number and amount are freely used by all writers as accusative of result produced (inner object). Horace, in common with other poets, extends this idiom farther and uses other adjectives freely in this relation, *e.g.* **dulce loquentem**, *sweetly prattling.*

36. The Dative.

a) The dative of agency occurs frequently with the perfect passive participle, as well as with the gerundive, *e.g. Odes*, i. 1. 24, **bella matribus detestata**, *wars hated by mothers.*

b) The dative is sometimes used to denote the direction, and even the limit, of motion, *e.g. Odes*, i. 24. 18, **nigro compulerit gregi**, *has gathered to his sable flock.*

c) In imitation of the Greek, the dative occurs frequently with verbs of *contending, differing, etc., e.g. Odes*, i. 3. 13, **Africum decertantem Aquilonibus**, *Africus fighting with Aquilo.*

---

[1] Under this head are considered only the most striking deviations from standard prose usage.

37. The Genitive.

a) The genitive is freely used to complete the meaning of many adjectives which in prose do not admit this construction, *e.g. Odes*, i. 22. 1, **integer vitae scelerisque purus**, *upright in life and free from guilt.*

b) In imitation of the Greek, the genitive is sometimes used to denote *separation, etc.*, *e.g. Odes*, iii. 27. 69, **abstineto irarum**, *refrain from anger!*

38. The Ablative.

a) The ablative of association occurs with verbs of *joining, mixing, changing*, and the like, *e.g. Odes*, iv. 9. 4, **verba socianda chordis**, *words to be linked with music.*

THE VERB.

39. Agreement. — Horace almost invariably uses a singular verb with a compound subject whose members are singular, *e.g. Odes*, ii. 13. 38, **Prometheus et Pelopis parens decipitur.**

40. The Tenses.

a) The gnomic perfect occasionally occurs. This is used of general truths, *e.g. Odes*, i. 34. 16, **hinc apicem rapax Fortuna sustulit**, *from this man Fortune takes away the crown.*

b) The perfect infinitive is sometimes used substantially with the force of the present, *e.g. Odes*, i. 1. 4, **pulverem Olympicum collegisse**, *to gather the Olympic dust.*

41. The Moods.

a) *Quamvis* with the indicative occurs occasionally, *e.g. Odes*, i. 28 (1), **quamvis concesserat**, *though he had yielded up.* If we omit two uncertain instances in Cicero and Nepos, this usage first appears in the Augustan poets, Virgil and Horace.

b) Clauses of characteristic following *sunt qui, est qui*, are sometimes in the indicative, *e.g. Odes*, i. 1. 3, **sunt quos iuvat.**

c) The infinitive is freely used with adjectives of the most various significations, to complete their meanings, *e.g. Odes*, iv. 2. 59, **niveus videri**.

d) The infinitive is occasionally used to denote purpose, *e.g. Odes*, i. 2. 8, **pecus egit altos visere montes**, *drove his flock to visit the lofty mountains.*

e) The infinitive without subject accusative occurs as object with a great variety of governing verbs that in prose do not admit this construction, *e.g. Odes*, i. 37. 22, **perire quaerens**.

42. Participles.

a) The future active participle, which in classical prose is regularly confined to combination with parts of the verb *esse* in the first periphrastic conjugation, occurs frequently in Horace, denoting purpose, inclination, or destiny, *e.g. Odes*, ii. 6. 1, **aditure**, *ready to go;* ii. 3. 4, **moriture**, *destined to die.*

b) The perfect passive participles of deponent verbs, regularly active in meaning, are not infrequently used passively, *e.g.* i. 1. 25, **detestata**, *hated.*

VII.

METRES.

Introductory.

GENERAL CHARACTER OF LATIN POETRY.

English poetry, as a rule, is based on *stress*, *i.e.* on a regular succession of accented and unaccented syllables. The versification of —

This is the forest primeval, the murmuring pines and the hemlocks,

depends entirely upon this alternation of accented and unaccented syllables, and the same thing is true of all ordinary English verse. This basis of English poetry, moreover, is a result of the very nature of the English language. Like all languages of the Teutonic group, our English speech is characterized by a strong word-accent.

Latin verse, on the other hand, was based on *quantity;* a line of Latin poetry consisted of a regular succession of long and short syllables, *i.e.* of syllables which it took a long or short time to pronounce. This basis of Latin poetry, as in the case of English poetry, is strictly in conformity with the character of the spoken language; for classical Latin was not a language in which there was a strong word-accent. The word-accent, in fact, must have been extremely weak. Different languages differ very greatly in this respect, and we ought to bear this fact in mind in thinking of Latin. In Latin, word-accent was so weak that it could not be made the basis of versification as it is in English, while, on the other hand, quantity was a strongly marked feature of the spoken language. Thus we see how it came about that quantity was made the basis of Latin verse, and why accent was not.

We are, then, to conceive of a line of Latin poetry as consisting simply of a regular arrangement of long and short syllables — nothing else. To read Latin poetry, therefore, it is necessary simply to pronounce the words with the proper quantity. This takes some patience and practice, but it is easily within the power of every pupil of Latin who can read Latin prose with quantitative accuracy. It is in Latin as in English: any one who can read prose with accuracy and fluency has no difficulty in reading poetry. The poet arranges the words in such wise that they make poetry of themselves, if they are only properly pronounced. No other kind of poetry was ever known in any language. No other is easily conceivable.

Of course it necessarily takes time for the student's ear

to become sensitive to quantitative differences and to acquire a feeling for the quantitative swing of Latin verse. Yet, with patience and abundant practice in careful pronunciation, the quantitative sense is bound to develop.

ICTUS.

Two views of ictus are held. According to one view, ictus is a stress accent. This makes Latin verse accentual precisely like English poetry. According to the other view, ictus is merely the quantitative prominence inherent in the long syllable of every fundamental foot, — the iambus, trochee, dactyl, and anapaest.

The editor of this volume advocates the second of these two theories,[1] as alone satisfying the conception of the quantitative character of Latin verse. For if ictus is stress, a dactyl, for example, becomes an accented syllable followed by two unaccented syllables, and Latin poetry thus depends for its rhythm upon accent, precisely like English verse; its rhythm thus has nothing to justify the quantitative character which its internal structure and all available evidence clearly show that it possessed.

It may take the student some time to appreciate the full force of the conception of ictus as simply quantity; but it is believed that careful and exact pronunciation will both make this definition plain, and do much to justify it.

WORD-ACCENT.

In reading Latin poetry, the ordinary accent of the words should not be neglected. But, as we have already seen above (p. xxv), the word-accent in Latin was exceedingly slight. We almost invariably accent Latin words altogether

---

[1] The full discussion of this view of ictus may be found in the *American Journal of Philology*, vol. xix. No. 76.

too strongly. As a result we destroy the quantity of the remaining syllables of a word. Thus, in a word like *ēvītābātur*, we are inclined to stress the penultimate syllable with such energy as to reduce the quantity of the vowel in each of the three preceding syllables. In this way the pupil says *ĕ-vĭ-tă-bā-tur*. Such a pronunciation is a fatal defect in reading. What we ought to do is to make the quantity prominent and the accent very slight. Where this is done, the accent will be felt to be subordinate to the quantity, as it ought to be, and as it must be if one is ever to acquire a feeling for the quantitative character of Latin poetry. If the quantity is not made more prominent than the accent, the accent is bound to be more prominent than the quantity, which will be fatal to the acquisition of a quantitative sense for the verse.

SPECIAL CAUTIONS TO BE OBSERVED IN ORDER TO SECURE CORRECT SYLLABIC QUANTITY IN READING.

Inasmuch as Latin poetry was based on the quantity of syllables, it is obvious that the greatest care must be taken in the pronunciation of the words with a view to securing an absolutely correct syllabic quantity. Otherwise the metrical (*i.e.* quantitative) character of the verse is violated, and the effect intended by the poet is lost. To ignore the proper quantity of the syllables is as disastrous in a line of Latin poetry as it would be in English poetry to misplace the word-accent. If one were to read the opening line of Longfellow's *Evangeline*, for example, as follows: —

Thís ís the forést prímeval

the result would be no more fatal than to read a line of Latin poetry with neglect of the quantity.

In reading Latin verse, there are two classes of errors to which the student is particularly liable, either one of which results in giving a wrong syllabic quantity.

Class First.

In 'Open'[1] Syllables.

Here the quantity of the syllable is always the same as the quantity of the vowel. Thus, in *mā-ter*, the first syllable is long; in *pă-ter*, the first syllable is short.

This being so, it is imperative that the pupil should in 'open' syllables scrupulously observe the quantity of the vowel. If he pronounces a short vowel long, or a long vowel short, he thereby gives a false quantity to the syllable, and thus wrecks the line completely. The pupil, therefore, must know the quantity of every vowel, and must pronounce in the light of his knowledge. He must not say *gērō, tērō, sērō* (for *gĕrō, tĕrō, sĕrō*); nor must he say *pāter, āger, nīsī, quōd, quībus, ingēnium, ēs* ('thou art'), *etc.* One such error in a verse is fatal to its metrical structure and the pupil who habitually commits such errors in reading is simply wasting valuable time.

Class Second.

In 'Closed'[2] Syllables.

It is a fundamental fact that a 'closed' syllable is long. But in order to be long it must *be actually closed in pronunciation.* Right here is where the pupil is apt to err.

---

[1] An 'open' syllable is one whose vowel is followed by a single consonant (or by a mute with *l* or *r*). This single consonant (or the mute with *l* or *r*) is joined with the vowel of the following syllable, thus leaving the previous syllable 'open.'

[2] A 'closed' syllable is one whose vowel is followed by two or more consonants (except a mute with *l* or *r*). The first of the two (or more) consonants is regularly joined in pronunciation with the preceding vowel, thus *closing* the preceding syllable. This is the real significance of the common rule that a syllable is long when a short vowel is followed by two consonants. It is because one of the consonants is joined to the preceding vowel, thus closing the syllable.

He fails to make the syllable 'closed,' *i.e.* he does not join the first of the two or more consonants to the *preceding* vowel, but joins all of the consonants with the *following* vowel. He thus leaves the preceding syllable 'open.' Hence, if the vowel itself is short, the syllable by this incorrect pronunciation is made short, where it ought to be made long. Thus the student is apt to say *tem-pe-stă-ti-bus* where he ought to say *tem-pes-tā-ti-bus, i.e.* he joins both the *s* and the *t* with the following vowel, where he ought to join the *s* with the preceding vowel (thus making a 'closed' syllable), and only the *t* with the following vowel.[1]

Errors of the kind referred to are so liable to occur that it seems best to classify them by groups: —

a) The commonest group consists of those words which contain a *short* vowel followed by doubled consonants (*pp, cc, tt, etc.*), — words of the type of *ap-parābat, ac-cipiēbam, at-tigerant, ges-sērunt, ter-rā-rum, an-nōrum, ad-diderat, flam-mārum, excel-lentia, ag-gerimus, etc.* In Latin, both of the doubled consonants were pronounced, one being combined with the previous vowel (thus closing the syllable and making it long), one with the following vowel. But in English we practically never have doubled consonants. We write them and print them, but we *do not pronounce* them. Thus, we write and print *kit-ty, fer-ry, etc.*, but we do not pronounce two *t*'s or two *r*'s in these words any more than in *pity*, which we write with one *t*, or in *very*, which we write with one *r*. Now, in pronouncing Latin the pupil is very apt to pronounce the doubled consonants of that language as single consonants, just as he does in English. Thus he naturally pronounces the words above

---

[1] This doctrine, to be sure, contradicts the rules given in grammars for division of words into syllables; but those rules apply only to writing, not to actual utterance. See Bennett, *Appendix to Latin Grammar*, § 35.

given, not *ap-pa-rā-bat, etc.*, but *ă-pa-rābat, ă-cipiēbam, ă-tigerant, gĕ-sērunt, tĕ-rārum, a-nōrum, ă-diderat, flă-mārum, excĕlentia, ă-gerimus.* In other words, the pupil pronounces only one consonant, where he ought to pronounce two, and that one consonant he joins with the following vowel. He thus leaves the preceding syllable 'open,' *i.e.* he makes it short when it ought to be long.

The effects of this pronunciation are disastrous in reading Latin poetry, for these doubled consonants occur on an average in every other line of Latin poetry.

b) The second group consists of words in which a short vowel is followed by *sp, sc, st*; also by *scl, scr, str*. In English, when the vowel following these combinations is accented, we usually combine the consonants with the following vowel. Thus we say *a-scríbe, a-stoúnding, etc.* Now, the Latin pupil is almost certain to do the same thing in pronouncing Latin, unless he is on his guard, *i.e.* he is likely to say *a-spérsus, i-stórum, tempe-stívus, coru-scābat, mi-scúerat, magi-strórum, a-scrípsit, etc.* What he ought to do is to join the *s* with the preceding vowel (thus making the syllable closed, and long), pronouncing *as-persus, is-tōrum, tempestīvus, corus-cābat, mis-cuerat, magis-trōrum, as-cripsit, etc.* By joining all the consonants to the following vowel he leaves the preceding syllable open. Hence, when the preceding vowel is short, the syllable also becomes short. This destroys the metre of the line.

c) The third group consists of words containing a short vowel followed by *r* and some consonant. In our common English utterance we are very apt to neglect the *r*. This tendency is all but universal in New England, and is widely prevalent in the Middle states. As a result, the pupil is apt to pronounce Latin with the same neglect of the *r* as he habitually practises in the vernacular. This omission occurs particularly where the preceding vowel is unaccented, *e.g.* in *portărum, terminorum, etc.* The pupil is likely to say *po(r)-tărum, te(r)-minorum, i.e.* he makes the preceding syllable 'open' and short, where it ought to be 'closed' and long. In order to close the syllable, a distinct articulation of the *r* is necessary. When this is overlooked, the quantity of the syllable is lost and the metrical character of the line is destroyed.

d) The fourth group of words consists of those ending in *s*, preceded by a short vowel and followed by words beginning with *c, p, t, v, m, n, f.* In English we are very apt to join the final *s* to the initial consonant of the following word. Thus we habitually say *grievou stale* for *grievous tale; Lewi sTaylor* for *Lewis Taylor, etc.* There is great danger of doing the same thing in Latin. Experience teaches that pupils often say *urbĭ sportās* for *urbis portās; capĭ scanem* for *capis canem;* even *urbĭ svīcī* for *urbis vīcī, etc.* Care must be taken to join the final *s* clearly with the preceding vowel. Otherwise the preceding syllable will be left 'open' and short where it ought to be 'closed' and long.

The foregoing cautions are not mere theoretical inventions. They are vital, and are based on experience of the errors which we as English-speaking people naturally commit when we pronounce Latin. It is only by a conscientious observance of the principles above laid down that any one can read Latin poetry quantitatively; and unless we do so read it, we necessarily fail to reproduce its true character.

Common Syllables.

As is well known, when a *short* vowel is followed by a mute with *l* or *r* (*pl, cl, tl; pr, cr, tr; etc.*), the syllable is common, *i.e.* it may be either long or short in verse at the option of the poet. The explanation of this peculiarity is as follows: —

In a word like *pătrem*, for example, it was recognized as legitimate to pronounce in two ways: either to combine the *tr* with the following vowel (*pa-trem*), thus leaving the preceding syllable 'open' and short, or to join the *t* with the preceding vowel (*patrem*), thus closing the preceding syllable and making it long. Hence, in the case of common syllables, the quantity in each individual instance depends upon the mode of pronunciation, *i.e.* the mode in which we divide the syllable. In reading Latin poetry, therefore, it will be necessary for the pupil to observe how the poet treats each common syllable, and to pronounce accordingly.

Elision.

The rule for Elision, as stated in our Latin grammars, is in substance as follows: "A final vowel, a final diphthong, or *m* with a preceding vowel,[1] is regularly elided before a word beginning with a vowel or *h*."

The exact nature of Elision, as observed by the ancients in reading Latin verse, is still very uncertain. The Romans may have slurred the words together in some way, or they may have omitted the elided part entirely. In practice, the latter procedure is probably the wiser one to follow.

Lyric Metres.

The various lyric metres employed by the Latin poets are, like the dactylic hexameter, imitated from the lyric metres of the Greeks. Greek lyric poetry, as its name implies, was primarily written for musical performance, *i.e.* for singing to the accompaniment of the lyre. Therefore, in the rendition of such poetry, the utterance of the words naturally conformed to the musical *tempo*. It accordingly not

[1] The elision of final *m* with a preceding vowel is sometimes called Ecthlipsis.

infrequently happened that the normal quantity of the syllables was either shortened or lengthened in order to secure such conformity. The performance of Greek lyric poetry, in other words, was entirely analogous to the performance of a modern song, in which a single syllable often extends in time over an entire measure, or even more.

Now, there is nothing to show that the Roman poets, in borrowing the lyric measures of the Greeks, employed them for the composition of poetry *which was intended to be sung to a musical accompaniment.* In fact, everything seems to point the other way, *viz.* to the fact that Roman lyric poetry was primarily intended for oral reading.[1] At all events, for the student the only practical thing is to *read* such poetry. He cannot sing it to a musical accompaniment, and the problem which confronts him is: How to read it.

Most of our American grammarians who touch on Latin prosody make Latin lyric metres conform to a strict musical notation. In carrying out this principle, they inculcate the frequent necessity of abnormally shortening some syllables and of abnormally lengthening others, as was above explained to be the regular practice in the rendition of Greek lyric poetry.

Thus, the opening line of Horace's first ode, in accordance with the doctrine alluded to, is divided as follows: —

— > | —◡ ◡ | ⌊ ‖ —◡ ◡ | — ◡ | ◡ ∧

Mae-cē|nās a-ta|vīs‖ē-di-te | rē-gi|bus

That is, the musical *tempo* of $\frac{3}{8}$ time is assumed as the basis of the construction of this poem, and the words are supposed to be artificially adapted to that movement. This is indicated by the notation above printed. The sign — > (the irrational spondee) indicates a spondee (really $\frac{4}{8}$) shortened

---

[1] The article by Otto Jahn in Hermes, ii, *Wie wurden die Oden des Horaz vorgetragen?* does not succeed in disproving this.

to $\frac{3}{8}$; —◡ ◡ (the cyclic dactyl) indicates a dactyl (really $\frac{4}{8}$), likewise shortened to $\frac{3}{8}$;[1] ⌞ is used to indicate that the long syllable (ordinarily $\frac{2}{8}$) is here equivalent to $\frac{3}{8}$; while the sign ∧ indicates a pause sufficient to prolong *-bus*, the final syllable (equal $\frac{1}{8}$), to the time of $\frac{3}{8}$. That is, in order, in reading, to make the verse conform to the prescribed musical notation, the student is obliged in every foot but one to introduce an artificial pronunciation at variance with the natural employment of the same words in everyday speech. Were the pupil *singing* the ode to musical accompaniment, such an artificiality would seem perfectly natural, since in singing the text is habitually made subordinate to the notes; but that in the *reading* of Latin lyric poetry there was any such artificial adaptation to a musical *tempo* is *a priori* inconceivable. No such process ever occurs in the poetry of any language. The poet simply takes the choicer words of familiar speech and employs them in their ordinary equivalence with their regular pronunciation. He must do so, for his appeal is to the many, not to a select handful who may have been initiated into the secret trick of his versification. In reading poetry in any language the reader gains sufficient consciousness of the metrical structure of the verse by pronouncing the words with their ordinary everyday values; he does not first hunt up the metrical scheme, and in his reading adapt the words to the scheme. So, too, one would naturally assume, it must have been in Latin.

Moreover, there is no evidence of any kind which intimates that the Romans did otherwise. The ancient grammarians, in fact, who wrote extensively on the subject of lyric poetry, particularly on the lyric metres of Horace, so far from suggesting a musical *tempo* as the basis of

---

[1] The exact distribution of the syllables is often explained by the musical notation .

lyric verse, group the syllables on entirely different principles.

· It would seem plain, therefore, that the Latin lyric poets, in adopting the *form* of Greek lyric poetry, did not also adopt the specifically *musical tempo* which, as above explained, was inherent in the musical lyric poetry of the Greeks.

Latin lyric poetry, accordingly, is to be read like poetry in any language. The reader is to pronounce the words with accuracy, endeavoring to attain a strictly quantitative pronunciation. If he does that, the metre will take care of itself, and an ear already accustomed to a correct quantitative reading of the dactylic hexameter will have no difficulty in at once apprehending the form of a Latin lyric even without the help of a metrical key; *i.e.* a correct pronunciation of the words in Latin, as in English, itself reveals the metrical structure of the verse; and the student who is curious to see the verse scheme set down in long and short syllables can easily deduce the scheme himself, and group the syllables into appropriate feet.

Rules for Reading.

1) Observe the quantity of each syllable scrupulously, taking care to observe the division of the syllables as indicated above, p. xxviii ff.

2) Make the word-accent light; subordinate it carefully to quantity.

3) Endeavor to cultivate the quantitative sense, *i.e.* to feel the verse as consisting of a succession of long and short intervals.

4) Do not attempt to give special expression to the *ictus* in any way. The *ictus* will care for itself if the syllables are properly pronounced.

Metres used by Horace.[1]

43. Alcaic Strophe.[2]

⏓ | – ⏑ | – – ‖ – ⏑ ⏑ | – ⏑ | ⏓ (twice)
⏓ | – ⏑ | – – | – ⏑ | – ⏓
– ⏑ ⏑ | – ⏑ ⏑ | – ⏑ | – ⏓

In the first two lines a diaeresis regularly occurs after the second complete foot, but this is sometimes neglected, *e.g.* *Odes*, i. 37. 14; iv. 14. 17.

The extra syllable at the beginning of the first three lines of each stanza is called an anacrusis.

This metre occurs in *Odes*, i. 9. 16. 17. 26. 27. 29. 31. 34. 35. 37; ii. 1. 3. 5. 7. 9. 11. 13. 14. 15. 17. 19. 20; iii. 1–6. 17. 21. 23. 26. 29; iv. 4. 9. 14. 15.

44. Sapphic and Adonic.[3]

– ⏑ | – – | – ‖ ⏑ ⏑ | – ⏑ | – ⏓ (three times)
– ⏑ ⏑ | – ⏓

The regular caesura of the first three lines falls after the long syllable of the dactyl; but a feminine caesura, after the first short of the dactyl, sometimes occurs. This is especially frequent in Book IV. of the *Odes*, and in the *Carmen Saeculare*.

Now and then we find a hypermetric verse, *e.g.* *Odes*, ii. 16. 34.

---

[1] For those who adhere to the theory of a musical tempo for Latin lyric poetry, alternative metrical schemes are given at the foot of the page.

[2] **43.** ⏓ ⁝ – ⏑ | – > ‖ ⌐⏑ ⏑ | – ⏑ | – ∧ (twice)
⏓ ⁝ – ⏑ | – > | – ⏑ | – ⏓
⌐⏑ ⏑ | ⌐⏑ ⏑ | – ⏑ | – ⏓

For the notation used in these schemes, see p. **xxxiii f.**

[3] **44.** – ⏑ | – > | – ‖ ⏑⏑ | – ⏑ | – ⏓ (three times)
⌐⏑ ⏑ | – ⏓

This metre occurs in *Odes*, i. 2. 10. 12. 20. 22. 25. 30. 32. 38; ii. 2. 4. 6. 8. 10. 16; iii. 8. 11. 14. 18. 20. 22. 27; iv. 2. 6. 11; *Carmen Saeculare.*

45. First Asclepiadean.[1]

— — | — ∪ ∪ | — ‖ — ∪ ∪ | — ∪ | ⏓

A diaeresis regularly occurs after the sixth syllable of the verse, but exceptions occur in *Odes*, ii. 12. 25, and iv. 8. 17.

This metre occurs in *Odes*, i. 1; iii. 30; iv. 8.

46. Second Asclepiadean.[2]

— — | — ∪ ∪ | — ∪ | ⏓
— — | — ∪ ∪ | — ‖ — ∪ ∪ | — ∪ | ⏓

The second line of the couplet is the First Asclepiadean. The special name Glyconic is given to the metre of the first line.

This metre occurs in *Odes*, i. 3. 13. 19. 36; iii. 9. 15. 19. 24. 25. 28; iv. 1. 3.

47. Third Asclepiadean.[3]

— — | — ∪ ∪ | — ‖ — ∪ ∪ | — ∪ | ⏓ (three times)
— — | — ∪ ∪ | — ∪ | ⏓

This consists of the First Asclepiadean and the Glyconic.

This metre occurs in *Odes*, i. 6. 15. 24. 33; ii. 12; iii. 10. 16; iv. 5. 12.

48. Fourth Asclepiadean.[4]

— — | — ∪ ∪ | — ‖ — ∪ ∪ | — ∪ | ⏓ (twice)
— — | — ∪ ∪ | — ⏓
— — | — ∪ ∪ | — ∪ | ⏓

---

[1] 45. — > | ⌐∪ ∪ | └ ‖ ⌐∪ ∪ | — ∪ | — Λ

[2] 46. — > | ⌐∪ ∪ | — ∪ | — Λ
— > | ⌐∪ ∪ | └ ‖ ⌐∪ ∪ | — ∪ | ⏓ Λ

[3] 47. — > | ⌐∪ ∪ | └ ‖ ⌐∪ ∪ | — ∪ | ⏓ Λ (three times)
— > | ⌐∪ ∪ | — ∪ | — Λ

[4] 48. — > | ⌐∪ ∪ | └ ‖ ⌐∪ ∪ | — ∪ | — Λ (twice)
— > | ⌐∪ ∪ | └ | — Λ
— > | ⌐∪ ∪ | — ∪ | — Λ

The first two lines are the First Asclepiadean. The third is called Pherecratean. The fourth is the Glyconic.

This metre occurs in *Odes*, i. 5. 14. 21. 23; iii. 7. 13; iv. 13.

49. Fifth Asclepiadean.[1]

— — | — ∪ ∪ | — ‖ — ∪ ∪ | — ‖ — ∪ ∪ | — ∪ | ⏒

This metre occurs in *Odes*, i. 11. 18; iv. 10.

50. Iambic Trimeter. — The strict scheme is: —

∪ — | ∪ — | ∪ ‖ — | ∪ — | ∪ — | ∪ —;

but the spondee is occasionally substituted for the iambus in the odd feet of the verse, and at times even other substitutes occur, *e.g.* the tribrach (∪ ∪ ∪), dactyl, and rarely the anapaest (∪ ∪ —). A caesura regularly occurs after the short syllable of the third foot (penthemimeral caesura), less frequently after the short syllable of the fourth foot (hepthemimeral caesura).

This metre occurs in *Epode* 17.

51. Iambic Strophe.

∪ — | ∪ — | ∪ ‖ — | ∪ — | ∪ — | ∪ —
∪ — | ∪ — | ∪ — | ∪ —

This consists of the iambic trimeter (see § 50) followed by the iambic dimeter, which admits the same substitutes as the trimeter.

This metre occurs in *Epodes* 1–10.

52. Alcmanic Strophe.

— ∪ ∪ | — ∪ ∪ | — ‖ ∪ ∪ | — ∪ ∪ | — ∪ ∪ | — ⏒
— ∪ ∪ | — ∪ ∪ | — ∪ ∪ | — ⏒

This consists of the dactylic hexameter followed by a dactylic tetrameter. The spondee is freely substituted for the dactyl as in Virgil.

This metre occurs in *Odes*, i. 7. 28; *Epode* 12.

---

[1] **49.** — > | —∪ ∪ | ⌞ ‖ —∪ ∪ | ⌞ ‖ —∪ ∪ | — ∪ | — ∧

53. First Pythiambic.

– ∪ ∪ | – ∪ ∪ | – ‖ ∪ ∪ | – ∪ ∪ | – ∪ ∪ | – ⏓
∪ – | ∪ – | ∪ – | ∪ –

A dactylic hexameter followed by an iambic dimeter (§ 51).

This metre occurs in *Epodes* 14, 15.

54. Second Pythiambic.

– ∪ ∪ | – ∪ ∪ | – ‖ ∪ ∪ | – ∪ ∪ | – ∪ ∪ | – ⏓
∪ – | ∪ – | ∪ ‖ – | ∪ – | ∪ – | ∪ –

A dactylic hexameter followed by an iambic trimeter (§ 50). In this metre no substitutes for the iambus are permitted.

This metre occurs in *Epode* 16.

55. First Archilochian.

– ∪ ∪ | – ∪ ∪ | – ‖ ∪ ∪ | – ∪ ∪ | – ∪ ∪ | – ⏓
– ∪ ∪ | – ∪ ∪ | –

A dactylic hexameter followed by a dactylic trimeter catalectic ('stopping short').

This metre occurs in *Odes*, iv. 7.

56. Second Archilochian.

– ∪ ∪ | – ∪ ∪ | – ‖ ∪ ∪ | – ∪ ∪ | – ∪ ∪ | – ⏓
∪ – | ∪ – | ∪ – | ∪ – ‖ – ∪ ∪ | – ∪ ∪ | –

A dactylic hexameter followed by a line consisting of an iambic dimeter combined with a dactylic trimeter catalectic (§ 55). In the first and third feet of the dimeter the spondee may take the place of the iambus.

This metre occurs in *Epode* 13.

57. Third Archilochian.

∪ ⏒ | ∪ – | ∪ ‖ – | ∪ – | ∪ – | ∪ –
– ∪ ∪ | – ∪ ∪ | – ‖ ∪ – | ∪ – | ∪ – | ∪ –

The first line is an iambic trimeter (§ 50). The second is the same as the second line of the Second Archilochian (§ 56), with the two parts reversed.

This metre occurs in *Epode* 11.

58. Fourth Archilochian Strophe.

— ⏑ ⏑ | — ⏑ ⏑ | — ‖ ⏑ ⏑ | — ⏑ ⏑ | — ⏑ | — ⏑ | — ⏑
⏑ — | ⏑ — | ⏑ ‖ — | ⏑ — | ⏑ — | ⏑

The first line is called a greater Archilochian, and admits the substitution of the spondee for the dactyl in the first three feet. The second line is an iambic trimeter catalectic ('stopping short'); *cf.* § 50.

This metre occurs in *Odes*, i. 4.

59. Second Sapphic Strophe.[1]

— ⏑ ⏑ | — ⏑ | — ⏓
— ⏑ | — — | — ‖ ⏑ ⏑ | — | — ⏑ ⏑ | — ⏑ | — ⏓

A so-called Aristophanic verse, followed by a greater Sapphic.

This metre occurs in *Odes*, i. 8.

60. Trochaic Strophe.

— ⏑ | — ⏑ | — ⏑ | —
⏑ — | ⏑ — | ⏑ — | ⏑ — | ⏑ — | ⏒

A so-called Euripidean verse, followed by an iambic trimeter catalectic ('stopping short'); *cf.* § 50.

This metre occurs in *Odes*, ii. 18.

61. Ionic a Minore.

⏑ ⏑ — — | ⏑ ⏑ — — | ⏑ ⏑ — — | ⏑ ⏑ ‐ ‐ — (twice)
⏑ ⏑ — — | ⏑ ⏑ — —

This metre occurs in *Odes*, iii. 12.

---

[1] 59. ⏖ ⏑ | — ⏑ | — ⏑
— ⏑ | — > | — ‖ ⏕ | ∟ ‖ ⏖ ⏑ | — ⏑ | — ⏑

Q. HORATI FLACCI
CARMINUM
LIBER PRIMUS.

I.

DEDICATION OF THE FIRST THREE BOOKS OF THE ODES TO MAECENAS.

1. Outline of the Poem: The poet enumerates some of the chief ambitions and pursuits of mankind, in order to bring out more clearly by contrast the nature of his own aspirations:

a) Some seek the glory of victory in the public games, 1–6;
b) Others aim at political distinction or success in trade, 7–18;
c) Self-indulgence, war, and hunting furnish attractions for others, 19–28;
d) As for Horace, his aspiration is to excel in poetry, more particularly in lyric composition, 29–36.

2. Time: 23 B.C.

3. Metre: First Asclepiadean. Introd. § 45.

Maecēnas atavis edite regibus,
O et praesidium et dulce decus meum,
Sunt quos curriculo pulverem Olympicum
Collegisse iuvat metaque fervidis
Evitata rotis palmaque nobilis
Terrarum dominos evehit ad deos;
Hunc, si mobilium turba Quirītium
Certat tergeminis tollere honoribus;

Illum, si proprio condidit horreo,
Quicquid de Libycis verritur areis.
Gaudentem patrios findere sarculo
Agros Attalicis condicionibus
Numquam demoveas, ut trabe Cypria
Myrtoum pavidus nauta secet mare.
Luctantem Icariis fluctibus Africum
Mercator metuens otium et oppidi
Laudat rura sui; mox reficit rates
Quassas, indocilis pauperiem pati.
Est qui nec veteris pocula Massici
Nec partem solido demere de die
Spernit, nunc viridi membra sub arbuto
Stratus, nunc ad aquae lene caput sacrae.
Multos castra iuvant et lituo tubae
Permixtus sonitus bellaque matribus
Detestata. Manet sub Iove frigido
Venator tenerae coniugis immemor,
Seu visa est catulis cerva fidelibus,
Seu rupit teretes Marsus aper plagas.
Me doctarum hederae praemia frontium
Dis miscent superis, me gelidum nemus
Nympharumque leves cum Satyris chori
Secernunt populo, si neque tibias
Euterpe cohibet nec Polyhymnia
Lesboum refugit tendere barbiton.
Quodsi me lyricis vatibus inseris,
Sublimi feriam sidera vertice.

II.

TO AUGUSTUS, THE DELIVERER AND HOPE OF THE STATE.

1. Occasion of the Poem: In January, 27 B.C., Octavian, who had just entered upon his seventh consulship, suddenly announced his intention of resigning the extraordinary powers with which he had previously been invested, and which he had exercised so effectively for the restoration and maintenance of public order. This announcement, though probably intended merely as a test of public opinion, was sufficient to arouse the keenest solicitude on the part of all patriotic citizens. Added to this, fierce storms had just visited the city, and the Tiber had risen in a wild flood above its banks. These portents naturally intensified the existing feeling, to which Horace gives eloquent expression in this ode.

2. Outline of the Poem:

a) Distress at the recent portents, 1–20;
b) Causes of the gods' displeasure, — the horrors of the civil wars, 21–24;
c) Who is the destined deliverer of the state? Is it Apollo? Or Venus? Or Mars? Or is it Mercury in the guise of Augustus? 25–44;
d) May Augustus long live to direct the destinies of Rome, 45–52.

3. Time: January, 27 B.C.

4. Metre: Sapphic and Adonic. Introd. § 44.

Iam satis terris nivis atque dirae
Grandinis misit Pater et rubente
Dextera sacras iaculatus arces
Terruit urbem,

Terruit gentis, grave ne rediret
Saeculum Pyrrhae nova monstra questae,
Omne cum Proteus pecus egit altos
Visere montes,

Piscium et summa genus haesit ulmo,
Nota quae sedes fuerat columbis,

Et superiecto pavidae natarunt
 Aequore dammae.

Vidimus flavom Tiberim, retortis
Litore Etrusco violenter undis,
Ire deiectum monumenta regis
 Templaque Vestae,

Iliae dum se nimium querenti
Iactat ultorem, vagus et sinistra
Labitur ripa, Iove non probante, ux-
 orius amnis.

Audiet civis acuisse ferrum,
Quo graves Persae melius perirent,
Audiet pugnas vitio parentum
 Rara iuventus.

Quem vocet divom populus ruentis
Imperi rebus? Prece qua fatigent
Virgines sanctae minus audientem
 Carmina Vestam?

Cui dabit partis scelus expiandi
Iuppiter? Tandem venias, precamur,
Nube candentis umeros amictus,
 Augur Apollo;

Sive tu mavis, Erycīna ridens,
Quam Iocus circum volat et Cupido;
Sive neclectum genus et nepotes
 Respicis, auctor,

Heu nimis longo satiate ludo,
Quem iuvat clamor galeaeque leves
Acer et Marsi peditis cruentum
 Voltus in hostem.

Sive mutata iuvenem figura
Ales in terris imitaris almae
Filius Maiae, patiens vocari
    Caesaris ultor:

Serus in caelum redeas, diuque
Laetus intersis populo Quirīni
Neve te nostris vitiis iniquom
    Ocior aura

Tollat;. hic magnos potius triumphos,
Hic ames dici pater atque princeps,
Neu sinas Medos equitare inultos,
    Te duce, Caesar.

III.

TO VIRGIL, SETTING OUT FOR GREECE.

1. **Outline of the Poem**:
   a) The poet wishes his friend a prosperous voyage, 1–8;
   b) Courage of him who first braved the perils of the deep, 9–20;
   c) Man's restless enterprise has ever led him to transgress proper bounds; consequences of this, 21–40.
2. **Time**: Uncertain; not after 23 B.C.
3. **Metre**: Second Asclepiadean. Introd. § 46.

Sic te diva potens Cypri,
  Sic fratres Helenae, lucida sidera,
Ventorumque regat pater
  Obstrictis aliis praeter Iāpyga,

Navis, quae tibi creditum
  Debes Vergilium; finibus Atticis
Reddas incolumem, precor,
  Et serves animae dimidium meae.

Illi robur et aes triplex
Circa pectus erat, qui fragilem truci
Commisit pelago ratem
Primus, nec timuit praecipitem Africum

Decertantem Aquilonibus
Nec tristis Hyadas nec rabiem Noti,
Quo non arbiter Hadriae
Maior, tollere seu ponere volt freta.

Quem mortis timuit gradum,
Qui siccis oculis monstra natantia,
Qui vidit mare turbidum et
Infamis scopulos, Acroceraunia?

Nequiquam deus abscidit
Prudens Oceano dissociabili
Terras, si tamen impiae
Non tangenda rates transiliunt vada.

Audax omnia perpeti
Gens humana ruit per vetitum nefas.
Audax Iapeti genus
Ignem fraude mala gentibus intulit.

Post ignem aetheria domo
Subductum macies et nova febrium
Terris incubuit cohors,
Semotique prius tarda necessitas

Leti corripuit gradum.
Expertus vacuom Daedalus aëra
Pinnis non homini datis;
Perrupit Acheronta Herculeus labor.

Nil mortalibus ardui est;
  Caelum ipsum petimus stultitia, neque
Per nostrum patimur scelus
  Iracunda Iovem ponere fulmina.

IV.

SPRING'S LESSON.

1. **Outline of the Poem:**

   a) Winter has fled; spring with its delights is again at hand, 1–12;
   b) Yet death comes sure to all, nor may we cherish hopes of a long existence here, 13–20.

2. **Time:** Probably 23 B.C.

3. **Metre:** Fourth Archilochian Strophe. Introd. § 58.

Solvitur acris hiems grata vice veris et Favoni,
  Trahuntque siccas machinae carinas,
Ac neque iam stabulis gaudet pecus aut arator igni,
  Nec prata canis albicant pruinis.

Iam Cytherēa choros ducit Venus imminente luna,
  Iunctaeque Nymphis Gratiae decentes
Alterno terram quatiunt pede, dum gravis Cyclōpum
  Volcanus ardens visit officinas.

Nunc decet aut viridi nitidum caput impedire myrto
  Aut flore, terrae quem ferunt solutae;
Nunc et in umbrosis Fauno decet immolare lucis,
  Seu poscat agna sive malit haedo.

Pallida Mors aequo pulsat pede pauperum tabernas
  Regumque turris. O beate Sesti,
Vitae summa brevis spem nos vetat incohare longam.
  Iam te premet nox fabulaeque Manes

Et domus exilis Plutonia; quo simul mearis,
Nec regna vini sortiere talis,
Nec tenerum Lycidan mirabere, quo calet iuventus
Nunc omnis et mox virgines tepebunt.

V.

TO A FLIRT.

1. Outline of the Poem:

a) What youth now courts thee, Pyrrha? 1–5;
b) Alas! he little knows how inconstant is thy fancy, 5–13;
c) I am thankful to have escaped betimes, 13–16.

2. Time: Uncertain; not after 23 B.C.

3. Metre: Fourth Asclepiadean. Introd. § 48.

Quis multa gracilis te puer in rosa
Perfusus liquidis urget odoribus
Grato, Pyrrha, sub antro?
Cui flavam religas comam,

Simplex munditiis? Heu quotiens fidem
Mutatosque deos flebit et aspera
Nigris aequora ventis
Emirabitur insolens,

Qui nunc te fruitur credulus aurea,
Qui semper vacuam, semper amabilem
Sperat, nescius aurae
Fallacis. Miseri, quibus

Intemptata nites. Me tabula sacer
Votiva paries indicat uvida
Suspendisse potenti
Vestimenta maris deo.

VI.

HORACE PLEADS HIS INABILITY WORTHILY TO SING THE PRAISES OF AGRIPPA.

1. **Occasion of the Poem**: Agrippa had asked Horace to write an epic poem in celebration of his own military successes and those of Octavian.

2. **Outline of the Poem**:

   a) Varius is the poet fittingly to celebrate thy achievements, Agrippa, 1–4;
   b) My lyric muse is unequal to epic themes, 5–16;
   c) Wine and love are the subjects of my song, 17–20.

3. **Time**: 29 B.C., or soon after.

4. **Metre**: Third Asclepiadean. Introd. § 47.

Scriberis Vario fortis et hostium
Victor, Maeonii carminis aliti,
Quam rem cumque ferox navibus aut equis
  Miles te duce gesserit.

Nos, Agrippa, neque haec dicere nec gravem
Pelidae stomachum cedere nescii
Nec cursus duplicis per mare Ulixei
  Nec saevam Pelopis domum

Conamur, tenues grandia, dum pudor
Imbellisque lyrae Musa potens vetat
Laudes egregii Caesaris et tuas
  Culpa deterere ingeni.

Quis Martem tunica tectum adamantina
Digne scripserit aut pulvere Troico
Nigrum Merionen aut ope Palladis
  Tydiden superis parem?

Nos convivia, nos proelia virginum
Sectis in iuvenes unguibus acrium
Cantamus, vacui, sive quid urimur,
Non praeter solitum leves.

VII.

FAIREST OF SPOTS, O PLANCUS, IS TIBUR. THERE, OR WHEREVER YOU MAY BE, DROWN CARE IN WINE.

1. **Outline of the Poem:**
   - *a*) Earth has many fair spots, — Rhodes, Mytilene, Ephesus, Corinth, Thebes, Tempe's vale, Athens, Argos, and Mycenæ, — but fairest of all is Tibur by the falls of the dashing Anio, 1–14;
   - *b*) Nature is not always sad; nor should man be, Plancus; so at your favorite Tibur (or wherever you may be) away with sorrow! Seek in mellow wine consolation for care! 15–21;
   - *c*) So did Teucer, when driven by Telamon from his native Salamis, 21–32.
2. **Time:** Uncertain; possibly as early as 32 B.C.
3. **Metre:** Alcmanic Strophe. Introd. § 52.

Laudabunt alii claram Rhodon aut Mytilēnen
Aut Ephesum bimarisve Corinthi
Moenia vel Baccho Thebas vel Apolline Delphos
Insignis aut Thessala Tempe.

Sunt quibus unum opus est, intactae Palladis urbem
Carmine perpetuo celebrare et
Undique decerptam fronti praeponere olivam.
Plurimus in Iunonis honorem

Aptum dicet equis Argos ditesque Mycēnas.
Me nec tam patiens Lacedaemon
Nec tam Larīsae percussit campus opimae,
Quam domus Albuneae resonantis

Et praeceps Anio ac Tiburni lucus et uda
Mobilibus pomaria rivis.
Albus ut obscuro deterget nubila caelo
Saepe Notus neque parturit imbris

Perpetuos, sic tu sapiens finire memento
Tristitiam vitaeque labores
Molli, Plance, mero, seu te fulgentia signis
Castra tenent seu densa tenebit

Tiburis umbra tui. Teucer Salamina patremque
Cum fugeret, tamen uda Lyaeo
Tempora populea fertur vinxisse corona,
Sic tristis adfatus amicos:

'Quo nos cumque feret melior fortuna parente,
Ibimus, o socii comitesque!
Nil desperandum Teucro duce et auspice Teucro!
Certus enim promisit Apollo

Ambiguam tellure nova Salamina futuram.
O fortes peioraque passi
Mecum saepe viri, nunc vino pellite curas;
Cras ingens iterabimus aequor.'

VIII.

SYBARIS'S INFATUATION FOR LYDIA.

1. **Outline of the Poem**:
   a) Lydia, why wilt thou ruin Sybaris by love? 1–3;
   b) Why has he abandoned all manly sports,—riding, swimming, and the discus? 3–12;
   c) Why is he skulking, as did once Achilles? 13–16.
2. **Time**: Uncertain; not after 23 B.C.
3. **Metre**: Second Sapphic Strophe. Introd. § 59.

Lydia, dic, per omnis
  Te deos oro, Sybarin cur properes amando
Perdere; cur apricum
  Oderit campum, patiens pulveris atque solis:

Cur neque militaris
  Inter aequalis equitet, Gallica nec lupatis
Temperet ora frenis.
  Cur timet flavom Tiberim tangere? Cur olivom

Sanguine viperino
  Cautius vitat, neque iam livida gestat armis
Bracchia, saepe disco,
  Saepe trans finem iaculo nobilis expedito?

Quid latet, ut marinae
  Filium dicunt Thetidis sub lacrimosa Troiae
Funera, ne virilis
  Cultus in caedem et Lycias proriperet catervas?

IX.

WINTER WITHOUT BIDS US MAKE MERRY WITHIN.

1. **Outline of the Poem:**

   a) The snow is deep; the frost is keen, 1–4;
   b) Pile high the hearth and bring out old wine, 5–8;
   c) Leave all else to the gods, 9–12;
   d) Think not of the morrow, but enjoy what fortune bestows, — love, the dance, and the other delights of youth, 13–24.

2. **Time**: Uncertain; not after 23 B.C.

3. **Metre**: Alcaic. Introd. § 43.

Like *Epode* 13, this ode is an imitation of a fragment of Alcaeus, and is thought to belong among the earliest of Horace's lyric compositions.

Vides ut alta stet nive candidum
Soracte, nec iam sustineant onus
  Silvae laborantes, geluque
    Flumina constiterint acuto.

Dissolve frigus ligna super foco
Large reponens atque benignius
  Deprome quadrimum Sabina,
    O Thaliarche, merum diota.

Permitte divis cetera, qui simul
Stravere ventos aequore fervido
  Deproeliantis, nec cupressi
    Nec veteres agitantur orni.

Quid sit futurum cras, fuge quaerere et
Quem Fors dierum cumque dabit, lucro
  Appone nec dulcis amores
    Sperne puer neque tu choreas,

Donec virenti canities abest
Morosa. Nunc et campus et areae
  Lenesque sub noctem susurri
    Composita repetantur hora,

Nunc et latentis proditor intumo
Gratus puellae risus ab angulo
  Pignusque dereptum lacertis
    Aut digito male pertinaci.

X.

HYMN TO MERCURY.

1. **Outline of the Poem:**
   - *a*) Thou, Mercury, didst endow primitive man with speech, and didst institute the palaestra, 1–4;
   - *b*) Thou didst invent the lyre, and wast ever clever to deceive, 5–12;
   - *c*) Thou wast Priam's trusty guide at Troy, and art the trusty messenger, not only of the gods above, but of those below as well, 13–20.
2. **Time:** Uncertain; not after 23 B.C.
3. **Metre:** Sapphic and Adonic. Introd. § 44.

Mercuri, facunde nepos Atlantis,
Qui feros cultus hominum recentum
Voce formasti catus et decorae
  More palaestrae,

Te canam, magni Iovis et deorum
Nuntium curvaeque lyrae parentem,
Callidum, quicquid placuit, iocoso
  Condere furto.

Te, boves olim nisi reddidisses
Per dolum amotas, puerum minaci
Voce dum terret, viduos pharetra
  Risit Apollo.

Quin et Atrīdas duce te superbos
Ilio dives Priamus relicto
Thessalosque ignis et iniqua Troiae
  Castra fefellit.

Tu pias laetis animas reponis
Sedibus virgaque levem coerces
Aurea turbam, superis deorum
  Gratus et imis.

XI.

'CARPE DIEM.'

1. **Outline of the Poem** :
   a) Seek not to learn by signs, Leuconoë, what limit of life the gods have granted thee, 1–6;
   b) Follow thy humble duties; enjoy the present hour, and put no trust in the future, 6–8.
2. **Time** : Uncertain; not after 23 B.C.
3. **Metre** : Fifth Asclepiadean. Introd. § 49.

Tu ne quaesieris — scire nefas — quem mihi, quem tibi
Finem di dederint, Leuconoë, nec Babylonios
Temptaris numeros. Ut melius, quicquid erit, pati!
Seu plures hiemes, seu tribuit Iuppiter ultimam,
Quae nunc oppositis debilitat pumicibus mare
Tyrrhenum. Sapias, vina liques, et spatio brevi
Spem longam reseces. Dum loquimur, fugerit invida
Aetas: carpe diem, quam minimum credula postero.

XII.

THE PRAISES OF AUGUSTUS.

1. **The Probable Occasion of the Ode**: In the year 24 B.C. Augustus adopted his nephew Marcellus as his son and gave him his daughter Julia in marriage. Probably he cherished the further purpose of making Marcellus his successor. Horace makes the union of Julia and Marcellus the occasion of glorifying the rule of Augustus and of voicing the general wish for its prosperous continuance.

2. **Outline of the Poem**:

a) Invocation to the Muse, 1–12;
b) Praise of the gods, — Jupiter first of all, then Pallas, Liber, Diana, Apollo, 13–24;
c) Praise of heroes, — Hercules, Castor and Pollux, 25–32;
d) Praise of Roman kings and patriots, Romulus, Pompilius, Tarquin, Cato, Regulus, Scaurus. Paulus, Fabricius, Curius, Camillus, 33–44;
e) Praise of the Marcelli and the Julian house, particularly Augustus, 45–60.

3. **Time**: 24 B.C.

4. **Metre**: Sapphic and Adonic. Introd. § 44.

Quem virum aut heroa lyra vel acri
Tibia sumis celebrare, Clio?
Quem deum? Cuius recinet iocosa
Nomen imago

Aut in umbrosis Heliconis oris
Aut super Pindo gelidove in Haemo,
Unde vocalem temere insecutae
Orphea silvae,

Arte materna rapidos morantem
Fluminum lapsus celerisque ventos,
Blandum et auritas fidibus canoris
Ducere quercus?

Quid prius dicam solitis parentis
Laudibus, qui res hominum ac deorum,
Qui mare et terras variisque mundum
Temperat horis?

Unde nil maius generatur ipso,
Nec viget quicquam simile aut secundum.
Proximos illi tamen occupavit
Pallas honores,

Proeliis audax; neque te silebo,
Liber, et saevis inimica virgo
Beluis, nec te, metuende certa
Phoebe sagitta.

Dicam et Alcīden puerosque Ledae,
Hunc equis, illum superare pugnis
Nobilem; quorum simul alba nautis
Stella refulsit,

Defluit saxis agitatus umor,
Concidunt venti fugiuntque nubes,
Et minax, quod sic voluere, ponto
Unda recumbit.

Romulum post hos prius an quietum
Pompili regnum memorem an superbos
Tarquini fasces, dubito, an Catonis
Nobile letum.

Regulum et Scauros animaeque magnae
Prodigum Paulum, superante Poeno,
Gratus insigni referam camena
Fabriciumque.

Hunc et intonsis Curium capillis
Utilem bello tulit et Camillum
Saeva paupertas et avitus arto
  Cum lare fundus.

Crescit occulte velut arbor aevo
Fama Marcelli; micat inter omnis
Iulium sidus, velut inter ignis
  Luna minores.

Gentis humanae pater atque custos,
Orte Saturno, tibi cura magni
Caesaris fatis data: tu secundo
  Caesare regnes.

Ille seu Parthos Latio imminentis
Egerit iusto domitos triumpho,
Sive subiectos Orientis orae
  Seras et Indos,

Te minor latum reget aequos orbem:
Tu gravi curru quaties Olympum,
Tu parum castis inimica mittes
  Fulmina lucis.

XIII.

JEALOUSY.

1. Outline of the Poem:

a) Thy praises of Telephus, Lydia, fill my heart with keenest jealousy, 1–8;
b) I kindle, too, at his savage treatment of thee, 9–12;
c) Believe not that he will be constant, 13–16;
d) Happy they whose union is perfect, untorn by dissension, 17–20.

2. Time: Uncertain; not after 23 B.C.

3. Metre: Second Asclepiadean. Introd. § 46.

Cum tu, Lydia, Telephi
  Cervicem roseam, cerea Telephi
Laudas bracchia, vae, meum
  Fervens difficili bile tumet iecur.

Tunc nec mens mihi nec color
  Certa sede manent, umor et in genas
Furtim labitur, arguens
  Quam lentis penitus macerer ignibus.

Uror, seu tibi candidos
  Turparunt umeros immodicae mero
Rixae, sive puer furens
  Impressit memorem dente labris notam.

Non, si me satis audias,
  Speres perpetuom dulcia barbare
Laedentem oscula, quae Venus
  Quinta parte sui nectaris imbuit.

Felices ter et amplius,
  Quos inrupta tenet copula nec malis
Divolsus querimoniis
  Suprema citius solvet amor die.

XIV.

TO THE SHIP OF STATE.

1. Occasion of the Ode: Some threatened renewal of civil strife, — possibly that which culminated in the rupture between Octavian and Antony in 32 B.C.

2. Outline of the Poem:

a) Beware, O ship, of fresh perils! Keep safely in harbor! Thy oars, mast, yards, and hull are no longer staunch, nor hast thou favoring deities to protect thee in distress, 1–10;

b) Despite thy noble name, the sailor trusts thee no more. Beware lest thou become the sport of the gale! Avoid, too, the treacherous reefs of the sea! 11–20.

3. Time: 32 B.C., if the references in the ode are to the approaching struggle between Octavian and Antonius.

4. Metre: Fourth Asclepiadean. Introd. § 48.

The allegorical character of this ode was recognized by the eminent rhetorician Quintilian (about 90 A.D.), who remarks, *Inst. Or.* viii. 6. 44, *navem pro republica, tempestates pro bellis civilibus, portum pro pace atque concordia dicit*. Still we must not undertake to carry the allegory too far. Many of the allusions apply to a ship only, and cannot be applied to existing political conditions.

O navis, referent in mare te novi
Fluctus. O quid agis! Fortiter occupa
Portum. Nonne vides, ut
Nudum remigio latus

Et malus celeri saucius Africo
Antemnaeque gemant, ac sine funibus
Vix durare carinae
Possint imperiosius

Aequor? Non tibi sunt integra lintea,
Non di, quos iterum pressa voces malo.
Quamvis Pontica pinus,
Silvae filia nobilis,

Iactes et genus et nomen inutile:
Nil pictis timidus navita puppibus
  Fidit. Tu, nisi ventis
    Debes ludibrium, cave.

Nuper sollicitum quae mihi taedium,
Nunc desiderium curaque non levis,
  Interfusa nitentis
    Vites aequora Cycladas.

XV.

THE PROPHECY OF NEREUS.

1. **Outline of Poem**: As Paris hurries from Sparta to Troy with Helen, Nereus stills the winds and prophesies:

  a) 'Tis under evil auspices that thou art taking home thy bride; Greece will avenge the wrong, and great war is in store for the race of Dardanus, 1–12;

  b) Vain will be Venus's protection; vain, too, the music of thy lyre; thou canst not escape the foe, 13–20;

  c) Heedest thou not Ulysses, Nestor, and the other Grecian warriors, Meriones and Diomede, from whom thou shalt fiy, as the deer flies from the wolf? 21–32;

  d) Though postponed for a while, Ilium's doom is inevitable, 33–36.

2. **Time**: Uncertain; not after 23 B.C.

3. **Metre**: Third Asclepiadean. Introd. § 47.

According to Porphyrio, the third century scholiast of Horace, this poem is an imitation of an ode of the Greek poet Bacchylides in which Cassandra is represented as prophesying the doom of Troy.

Pastor cum traheret per freta navibus
Idaeis Helenen perfidus hospitam,
Ingrato celeris obruit otio
  Ventos, ut caneret fera

Nereus fata: 'Mala ducis avi domum,
Quam multo repetet Graecia milite,
Coniurata tuas rumpere nuptias
  Et regnum Priami vetus.

Eheu, quantus equis, quantus adest viris
Sudor! quanta moves funera Dardanae
Genti! Iam galeam Pallas et aegida
  Currusque et rabiem parat.

Nequicquam Veneris praesidio ferox
Pectes caesariem grataque feminis
Imbelli cithara carmina divides;
  Nequicquam thalamo gravis

Hastas et calami spicula Cnosii
Vitabis strepitumque et celerem sequi
Aiacem: tamen, heu serus! adulteros
  Crines pulvere collines.

Non Laërtiaden, exitium tuae
Gentis, non Pylium Nestora respicis?
Urgent impavidi te Salaminius
  Teucer, te Sthenelus, sciens

Pugnae, sive opus est imperitare equis,
Non auriga piger. Merionen quoque
Nosces. Ecce furit te reperire atrox
  Tydīdes melior patre,

Quem tu, cervos uti vallis in altera
Visum parte lupum graminis immemor,
Sublimi fugies mollis anhelitu,
  Non hoc pollicitus tuae.

Iracunda diem proferet Ilio
Matronisque Phrygum classis Achillei;
Post certas hiemes uret Achaicus
Ignis Pergameas domos.'

XVI.

THE POET'S RECANTATION.

1. **Occasion of the Poem**: The poet had offended some fair one by the intemperate utterances of his verse; he now seeks forgiveness for the fault.

2. **Outline of the Poem**:

a) Destroy the guilty verses as thou wilt, 1–4;
b) The violence of anger surpasses all else; 'tis the 'mad lion' in our natures, and has ever brought ruin to kings and nations, 5–22;
c) I too once yielded to its fury; but now I repent and beg forgiveness, 22–28.

3. **Time**: Uncertain; not after 23 B.C.

4. **Metre**: Alcaic. Introd. § 43.

O matre pulchra filia pulchrior,
Quem criminosis cumque voles modum
Pones iambis, sive flamma
Sive mari libet Hadriano.

Non Dindymēne, non adytis quatit
Mentem sacerdotum incola Pythius,
Non Liber aeque, non acuta
Sic geminant Corybantes aera,

Tristes ut irae, quas neque Noricus
Deterret ensis nec mare naufragum
Nec saevos ignis nec tremendo
Iuppiter ipse ruens tumultu.

Fertur Prometheus addere principi
Limo coactus particulam undique
Desectam et insani leonis
Vim stomacho apposuisse nostro.

Irae Thyesten exitio gravi
Stravere et altis urbibus ultimae
Stetere causae, cur perirent
Funditus imprimeretque muris

Hostile aratrum exercitus insolens.
Compesce mentem: me quoque pectoris
Temptavit in dulci iuventa
Fervor et in celeres iambos

Misit furentem; nunc ego mitibus
Mutare quaero tristia, dum mihi
Fias recantatis amica
Opprobriis animumque reddas.

XVII.

AN INVITATION TO TYNDARIS TO ENJOY THE DELIGHTS OF THE COUNTRY.

1. **Outline of the Poem**:
   a) Faunus often delights to come to fair Lucretilis and bless it with his presence, 1–12.
   b) Hither come, my Tyndaris: here thou shalt find rustic plenty, cool air, song, and wine, freedom, too, from the cruelties of an ill-matched lover, Cyrus, 13–28.
2. **Time**: Uncertain; not after 23 B.C.
3. **Metre**: Alcaic. Introd. § 43.

Tyndaris, apparently is some *meretrix*, accustomed to the boisterous conviviality of the city. Horace pictures to her the idyllic delights of the country as exhibited by his own Sabine farm.

Velox amoenum saepe Lucretilem
Mutat Lycaeo Faunus et igneam
Defendit aestatem capellis
Usque meis pluviosque ventos.

Impune tutum per nemus arbutos
Quaerunt latentis et thyma deviae
Olentis uxores mariti,
Nec viridis metuont colubras

Nec Martialis haediliae lupos,
Utcumque dulci, Tyndari, fistula
Valles et Ustīcae cubantis
Levia personuere saxa.

Di me tuentur, dis pietas mea
Et Musa cordi est. Hic tibi copia
Manabit ad plenum benigno
Ruris honorum opulenta cornu.

Hic in reducta valle Caniculae
Vitabis aestus, et fide Teia
Dices laborantis in uno
Penelopen vitreamque Circen;

Hic innocentis pocula Lesbii
Duces sub umbra, nec Semeleius
Cum Marte confundet Thyōneus
Proelia, nec metues protervom

Suspecta Cyrum, ne male dispari
Incontinentis iniciat manus
Et scindat haerentem coronam
Crinibus immeritamque vestem.

XVIII.

THE PRAISES OF WINE.

1. **Outline of the Poem:**
   a) The blessings that wine brings, 1–6;
   b) Yet Bacchus's gifts are not to be profaned in riotous brawl, 7–16.

2. **Time:** Uncertain; not after 23 B.C.

3. **Metre:** Fifth Asclepiadean. Introd. § 49.

The ode is apparently, in part at least, an imitation of a similar ode by Alcaeus.

Nullam, Vare, sacra vite prius severis arborem
Circa mite solum Tiburis et moenia Catili;
Siccis omnia nam dura deus proposuit neque
Mordaces aliter diffugiunt sollicitudines.
Quis post vina gravem militiam aut pauperiem crepat?
Quis non te potius, Bacche pater, teque, decens Venus?
Ac nequis modici transiliat munera Liberi,
Centaurea monet cum Lapithis rixa super mero
Debellata, monet Sithoniis non levis Euhius,
Cum fas atque nefas exiguo fine libidinum
Discernunt avidi. Non ego te, candide Bassareu,
Invitum quatiam nec variis obsita frondibus
Sub divom rapiam. Saeva tene cum Berecyntio
Cornu tympana, quae subsequitur caecus Amor sui
Et tollens vacuom plus nimio Gloria verticem
Arcanique Fides prodiga, perlucidior vitro.

XIX.

THE CHARMS OF GLYCERA.

1. **Outline of the Poem**:
   - *a*) I am constrained to yield again to the might of love, 1-4;
   - *b*) 'Tis radiant Glycĕra's beauty that charms me, 5-8;
   - *c*) Venus's power prevents my giving heed to other things, 9-12;
   - *d*) I will appease the goddess by incense and a sacrifice; so will she relent, 13-16.
2. **Time**: Uncertain; not after 23 B.C.
3. **Metre**: Second Asclepiadean. Introd. § 46.

Mater saeva Cupidinum
  Thebanaeque iubet me Semelae puer
Et lasciva Licentia
  Finitis animum reddere amoribus.

Urit me Glycĕrae nitor,
  Splendentis Pario marmore purius,
Urit grata protervitas
  Et voltus nimium lubricus aspici.

In me tota ruens Venus
  Cyprum deseruit, nec patitur Scythas
Et versis animosum equis
  Parthum dicere, nec quae nihil attinent.

Hic vivom mihi caespitem, hic
  Verbenas, pueri, ponite turaque
Bimi cum patera meri:
  Mactata veniet lenior hostia.

XX.

'TWILL BE PLAIN FARE, MAECENAS.

1. Occasion of the Poem: The ode is evidently written in reply to a letter from Maecenas stating that he was coming to visit the poet.

2. Outline of the Poem:

a) 'Twill be plain wine, Maecenas, thou shalt drink with me, yet 'twas put up on a day thou well rememberest, 1–8;
b) Better vintages thou hast at home than any that fill my goblets, 9–12.

3. Time: Between 30 and 23 B.C.

4. Metre: Sapphic and Adonic. Introd. § 44.

Vile potabis modicis Sabinum
Cantharis, Graeca quod ego ipse testa
Conditum levi, datus in theatro
   Cum tibi plausus,

Care Maecēnas eques, ut paterni
Fluminis ripae simul et iocosa
Redderet laudes tibi Vaticani
   Montis imago.

Caecubum et prelo domitam Caleno
Tu bibas uvam: mea nec Falernae
Temperant vites neque Formiani
   Pocula colles.

XXI.

IN PRAISE OF LATONA AND HER CHILDREN.

1. Outline of the Poem:

a) Praise Diana, O ye maidens! Praise, O boys, Apollo! Praise Latona, beloved of Jove! 1–4;
b) Praise Diana who delights in stream and wood! Praise Tempe, Apollo's haunt, and Delos his birthplace, 5–12;
c) May they ward off from Rome war, plague, and famine, and turn them against the foe, 13–16.

2. Time: Probably 27 B.C.

3. Metre: Fourth Asclepiadean. Introd. § 48.

Dianam tenerae dicite virgines,
Intonsum, pueri, dicite Cynthium
  Latonamque supremo
    Dilectam penitus Iovi.

Vos laetam fluviis et nemorum coma,
Quaecumque aut gelido prominet Algido,
  Nigris aut Erymanthi
    Silvis aut viridis Cragi;

Vos Tempe totidem tollite laudibus
Natalemque, mares, Delon Apollinis,
  Insignemque pharetra
    Fraternaque umerum lyra.

Hic bellum lacrimosum, hic miseram famem
Pestemque a populo et principe Caesare in
  Persas atque Britannos
    Vestra motus aget prece.

XXII.

FROM THE RIGHTEOUS MAN EVEN THE WILD BEASTS RUN AWAY.

1. **Outline of the Poem** :
   a) The upright man needs no weapon, Fuscus, wherever his path may lead him, 1–8 ;
   b) The proof : A wild wolf fled from *me* in the Sabine wood as I roamed about unprotected, 9–16 ;
   c) So, wherever my lot is cast, — in the cold north or under a tropic sun, — I will love my Lalage, 17–24.
2. **Time** : Uncertain ; not after 23 B.C.
3. **Metre** : Sapphic and Adonic. Introd. § 44.

This ode is manifestly intended by the poet merely as a humorous glorification of his own virtue. The exaggerated description of the wolf, along with the sportive stanzas at the close, tally admirably with the mock philosophical reflections of the opening strophes.

Integer vitae scelerisque purus
Non eget Mauris iaculis neque arcu
Nec venenatis gravida sagittis,
Fusce, pharetra,

Sive per Syrtis iter aestuosas
Sive facturus per inhospitalem
Caucasum vel quae loca fabulosus
Lambit Hydaspes.

Namque me silva lupus in Sabina,
Dum meam canto Lalagen et ultra
Terminum curis vagor expeditis,
Fugit inermem;

Quale portentum neque militaris
Daunias latis alit aesculetis
Nec Iubae tellus generat, leonum
Arida nutrix.

Pone me pigris ubi nulla campis
Arbor aestiva recreatur aura,
Quod latus mundi nebulae malusque
Iuppiter urget;

Pone sub curru nimium propinqui
Solis in terra domibus negata:
Dulce ridentem Lalagen amabo,
Dulce loquentem.

XXIII.

FEAR ME NOT, CHLOE!

1. Outline of the Poem:

a) Thou shunnest me like a timid fawn that seeks its mother on the trackless mountain and trembles at the rustling bramble or the darting lizard, 1–8;

b) I'll do thee no harm. Cease to cling to thy mother! Thou art ripe for a mate, 9–12.

2. Time: Uncertain; not after 23 B.C.

3. Metre: Fourth Asclepiadean. Introd. § 48

Vitas hinnuleo me similis, Chloë,
Quaerenti pavidam montibus aviis
Matrem non sine vano
Aurarum et siluae metu.

Nam seu mobilibus vepris inhorruit
Ad ventos foliis, seu virides rubum
Dimovere lacertae,
Et corde et genibus tremit.

Atqui non ego te tigris ut aspera
Gaetulusve leo frangere persequor:
Tandem desine matrem
Tempestiva sequi viro.

XXIV.

A DIRGE FOR QUINTILIUS.

1. **Outline of the Poem** :

a) 'Tis meet to indulge our sorrow for our lost Quintilius, 1–4;
b) Is he, then, really gone, he who had no peer in honor, in loyalty, and truth? 5–8;
c) Dear he was to many, yet dearest to thee, O Virgil, 9, 10;
d) In vain dost thou pray for his return to earth; wert thou to play the lyre of Orpheus more sweetly than the bard himself, thou couldst not bring back the dead to life, 11–18;
e) 'Tis hard to bear; yet suffering softens pain, 19, 20.

2. **Time**: 24 B.C.

3. **Metre**: Third Asclepiadean. Introd. § 47.

Quis desiderio sit pudor aut modus
Tam cari capitis? Praecipe lugubris
Cantus, Melpomene, cui liquidam pater
Vocem cum cithara dedit.

Ergo Quintilium perpetuos sopor
Urget? Cui Pudor et Iustitiae soror,
Incorrupta Fides, nudaque Veritas
Quando ullum inveniet parem?

Multis ille bonis flebilis occidit,
Nulli flebilior quam tibi, Vergili.
Tu frustra pius heu non ita creditum
Poscis Quintilium deos.

Quid, si Threicio blandius Orpheo
Auditam moderere arboribus fidem?
Num vanae redeat sanguis imagini,
Quam virga semel horrida,

Non lenis precibus fata recludere,
Nigro compulerit Mercurius gregi?
Durum: sed levius fit patientia,
Quicquid corrigere est nefas.

XXV.

LYDIA, THY CHARMS ARE PAST.

1. **Outline of the Poem**:

a) Admirers come less often, and thou hearest their plaints less frequently than of old, 1–8;

b) Thou in turn shalt pine for them, complaining that they prefer youth's freshness to withered age, 9–20.

2. **Time**: Uncertain; not after 23 B.C.

3. **Metre**: Sapphic and Adonic. Introd. § 44.

Parcius iunctas quatiunt fenestras
Ictibus crebris iuvenes protervi,
Nec tibi somnos adimunt, amatque
Ianua limen,

Quae prius multum facilis movebat
Cardines. Audis minus et minus iam:
'Me tuo longas pereunte noctes,
Lydia, dormis?'

Invicem moechos anus arrogantis
Flebis in solo levis angiportu,
Thracio bacchante magis sub inter-
lunia vento,

Cum tibi flagrans amor et libido,
Quae solet matres furiare equorum,
Saeviet circa iecur ulcerosum,
Non sine questu,

Laeta quod pubes hedera virenti
Gaudeat pulla magis atque myrto,
Aridas frondes Hiemis sodali
Dedicet Euro.

XXVI.

IMMORTALIZE LAMIA, YE MUSES.

1. Outline of the Poem :

a) The Muse's favor bids me heed not wars and rumors of wars, 1–6;

b) Rather will I call on thee, O Muse, to aid me in weaving a worthy chaplet in verse to honor my Lamia, 6–12.

2. Time : 30 B.C.

3. Metre : Alcaic. Introd. § 43.

Musis amicus tristitiam et metus
Tradam protervis in mare Creticum
Portare ventis, quis sub Arcto
Rex gelidae metuatur orae,

Quid Tiridāten terreat, unice
Securus. O quae fontibus integris
Gaudes, apricos necte flores,
Necte meo Lamiae coronam,

Pimplei dulcis. Nil sine te mei
Prosunt honores: hunc fidibus novis,
Hunc Lesbio sacrare plectro
Teque tuasque decet sorores.

XXVII.

LET MODERATION REIGN!

1. Outline of the Poem:

a) Away with strife and quarrels from the festal board! 1–8;
b) I'll drain my bumper of stout Falernian on one condition only: Let Megylla's brother confide to my trusty ear the object of his affections. — Ah, luckless wight, worthy of a better maiden, I fear thy case is hopeless, 9–24.

2. Time: Uncertain; before 23 B.C.

3. Metre: Alcaic. Introd. § 43.

The poem is apparently an imitation of an ode of Anacreon, part of which is preserved.

Natis in usum laetitiae scyphis
Pugnare Thracum est: tollite barbarum
Morem, verecundumque Bacchum
Sanguineis prohibete rixis.

Vino et lucernis Medus acinaces
Immane quantum discrepat: impium
Lenite clamorem, sodales,
Et cubito remanete presso.

Voltis severi me quoque sumere
Partem Falerni? Dicat Opuntiae
Frater Megyllae, quo beatus
Volnere, qua pereat sagitta.

Cessat voluntas? Non alia bibam
Mercede. Quae te cumque domat Venus,
Non erubescendis adurit
Ignibus ingenuoque semper

Amore peccas. Quicquid habes, age,
Depone tutis auribus. — A miser,
  Quanta laboras in Charybdi,
    Digne puer meliore flamma!

Quae saga, quis te solvere Thessalis
Magus venenis, quis poterit deus?
  Vix inligatum te triformi
    Pegasus expediet Chimaera.

XXVIII., 1.

DEATH THE DOOM OF ALL.

1. **Outline of the Poem**:
   a) Thou, Archytas, art now confined by a small mound of earth, and it avails thee naught to have explored in life the realms of space, and to have measured the earth and sea, 1–6;
   b) So all the great have passed away, — Pelops and Tithonus, Minos and Pythagoras; Death's path must be trodden by us all, 7–20.
2. **Time**: Uncertain; not after 23 B.C.
3. **Metre**: Alcmanic Strophe. Introd. § 52.

In the Mss., and in most editions of Horace, this ode appears as a part of the following, but it is practically impossible to interpret the two as constituting a single poem.

Te maris et terrae numeroque carentis harenae
  Mensorem cohibent, Archȳta,
Pulveris exigui prope litus parva Matinum
  Munera, nec quicquam tibi prodest

Aërias temptasse domos animoque rotundum
  Percurrisse polum morituro.
Occidit et Pelopis genitor, conviva deorum,
  Tithōnusque remotus in auras

Et Iovis arcanis Minos admissus, habentque
  Tartara Panthoiden iterum Orco
Demissum, quamvis clipeo Troiana refixo
  Tempora testatus nihil ultra

Nervos atque cutem morti concesserat atrae,
  Iudice te non sordidus auctor
Naturae verique. Sed omnis una manet nox,
  Et calcanda semel via leti.

Dant alios Furiae torvo spectacula Marti,
  Exitio est avidum mare nautis;
Mixta senum ac iuvenum densentur funera, nullum
  Saeva caput Proserpina fugit.

XXVIII., 2.

A PETITION FOR SEPULTURE.

1. Outline of the Poem :

a) I am another victim of the Adriatic wave; but do thou, O mariner, cast a bit of sand upon my unburied head, 1–5;

b) So may all blessings be showered upon thee by Jove and Neptune! Neglect not the duty! Three handfuls of sand suffice, 5–16.

2. Time: Uncertain; not after 23 B.C.

3. Metre: Alcmanic Strophe. Introd. § 52.

In the Mss., and in most editions of Horace, this ode appears as a part of the preceding, but it is practically impossible to interpret the two as constituting a single poem.

Me quoque devexi rapidus comes Orīonis
  Illyricis Notus obruit undis.
At tu, nauta, vagae ne parce malignus harenae
  Ossibus et capiti inhumato

Particulam dare: sic, quodcumque minabitur Eurus
Fluctibus Hesperiis, Venusinae
Plectantur silvae te sospite, multaque merces,
Unde potest, tibi defluat aequo

Ab Iove Neptunoque sacri custode Tarenti.
Neclegis immeritis nocituram
Postmodo te natis fraudem committere? Fors et
Debita iura vicesque superbae

Te maneant ipsum: precibus non linquar inultis,
Teque piacula nulla resolvent.
Quamquam festinas, non est mora longa; licebit
Iniecto ter pulvere curras.

XXIX.

THE SCHOLAR TURNED ADVENTURER.

1. **Outline of the Poem:**

   a) Can it be, Iccius, that in eagerness for wealth you are preparing to join the expedition against Arabia, with the possibility of later enterprises against the Parthians? 1–5;

   b) I picture your successes in my mind; maids and youths of high degree shall be your booty, 5–10;

   c) Nothing is impossible. Even rivers may be expected to flow up hill, when a man of your fair promise changes philosophy for coat of mail, 10–16.

2. **Time**: 27 B.C.

3. **Metre**: Alcaic. Introd. § 43.

The expedition alluded to in the ode was that of Aelius Gallus, prefect of Egypt. Egypt had been subdued in 29 B.C., and ever since that time the fabulous wealth of Arabia had offered an alluring and apparently easy field for Roman conquest. A pestilence, however, broke out among Gallus's troops, and the undertaking ended in failure.

Icci, beatis nunc Arabum invides
Gazis et acrem militiam paras
Non ante devictis Sabaeae
Regibus, horribilique Medo

Nectis catenas? Quae tibi virginum
Sponso necato barbara serviet?
Puer quis ex aula capillis
Ad cyathum statuetur unctis,

Doctus sagittas tendere Sericas
Arcu paterno? Quis neget arduis
Pronos relabi posse rivos
Montibus et Tiberim reverti,

Cum tu coëmptos undique nobilis
Libros Panaeti, Socraticam et domum
Mutare loricis Hiberis,
Pollicitus meliora, tendis?

XXX.

INVOCATION TO VENUS.

1. **Outline of the Poem**: Come, Venus, to Glycera's chapel; and with thee come Cupid, the Graces, the nymphs, Youth, and Mercury.

2. **Time**: Uncertain; not after 23 B.C.

3. **Metre**: Sapphic and Adonic. Introd. § 44.

O Venus, regina Cnidi Paphique,
Sperne dilectam Cypron et vocantis
Ture te multo Glycĕrae decoram
Transfer in aedem.

Fervidus tecum puer et solutis
Gratiae zonis properentque nymphae
Et parum comis sine te Iuventas
Mercuriusque.

XXXI.

THE POET'S PRAYER.

1. Occasion of the Poem: In the year 28 B.C. (October 24) Augustus dedicated to Apollo the splendid temple which had been eight years in process of building. The structure was one of the most magnificent Rome had ever known. Its pillars were of solid marble, and the interior was lavishly decorated with the most costly works of art. Connected with the temple were two libraries, one of Greek books, the other of Latin. Doubtless this evidence of Augustus's interest in the literary life of Rome heightened Horace's interest in the auspicious occasion.

2. Outline of the Poem:

a) What wish do I cherish as I pour new wine at the dedication of Apollo's shrine? Not herds, nor gold, nor ivory, nor lands, nor costly wines, 1–15;

b) My simple fare is of olives, endive, and wholesome mallows; and my prayer to the god begs only for health of body and of mind, contentment with what Fortune gives, and an old age of honor and of song, 15–20.

3. Time: October, 28 B.C.

4. Metre: Alcaic. Introd. § 43.

Quid dedicatum poscit Apollinem
Vates? Quid orat, de patera novom
  Fundens liquorem? Non opimae
    Sardiniae segetes feraces,

Non aestuosae grata Calabriae
Armenta, non aurum aut ebur Indicum,
  Non rura, quae Liris quieta
    Mordet aqua taciturnus amnis.

Premant Calena falce quibus dedit
Fortuna vitem, dives ut aureis
  Mercator exsiccet culillis
    Vina Syra reparata merce,

Dis carus ipsis, quippe ter et quater
Anno revisens aequor Atlanticum
Impune. Me pascunt olivae,
Me cichorea levesque malvae.

Frui paratis et valido mihi,
Latoe, dones et, precor, integra
Cum mente, nec turpem senectam
Degere nec cithara carentem.

XXXII.

INVOCATION TO THE LYRE.

1. **Outline of the Poem**: I am asked for a song. Lend me thy aid to sing a genuine Roman lay that shall be immortal, thou, O lyre, first tuned by Alcaeus, who, in storm and stress, was ever faithful to the Muse. Do thou, glory of Apollo and honored of Jove, lend me thy aid whenever I invoke thee duly.

2. **Time**: Uncertain; not after 23 B.C.

3. **Metre**: Sapphic and Adonic. Introd. § 44.

Poscimur. Siquid vacui sub umbra
Lusimus tecum, quod et hunc in annum
Vivat et pluris, age dic Latinum,
Barbite, carmen,

Lesbio primum modulate civi,
Qui ferox bello tamen inter arma,
Sive iactatam religarat udo
Litore navim,

Liberum et Musas Veneremque et illi
Semper haerentem puerum canebat,
Et Lycum nigris oculis nigroque
Crine decorum.

O decus Phoebi et dapibus supremi
Grata testudo Iovis, o laborum
Dulce lenimen medicumque, salve
Rite vocanti!

XXXIII.

THE FAITHLESS FAIR.

1. **Outline of the Poem** :

a) Grieve not o'ermuch, Tibullus, over the faithless Glycĕra, 1–4;
b) So is it ever; Lycoris yearns for Cyrus, Cyrus for Pholoë, yet Pholoë shuns his suit. Venus in cruel sport delights to bring to her yoke ill-mated hearts, 5–12;
c) I, too, have known this fate. Despite the allurements of a worthier love, the shrewish Myrtale has held me fast in her fetters, 13–16.

2. **Time** : Uncertain; before 23 B.C.

3. **Metre** : Third Asclepiadean. Introd. § 47.

Albi, ne doleas plus nimio memor
Immitis Glycĕrae neu miserabilis
Decantes elegos, cur tibi iunior
Laesa praeniteat fide.

Insignem tenui fronte Lycōrida
Cyri torret amor, Cyrus in asperam
Declinat Pholoën: sed prius Apulis
Iungentur capreae lupis,

Quam turpi Pholoë peccet adultero.
Sic visum Veneri, cui placet imparis
Formas atque animos sub iuga aënea
Saevo mittere cum ioco.

Ipsum me melior cum peteret Venus,
Grata detinuit compede Myrtale
Libertina, fretis acrior Hadriae
Curvantis Calabros sinus.

XXXIV.

THE POET'S CONVERSION FROM ERROR.

1. Outline of the Poem :

a) I am compelled to renounce my former errors of belief and to make sail for a new haven, 1–5;
b) The cause: Jove recently hurled his thunderbolts with a mighty crash through the clear sky, 5–12;
c) The god *has* power; he can abase the high and exalt the lowly; from one man he swiftly takes away the crown, to bestow it on another, 12–16.

2. Time: Probably between 29 and 25 B.C.

3. Metre: Alcaic. Introd. § 43.

Parcus deorum cultor et infrequens,
Insanientis dum sapientiae
Consultus erro, nunc retrorsum
Vela dare atque iterare cursus

Cogor relictos: namque Diespiter,
Igni corusco nubila dividens
Plerumque, per purum tonantis
Egit equos volucremque currum;

Quo bruta tellus et vaga flumina
Quo Styx et invisi horrida Taenari
Sedes Atlanteusque finis
Concutitur. Valet ima summis

Mutare et insignem attenuat deus,
Obscura promens; hinc apicem rapax
Fortuna cum stridore acuto
Sustulit, hic posuisse gaudet.

XXXV.

TO FORTUNA.

1. Occasion of the Poem: In the year 27 B.C. Augustus began preparations for two expeditions, one against the Britons, the other under Aelius Gallus against Arabia Felix (see i. 29). The poet invokes the protection of the goddess Fortuna for both undertakings. Inasmuch as the *Fortuna Antias*, who is here addressed, was sometimes consulted for oracular deliverances, it is possible that Augustus had consulted her with reference to one or both of these two enterprises, and that this circumstance was the immediate cause of the ode.

2. Outline of the Poem:

a) O goddess, that art omnipotent to determine the affairs of men, all acknowledge thy might, all court, all fear, 1–16;

b) Thy attendant is Necessity, with her emblems of power; Hope and rare Faith, too, cherish thee, when in hostile mood thou bringest trouble upon the great, and when others, alas, prove faithless, 17–28;

c) Preserve, O goddess, our Caesar, who is setting forth against the Britons, and the soldiers who are departing for Arabia and Parthia, 29–32;

d) Forgive our past iniquity, and guide our weapons against the foe, 33–40.

3. Time: 27 B.C.

4. Metre: Alcaic. Introd. § 43.

O diva, gratum quae regis Antium,
Praesens vel imo tollere de gradu
Mortale corpus vel superbos
Vertere funeribus triumphos,

Te pauper ambit sollicita prece
Ruris colonus, te dominam aequoris,
Quicumque Bithyna lacessit
Carpathium pelagus carina,

Te Dacus asper, te profugi Scythae
Urbesque gentesque et Latium ferox
Regumque matres barbarorum et
Purpurei metuont tyranni,

Iniurioso ne pede proruas
Stantem columnam, neu populus frequens
Ad arma cessantis, ad arma
Concitet imperiumque frangat.

Te semper antit saeva Necessitas,
Clavos trabalis et cuneos manu
Gestans aëna, nec severus
Uncus abest liquidumque plumbum.

Te Spes et albo rara Fides colit
Velata panno, nec comitem abnegat,
Utcumque mutata potentis
Veste domos inimica linquis.

At volgus infidum et meretrix retro
Periura cedit, diffugiunt cadis
Cum faece siccatis amici,
Ferre iugum pariter dolosi.

Serves iturum Caesarem in ultimos
Orbis Britannos et iuvenum recens
Examen, Eois timendum
Partibus Oceanoque rubro.

Eheu, cicatricum et sceleris pudet
Fratrumque. Quid nos dura refugimus
Aetas? Quid intactum nefasti
Liquimus? Unde manum iuventus

Metu deorum continuit? Quibus
Pepercit aris? O utinam nova
Incude diffingas retusum in
Massagetas Arabasque ferrum!

XXXVI.

A JOYFUL RETURN.

1. Outline of the Poem:

a) Let us make sacrifice in celebration of Numida's safe return. Dear is he to many, yet dearest of all to Lamia, his old schoolmate and friend, 1–9;

b) A white mark to commemorate the day, and let indulgence in wine and the dance know no bound; let roses, parsley, and lilies grace our banquet; let even Bassus drink generously to-day and not be outdone by Damalis, the fair, 10–20.

2. Time: Possibly 24 B.C.

3. Metre: Second Asclepiadean. Introd. § 46.

Et ture et fidibus iuvat
 Placare et vituli sanguine debito
Custodes Numidae deos,
 Qui nunc Hesperia sospes ab ultima

Caris multa sodalibus,
 Nulli plura tamen dividit oscula
Quam dulci Lamiae, memor
 Actae non alio rege puertiae

Mutataeque simul togae.
 Cressa ne careat pulchra dies nota,
Neu promptae modus amphorae,
 Neu morem in Salium sit requies pedum,

Neu multi Damalis meri
 Bassum Threicia vincat amystide.
Neu desint epulis rosae
 Neu vivax apium neu breve lilium;

Omnes in Damalin putris
  Deponent oculos, nec Damalis novo
Divelletur adultero,
  Lascivis hederis ambitiosior.

XXXVII.

THE FALL OF CLEOPATRA.

1. Occasion of the Poem: In September of 31 B.C. Augustus had defeated at Actium the fleets of Antony and Cleopatra. Although this success almost completely annihilated the naval resources of Antony and Cleopatra, they still remained masters of formidable land forces. When these were finally defeated and Augustus entered Alexandria in August of 30 B.C., Antony and Cleopatra both committed suicide. Thus was removed what at one time had constituted a serious menace to the welfare of Rome, and Horace gives voice to the sentiments of his countrymen in the following stirring ode.

2. Outline of the Poem:

a) Now is the time for drinking and dancing, now for offering to the gods our grateful thanksgiving; an earlier day had been premature, so long as a foreign queen was planning ruin against our Roman temples, 1–12;

b) But her crushing defeat at Actium sobered her wild dreams of conquest, and fear of Caesar drove her in terror over the sea, 12–21;

c) Yet her death was heroic; she showed no fear, and boldly took the serpent to her bosom, too proud to deign to grace the triumph of her conqueror, 21–32.

3. Time: September, 30 B.C.

4. Metre: Alcaic. Introd. § 43.

Nunc est bibendum, nunc pede libero
Pulsanda tellus, nunc Saliaribus
  Ornare pulvinar deorum
    Tempus erat dapibus, sodales.

Antehac nefas depromere Caecubum
Cellis avitis, dum Capitolio
Regina dementis ruinas,
Funus et imperio parabat

Contaminato cum grege turpium
Morbo virorum, quidlibet impotens
Sperare fortunaque dulci
Ebria. Sed minuit furorem

Vix una sospes navis ab ignibus,
Mentemque lymphatam Mareotico
Redegit in veros timores
Caesar, ab Italia volantem

Remis adurgens, accipiter velut
Mollis columbas aut leporem citus
Venator in campis nivalis
Haemoniae, daret ut catenis

Fatale monstrum. Quae generosius
Perire quaerens nec muliebriter
Expavit ensem nec latentis
Classe cita reparavit oras.

Ausa et iacentem visere regiam
Voltu sereno, fortis et asperas
Tractare serpentes, ut atrum
Corpore combiberet venenum,

Deliberata morte ferocior;
Saevis Liburnis scilicet invidens
Privata deduci superbo
Non humilis mulier triumpho.

XXXVIII.

AWAY WITH ORIENTAL LUXURY!

1. Outline of the Poem: Away with oriental luxury! Bring hither no linden garlands nor wreaths of late-blooming roses. Chaplets of simple myrtle are enough, alike for master and for man.

2. Time: Uncertain; not after 23 B.C.

3. Metre: Sapphic and Adonic. Introd. § 44.

Persicos odi, puer, apparatus,
Displicent nexae philyra coronae;
Mitte sectari, rosa quo locorum
  Sera moretur.

Simplici myrto nihil adlabores
Sedulus, cura: neque te ministrum
Dedecet myrtus neque me sub arta
  Vite bibentem.

CARMINUM
LIBER ALTER.

I.

TO POLLIO WRITING A HISTORY OF THE CIVIL WARS.

1. Outline of the Poem:

a) Thou art chronicling the details of the civil commotions that began with the first Triumvirs, — a task full of danger and hazard, 1–8;

b) But withdraw not thy energies for long from the tragic muse, O Pollio, famed at the bar, in council, and in the field, 9–16;

c) In imagination already I seem to see the martial deeds described in thy story; I hear the sound of trumpets and clarions, the clash of arms and behold the flight of horses, — great leaders, too, begrimed with the dust of battle, and all the world at Caesar's feet save dauntless Cato, 17–24;

d) Well may our civil strife be regarded as satisfaction to Jugurtha's shade. What field, or stream, or sea has not been stained with Roman blood? 25–36;

e) But a truce to such dismal themes! Assume, O Muse, a lighter mood! 37–40.

2. Time: Uncertain; probably before Actium (31 B.C.).

3. Metre: Alcaic. Introd. § 43.

Motum ex Metello consule civicum
Bellique causas et vitia et modos
Ludumque Fortunae gravisque
Principum amicitias et arma

Nondum expiatis uncta cruoribus,
Periculosae plenum opus aleae,
Tractas et incedis per ignes
Suppositos cineri doloso.

Paulum severae Musa tragoediae
Desit theatris: mox, ubi publicas
Res ordinaris, grande munus
Cecropio repetes coturno,

Insigne maestis praesidium reis
Et consulenti, Pollio, curiae,
Cui laurus aeternos honores
Delmatico peperit triumpho.

Iam nunc minaci murmure cornuum
Perstringis auris, iam litui strepunt,
Iam fulgor armorum fugacis
Terret equos equitumque voltus.

Audire magnos iam videor duces,
Non indecoro pulvere sordidos,
Et cuncta terrarum subacta
Praeter atrocem animum Catonis.

Iuno et, deorum quisquis amicior
Afris inulta cesserat impotens
Tellure, victorum nepotes
Rettulit inferias Iugurthae.

Quis non Latino sanguine pinguior
Campus sepulcris impia proelia
Testatur auditumque Medis
Hesperiae sonitum ruinae?

Qui gurges aut quae flumina lugubris
Ignara belli? Quod mare Dauniae
Non decoloravere caedes?
Quae caret ora cruore nostro?

Sed ne relictis, Musa, procax iocis
Ceae retractes munera neniae,
Mecum Dionaeo sub antro
Quaere modos leviore plectro.

II.

MONEY, — ITS USE AND ABUSE.

1. **Outline of the Poem:**
   a) Money, Sallust, is of no worth, unless it be put to wise uses; imitate the example of generous Proculeius, 1–8;
   b) To subdue one's own desire for more is better than the widest dominion of the world; resist the passion, lest it become a dire disease increasing by indulgence, 9–16;
   c) 'Tis not the mighty potentate that is really happy; rather he who can gaze upon vast treasure without envy, 17–24.

2. **Time**: 25 B.C., or soon after.

3. **Metre**: Sapphic and Adonic. Introd. § 44.

The ode is an embodiment of the Stoic doctrine often emphasized by Horace, that the wise man (the ideal *sapiens* of the Stoics) alone is happy and worthy.

Nullus argento color est avaris
Abdito terris, inimice lamnae
Crispe Sallusti, nisi temperato
Splendeat usu.

Vivet extento Proculeius aevo,
Notus in fratres animi paterni:
Illum aget pinna metuente solvi
Fama superstes.

Latius regnes avidum domando
Spiritum, quam si Libyam remotis
Gadibus iungas et uterque Poenus
  Serviat uni.

Crescit indulgens sibi dirus hydrops,
Nec sitim pellit, nisi causa morbi
Fugerit venis et aquosus albo
  Corpore languor.

Redditum Cyri solio Phraāten
Dissidens plebi numero beatorum
Eximit Virtus populumque falsis
  Dedocet uti

Vocibus, regnum et diadema tutum
Deferens uni propriamque laurum,
Quisquis ingentis oculo inretorto
  Spectat acervos.

III.

'CARPE DIEM.'

1. Outline of the Poem:

a) Be courageous in adversity, modest in prosperity, 1–8;
b) Nature's charms are for man to enjoy; let us seek them while we may, 9–16;
c) Be we rich or poor, high or low, our days on earth are numbered, 17–28.

2. Time: Probably between 29 and 23 B.C.

3. Metre: Alcaic. Introd. § 43.

Aequam memento rebus in arduis
Servare mentem, non secus in bonis
  Ab insolenti temperatam
    Laetitia, moriture Delli,

Seu maestus omni tempore vixeris,
Seu te in remoto gramine per dies
Festos reclinatum bearis
Interiore nota Falerni.

Quo pinus ingens albaque populus
Umbram hospitalem consociare amant
Ramis? Quid obliquo laborat
Lympha fugax trepidare rivo?

Huc vina et unguenta et nimium brevis
Flores amoenae ferre iube rosae,
Dum res et aetas et sororum
Fila trium patiuntur atra.

Cedes coëmptis saltibus et domo
Villaque, flavos quam Tiberis lavit,
Cedes, et exstructis in altum
Divitiis potietur heres.

Divesne, prisco natus ab Inacho,
Nil interest an pauper et infima
De gente sub divo moreris;
Victima nil miserantis Orci.

Omnes eodem cogimur, omnium
Versatur urna serius ocius
Sors exitura et nos in aeternum
Exsilium impositura cumbae.

IV.

ON XANTHIAS'S LOVE FOR A SLAVE-GIRL.

1. Outline of the Poem:

a) Be not ashamed, O Xanthias, of thy love for a slave-maiden; thou'rt not the first to cherish such a passion, 1–12;
b) Doubtless she comes of a noble ancestry; her beauty, her devotion, her dignity, all betoken this, 13–20;
c) Suspect me not; I praise her charms from no unworthy motive, 21–24.

2. Time: 25 B.C.

3. Metre: Sapphic and Adonic. Introd. § 44.

Ne sit ancillae tibi amor pudori,
Xanthia Phoceu. Prius insolentem
Serva Brisēis niveo colore
Movit Achillem;

Movit Aiacem Telamone natum
Forma captivae dominum Tecmessae;
Arsit Atrides medio in triumpho
Virgine rapta,

Barbarae postquam cecidere turmae
Thessalo victore et ademptus Hector
Tradidit fessis leviora tolli
Pergama Grais.

Nescias an te generum beati
Phyllidis flavae decorent parentes:
Regium certe genus, et penatis
Maeret iniquos.

Crede non illam tibi de scelesta
Plebe dilectam neque sic fidelem,
Sic lucro aversam potuisse nasci
Matre pudenda.

Bracchia et voltum teretisque suras
Integer laudo; fuge suspicari,
Cuius octavom trepidavit aetas
Claudere lustrum.

V.

NOT YET!

1. **Outline of the Poem**:
   a) The maid thou lovest is still too young to return thy passion, 1–10;
   b) Soon 'twill be otherwise; she shall seek thee of her own accord, 10–16;
   c) None shalt thou cherish more than her, 17–24.
2. **Time**: Uncertain; not after 23 B.C.
3. **Metre**: Alcaic. Introd. § 43.

Nondum subacta ferre iugum valet
Cervice, nondum munia comparis
Aequare nec tauri ruentis
In venerem tolerare pondus.

Circa virentis est animus tuae
Campos iuvencae, nunc fluviis gravem
Solantis aestum, nunc in udo
Ludere cum vitulis salicto

Praegestientis. Tolle cupidinem
Immitis uvae: iam tibi lividos
Distinguet autumnus racemos
Purpureo varius colore.

Iam te sequetur (currit enim ferox
Aetas, et illi, quos tibi dempserit,
Apponet annos), iam proterva
Fronte petet Lalage maritum,

Dilecta, quantum non Pholoë fugax,
Non Chloris, albo sic umero nitens,
Ut pura nocturno renidet
Luna mari Cnidiusve Gyges,

Quem si puellarum insereres choro,
Mire sagacis falleret hospites
Discrimen obscurum solutis
Crinibus ambiguoque voltu.

VI.

FAIREST OF ALL IS TIBUR. YET TARENTUM, TOO, IS FAIR.

1. **Outline of the Poem**:

a) Be Tibur the haven of my old age, 1–8;
b) If the Fates keep me from there, I'll seek salubrious Tarentum, with its honey, oil, and wine, 9–20;
c) Tarentum invites us both, Septimius; there shall my ashes rest, 21–24.

2. **Time**: 25–23 B.C.
3. **Metre**: Sapphic and Adonic. Introd. § 44.

Septimi, Gadis aditure mecum et
Cantabrum indoctum iuga ferre nostra et
Barbaras Syrtis, ubi Maura semper
Aestuat unda,

Tibur Argeo positum colono
Sit meae sedes utinam senectae,
Sit modus lasso maris et viarum
Militiaeque.

Unde si Parcae prohibent iniquae,
Dulce pellitis ovibus Galaesi
Flumen et regnata petam Laconi
Rura Phalantho.

Ille terrarum mihi praeter omnis
Angulus ridet, ubi non Hymetto
Mella decedunt viridique certat
Baca Venāfro;

Ver ubi longum tepidasque praebet
Iuppiter brumas, et amicus Aulon
Fertili Baccho minimum Falernis
Invidet uvis.

Ille te mecum locus et beatae
Postulant arces; ibi tu calentem
Debita sparges lacrima favillam
Vatis amici.

VII.

A JOYFUL RETURN.

1. Outline of the Poem:

a) Greetings on thy return, O Pompey, old comrade in pleasure and in arms, 1–12;
b) Since Philippi's day our ways have lain apart, 13–16;
c) Now, then, give thanks to Jove; fill up the cup; let us have perfumes, garlands, a master of the feast, and let our joy know no restraint, 17–28.

2. Time: 29 B.C.

3. Metre: Alcaic. Introd. § 43.

O saepe mecum tempus in ultimum
Deducte Bruto militiae duce,
Quis te redonavit Quiritem
Dis patriis Italoque caelo,

Pompei, meorum prime sodalium,
Cum quo morantem saepe diem mero
Fregi, coronatus nitentis
Malobathro Syrio capillos?

Tecum Philippos et celerem fugam
Sensi relicta non bene parmula,
Cum fracta virtus et minaces
Turpe solum tetigere mento.

Sed me per hostis Mercurius celer
Denso paventem sustulit aëre;
Te rursus in bellum resorbens
Unda fretis tulit aestuosis.

Ergo obligatam redde Iovi dapem,
Longaque fessum militia latus
Depone sub lauru mea nec
Parce cadis tibi destinatis.

Oblivioso levia Massico
Ciboria exple, funde capacibus
Unguenta de conchis. Quis udo
Deproperare apio coronas

Curatve myrto? Quem Venus arbitrum
Dicet bibendi? Non ego sanius
Bacchabor Edonis: recepto
Dulce mihi furere est amico.

VIII.

THE BALEFUL CHARMS OF BARINE.

1. Outline of the Poem :

a) Faithless art thou, Barine; yet not less fair than faithless, 1–8;
b) Thou profitest by violating the most solemn pledges; Venus, too, and the nymphs, and Cupid lend thee encouragement, 9–16;
c) Not only dost thou hold the slaves thou hast, but the new generation growing up seems doomed to yield to thy enchantments, 17–24.

2. Time : Uncertain; not later than 23 B.C.

3. Metre : Sapphic and Adonic. Introd. § 44.

Ulla si iuris tibi peierati
Poena, Barīne, nocuisset umquam,
Dente si nigro fieres vel uno
Turpior ungui,

Crederem. Sed tu simŭl obligasti
Perfidum votis caput, enitescis
Pulchrior multo iuvenumque prodis
Publica cura.

Expedit matris cineres opertos
Fallere et toto taciturna noctis
Signa cum caelo gelidaque divos
Morte carentis.

Ridet hoc, inquam, Venus ipsa; rident
Simplices Nymphae ferus et Cupido,
Semper ardentis acuens sagittas
Cote cruenta.

Adde quod pubes tibi crescit omnis,
Servitus crescit nova, nec priores
Impiae tectum dominae relinquont,
Saepe minati.

Te suis matres metuont iuvencis,
Te senes parci miseraeque, nuper
Virgines, nuptae, tua ne retardet
Aura maritos.

IX.

A TRUCE TO SORROW, VALGIUS!

1. **Outline of the Poem**:
   a) Nature's phases, Valgius, are not always those of gloom, 1–8;
   b) Yet thou art ever sorrowful, 9–12;
   c) Others have found consolation in their bereavement, 13–17;
   d) Cease thy laments, therefore; let us sing the glories of great Caesar, 17–24.
2. **Time**: Probably 24 B.C.
3. **Metre**: Alcaic. Introd. § 43.

Non semper imbres nubibus hispidos
Manant in agros aut mare Caspium
Vexant inaequales procellae
Usque nec Armeniis in oris,

Amice Valgi, stat glacies iners
Menses per omnis, aut Aquilonibus
Querqueta Gargāni laborant
Et foliis viduantur orni:

Tu semper urges flebilibus modis
Mysten ademptum, nec tibi Vespero
Surgente decedunt amores
Nec rapidum fugiente solem.

At non ter aevo functus amabilem
Ploravit omnis Antilochum senex
Annos, nec impubem parentes
Troilon aut Phrygiae sorores

Flevere semper. Desine mollium
Tandem querellarum, et potius nova
Cantemus Augusti tropaea
Caesaris, et rigidum Niphāten

Medumque flumen gentibus additum
Victis minores volvere vertices,
Intraque praescriptum Gelōnos
Exiguis equitare campis.

X.

PRAISE OF 'THE GOLDEN MEAN.'

1. **Outline of the Poem**:
   a) Not too far out to sea, Licinius, nor yet too near the shore; so let thy dwelling be neither a hovel nor a palace, 1–8;
   b) The loftier thy aspirations, the greater the possible disaster, 9–12;
   c) Be on thy guard in prosperity; in adversity cherish hope. Nature is not ever sad; nor the gods always hostile, 13–24.
2. **Time**: Before 23 B.C.
3. **Metre**: Sapphic and Adonic. Introd. § 44.

Rectius vives, Licini, neque altum
Semper urgendo neque, dum procellas
Cautus horrescis, nimium premendo
Litus iniquom.

Auream quisquis mediocritatem
Diligit, tutus caret obsoleti
Sordibus tecti, caret invidenda
Sobrius aula.

Saepius ventis agitatur ingens
Pinus et celsae graviore casu
Decidunt turres feriuntque summos
  Fulgura montis.

Sperat infestis, metuit secundis
Alteram sortem bene praeparatum
Pectus. Informis hiemes reducit
  Iuppiter; idem

Summovet. Non, si male nunc, et olim
Sic erit: quondam cithara tacentem
Suscitat Musam neque semper arcum
  Tendit Apollo.

Rebus angustis animosus atque
Fortis appare: sapienter idem
Contrahes vento nimium secundo
  Turgida vela.

XI.

'CARPE DIEM.'

1. Outline of the Poem:

a) Away with all useless worry, Hirpinus; youth and beauty are gliding swiftly by; nothing endures, 1–12;

b) Rather under plane and pine let us have garlands and perfumes, wine and music, 13–24.

2. Time: Somewhere between 26 and 24 B.C.

3. Metre: Alcaic. Introd. § 43.

Quid bellicosus Cantaber et Scythes,
Hirpīne Quincti, cogitet Hadria
  Divisus obiecto, remittas
    Quaerere, nec trepides in usum

Poscentis aevi pauca: fugit retro
Levis iuventas et decor, arida
  Pellente lascivos amores
    Canitie facilemque somnum.

Non semper idem floribus est honor
Vernis, neque uno luna rubens nitet
  Voltu: quid aeternis minorem
    Consiliis animum fatigas?

Cur non sub alta vel platano vel hac
Pinu iacentes sic temere et rosa
  Canos odorati capillos,
    Dum licet, Assyriaque nardo

Potamus uncti? Dissipat Euhius
Curas edacis. Quis puer ocius
  Restinguet ardentis Falerni
    Pocula praetereunte lympha?

Quis devium scortum eliciet domo
Lyden? Eburna, dic age, cum lyra
  Maturet, incomptam Lacaenae
    More comam religata nodo!

XII.

THE CHARMS OF TERENTIA.

1. Occasion of the Ode: In the year 29 B.C., Augustus celebrated a triple triumph commemorative of his victories at Actium, in Egypt, and in Pannonia. Maecenas seems at that time to have called upon Horace to commemorate these achievements in lyric verse, a task which the poet declined on the ground that history was ill suited to the lyric Muse. As compensation for his refusal, however, he describes the charms of Maecenas's wife Terentia, here designated by the pseudonym *Licymnia*.

2. Outline of the Poem:

a) No one would choose lyric poetry to describe events of history or of mythologic legend, 1–8;

b) Let prose be the vehicle of celebrating Augustus's glory, and do thou, not I, Maecenas, essay the task, 9–12;

c) As for me, let me rather sing the praises of thy consort Licymnia, her lustrous eyes, her true heart, and her winsome ways, 13–28.

3. Time: Between 29 and 24 B.C.

4. Metre: Third Asclepiadean. Introd. § 47.

Nolis longa ferae bella Numantiae
Nec durum Hannibalem nec Siculum mare
Poeno purpureum sanguine mollibus
  Aptari citharae modis,

Nec saevos Lapithas et nimium mero
Hylaeum domitosque Herculea manu
Telluris iuvenes, unde periculum
  Fulgens contremuit domus

Saturni veteris: tuque pedestribus
Dices historiis proelia Caesaris,
Maecenas, melius ductaque per vias
  Regum colla minacium.

Me dulcis dominae Musa Licymniae
Cantus, me voluit dicere lucidum
Fulgentis oculos et bene mutuis
  Fidum pectus amoribus;

Quam nec ferre pedem dedecuit choris
Nec certare ioco nec dare bracchia
Ludentem nitidis virginibus sacro
  Dianae celebris die.

Num tu qūae tenuit dives Achaemenes
Aut pinguis Phrygiae Mygdonias opes
Permutare velis crine Licymniae,
Plenas aut Arabum domos,

Cum flagrantia detorquet ad oscula
Cervicem, aut facili saevitia negat,
Quae poscente magis gaudeat eripi,
Interdum rapere occupat?

XIII.

A NARROW ESCAPE.

1. Occasion of the Poem: On the 1st of March, 30 B.C., Horace had narrowly escaped death by the fall of a tree on his Sabine estate.

2. Outline of the Poem:

a) 'Twas on an ill-omened day that thou wast planted, O tree; and with a sacrilegious hand wast thou reared, 1–12;

b) Man never realizes the unseen dangers that threaten from every side, 13–20;

c) How narrowly did I escape passing to the realms of Proserpine, where Sappho and Alcaeus charm the shades with the music of their lyres, 21–40.

3. Time: Probably 30 B.C.

4. Metre: Alcaic. Introd. § 43.

The ode falls into two distinct parts, the first on the uncertainty of human existence, the second on the glory of poetry.

Ille et nefasto te posuit die,
Quicumque primum, et sacrilega manu
Produxit, arbos, in nepotum
Perniciem opprobriumque pagi.

Illum et parentis crediderim sui
Fregisse cervicem et penetralia
Sparsisse nocturno cruore
Hospitis; ille venena Colcha

Et quicquid usquam concipitur nefas
Tractavit, agro qui statuit meo
Te, triste lignum, te caducum
In domini caput immerentis.

Quid quisque vitet, numquam homini satis
Cautum est in horas: navita Bosphorum
Poenus perhorrescit neque ultra
Caeca timet aliunde fata;

Miles sagittas et celerem fugam
Parthi, catenas Parthus et Italum
Robur; sed improvisa leti
Vis rapuit rapietque gentis.

Quam paene furvae regna Proserpinae
Et iudicantem vidimus Aeacum
Sedesque discriptas piorum et
Aeoliis fidibus querentem

Sappho puellis de popularibus
Et te sonantem plenius aureo,
Alcaee, plectro dura navis,
Dura fugae mala, dura belli.

Utrumque sacro digna silentio
Mirantur umbrae dicere; sed magis
Pugnas et exactos tyrannos
Densum umeris bibit aure volgus.

Quid mirum, ubi illis carminibus stupens
Demittit atras belua centiceps
Auris, et intorti capillis
Eumenidum recreantur angues?

Quin et Promētheus et Pelopis parens
Dulci laborum decipitur sono,
Nec curat Orion leones
Aut timidos agitare lyncas.

XIV.

DEATH INEVITABLE.

1. Outline of the Poem:

a) Nothing, Postumus, avails to withstand the approach of death; not goodness, nor sacrifices, nor lofty station, 1–12;

b) In vain do we evade the dangers of this life, — war, shipwreck, and disease; death's dark night is the final doom of all, 13–20;

c) The joys of this life, — lands, homes, family, — are ours only to be renounced, and handed over to worthier successors, 21–28.

2. Time: Uncertain; probably about 30 B.C.

3. Metre: Alcaic. Introd. § 43.

Eheu fugaces, Postume, Postume,
Labuntur anni, nec pietas moram
Rugis et instanti senectae
Adferet indomitaeque morti;

Non, si trecenis, quotquot eunt dies,
Amice, places inlacrimabilem
Plutona tauris, qui ter amplum
Geryonen Tityonque tristi

Compescit unda, scilicet omnibus,
Quicumque terrae munere vescimur,
Enaviganda, sive reges
Sive inopes erimus coloni.

Frustra cruento Marte carebimus
Fractisque rauci fluctibus Hadriae,
Frustra per autumnos nocentem
Corporibus metuemus Austrum:

Visendus ater flumine languido
Cocȳtos errans et Danai genus
Infame damnatusque longi
Sisyphus Aeolides laboris.

Linquenda tellus et domus et placens
Uxor, neque harum, quas colis, arborum
Te praeter invisas cupressos
Ulla brevem dominum sequetur.

Absumet heres Caecuba dignior
Servata centum clavibus et mero
Tinguet pavimentum superbis
Pontificum potiore cenis.

XV.

AGAINST LUXURY.

1. Outline of the Poem:

a) Our princely estates with their fish-ponds bid fair to banish farming from the land; plane-trees, myrtle, and violets threaten to supplant the vine and olive, 1–10;

b) Far different was it in the days of old; then private wealth was small, and simple were men's abodes; but rich was the state and splendid were the public buildings, 10–20 (*cf.* Cic. *pro Murena* 36. 76, *odit populus Romanus privatam luxuriam, publicam magnificentiam diligit*).

2. **Time**: Probably 28 B.C.

3. **Metre**: Alcaic. Introd. § 43.

This poem stands alone among Horace's odes in that it is not addressed to any individual.

Iam pauca aratro iugera regiae
Moles relinquent, undique latius
Extenta visentur Lucrino
Stagna lacu, platanusque caelebs

Evincet ulmos; tum violaria et
Myrtus et omnis copia narium
Spargent olivetis odorem
Fertilibus domino priori.

Tum spissa ramis laurea fervidos
Excludet ictus. Non ita Romuli
Praescriptum et intonsi Catonis
Auspiciis veterumque norma.

Privatus illis census erat brevis,
Commune magnum: nulla decempedis
Metata privatis opacam
Porticus excipiebat Arcton,

Nec fortuitum spernere caespitem
Leges sinebant, oppida publico
Sumptu iubentes et deorum
Templa novo decorare saxo.

XVI.

CONTENTMENT WITH OUR LOT THE ONLY TRUE HAPPINESS.

1. **Outline of the Poem**:

a) Peace and happiness, O Grosphus, are the quest of all, 1–6;
b) But these cannot be bought with jewels or with gold; wealth avails not to still the restless tumults of the soul, 7–12;
c) Simple tastes and self-restraint must be the means, not eager striving for more, nor yet roving in foreign lands; let our hearts enjoy the present, meet its ills with resignation, and refuse to borrow care for the future, 13–27;
d) Yet no one can be altogether happy; witness Achilles and Tithonus. Fortune, too, grants to one man what she denies another; to thee she has given lands and kine, horses, and purple; me she has endowed with the glorious gift of song, 27–40.

2. **Time**: Probably 28 B.C.

3. **Metre**: Sapphic and Adonic. Introd. § 44.

Otium divos rogat in patenti
Prensus Aegaeo, simul atra nubes
Condidit lunam neque certa fulgent
Sidera nautis;

Otium bello furiosa Thrace,
Otium Medi pharetra decori,
Grosphe, non gemmis neque purpura ve-
nale neque auro.

Non enim gazae neque consularis
Summovet lictor miseros tumultus
Mentis et curas laqueata circum
Tecta volantis.

Vivitur parvo bene, cui paternum
Splendet in mensa tenui salinum
Nec levis somnos timor aut cupido
Sordidus aufert.

Quid brevi fortes iaculamur aevo
Multa? Quid terras alio calentis
Sole mutamus? Patriae quis exsul
Se quoque fugit?

Scandit aeratas vitiosa navis
Cura nec turmas equitum relinquit,
Ocior cervis et agente nimbos
Ocior Euro.

Laetus in praesens animus quod ultra est
Oderit curare et amara lento
Temperet risu. Nihil est ab omni
Parte beatum.

Abstulit clarum cita mors Achillem,
Longa Tithōnum minuit senectus;
Et mihi forsan, tibi quod negarit,
Porriget hora.

Te greges centum Siculaeque circum
Mugiunt vaccae, tibi tollit hinnitum
Apta quadrigis equa, te bis Afro
Murice tinctae

Vestiunt lanae; mihi parva rura et
Spiritum Graiae tenuem Camenae
Parca non mendax dedit et malignum
Spernere volgus.

XVII.

DESPAIR NOT, MAECENAS! ONE STAR LINKS OUR DESTINIES.

1. Occasion of the Poem: The ode seems to have been called forth by a serious illness which befell Maecenas in the fall of 30 B.C. and threatened to prove fatal.

2. Outline of the Poem:

a) Think not that thou shalt die before me, Maecenas! Why should I linger after thee? One and the same day shall see us enter on that final journey, nor shall any power of earth or hell tear me from thee, 1–16;

b) Whatever planet guides our destinies, our fates are surely linked together. Thee Jove, me Faunus, saved from destruction, 17–30;

c) And so an offering to the gods in commemoration of their favor! 30–32.

3. Time: 30 B.C.

4. Metre: Alcaic. Introd. § 43.

Cur me querellis exanimas tuis?
Nec dis amicum est nec mihi te prius
Obire, Maecenas, mearum
Grande decus columenque rerum.

A, te meae si partem animae rapit
Maturior vis, quid moror altera,
Nec carus aeque nec superstes
Integer? Ille dies utramque

Ducet ruinam. Non ego perfidum
Dixi sacramentum: ibimus, ibimus,
Utcumque praecedes, supremum
Carpere iter comites parati.

Me nec Chimaerae spiritus igneae
Nec, si resurgat, centimanus Gyas
Divellet umquam: sic potenti
Iustitiae placitumque Parcis.

Seu Libra seu me Scorpios adspicit
Formidolosus pars violentior
Natalis horae seu tyrannus
Hesperiae Capricornus undae,

Utrumque nostrum incredibili modo
Consentit astrum. Te Iovis impio
Tutela Saturno refulgens
Eripuit volucrisque Fati

Tardavit alas, cum populus frequens
Laetum theatris ter crepuit sonum;
Me truncus inlapsus cerebro
Sustulerat, nisi Faunus ictum

Dextra levasset, Mercurialium
Custos virorum. Reddere victimas
Aedemque votivam memento;
Nos humilem feriemus agnam.

XVIII.

THE VANITY OF RICHES.

1. Outline of the Poem:

a) No glittering splendor of gold and ivory and marble marks my house, 1–8;
b) But loyal devotion to my friends and the inspiration of the muse are mine; these make me content with my little Sabine farm, 9–14;
c) Others, heedless of time's swift passage, think only of rearing splendid palaces, encroaching now on the sea's domain, now on the lands of their helpless tenants, 15–28;
d) Yet Death is the doom of all alike, — of the rich lord no less than the poor peasant, 29–40.

2. Time: Uncertain; probably soon after the gift of the Sabine farm (about 33 B.C.).

3. Metre: Trochaic Strophe. Introd. § 60.

Non ebur neque aureum
  Mea renidet in domo lacunar,
Non trabes Hymettiae
  Premunt columnas ultima recisas

Africa, neque Attali
  Ignotus heres regiam occupavi,
Nec Laconicas mihi
  Trahunt honestae purpuras clientae.

At fides et ingeni
  Benigna vena est, pauperemque dives
Me petit: nihil supra
  Deos lacesso nec potentem amicum

Largiora flagito,
  Satis beatus unicis Sabinis.
Truditur dies die,
  Novaeque pergunt interire lunae.

Tu secanda marmora
  Locas sub ipsum funus et sepulcri
Immemor struis domos,
  Marisque Bais obstrepentis urges

Summovere litora,
  Parum locuples continente ripa.
Quid quod usque proximos
  Revellis agri terminos et ultra

Limites clientium
  Salis avarus? Pellitur paternos
In sinu ferens deos
  Et uxor et vir sordidosque natos.

Nulla certior tamen
  Rapacis Orci fine destinata
Aula divitem manet
  Erum. Quid ultra tendis? Aequa tellus

Pauperi recluditur
  Regumque pueris, nec satelles Orci
Callidum Promēthea
  Revexit auro captus. Hic superbum

Tantalum atque Tantali
  Genus coercet, hic levare functum
Pauperem laboribus
  Vocatus atque non vocatus audit.

XIX.

BACCHUS, THINE'S THE POWER!

1. Outline of the Poem:

a) My heart still thrills with delight at my recent glimpse of Bacchus amid the rocks teaching the nymphs and satyrs, 1–8;

b) And so I am moved to sing of the votaries of the god and of the wine, the milk, the honey that flow forth at his bidding; of Ariadne, too, his deified consort; of the dire fates of Pentheus and Lycurgus, 9–16;

c) Thy power, O Bacchus, is universal; river and sea, man and god, confess thy might; even Cerberus stood in awe of thee, 17–32.

2. Time: Uncertain; not later than 23 B.C.

3. Metre: Alcaic. Introd. § 43.

In its wild enthusiasm this ode suggests that Horace is here imitating some Greek dithyramb.

Bacchum in remotis carmina rupibus
Vidi docentem — credite posteri —
Nymphasque discentis et auris
Capripedum Satyrorum acutas.

Euhoe, recenti mens trepidat metu,
Plenoque Bacchi pectore turbidum
Laetatur. Euhoe, parce, Liber,
Parce, gravi metuende thyrso.

Fas pervicacis est mihi Thyiadas
Vinique fontem lactis et uberes
Cantare rivos atque truncis
Lapsa cavis iterare mella;

Fas et beatae coniugis additum
Stellis honorem tectaque Penthei
Disiecta non leni ruina
Thracis et exitium Lycurgi.

Tu flectis amnes, tu mare barbarum,
Tu separatis uvidus in iugis
Nodo coerces viperino
Bistonidum sine fraude crinis.

Tu, cum parentis regna per arduom
Cohors Gigantum scanderet impia,
Rhoetum retorsisti leonis
Unguibus horribilique mala;

Quamquam choreis aptior et iocis
Ludoque dictus non sat idoneus
Pugnae ferebaris; sed idem
Pacis eras mediusque belli.

Te vidit insons Cerberus aureo
Cornu decorum, leniter atterens
Caudam, et recedentis trilingui
Ore pedes tetigitque crura.

XX.

THE POET PROPHESIES HIS OWN IMMORTALITY.

1. **Outline of the Poem**:
   a) On mighty pinion I shall mount aloft, soaring above the cities of earth and the envy of men, escaping the Stygian wave, 1–8;
   b) Already I feel the plumage of my new form, 9–12;
   c) North and south, east and west, shall I fly in my course, 13–20;
   d) Therefore refrain from tears and weeping; and rear no tomb in my honor when I seem to be gone, 21–24.
2. **Time**: Uncertain; not later than 23 B.C.
3. **Metre**: Alcaic. Introd. § 43.

Non usitata nec tenui ferar
Pinna biformis per liquidum aethera
Vates, neque in terris morabor
Longius invidiaque maior

Urbes relinquam. Non ego, pauperum
Sanguis parentum, non ego, quem vocas,
Dilecte Maecenas, obibo
Nec Stygia cohibebor unda.

Iam iam residunt cruribus asperae
Pelles, et album mutor in alitem
Superne, nascunturque leves
Per digitos umerosque plumae.

Iam Daedaleo tutior Icaro
Visam gementis litora Bosphori
Syrtisque Gaetulas canorus
Ales Hyperboreosque campos.

Me Colchus et, qui dissimulat metum
Marsae cohortis, Dacus et ultimi
Noscent Geloni, me peritus
Discet Hiber Rhodanique potor.

Absint inani funere neniae
Luctusque turpes et querimoniae;
Compesce clamorem ac sepulcri
Mitte supervacuos honores.

CARMINUM

LIBER TERTIUS.

THE FIRST SIX ODES.

The first six odes of Book III. form an organic whole. This is clear, not merely from the special lyrical form (Alcaic) in which they all are cast, but more particularly from their content. These six poems all emphasize the cardinal Roman virtues, which had made Rome great in the past, and to which, the poet declares, the rising generation must steadfastly cling to ensure the perpetuation of that greatness for the future. These virtues, in the order of their presentation in the successive odes, are simplicity of living (*frugalitas*), Ode I.; endurance (*patientia*) and fidelity to a trust (*fides*), Ode II.; steadfastness of purpose in a righteous cause (*iustitia atque constantia*), Ode III.; wisdom and deliberation in action (*consilium*), Ode IV.; martial courage (*virtus*, *fortitudo*), Ode V.; reverence for the gods and righteous doing (*pietas*, *castitas*), Ode VI. As befits a poet, Horace urges the importance of these fundamental virtues, not by way of systematic treatment or detailed analysis, but rather by a wealth of poetic illustration. The special theme of each ode is nowhere obtruded upon the reader; in some of the odes, indeed, as, for example, the fourth, the central thought is kept carefully in the background, not being suggested till near the close. Nowhere has the poet evinced more art than in the opening odes of this book; with fine instinct he has embodied the advocacy and enforcement of the loftiest ethical ideals in stanzas which, apart from the high purposes of his teaching, constitute some of the choicest verse he ever wrote.

Whether or not composed at the express solicitation of Augustus, it is clear that these odes were intended to indorse and support the emperor in the social and religious reforms which he had inaugurated for promoting the stability and perpetuity of the Roman state.

I.

FRUGALITAS.

1. Outline of the Poem :

a) Introductory to the series of the six odes, 1–4 ;

b) As kings hold sway over their subjects, and as Jove holds sway over kings, so upon all men, despite their differences of outward station, does inexorable Destiny pronounce her decrees, 5–16 ;

c) Not choice viands nor sound of music can bring sweet sleep, but only contentment with our humble lot and indifference to the blows of Fortune, 17–32 ;

d) No palace, no galley, however swift, no purple, or wines, or perfumes, can secure us from fear and care ; and so why should I exchange my Sabine valley for a palace reared in the splendid fashion of the day ? 33–48.

2. Time : Probably about 27 B.C.

3. Metre : Alcaic. Introd. § 43.

'Odi profanum volgus et arceo;
Favete linguis.' Carmina non prius
Audita Musarum sacerdos
Virginibus puerisque canto.

Regum timendorum in proprios greges,
Reges in ipsos imperium est Iovis,
Clari Giganteo triumpho,
Cuncta supercilio moventis.

Est ut viro vir latius ordinet
Arbusta sulcis, hic generosior
Descendat in Campum petitor,
Moribus hic meliorque fama

Contendat, illi turba clientium
Sit maior; aequa lege Necessitas
Sortitur insignis et imos;
Omne capax movet urna nomen.

Destrictus ensis cui super impia
Cervice pendet, non Siculae dapes
Dulcem elaborabunt saporem,
Non avium citharaeque cantus

Somnum reducent. Somnus agrestium
Lenis virorum non humilis domos
Fastidit umbrosamque ripam,
Non zephyris agitata Tempe.

Desiderantem quod satis est neque
Tumultuosum sollicitat mare
Nec saevos Arctūri cadentis
Impetus aut orientis Haedi,

Non verberatae grandine vineae
Fundusque mendax, arbore nunc aquas
Culpante, nunc torrentia agros
Sidera, nunc hiemes iniquas.

Contracta pisces aequora sentiunt
Iactis in altum molibus: huc frequens
Caementa demittit redemptor
Cum famulis dominusque terrae

Fastidiosus. Sed Timor et Minae
Scandunt eodem quo dominus, neque
Decedit aerata triremi et
Post equitem sedet atra Cura.

Quodsi dolentem nec Phrygius lapis
Nec purpurarum sidere clarior
Delenit usus nec Falerna
Vitis Achaemeniumque costum:

Cur invidendis postibus et novo
Sublime ritu moliar atrium?
Cur valle permutem Sabina
Divitias operosiores?

II.

PATIENTIA, VIRTUS, FIDES.

1. Outline of the Poem:

a) Let our young soldiers learn to endure with patience the privations of the field, and may they prove a terror to our foes; for sweet and glorious is it to die for fatherland, while cowardice can expect only its just reward, 1–16;

b) True worth, self-poised, recks not the judgment of the mob, but pursues serenely its own lofty course, 17–24;

c) Praiseworthy, too, is he who is faithful to his trust; let no other share my hearth. Though the outraged god at times may not spare the innocent, yet the guilty never escape, 25–32.

2. Time: Probably about 27 B.C.

3. Metre: Alcaic. Introd. § 43.

Angustam amice pauperiem pati
Robustus acri militia puer
Condiscat et Parthos ferocis
Vexet eques metuendus hasta,

Vitamque sub divo et trepidis agat
In rebus. Illum ex moenibus hosticis
Matrona bellantis tyranni
Prospiciens et adulta virgo

Suspiret: 'eheu, ne rudis agminum
Sponsus lacessat regius asperum
Tactu leonem, quem cruenta
Per medias rapit ira caedes.'

Dulce et decorum est pro patria mori.
Mors et fugacem persequitur virum,
Nec parcit imbellis iuventae
Poplitibus timidove tergo.

Virtus, repulsae nescia sordidae,
Intaminatis fulget honoribus,
Nec sumit aut ponit securis
Arbitrio popularis aurae.

Virtus, recludens immeritis mori
Caelum, negata temptat iter via,
Coetusque volgaris et udam
Spernit humum fugiente pinna.

Est et fideli tuta silentio
Merces: vetabo, qui Cereris sacrum
Volgarit arcanae, sub isdem
Sit trabibus fragilemque mecum

Solvat phaselon; saepe Diespiter
Neclectus incesto addidit integrum,
Raro antecedentem scelestum
Deseruit pede Poena claudo.

III.

JUSTITIA ET CONSTANTIA.

1. Outline of the Poem:

a) The man tenacious of his purpose in a righteous cause, no terrors of earth or heaven can move from his course, 1–8;

b) 'Twas such merit that won divine honors for Pollux and Hercules and Bacchus; 'twas such merit on the part of Romulus that induced Juno to admit him to the ranks of the celestials, 9–36;

c) But the goddess imposed conditions: 'Provided a wide sea roll between Rome and Ilium; provided the cattle and wild beasts roam with impunity over the site of ancient Troy and the ashes of Priam, let Rome extend her name and prowess to the confines of the world; but let her never, in excess of devotion, think of restoring the walls of the ancient city. Should Troy thrice rise, thrice should she be destroyed by my Greeks,' 37–68.

d) But cease, O Muse, to repeat the words of the gods, and to belittle great themes with thy trivial song! 69–72.

2. Time: About 27 B.C.

3. Metre: Alcaic. Introd. § 43.

Iustum et tenacem propositi virum
Non civium ardor prava iubentium,
Non voltus instantis tyranni
Mente quatit solida neque Auster,

Dux inquieti turbidus Hadriae,
Nec fulminantis magna manus Iovis;
Si fractus inlabatur orbis,
Impavidum ferient ruinae.

Hac arte Pollux et vagus Hercules
Enisus arces attigit igneas,
Quos inter Augustus recumbens
Purpureo bibet ore nectar.

Hac te merentem, Bacche pater, tuae
Vexere tigres, indocili iugum
Collo trahentes; hac Quirīnus
Martis equis Acheronta fugit,

Gratum elocuta consiliantibus
Iunone divis: ‘Ilion, Ilion
Fatalis incestusque iudex
Et mulier peregrina vertit

In pulverem, ex quo destituit deos
Mercede pacta Laomedon, mihi
Castaeque damnatum Minervae
Cum populo et duce fraudulento.

Iam nec Lacaenae splendet adulterae
Famosus hospes nec Priami domus
Periura pugnaces Achivos
Hectoreis opibus refringit,

Nostrisque ductum seditionibus
Bellum resedit. Protinus et gravis
Iras et invisum nepotem,
Troica quem peperit sacerdos,

Marti redonabo; illum ego lucidas
Inire sedes, ducere nectaris
Sucos et adscribi quietis
Ordinibus patiar deorum.

Dum longus inter saeviat Ilion
Romamque pontus, qualibet exsules
In parte regnanto beati;
Dum Priami Paridisque busto

Insultet armentum et catulos ferae
Celent inultae, stet Capitolium
Fulgens triumphatisque possit
Roma ferox dare iura Medis.

Horrenda late nomen in ultimas
Extendat oras, qua medius liquor
Secernit Europen ab Afro,
Qua tumidus rigat arva Nilus,

Aurum inrepertum et sic melius situm,
Cum terra celat, spernere fortior
Quam cogere humanos in usus
Omne sacrum rapiente dextra.

Quicumque mundo terminus obstitit,
Hunc tangat armis, visere gestiens,
Qua parte debacchentur ignes,
Qua nebulae pluviique rores.

Sed bellicosis fata Quiritibus
Hac lege dico, ne nimium pii
Rebusque fidentes avitae
Tecta velint reparare Troiae.

Troiae renascens alite lugubri
Fortuna tristi clade iterabitur
Ducente victrices catervas
Coniuge me Iovis et sorore.

Ter si resurgat murus aëneus
Auctore Phoebo, ter pereat meis
Excisus Argivis, ter uxor
Capta virum puerosque ploret.'

Non hoc iocosae conveniet lyrae:
Quo, Musa, tendis? Desine pervicax
Referre sermones deorum et
Magna modis tenuare parvis.

IV

CONSILIUM ET TEMPERANTIA.

1. **Outline of the Poem:**

   a) Invocation to the Muse, 1–8;
   b) Horace's boyhood adventure on Mt. Vultur, 9–20;
   c) His devotion to the Muses; 'tis as their minister that he visits his Sabine farm, his villa at Tivoli, or fair Baiae; 'tis their care that has watched over him in the past and gives him heart to face the future, 21–36;
   d) The Muses lend cheer and comfort to Caesar, too; more than that, they impart wise counsel also, against which no forces of evil can prevail, — no more than the Titans could prevail against the wisdom of the gods of Olympus, 37–64;
   e) Wisely ordered might will ever prosper, while brute force falls with its own weight, — witness the fates of Gyas, of Orion, of the giants, Tityos, and Pirithous, 65–80.

2. **Time:** Probably about 27 B.C.

3. **Metre:** Alcaic. Introd. § 43.

Descende caelo et dic age tibia
Regina longum Calliope melos,
Seu voce nunc mavis acuta
Seu fidibus citharaque Phoebi.

Auditis, an me ludit amabilis
Insania? Audire et videor pios
Errare per lucos, amoenae
Quos et aquae subeunt et aurae.

Me fabulosae Volture in avio
Nutricis extra limen Apuliae
  Ludo fatigatumque somno
    Fronde nova puerum palumbes

Texere, mirum quod foret omnibus,
Quicumque celsae nidum Acherontiae
  Saltusque Bantinos et arvom
    Pingue tenent humilis Forenti,

Ut tuto ab atris corpore viperis
Dormirem et ursis, ut premerer sacra
  Lauroque conlataque myrto,
    Non sine dis animosus infans.

Vester, Camenae, vester in arduos
Tollor Sabinos, seu mihi frigidum
  Praeneste seu Tibur supinum
    Seu liquidae placuere Baiae.

Vestris amicum fontibus et choris
Non me Philippis versa acies retro,
  Devota non extinxit arbor,
    Nec Sicula Palinūrus unda.

Utcumque mecum vos eritis, libens
Insanientem navita Bosphorum
  Temptabo et urentis harenas
    Litoris Assyrii viator;

Visam Britannos hospitibus feros
Et laetum equino sanguine Concanum,
  Visam pharetratos Gelōnos
    Et Scythicum inviolatus amnem.

Vos Caesarem altum, militia simul
Fessas cohortes addidit oppidis,
Finire quaerentem labores,
Pierio recreatis antro.

Vos lene consilium et datis et dato
Gaudetis, almae. Scimus, ut impios
Titanas immanemque turbam
Fulmine sustulerit caduco,

Qui terram inertem, qui mare temperat
Ventosum et urbes regnaque tristia,
Divosque mortalisque turmas
Imperio regit unus aequo.

Magnum illa terrorem intulerat Iovi
Fidens iuventus horrida bracchiis
Fratresque tendentes opaco
Pelion imposuisse Olympo.

Sed quid Typhōeus et validus Mimas,
Aut quid minaci Porphyrion statu,
Quid Rhoetus evolsisque truncis
Enceladus iaculator audax

Contra sonantem Palladis aegida
Possent ruentes? Hinc avidus stetit
Volcanus, hinc matrona Iuno et
Numquam umeris positurus arcum,

Qui rore puro Castaliae lavit
Crinis solutos, qui Lyciae tenet
Dumeta natalemque silvam,
Delius et Patareus Apollo.

Vis consili expers mole ruit sua:
Vim temperatam di quoque provehunt
In maius; idem odere viris
Omne nefas animo moventis.

Testis mearum centimanus Gyas
Sententiarum, notus et integrae
Temptator Orīon Dianae,
Virginea domitus sagitta.

Iniecta monstris Terra dolet suis
Maeretque partus fulmine luridum
Missos ad Orcum; nec peredit
Impositam celer ignis Aetnen,

Incontinentis nec Tityi iecur
Reliquit ales, nequitiae additus
Custos; amatorem trecentae
Pirithoum cohibent catenae.

V.

VIRTUS, FORTITUDO.

1. Outline of the Poem:

a) Jove's thunders proclaim him god of the sky; but Augustus will be recognized as a god on earth for his subjugation of the Britons and the Parthians, 1–4;

b) The decay of Roman courage, as exemplified by the conduct of Crassus's troops, — men who forgot their Roman birthright, 5–12;

c) 'Twas no such spirit that Regulus displayed in the good old days. 'Victory or death,' was then the watchword. 'Ransom not the man who has once surrendered!' he urged; 'such a one will never again display true courage, no more than the wool once dyed can regain its whiteness; no more than the deer will fight the hounds,' 13–40;

d) The departure of Regulus: sternly repulsing wife and child, kinsmen and friends, he went away, well knowing to what doom. 41–56.

2. **Time**: Probably about 27 B.C.

3. **Metre**: Alcaic. Introd. § 43.

Caelo tonantem credidimus Iovem
Regnare; praesens divos habebitur
Augustus adiectis Britannis
Imperio gravibusque Persis.

Milesne Crassi coniuge barbara
Turpis maritus vixit et hostium
(Pro curia inversique mores!)
Consenuit socerorum in armis

Sub rege Medo, Marsus et Apulus,
Anciliorum et nominis et togae
Oblitus aeternaeque Vestae,
Incolumi Iove et urbe Roma?

Hoc caverat mens provida Reguli
Dissentientis condicionibus
Foedis et exemplo trahenti
Perniciem veniens in aevom,

Si non periret immiserabilis
Captiva pubes. 'Signa ego Punicis
Adfixa delubris et arma
Militibus sine caede' dixit

'Derepta vidi, vidi ego civium
Retorta tergo bracchia libero
Portasque non clausas et arva
Marte coli populata nostro.

Auro repensus scilicet acrior
Miles redibit. Flagitio additis
Damnum: neque amissos colores
Lana refert medicata fuco,

Nec vera virtus, cum semel excidit,
Curat reponi deterioribus.
Si pugnat extricata densis
Cerva plagis, erit ille fortis

Qui perfidis se credidit hostibus,
Et Marte Poenos proteret altero,
Qui lora restrictis lacertis
Sensit iners timuitque mortem.

Hic, unde vitam sumeret inscius,
Pacem duello miscuit. O pudor!
O magna Carthago, probrosis
Altior Italiae ruinis!'

Fertur pudicae coniugis osculum
Parvosque natos ut capitis minor
Ab se removisse et virilem
Torvos humi posuisse voltum,

Donec labantis consilio patres
Firmaret auctor numquam alias dato,
Interque maerentis amicos
Egregius properaret exsul.

Atqui sciebat quae sibi barbarus
Tortor pararet. Non aliter tamen
Dimovit obstantis propinquos
Et populum reditus morantem,

Quam si clientum longa negotia
Diiudicata lite relinqueret,
Tendens Venafranos in agros
Aut Lacedaemonium Tarentum.

VI

PIETAS, CASTITAS.

1. **Outline of the Poem** :
   a) Restore, O Roman, the crumbling shrines and statues of the gods ; all that thou art thou owest to the gods ; their neglect has already brought upon Hesperia many woes, — from Parthian, Dacian, and Numidian, 1-16 ;
   b) From the family and the home threaten the greatest dangers. Our women are no longer pure, 17–32 ;
   c) Not of such parentage were the warriors who in former days dyed the waves with Punic blood and crushed Antiochus and Hannibal, 33–44 ;
   d) Alas the ravages of time ! As we are less worthy than our sires, so our offspring promise to be more degenerate than we, 45–48.
2. **Time** : Probably about 27 B.C.
3. **Metre** : Alcaic. Introd. § 43.

Delicta maiorum immeritus lues,
Romane, donec templa refeceris
Aedisque labentis deorum et
Foeda nigro simulacra fumo.

Dis te minorem quod geris, imperas:
Hinc omne principium; huc refer exitum.
Di multa neclecti dederunt
Hesperiae mala luctuosae.

Iam bis Monaeses et Pacori manus
Non auspicatos contudit impetus
Nostros et adiecisse praedam
Torquibus exiguis renidet.

Paene occupatam seditionibus
Delevit urbem Dacus et Aethiops,
Hic classe formidatus, ille
Missilibus melior sagittis.

Fecunda culpae saecula nuptias
Primum inquinavere et genus et domos:
Hoc fonte derivata clades
In patriam populumque fluxit.

Motus doceri gaudet Ionicos
Matura virgo et fingitur artibus
Iam nunc et incestos amores
De tenero meditatur ungui.

Mox iuniores quaerit adulteros
Inter mariti vina, neque eligit
Cui donet impermissa raptim
Gaudia luminibus remotis,

Sed iussa coram non sine conscio
Surgit marito, seu vocat institor
Seu navis Hispanae magister,
Dedecorum pretiosus emptor.

Non his iuventus orta parentibus
Infecit aequor sanguine Punico
Pyrrhumque et ingentem cecidit
Antiochum Hannibalemque dirum;

Sed rusticorum mascula militum
Proles, Sabellis docta ligonibus
Versare glaebas et severae
Matris ad arbitrium recisos

Portare fustis, Sol ubi montium
Mutaret umbras et iuga demeret
Bobus fatigatis, amicum
Tempus agens abeunte curru.

Damnosa quid non imminuit dies?
Aetas parentum, peior avis, tulit
Nos nequiores, mox daturos
Progeniem vitiosiorem.

VII.

CONSTANCY, ASTERIE!

1. **Outline of the Poem:**

   a) Weep not, Asterie! With spring's first zephyrs thy lover will be back again, 1–5;

   b) Meanwhile he longs for thee, and yields not to the arts of those who plot to steal his love, 5–22;

   c) But do thou thyself have a care lest thy affection be won by thy neighbor, Enipeus; mighty he is in prowess; but yield not to his advances, 22–32.

2. **Time:** Uncertain; not later than 23 B.C.

3. **Metre:** Fourth Asclepiadean. Introd. § 48.

Quid fles, Asterie, quem tibi candidi
Primo restituent vere Favonii
Thyna merce beatum,
Constantis iuvenem fide,

Gygen? Ille Notis actus ad Oricum
Post insana Caprae sidera frigidas
Noctes non sine multis
Insomnis lacrimis agit.

Atqui sollicitae nuntius hospitae,
Suspirare Chloen et miseram tuis
Dicens ignibus uri,
Temptat mille vafer modis.

Ut Proetum mulier perfida credulum
Falsis impulerit criminibus nimis
Casto Bellerophontae
Maturare necem refert;

Narrat paene datum Pelea Tartaro,
Magnessam Hippolyten dum fugit abstinens;
Et peccare docentis
Fallax historias movet.

Frustra: nam scopulis surdior Icari
Voces audit adhuc integer. At tibi
Ne vicinus Enīpeus
Plus iusto placeat cave;

Quamvis non alius flectere equom sciens
Aeque conspicitur gramine Martio,
Nec quisquam citus aeque
Tusco denatat alveo.

Prima nocte domum claude neque in vias
Sub cantu querulae despice tibiae,
Et te saepe vocanti
Duram difficilis mane.

VIII.

A GLAD ANNIVERSARY.

1. Outline of the Poem:

a) **What mean my flowers and offerings? 'Tis in commemoration of my escape from the falling tree, 1–8;**

b) **This anniversary shall ever be the signal for good cheer, 9–12;**

c) **Share thou my celebration, O Maecenas! Leave meanwhile the cares of state! Naught threatens from without; our foes are quelled; enjoy the passing hour! 13–28.**

2. Time: 29 B.C.

3. Metre: Sapphic and Adonic. Introd. § 44.

Martiis caelebs quid agam Kalendis,
Quid velint flores et acerra turis
Plena miraris positusque carbo in
  Caespite vivo,

Docte sermones utriusque linguae.
Voveram dulcis epulas et album
Libero caprum prope funeratus
  Arboris ictu.

Hic dies anno redeunte festus
Corticem adstrictum pice demovebit
Amphorae fumum bibere institutae
  Consule Tullo.

Sume, Maecenas, cyathos amici
Sospitis centum et vigiles lucernas
Perfer in lucem: procul omnis esto
  Clamor et ira.

Mitte civilis super urbe curas:
Occidit Daci Cotisonis agmen,
Medus infestus sibi luctuosis
  Dissidet armis,

Servit Hispanae vetus hostis orae
Cantaber, sera domitus catena,
Iam Scythae laxo meditantur arcu
  Cedere campis.

Neclegens, nequa populus laboret,
Parce privatus nimium cavere et
Dona praesentis cape laetus horae ac
  Linque severa.

IX.

RECONCILIATION.

1. Outline of the Poem:

a) The Lover: 'While I was dearer than all others to thee, my happiness knew no bounds,' 1–4;
b) Lydia: 'Nor mine, while I was thy only flame,' 5–8;
c) The Lover: 'Chloe is my mistress now, and for her I'd suffer death itself.' 9–12;
d) Lydia: 'Calais is *my* lover; twice would I die for him,' 13–16;
e) The Lover: 'What if the old love be renewed, and Lydia be welcomed again?' 17–20;
f) Lydia: 'Fair though he be, and fickle thou, with thee will I cast my lot,' 21–24.

2. Time: Uncertain; not later than 23 B.C.

3. Metre: Second Asclepiadean. Introd. § 46.

'Donec gratus eram tibi
  Nec quisquam potior bracchia candidae
Cervici iuvenis dabat,
  Persarum vigui rege beatior.'

'Donec non alia magis
  Arsisti neque erat Lydia post Chloen,
Multi Lydia nominis
  Romana vigui clarior Ilia.'

'Me nunc Thressa Chloe regit,
  Dulcis docta modos et citharae sciens,
Pro qua non metuam mori,
  Si parcent animae fata superstiti.'

'Me torret face mutua
  Thurini Calais filius Ornyti,
Pro quo bis patiar mori,
  Si parcent puero fata superstiti.'

'Quid si prisca redit Venus
  Diductosque iugo cogit aëneo?
Si flava excutitur Chloe
  Reiectaeque patet ianua Lydiae?'

'Quamquam sidere pulchrior
  Ille est, tu levior cortice et improbo
Iracundior Hadria,
  Tecum vivere amem, tecum obeam libens!'

X.

A LOVER'S COMPLAINT.

1. **Outline of the Poem**:
   a) No barbarian, Lyce, would be so cruel as art thou to let me lie outside thy door in wind and cold, 1–8;
   b) Banish thy haughty disdain, and have compassion on thy suppliant; not alway will I submit to such harsh treatment, 9–20.
2. **Time**: Uncertain; not later than 23 B.C.
3. **Metre**: Third Asclepiadean. Introd. § 47.

Extremum Tanain si biberes, Lyce,
Saevo nupta viro, me tamen asperas
Porrectum ante fores obicere incolis
  Plorares Aquilonibus.

Audis, quo strepitu ianua, quo nemus
Inter pulchra satum tecta remugiat
Ventis, et positas ut glaciet nives
  Puro numine Iuppiter?

Ingratam Veneri pone superbiam,
Ne currente retro funis eat rota:
Non te Penelopen difficilem procis
  Tyrrhenus genuit parens.

O quamvis neque te munera nec preces
Nec tinctus viola pallor amantium
Nec vir Pieria paelice saucius
  Curvat, supplicibus tuis

Parcas, nec rigida mollior aesculo
Nec Mauris animum mitior anguibus.
Non hoc semper erit liminis aut aquae
  Caelestis patiens latus.

XI.

TAKE WARNING, LYDE, FROM THE DANAIDS!

1. **Outline of the Poem**:

a) O lyre of Mercury, cast the magic of thy spell upon the stubborn Lyde, who now resists the claims of Cupid, 1–12;

b) Thy might, O lyre, can tame the tigers and stay the course of torrents; it can even still the torment of those in Tartarus, — Ixion, Tityos, and the Danaids, 13–24;

c) Let Lyde heed the fate of these, impious all but one, who, "gloriously false" to her pledge, saved her lover, well knowing the risk it meant, 25–52.

2. **Time**: Uncertain; not later than 23 B.C.

3. **Metre**: Sapphic and Adonic. Introd. § 44.

Mercuri (nam te docilis magistro
Movit Amphīon lapides canendo),
Tuque testudo resonare septem
  Callida nervis,

Nec loquax olim neque grata, nunc et
Divitum mensis et amica templis,
Dic modos, Lyde quibus obstinatas
  Applicet auris,

Quae velut latis equa trima campis
Ludit exsultim metuitque tangi,
Nuptiarum expers et adhuc protervo
  Cruda marito.

Tu potes tigris comitesque silvas
Ducere et rivos celeres morari;
Cessit immanis tibi blandienti
  Ianitor aulae,

Cerberus, quamvis furiale centum
Muniant angues caput eius atque
Spiritus taeter saniesque manet
Ore trilingui.

Quin et Ixīon Tityosque voltu
Risit invito, stetit urna paulum
Sicca, dum grato Danai puellas
Carmine mulces.

Audiat Lyde scelus atque notas
Virginum poenas et inane lymphae
Dolium fundo pereuntis imo
Seraque fata,

Quae manent culpas etiam sub Orco.
Impiae (nam quid potuere maius?)
Impiae sponsos potuere duro
Perdere ferro.

Una de multis face nuptiali
Digna periurum fuit in parentem
Splendide mendax et in omne virgo
Nobilis aevom,

'Surge' quae dixit iuveni marito,
'Surge, ne longus tibi somnus, unde
Non times, detur; socerum et scelestas
Falle sorores,

Quae, velut nanctae vitulos leaenae,
Singulos eheu lacerant: ego illis
Mollior nec te feriam neque intra
Claustra tenebo.

Me pater saevis oneret catenis,
Quod viro clemens misero peperci;
Me vel extremos Numidarum in agros
  Classe releget.

I, pedes quo te rapiunt et aurae,
Dum favet Nox et Venus; i secundo
Omine, et nostri memorem sepulcro
  Scalpe querellam.'

XII.

NEOBULE'S PLAINT.

1. **Outline of the Poem**:
   - *a*) Hard is the lot of maidens who may not indulge Love's fancy or drown their cares in wine, for fear of being chidden by some stern guardian, 1–3;
   - *b*) Ah me! all heart for my wonted tasks is driven away by the beauty of radiant Hebrus, who excels alike in feats of skill and prowess, 4–12.
2. **Time**: Uncertain; not later than 23 B.C.
3. **Metre**: Ionic a Minore. Introd. § 61.

Miserarum est neque amori dare ludum neque dulci
Mala vino lavere aut exanimari metuentis
  Patruae verbera linguae.

Tibi qualum Cytherĕae puer ales, tibi telas
Operosaeque Minervae studium aufert, Neobūle,
  Liparaei nitor Hebri,

Simul unctos Tiberinis umeros lavit in undis,
Eques ipso melior Bellerophonte, neque pugno
  Neque segni pede victus,

Catus idem per apertum fugientis agitato
Grege cervos iaculari et celer arto latitantem
  Fruticeto excipere aprum.

XIII.

TO THE FOUNTAIN BANDUSIA.

1. **Outline of the Poem**:

a) To-morrow, beauteous fount, shalt thou receive thy annual sacrifice, 1–8;

b) Thy gracious coolness is vouchsafed to flock and herd; immortal shalt thou be through the tribute of my verse, 9–16.

2. **Time**: Uncertain; not later than 23 B.C.

3. **Metre**: Fourth Asclepiadean. Introd. § 48.

O fons Bandusiae, splendidior vitro,
Dulci digne mero non sine floribus,
Cras donaberis haedo,
Cui frons turgida cornibus

Primis et venerem et proelia destinat.
Frustra: nam gelidos inficiet tibi
Rubro sanguine rivos
Lascivi suboles gregis.

Te flagrantis atrox hora Caniculae
Nescit tangere, tu frigus amabile
Fessis vomere tauris
Praebes et pecori vago.

Fies nobilium tu quoque fontium,
Me dicente cavis impositam ilicem
Saxis, unde loquaces
Lymphae desiliunt tuae.

XIV.

THE RETURN OF AUGUSTUS.

1. **Outline of the Poem**:
   a) Augustus is returning in triumph from his Spanish victories, 1–4;
   b) Let all rejoice, his consort and his sister, matrons, boys, and maids, 5–12;
   c) This glorious day shall banish gloomy care for me; my lad, bring perfumes hither, wine, and garlands; command Neaera, too, to hasten to the feast; but linger not, if she delay; in other days I had not brooked refusal, 13–28.
2. **Time**: 24 B.C.
3. **Metre**: Sapphic and Adonic. Introd. § 44.

Herculis ritu modo dictus, o plebs,
Morte venalem petiisse laurum
Caesar Hispana repetit penatis
Victor ab ora.

Unico gaudens mulier marito
Prodeat iustis operata divis
Et soror clari ducis et decorae
Supplice vitta

Virginum matres iuvenumque nuper
Sospitum. Vos, o pueri et puellae
Non virum expertae, maleominatis
Parcite verbis.

Hic dies vere mihi festus atras
Eximet curas; ego nec tumultum
Nec mori per vim metuam tenente
Caesare terras.

I, pete unguentum, puer, et coronas
Et cadum Marsi memorem duelli,
Spartacum siqua potuit vagantem
  Fallere testa.

Dic et argutae properet Neaerae
Murreum nodo cohibere crinem;
Si per invisum mora ianitorem
  Fiet, abito.

Lenit albescens animos capillus
Litium et rixae cupidos protervae;
Non ego hoc ferrem calidus iuventa
  Consule Planco.

XV.

OLD AND YOUNG.

1. **Outline of the Poem**:
   a) A truce to thy shameless flirtations, Chloris! Cease longer to frolic among maidens, and cast a shadow on their fair company, 1–8;
   b) Leave such gayety to thy daughter Pholoë; thee household tasks become, — not the lyre, the rose, and jars of wine, 8–16.
2. **Time**: Uncertain; not later than 23 B.C.
3. **Metre**: Second Asclepiadean. Introd. § 46.

Uxor pauperis Ibyci,
  Tandem nequitiae fige modum tuae
Famosisque laboribus;
  Maturo propior desine funeri

Inter ludere virgines
  Et stellis nebulam spargere candidis.
Non, siquid Pholoen, satis
  Et te, Chlori, decet: filia rectius

Expugnat iuvenum domos,
Pulso Thyias uti concita tympano.
Illam cogit amor Nothi
Lascivae similem ludere capreae;

Te lanae prope nobilem
Tonsae Luceriam, non citharae decent
Nec flos purpureus rosae
Nec poti vetulam faece tenus cadi.

XVI.

CONTENTMENT.

1. **Outline of the Poem :**
   a) The power of gold : It laughed at Acrisius's towers and guards; it corrupts courts; destroys citadels; works the ruin of prophets even; lays cities and dynasties in the dust; and sounds the doom of famous captains, 1–16;
   b) But its possession brings care and restlessness; true riches is to be contented with a little; my Sabine farm gives me more joy than would a fertile province; happy he to whom the god with sparing hand has given just enough, 17–44.

2. **Time**: Uncertain; not later than 23 B.C.

3. **Metre**: Third Asclepiadean. Introd. § 47.

Inclusam Danaen turris aënea
Robustaeque fores et vigilum canum
Tristes excubiae munierant satis
Nocturnis ab adulteris,

Si non Acrisium virginis abditae
Custodem pavidum Iuppiter et Venus
Risissent: fore enim tutum iter et patens
Converso in pretium deo.

Aurum per medios ire satellites
Et perrumpere amat saxa, potentius
Ictu fulmineo: concidit auguris
  Argivi domus, ob lucrum

Demersa exitio; diffidit urbium
Portas vir Macedo et subruit aemulos
Reges muneribus; munera navium
  Saevos inlaqueant duces.

Crescentem sequitur cura pecuniam
Maiorumque fames. Iure perhorrui
Late conspicuom tollere verticem,
  Maecenas, equitum decus.

Quanto quisque sibi plura negaverit,
Ab dis plura feret: nil cupientium
Nudus castra peto et transfuga divitum
  Partis linquere gestio,

Contemptae dominus splendidior rei,
Quam si, quidquid arat impiger Apulus,
Occultare meis dicerer horreis,
  Magnas inter opes inops.

Purae rivos aquae silvaque iugerum
Paucorum et segetis certa fides meae
Fulgentem imperio fertilis Africae
  Fallit sorte beatior.

Quamquam nec Calabrae mella ferunt apes,
Nec Laestrygonia Bacchus in amphora
Languescit mihi, nec pinguia Gallicis
  Crescunt vellera pascuis:

Importuna tamen pauperies abest,
Nec si plura velim tu dare deneges.
Contracto melius parva cupidine
Vectigalia porrigam,

Quam si Mygdoniis regnum Alyattei
Campis continuem. Multa petentibus
Desunt multa: bene est, cui deus obtulit
Parca quod satis est manu.

XVII.

PREPARE FOR A RAINY MORROW.

1. **Outline of the Poem**: The crow foretells a rainy morrow, Lamia. Gather some firewood while you may, and make ready for a merry time within the house.

2. **Time**: Uncertain; not later than 23 B.C.

3. **Metre**: Alcaic. Introd. § 43.

Aeli vetusto nobilis ab Lamo,
Quando et priores hinc Lamias ferunt
Denominatos et nepotum
Per memores genus omne fastos;

Auctore ab illo ducis originem,
Qui Formiarum moenia dicitur
Princeps et innantem Maricae
Litoribus tenuisse Lirim,

Late tyrannus. Cras foliis nemus
Multis et alga litus inutili
Demissa tempestas ab Euro
Sternet, aquae nisi fallit augur

Annosa cornix. Dum potes, aridum
Compone lignum: cras Genium mero
Curabis et porco bimenstri
Cum famulis operum solutis.

XVIII.

THY BLESSING, FAUNUS!

1. Outline of the Poem:

a) Lend the blessing of thy presence to my flocks and fields, O Faunus, if duly I pay thy annual sacrifice, 1–8;

b) When thou art near, the whole countryside is glad, flock and herd, and woodland, too, 9–16.

2. Time: Uncertain; not after 23 B.C.

3. Metre: Sapphic and Adonic. Introd. § 44.

Faune, Nympharum fugientum amator,
Per meos finis et aprica rura
Lenis incedas abeasque parvis
Aequos alumnis,

Si tener pleno cadit haedus anno,
Larga nec desunt Veneris sodali
Vina craterae, vetus ara multo
Fumat odore.

Ludit herboso pecus omne campo,
Cum tibi nonae redeunt Decembres;
Festus in pratis vacat otioso
Cum bove pagus;

Inter audaces lupus errat agnos;
Spargit agrestis tibi silva frondes;
Gaudet invisam pepulisse fossor
Ter pede terram.

XIX.

INVITATION TO A DRINKING-BOUT.

1. Outline of the Poem:

a) No more learned lore! Consider rather when and where we may hold glad revel, 1–8;

b) A health to the day, the hour, and our host Murena, 9–11;

c) Let each drink much or little as he will, 11–17;

d) But let jollity rule the hour, with flute and lyre, and roses, that our neighbors may hear the din, with Rhode by thy side, Glycera by mine, 18–28.

2. Time: Uncertain; not after 23 B.C.

3. Metre: Second Asclepiadean. Introd. § 46.

Quantum distet ab Inacho
  Codrus pro patria non timidus mori
Narras et genus Aeaci
  Et pugnata sacro bella sub Ilio;

Quo Chium pretio cadum
  Mercemur, quis aquam temperet ignibus,
Quo praebente domum et quota
  Paelignis caream frigoribus, taces.

Da lunae propere novae,
  Da noctis mediae, da, puer, auguris
Murenae: tribus aut novem
  Miscentor cyathis pocula commodis.

Qui Musas amat imparis,
  Ternos ter cyathos attonitus petet
Vates; tris prohibet supra
  Rixarum metuens tangere Gratia

Nudis iuncta sororibus.
  Insanire iuvat: cur Berecyntiae
Cessant flamina tibiae?
  Cur pendet tacita fistula cum lyra?

Parcentis ego dexteras
  Odi: sparge rosas; audiat invidus
Dementem strepitum Lycus
  Et vicina seni non habilis Lyco.

Spissa te nitidum coma,
  Puro te similem, Telephe, vespero
Tempestiva petit Rhode;
  Me lentus Glycerae torret amor meae.

XX.

THE RIVALS.

1. **Outline of the Poem:**

   a) 'Tis at great peril, Pyrrhus, that thou possessest thyself of young Nearchus. Soon the maid who claims him for her own will descend upon thee, and a pretty fight there'll be, 1–8;

   b) But Nearchus is indifferent to the outcome, standing with flowing locks kissed by the breezes, as fair as Nireus or Ganymede, 9–16.

2. **Time:** Uncertain; not after 23 B.C.

3. **Metre:** Sapphic and Adonic. Introd. § 41.

Non vides, quanto moveas periclo,
Pyrrhe, Gaetulae catulos leaenae?
Dura post paulo fugies inaudax
  Proelia raptor,

Cum per obstantis iuvenum catervas
Ibit insignem repetens Nearchum:
Grande certamen, tibi praeda cedat,
Maior an illa.

Interim, dum tu celeris sagittas
Promis, haec dentes acuit timendos,
Arbiter pugnae posuisse nudo
Sub pede palmam

Fertur et leni recreare vento
Sparsum odoratis umerum capillis,
Qualis aut Nireus fuit aut aquosa
Raptus ab Ida.

XXI.

IN PRAISE OF WINE.

1. **Outline of the Poem:**
   a) O goodly jar of Massic wine, fraught with whatever destiny, descend from thy store-room at the bidding of Corvinus, who'll not ignore thy claims, 1–12;
   b) Manifold are thy powers, O wine; thou makest stubborn hearts to yield; the secrets of the wise thou dost unlock, lending hope and courage to the troubled and the weak, 13–20;
   c) If Liber, Venus, and the Graces but attend, we'll bide by thee till morn, 21–24.
2. **Time:** Uncertain; not after 23 B.C.
3. **Metre:** Alcaic. Introd. § 43.

O nata mecum consule Manlio,
Seu tu querellas sive geris iocos
Seu rixam et insanos amores
Seu facilem, pia testa, somnum,

Quocumque lectum nomine Massicum
Servas, moveri digna bono die,
Descende Corvino iubente
Promere languidiora vina.

Non ille, quamquam Socraticis madet
Sermonibus, te negleget horridus:
Narratur et prisci Catonis
Saepe mero caluisse virtus.

Tu lene tormentum ingenio admoves
Plerumque duro; tu sapientium
Curas et arcanum iocoso
Consilium retegis Lyaeo;

Tu spem reducis mentibus anxiis
Viresque et addis cornua pauperi,
Post te neque iratos trementi
Regum apices neque militum arma.

Te Liber et si laeta aderit Venus
Segnesque nodum solvere Gratiae
Vivaeque producent lucernae,
Dum rediens fugat astra Phoebus.

XXII.

THY BLESSING ON MY PINE, DIANA!

1. **Outline of the Poem**: O maiden goddess, helper of women in travail, bless the pine tree that overhangs my home! I promise in return the yearly offering of a boar.

2. **Time**: Uncertain; not after 23 B.C.

3. **Metre**: Sapphic and Adonic. Introd. § 44.

Montium custos nemorumque, Virgo,
Quae laborantis utero puellas
Ter vocata audis adimisque leto,
  Diva triformis,

Imminens villae tua pinus esto,
Quam per exactos ego laetus annos
Verris obliquom meditantis ictum
  Sanguine donem.

XXIII.

THE GODS LOVE THE GIVER, NOT THE GIFT.

1. **Outline of the Poem**:
   a) A simple offering, Phidyle, insures thy crops and vines from blight, thy lambs from dire disease, 1–8;
   b) The sheep now grazing on Mt. Algidus is destined for the priests, not thee, 9–16;
   c) Thou needst no costly sacrifice to make thy gods propitious; a bit of salted meal suffices, 17–20.

2. **Time**: Uncertain; not after 23 B.C.

3. **Metre**: Alcaic. Introd. § 43.

Caelo supinas si tuleris manus
Nascente luna, rustica Phidyle,
  Si ture placaris et horna
    Fruge Lares avidaque porca:

Nec pestilentem sentiet Africum
Fecunda vitis nec sterilem seges
  Robiginem aut dulces alumni
    Pomifero grave tempus anno.

Nam quae nivali pascitur Algido
Devota quercus inter et ilices
  Aut crescit Albanis in herbis
    Victima, pontificum securis

Cervice tinguet: te nihil attinet
Temptare multa caede bidentium
  Parvos coronantem marino
    Rore deos fragilique myrto.

Immunis aram si tetigit manus,
Non sumptuosa blandior hostia,
  Mollivit aversos Penatis
    Farre pio et saliente mica.

XXIV.

THE CURSE OF MAMMON.

1. Outline of the Poem :

a) Though richer than the treasures of the Arabs or of India, thou canst not free thy soul from terror or the snare of Death, 1–8;

b) Better the simple ways of Scythians or the Getae, whose homes are but their rolling wains, and whose dower but chastity and virtue, 9–24;

c) Truest service will he render to the state, who shall curb our present license; character, not laws, is what we need; our thirst for wealth sends us to the four corners of the earth, and drives us far from Virtue's path, 25–44;

d) To the temples or the sea with our useless gauds, the cause of all our woe! Let our lads learn hardihood, and their parents truth and justice, 45–64.

2. Time: Probably about 28 B.C.

3. Metre: Second Asclepiadean. Introd. § 46.

Intactis opulentior
  Thesauris Arabum et divitis Indiae
Caementis licet occupes
  Tyrrhenum omne tuis et mare Apulicum;

Si figit adamantinos
  Summis verticibus dira Necessitas
Clavos, non animum metu,
  Non mortis laqueis expedies caput.

Campestres melius Scythae,
  Quorum plaustra vagas rite trahunt domos,
Vivont et rigidi Getae,
  Immetata quibus iugera liberas

Fruges et Cererem ferunt,
  Nec cultura placet longior annua,
Defunctumque laboribus
  Aequali recreat sorte vicarius.

Illic matre carentibus
  Privignis mulier temperat innocens,
Nec dotata regit virum
  Coniunx nec nitido fidit adultero.

Dos est magna parentium
  Virtus et metuens alterius viri
Certo foedere castitas,
  Et peccare nefas aut pretium est mori.

O quisquis volet impias
  Caedes et rabiem tollere civicam,
Si quaeret 'Pater urbium'
  Subscribi statuis, indomitam audeat

Refrenare licentiam,
  Clarus postgenitis: quatenus, heu nefas,
Virtutem incolumem odimus,
  Sublatam ex oculis quaerimus, invidi.

Quid tristes querimoniae,
  Si non supplicio culpa reciditur;
Quid leges sine moribus
  Vanae proficiunt? si neque fervidis

Pars inclusa caloribus
  Mundi nec Boreae finitimum latus
Durataeque solo nives
  Mercatorem abigunt, horrida callidi

Vincunt aequora navitae,
  Magnum pauperies opprobrium iubet
Quidvis et facere et pati,
  Virtutisque viam deserit arduae.

Vel nos in Capitolium,
  Quo clamor vocat et turba faventium,
Vel nos in mare proximum
  Gemmas et lapides aurum et inutile,

Summi materiem mali,
  Mittamus, scelerum si bene paenitet.
Eradenda cupidinis
  Pravi sunt elementa et tenerae nimis

Mentes asperioribus
  Formandae studiis. Nescit equo rudis
Haerere ingenuos puer
  Venarique timet, ludere doctior,

Seu Graeco iubeas trocho,
  Seu malis vetita legibus alea,
Cum periura patris fides
  Consortem socium fallat et hospites

Indignoque pecuniam
  Heredi properet. Scilicet improbae
Crescunt divitiae; tamen
  Curtae nescio quid semper abest rei.

XXV.

A DITHYRAMB.

1. **Outline of the Poem**:
   a) Whither, Bacchus, dost thou hurry me through wood and glen in fresh inspiration, planning to sing great Caesar's praise? 1–8;
   b) Like a Bacchanal beholding Hebrus's flood and the snowy plains of Thrace, I love to gaze on grove and river bank. Suffer me, O mighty God, to strike no mortal note, as I follow thee, my temples wreathed with vine leaves, 9–20.
2. **Time**: Uncertain; not after 23 B.C.
3. **Metre**: Second Asclepiadean. Introd. § 46.

Quo me, Bacche, rapis tui
  Plenum? Quae nemora aut quos agor in specus,
Velox mente nova? Quibus
  Antris egregii Caesaris audiar

Aeternum meditans decus
  Stellis inserere et consilio Iovis?
Dicam insigne, recens, adhuc
  Indictum ore alio. Non secus in iugis

Exsomnis stupet Euhias,
Hebrum prospiciens et nive candidam
Thracen ac pede barbaro
Lustratam Rhodopen, ut mihi devio

Ripas et vacuom nemus
Mirari libet. O Naiadum potens
Baccharumque valentium
Proceras manibus vertere fraxinos,

Nil parvom aut humili modo,
Nil mortale loquar. Dulce periculum est,
O Lenaee, sequi deum
Cingentem viridi tempora pampino.

XXVI.

LOVE'S TRIUMPHS ARE ENDED.

1. **Outline of the Poem** :
   a) Not long ago I served with glory in the lists of Love; but now I offer up at Venus's shrine all tokens of my former triumphs, — lyre, and torch, and bar, 1–8;
   b) But yet, one final boon; touch Chloe's stubborn heart, before I go, 9–12.
2. **Time** : Uncertain; not later than 23 B.C.
3. **Metre** : Alcaic. Introd. § 43.

Vixi duellis nuper idoneus
Et militavi non sine gloria;
Nunc arma defunctumque bello
Barbiton hic paries habebit,

Laevom marinae qui Veneris latus
Custodit. Hic, hic ponite lucida
Funalia et vectes et arcus
Oppositis foribus minacis.

O quae beatam diva tenes Cyprum et
Memphin carentem Sithonia nive,
Regina, sublimi flagello
Tange Chloen semel arrogantem.

XXVII.

BON VOYAGE!

1. Outline of the Poem:

a) May evil omens attend the wicked, fair ones my friends. A blessing on thee, Galatea, wherever thou goest, and may no ill betide, 1–16;

b) Yet beware the rising storm. 'Twas such rashness sealed Europa's doom, 17–28;

c) Europa's lament: 'Whence, whither, have I come, abandoning home and duty? One death is too little for such a sin. Do I wake, or am I dreaming? Let me become the prey of lions or of tigers! Or swing my body from the limb of yonder ash, or cast it on the jagged rocks!' 29–66;

d) But Venus: 'Thou art the spouse of Jove invincible. Come, stay thy sobs! A district of the world shall bear thy name,' 66–76.

2. Time: Uncertain; not after 23 B.C.

3. Metre: Sapphic and Adonic. Introd. § 44.

Impios parrae recinentis omen
Ducat et praegnas canis aut ab agro
Rava decurrens lupa Lanuvino
Fetaque volpes;

Rumpat et serpens iter institutum,
Si per obliquom similis sagittae
Terruit mannos: ego cui timebo,
Providus auspex,

Antequam stantis repetat paludes
Imbrium divina avis imminentum,
Oscinem corvom prece suscitabo
Solis ab ortu.

Sis licet felix, ubicumque mavis,
Et memor nostri, Galatea, vivas;
Teque nec laevos vetet ire picus
Nec vaga cornix.

Sed vides, quanto trepidet tumultu
Pronus Orion. Ego quid sit ater
Hadriae novi sinus et quid albus
Peccet Iapyx.

Hostium uxores puerique caecos
Sentiant motus orientis Austri et
Aequoris nigri fremitum et trementis
Verbere ripas.

Sic et Europe niveum doloso
Credidit tauro latus et scatentem
Beluis pontum mediasque fraudes
Palluit audax.

Nuper in pratis studiosa florum et
Debitae Nymphis opifex coronae
Nocte sublustri nihil astra praeter
Vidit et undas.

Quae simul centum tetigit potentem
Oppidis Creten, "Pater, o relictum
Filiae nomen pietasque" dixit
"Victa furore.

Unde quo veni? Levis una mors est
Virginum culpae. Vigilansne ploro
Turpe commissum an vitiis carentem
  Ludit imago

Vana, quae porta fugiens eburna
Somnium ducit? Meliusne fluctus
Ire per longos fuit an recentis
  Carpere flores?

Siquis infamem mihi nunc iuvencum
Dedat iratae, lacerare ferro et
Frangere enitar modo multum amati
  Cornua monstri.

Impudens liqui patrios Penates,
Impudens Orcum moror. O deorum
Siquis haec audis, utinam inter errem
  Nuda leones!

Antequam turpis macies decentis
Occupet malas teneraeque sucus
Defluat praedae, speciosa quaero
  Pascere tigris.

'Vilis Europe,' pater urget absens:
'Quid mori cessas? Potes hac ab orno
Pendulum zona bene te secuta
  Laedere collum.

Sive te rupes et acuta leto
Saxa delectant, age te procellae
Crede veloci, nisi erile mavis
  Carpere pensum

Regius sanguis dominaeque tradi
Barbarae paelex.' " Aderat querenti
Perfidum ridens Venus et remisso
Filius arcu.

Mox ubi lusit satis, "abstineto"
Dixit "irarum calidaeque rixae,
Cum tibi invisus laceranda reddet
Cornua taurus.

Uxor invicti Iovis esse nescis.
Mitte singultus, bene ferre magnam
Disce fortunam; tua sectus orbis
Nomina ducet."

XXVIII.

IN NEPTUNE'S HONOR.

1. **Outline of the Poem**:
   a) Bring forth for Neptune's feast a jar of mellow Caecuban, and storm the stronghold of sobriety, 1–8;
   b) Then let us sing in turn of Neptune and the Nereids, Latona and Diana's shafts, Venus and Night, 9–16.
2. **Time**: Uncertain; not after 23 B.C.
3. **Metre**: Second Asclepiadean. Introd. § 46.

Festo quid potius die
Neptuni faciam? Prome reconditum,
Lyde, strenua Caecubum
Munitaeque adhibe vim sapientiae.

Inclinare meridiem
Sentis ac, veluti stet volucris dies,
Parcis deripere horreo
Cessantem Bibuli consulis amphoram.

Nos cantabimus invicem
  Neptunum et viridis Nereidum comas;
Tu curva recines lyra
  Latonam et celeris spicula Cynthiae;

Summo carmine, quae Cnidon
  Fulgentisque tenet Cycladas et Paphum
Iunctis visit oloribus;
  Dicetur merita Nox quoque nenia.

XXIX.

A CLEAR CONSCIENCE MAKES US SUPERIOR TO FORTUNE.

1. **Outline of the Poem:**
   a) A freshly opened jar awaits thee at my home, Maecenas; come tear thyself away from cares of state and taste of country joys, 1–28;
   b) The future we may not guess: but each day's duty rightly met brings tranquil peace; what once we've had, no power can take away; while Fortune bides, I bless her; when she takes her flight, I trust the gods to bear me safe through every gale, 29–64.
2. **Time**: 29 B.C.
3. **Metre**: Alcaic. Introd. § 43.

Tyrrhena regum progenies, tibi
Non ante verso lene merum cado
  Cum flore, Maecenas, rosarum et
    Pressa tuis balanus capillis

Iamdudum apud me est: eripe te morae,
Ne semper udum Tibur et Aefulae
  Declive contempleris arvom et
    Telegoni iuga parricidae.

Fastidiosam desere copiam et
Molem propinquam nubibus arduis,
  Omitte mirari beatae
    Fumum et opes strepitumque Romae.

Plerumque gratae divitibus vices
Mundaeque parvo sub lare pauperum
  Cenae sine aulaeis et ostro
    Sollicitam explicuere frontem.

Iam clarus occultum Andromedae pater
Ostendit ignem, iam Procyon furit
  Et stella vesani Leonis
    Sole dies referente siccos;

Iam pastor umbras cum grege languido
Rivomque fessus quaerit et horridi
  Dumeta Silvani, caretque
    Ripa vagis taciturna ventis.

Tu civitatem quis deceat status
Curas et urbi sollicitus times,
  Quid Seres et regnata Cyro
    Bactra parent Tanaisque discors.

Prudens futuri temporis exitum
Caliginosa nocte premit deus,
  Ridetque si mortalis ultra
    Fas trepidat. Quod adest memento

Componere aequos; cetera fluminis
Ritu feruntur, nunc medio alveo
  Cum pace delabentis Etruscum
    In mare, nunc lapides adesos

Stirpesque raptas et pecus et domos
Volventis una non sine montium
Clamore vicinaeque silvae,
Cum fera diluvies quietos

Inritat amnis. Ille potens sui
Laetusque deget, cui licet in diem
Dixisse 'vixi: cras vel atra
Nube polum pater occupato

Vel sole puro; non tamen irritum,
Quodcumque retro est, efficiet, neque
Diffinget infectumque reddet,
Quod fugiens semel hora vexit.

Fortuna saevo laeta negotio et
Ludum insolentem ludere pertinax
Transmutat incertos honores,
Nunc mihi, nunc alii benigna.

Laudo manentem; si celeris quatit
Pinnas, resigno quae dedit et mea
Virtute me involvo probamque
Pauperiem sine dote quaero.

Non est meum, si mugiat Africis
Malus procellis, ad miseras preces
Decurrere et votis pacisci,
Ne Cypriae Tyriaeque merces

Addant avaro divitias mari:
Tum me biremis praesidio scaphae
Tutum per Aegaeos tumultus
Aura feret geminusque Pollux.'

XXX.

THE POET'S IMMORTAL FAME.

1. Outline of the Poem :

a) These lays, I ween, will be a loftier monument than brazen tablets or the pyramids' royal pile, indestructible by storm or time, 1–5 ;

b) I shall not die, but, while great Rome endures, my fame shall be imperishable, 6–14 ;

c) Accept, O Muse, the tribute richly earned, and crown my locks with Apollo's bays, 14–16.

2. Time : 23 B.C.

3. Metre : First Asclepiadean. Introd. § 45.

Exegi monumentum aere perennius
Regalique situ pyramidum altius,
Quod non imber edax, non Aquilo impotens
Possit diruere aut innumerabilis
Annorum series et fuga temporum.
Non omnis moriar multaque pars mei
Vitabit Libitinam: usque ego postera
Crescam laude recens. Dum Capitolium
Scandet cum tacita virgine pontifex,
Dicar, qua violens obstrepit Aufidus
Et qua pauper aquae Daunus agrestium
Regnavit populorum, ex humili potens
Princeps Aeolium carmen ad Italos
Deduxisse modos. Sume superbiam
Quaesitam meritis et mihi Delphica
Lauro cinge volens, Melpomene, comam.

CARMINUM

LIBER QUARTUS.

I.

VENUS, FORBEAR!

1. **Outline of the Poem:**
   a) Cease, O goddess, to lure me again into the snares of passion! 1–7;
   b) Seek the hearts of younger men! Paulus is meet to be thy standard-bearer. Flushed with triumph in thy cause, he shall build thee a glorious temple near the Alban Lake, where lads and maidens shall duly praise thy power with song and sacrifice, 8–28;
   c) Me, neither maid nor boy nor wine nor garland longer delights, barring, my Ligurinus, one final pang for thee, 29–40.

2. **Time:** About 13 B.C.

3. **Metre:** Second Asclepiadean.. Introd. § 46.

Intermissa, Venus, diu
  Rursus bella moves. Parce, precor, precor.
Non sum qualis eram bonae
  Sub regno Cinarae. Desine, dulcium

Mater saeva Cupidinum,
  Circa lustra decem flectere mollibus
Iam durum imperiis: abi,
  Quo blandae iuvenum te revocant preces.

Tempestivius in domum
  Pauli, purpureis ales oloribus,
Comissabere Maximi,
  Si torrere iecur quaeris idoneum.

Namque et nobilis et decens
  Et pro sollicitis non tacitus reis
Et centum puer artium
  Late signa feret militiae tuae;

Et quandoque potentior
  Largi muneribus riserit aemuli,
Albanos prope te lacus
  Ponet marmoream sub trabe citrea.

Illic plurima naribus
  Duces tura lyraeque et Berecyntiae
Delectabere tibiae
  Mixtis carminibus non sine fistula;

Illic bis pueri die
  Numen cum teneris virginibus tuom
Laudantes pede candido
  In morem Salium ter quatient humum.

Me nec femina nec puer
  Iam nec spes animi credula mutui
Nec certare iuvat mero
  Nec vincire novis tempora floribus.

Sed cur heu, Ligurine, cur
  Manat rara meas lacrima per genas?
Cur facunda parum decoro
  Inter verba cadit lingua silentio?

Nocturnis ego somniis
  Iam captum teneo, iam volucrem sequor
Te per gramina Martii
  Campi, te pĕr aquas, dure, volubilis.

II.

THOU, NOT I, ANTONIUS, SHOULDST SING GREAT CAESAR'S PRAISE.

1. **Occasion of the Poem:** In the year 16 B.C. the Sygambrians and other German tribes had crossed the Rhine and created consternation by a formidable invasion of Gaul. Augustus repaired to the scene of disturbance, and remained there for the next three years, until the subjugation of the invaders was complete. In anticipation of his return, Julus Antonius (son of Mark Antony, and step-son of Octavia, the sister of Augustus) calls upon Horace to compose a triumphal ode. Horace declines the task in favor of Antonius, who was not merely a poet of merit, but also a special favorite of the Emperor.

2. **Outline of the Poem:**

a) Hazardous were the attempt to rival mighty Pindar in dithyramb, in ode, in hymn, or mournful elegy, 1–27;

b) Far less ambitious must be the efforts of my humble Muse, 27–32;

c) Thine be the task, Antonius, to sing the triumphs of glorious Caesar, than whom the gods have given to earth no greater blessing, 33–44;

d) To thy loftier song, some simple lay I then may add, and join thee with my humble sacrifice, 45–60.

3. **Time:** 13 B.C.

4. **Metre:** Sapphic and Adonic. Introd. § 44.

Pindarum quisquis studet aemulari,
Iule, ceratis ope Daedalea
Nititur pinnis vitreo daturus
  Nomina ponto.

Monte decurrens velut amnis, imbres
Quem super notas aluere ripas,
Fervet immensusque ruit profundo
Pindarus ore,

Laurea donandus Apollinari,
Seu per audacis nova dithyrambos
Verba devolvit numerisque fertur
Lege solutis,

Seu deos regesve canit, deorum
Sanguinem, per quos cecidere iusta
Morte Centauri, cecidit tremendae
Flamma Chimaerae,

Sive quos Elea domum reducit
Palma caelestis pugilemve equomve
Dicit et centum potiore signis
Munere donat,

Flebili sponsae iuvenemve raptum
Plorat et viris animumque moresque
Aureos educit in astra nigroque
Invidet Orco.

Multa Dircaeum levat aura cycnum,
Tendit, Antoni, quotiens in altos
Nubium tractus. Ego apis Matinae
More modoque

Grata carpentis thyma per laborem
Plurimum circa nemus uvidique
Tiburis ripas operosa parvos
Carmina fingo.

Concines maiore poeta plectro
Caesarem, quandoque trahet ferocis
Per sacrum clivom merita decorus
  Fronde Sygambros;

Quo nihil maius meliusve terris
Fata donavere bonique divi,
Nec dabunt, quamvis redeant in aurum
  Tempora priscum.

Concines laetosque dies et urbis
Publicum ludum super impetrato
Fortis Augusti reditu forumque
  Litibus orbum.

Tum meae, siquid loquar audiendum,
Vocis accedet bona pars, et 'O sol
Pulcher, o laudande!' canam recepto
  Caesare felix.

Tuque dum procedis, 'Io triumphe!'
Non semel dicemus, 'io triumphe!'
Civitas omnis dabimusque divis
  Tura benignis.

Te decem tauri totidemque vaccae,
Me tener solvet vitulus, relicta
Matre qui largis iuvenescit herbis
  In mea vota,

Fronte curvatos imitatus ignis
Tertium lunae referentis ortum,
Qua notam duxit, niveus videri,
  Cetera fulvos.

III.

MY GLORY IS THY GIFT, O MUSE.

1. **Outline of the Poem**:

a) The child of thy choice, Melpomene, is destined not for victory in boxing, in racing, or in war. Contemplation of stream and grove shall form his voice for song, 1–12;

b) O mighty mistress of the golden lute, 'tis from thee alone that all my glory springs, 13–24.

2. **Time**: Between 23 and 13 B.C.

3. **Metre**: Second Asclepiadean. Introd. § 46.

Quem tu, Melpomene, semel
  Nascentem placido lumine videris,
Illum non labor Isthmius
  Clarabit pugilem, non equos impiger

Curru ducet Achaico
  Victorem, neque res bellica Deliis
Ornatum foliis ducem,
  Quod regum tumidas contuderit minas,

Ostendet Capitolio;
  Sed quae Tibur aquae fertile praefluont
Et spissae nemorum comae
  Fingent Aeolio carmine nobilem.

Romae principis urbium
  Dignatur suboles inter amabilis
Vatum ponere me choros,
  Et iam dente minus mordeor invido.

O testudinis aureae
  Dulcem quae strepitum, Pieri, temperas,
O mutis quoque piscibus
  Donatura cycni, si libeat, sonum,

Totum muneris hoc tui est,
Quod monstror digito praetereuntium
Romanae fidicen lyrae:
Quod spiro et placeo, si placeo, tuom est.

IV.

DRUSUS AND THE CLAUDIAN HOUSE.

1. Occasion of the Poem: For some years the Vindelici and Raeti, two northern tribes, had ravaged the Roman frontiers by their frequent incursions. At length in 15 B.C. they were defeated by Drusus, the step-son of Augustus.

2. Outline of the Poem:

a) Like a young eagle swooping down upon the fold, or like a lion mangling a grazing roe, so did Drusus descend upon the Raetians and Vindelici, and show these long victorious hordes how resistless are the head and heart nurtured by Augustus's love and counsel, 1–28;

b) Not birth alone suffices; there must be wise breeding, too; else disgrace ensues, 29–36;

c) To the Claudian house, O Rome, thy debt is great. Think only of Metaurus's fight, of slain Hasdrubal, and Hannibal's great tribute to the race that thrives best when with disaster crowned, 37–72;

d) No failure can befall the Claudian arms, blessed as they are with the favor of Jove and the wise direction of our Emperor, 73–76.

3. Time: 15 B.C.

4. Metre: Alcaic. Introd. § 43.

Qualem ministrum fulminis alitem,
Cui rex deorum regnum in avis vagas
Permisit expertus fidelem
Iuppiter in Ganymēde flavo,

Olim iuventas et patrius vigor
Nido laborum propulit inscium,
Vernique iam nimbis remotis
Insolitos docuere nisus

Venti paventem, mox in ovilia
Demisit hostem vividus impetus,
Nunc in reluctantis dracones
Egit amor dapis atque pugnae;

Qualemve laetis caprea pascuis
Intenta fulvae matris ab ubere
Iam lacte depulsum leonem
Dente novo peritura vidit:

Videre Raetis bella sub Alpibus
Drusum gerentem Vindelici; (quibus
Mos unde deductus per omne
Tempus Amazonia securi

Dextras obarmet, quaerere distuli,
Nec scire fas est omnia) sed diu
Lateque victrices catervae
Consiliis iuvenis revictae

Sensere, quid mens, rite quid indoles
Nutrita faustis sub penetralibus
Posset, quid Augusti paternus
In pueros animus Nerones.

Fortes creantur fortibus et bonis;
Est in iuvencis, est in equis patrum
Virtus, neque imbellem feroces
Progenerant aquilae columbam.

Doctrina sed vim promovet insitam,
Rectique cultus pectora roborant;
Utcumque defecere mores,
Indecorant bene nata culpae.

Quid debeas, o Roma, Neronibus,
Testis Metaurum flumen et Hasdrubal
Devictus et pulcher fugatis
Ille dies Latio tenebris,

Qui primus alma risit adorea,
Dirus per urbes Afer ut Italas
Ceu flamma per taedas vel Eurus
Per Siculas equitavit undas.

Post hoc secundis usque laboribus
Romana pubes crevit, et impio
Vastata Poenorum tumultu
Fana deos habuere rectos.

Dixitque tandem perfidus Hannibal:
'Cervi luporum praeda rapacium,
Sectamur ultro, quos opimus
Fallere et effugere est triumphus.

Gens, quae cremato fortis ab Ilio
Iactata Tuscis aequoribus sacra
Natosque maturosque patres
Pertulit Ausonias ad urbes,

Duris ut ilex tonsa bipennibus
Nigrae feraci frondis in Algido,
Per damna, per caedes ab ipso
Ducit opes animumque ferro.

Non hydra secto corpore firmior
Vinci dolentem crevit in Herculem,
Monstrumve submisere Colchi
Maius Echioniaeve Thebae.

Merses profundo, pulchrior evenit;
Luctere, multa proruit integrum
  Cum laude victorem geritque
    Proelia coniugibus loquenda.

Carthagini iam non ego nuntios
Mittam superbos: occidit, occidit
  Spes omnis et fortuna nostri
    Nominis Hasdrubale interempto.'

Nil Claudiae non perficient manus,
Quas et benigno numine Iuppiter
  Defendit et curae sagaces
    Expediunt per acuta belli.

V.

THE BLESSINGS OF AUGUSTUS'S SWAY.

1. **Occasion of the Poem**: The ode seems to have been prompted by the longing of the people for the return of Augustus from his northern campaign (16–13 B.C.); see Introd. to Ode II.

2. **Outline of the Poem**:

a) Return to thy people, O guardian of the race of Romulus, for whom we yearn as a mother for her son long absent across the sea, 1–16;

b) Under thy benign sway, fertility, peace, uprightness, chastity reign everywhere; yea, we even entreat thy name in prayer and beg the gods that long thou mayest live to bless Hesperia 17–40.

3. **Time**: 13 B.C.

4. **Metre**: Third Asclepiadean. Introd. § 47.

Divis orte bonis, optume Romulae
Custos gentis, abes iam nimium diu;
Maturum reditum pollicitus patrum
  Sancto concilio redi.

Lucem redde tuae, dux bone, patriae:
Instar veris enim voltus ubi tuos
Adfulsit populo, gratior it dies
   Et soles melius nitent.

Ut mater iuvenem, quem Notus invido
Flatu Carpathii trans maris aequora
Cunctantem spatio longius annuo
   Dulci distinet a domo,

Votis ominibusque et precibus vocat,
Curvo nec faciem litore demovet:
Sic desideriis icta fidelibus
   Quaerit patria Caesarem.

Tutus bos etenim rura perambulat,
Nutrit rura Ceres almaque Faustitas,
Pacatum volitant per mare navitae;
   Culpari metuit fides,

Nullis polluitur casta domus stupris,
Mos et lex maculosum edomuit nefas,
Laudantur simili prole puerperae,
   Culpam poena premit comes.

Quis Parthum paveat, quis gelidum Scythen,
Quis Germania quos horrida parturit
Fetus, incolumi Caesare? quis ferae
   Bellum curet Hiberiae?

Condit quisque diem collibus in suis,
Et vitem viduas ducit ad arbores;
Hinc ad vina redit laetus et alteris
   Te mensis adhibet deum;

Te multa prece, te prosequitur mero
Defuso pateris, et Laribus tuom
Miscet numen, uti Graecia Castoris
  Et magni memor Herculis.

'Longas o utinam, dux bone, ferias
Praestes Hesperiae!' dicimus integro
Sicci mane die, dicimus uvidi,
  Cum sol Oceano subest.

VI.

INVOCATION TO APOLLO.

1. Occasion of the Poem: In the year 17 B.C. Augustus commissioned Horace to write the *Carmen Saeculare*, a hymn to be sung at the Saecular festival occurring that year. The present ode is an invocation to Apollo, begging help and inspiration for that important task.

2. Outline of the Poem:

a) O mighty god, punisher of proud Niobe and Tityos, director of the hand that laid Achilles low, master of the lyre, lend thy inspiration to my humble song, 1–28;

b) O boys and maidens, keep the time of my Lesbian measure, as ye hymn the praises of Latona's children. In after years the memory of this day may mean no little glory, 29–44.

3. Time: 17 B.C.

4. Metre: Sapphic and Adonic. Introd. § 44.

Dive, quem proles Niobea magnae
Vindicem linguae Tityosque raptor
Sensit et Troiae prope victor altae
  Phthius Achilles,

Ceteris maior, tibi miles impar,
Filius quamvis Thetidis marinae
Dardanas turris quateret tremenda
  Cuspide pugnax.

Ille, mordaci velut icta ferro
Pinus aut impulsa cupressus Euro,
Procidit late posuitque collum in
  Pulvere Teucro.

Ille non inclusus equo Minervae
Sacra mentito male feriatos
Troas et laetam Priami choreis
  Falleret aulam;

Sed palam captis gravis, heu nefas, heu,
Nescios fari pueros Achivis
Ureret flammis, etiam latentem
  Matris in alvo,

Ni tuis victus Venerisque gratae
Vocibus divom pater adnuisset
Rebus Aeneae potiore ductos
  Alite muros.

Doctor argutae fidicen Thaliae,
Phoebe, qui Xantho lavis amne crinis,
Dauniae defende decus Camenae,
  Levis Agyieu.

Spiritum Phoebus mihi, Phoebus artem
Carminis nomenque dedit poetae.
Virginum primae puerique claris
  Patribus orti,

Deliae tutela deae, fugacis
Lyncas et cervos cohibentis arcu,
Lesbium servate pedem meique
  Pollicis ictum,

Rite Latonae puerum canentes,
Rite crescentem face Noctilucam,
Prosperam frugum celeremque pronos
Volvere mensis.

Nupta iam dices 'Ego dis amicum,
Saeculo festas referente luces,
Reddidi carmen docilis modorum
Vatis Horati.'

VII.

THE LESSON OF SPRING'S RETURN.

1. **Outline of the Poem**:
   a) The snows have sped, Nature again clothes herself in living green, and Nymphs and Graces lead again the dancing bands, 1–6;
   b) The changing seasons bid us reflect how brief is our earthly life, 7–18;
   c) Lay not up treasure for some eager heir! Enjoy rather thy present stores! Death's fetters know no loosing, 19–28.
2. **Time**: Uncertain; between 23 and 13 B.C.
3. **Metre**: First Archilochian. Introd. § 55.

Diffugere nives, redeunt iam gramina campis
Arboribusque comae;
Mutat terra vices et decrescentia ripas
Flumina praetereunt;

Gratia cum Nymphis geminisque sororibus audet
Ducere nuda choros.
Immortalia ne speres, monet annus et almum
Quae rapit hora diem.

Frigora mitescunt zephyris, ver proterit aestas
Interitura, simul
Pomifer autumnus fruges effuderit, et mox
Bruma recurrit iners.

Damna tamen celeres reparant caelestia lunae;
Nos ubi decidimus,
Quo pius Aeneas, quo Tullus dives et Ancus,
Pulvis et umbra sumus.

Quis scit an adiciant hodiernae crastina summae
Tempora di superi?
Cuncta manus avidas fugient heredis, amico
Quae dederis animo.

Cum semel occideris et de te splendida Minos
Fecerit arbitria,
Non, Torquāte, genus, non te facundia, non te
Restituet pietas;

Infernis neque enim tenebris Diana pudicum
Liberat Hippolytum,
Nec Lethaea valet Theseus abrumpere caro
Vincula Pirithoo.

VIII.

IN PRAISE OF POESY.

1. **Outline of the Poem**:

a) Gladly, O Censorinus, would I give bowls and bronzes, tripods, and statues such as Scopas chiselled, had I but store of these, 1–8;

b) But I have not, nor carest thou for such; a better gift I have, — my verse, 9–12;

c) 'Tis the poet that lendeth glory to the great; how else were Scipio, and Romulus, and Aeacus saved from oblivion? 13–34.

2. **Time**: Uncertain; between 23 and 13 B.C.

3. **Metre**: First Asclepiadean. Introd. § 45.

Donarem pateras grataque commodus,
Censorīne, meis aera sodalibus,
Donarem tripodas, praemia fortium
Graiorum, neque tu pessuma munerum
Ferres, divite me scilicet artium,
Quas aut Parrhasius protulit aut Scopas,
Hic saxo, liquidis ille coloribus
Sollers nunc hominem ponere, nunc deum.
Sed non haec mihi vis, non tibi talium
Res est aut animus deliciarum egens.
Gaudes carminibus; carmina possumus
Donare et pretium dicere muneri.
Non incisa notis marmora publicis,
Per quae spiritus et vita redit bonis
Post mortem ducibus, non celeres fugae
Reiectaeque retrorsum Hannibalis minae,
Non incendia Carthaginis impiae
Eius, qui domita nomen ab Africa
Lucratus rediit, clarius indicant
Laudes quam Calabrae Pierides neque,

Si chartae sileant quod bene feceris,
Mercedem tuleris. Quid foret Iliae
Mavortisque puer, si taciturnitas
Obstaret meritis invida Romuli?
Ereptum Stygiis fluctibus Aeacum
Virtus et favor et lingua potentium
Vatum divitibus consecrat insulis.
Dignum laude virum Musa vetat mori.
Caelo Musa beat. Sic Iovis interest
Optatis epulis impiger Hercules,
Clarum Tyndaridae sidus ab infimis
Quassas eripiunt aequoribus rates,
Ornatus viridi tempora pampino
Liber vota bonos ducit ad exitus.

IX.

IN PRAISE OF LOLLIUS.

1. **Outline of the Poem:**
   a) Think not that my verse shall perish. Homer, 'tis true, is first of bards; yet the songs of other poets may hope to live as well, 1-12;
   b) Helen was not the first to yield to the persuasive words of a paramour, and many a brave hero lived before Agamemnon's day. Why do we know them not? They lacked the bard to chronicle their deeds, 13-30;
   c) Thee, O Lollius, I'll save from such a fate. Here be thy lofty soul, thy wisdom, thy integrity, fit subject of my song! 30-52.
2. **Time:** About 16 B.C.
3. **Metre:** Alcaic. Introd. § 43.

Ne forte credas interitura quae
Longe sonantem natus ad Aufidum
  Non ante volgatas per artis
    Verba loquor socianda chordis:

Non, si priores Maeonius tenet
Sedes Homerus, Pindaricae latent
Ceaeque et Alcaei minaces
Stesichorique graves Camenae;

Nec siquid olim lusit Anacreon
Delevit aetas; spirat adhuc amor
Vivontque commissi calores
Aeoliae fidibus puellae.

Non sola comptos arsit adulteri
Crinis et aurum vestibus illitum
Mirata regalisque cultus
Et comites Helene Lacaena,

Primusve Teucer tela Cydonio
Direxit arcu; non semel Ilios
Vexata; non pugnavit ingens
Idomeneus Sthenelusve solus

Dicenda Musis proelia; non ferox
Hector vel acer Deiphobus graves
Excepit ictus pro pudicis
Coniugibus puerisque primus.

Vixere fortes ante Agamemnona
Multi; sed omnes inlacrimabiles
Urgentur ignotique longa
Nocte, carent quia vate sacro.

Paulum sepultae distat inertiae
Celata virtus. Non ego te meis
Chartis inornatum silebo,
Totve tuos patiar labores

Impune, Lolli, carpere lividas
Obliviones. Est animus tibi
Rerumque prudens et secundis
Temporibus dubiisque rectus,

Vindex avarae fraudis et abstinens
Ducentis ad se cuncta pecuniae,
Consulque non unius anni,
Sed quotiens bonus atque fidus

Iudex honestum praetulit utili,
Reiecit alto dona nocentium
Voltu, per obstantis catervas
Explicuit sua victor arma.

Non possidentem multa vocaveris
Recte beatum; rectius occupat
Nomen beati, qui deorum
Muneribus sapienter uti

Duramque callet pauperiem pati
Peiusque leto flagitium timet,
Non ille pro caris amicis
Aut patria timidus perire.

X.

BEAUTY IS FLEETING.

1. **Outline of the Poem**: Thy flowing locks and rosy cheeks, O Ligurinus, will soon have passed away. Then shalt thou regret thy present haughtiness.
2. **Time**: Uncertain; between 23 and 13 B.C.
3. **Metre**: Fifth Asclepiadean. Introd. § 49.

O crudelis adhuc et Veneris muneribus potens,
Insperata tuae cum veniet pluma superbiae
Et, quae nunc umeris involitant, deciderint comae
Nunc et qui color est puniceae flore prior rosae
Mutatus, Ligurīne, in faciem verterit hispidam:
Dices 'Heu,' quotiens te speculo videris alterum,
'Quae mens est hodie, cur eadem non puero fuit,
Vel cur his animis incolumes non redeunt genae?

XI.

A JOYOUS BIRTHDAY.

1. **Outline of the Poem**:
   a) With wine, and garlands, Phyllis, and a sacrifice, I'm making ready for a joyous feast, none other than the birthday of my dear Maecenas, 1–20;
   b) Forget all thoughts of Telephus! Another's pleasing fetters hold him fast. Come learn the lay I meant for thee, and banish care with song! 21–36.
2. **Time**: Uncertain; between 23 and 13 B.C.
3. **Metre**: Sapphic and Adonic. Introd. § 44.

Est mihi nonum superantis annum
Plenus Albani cadus; est in horto,
Phylli, nectendis apium coronis;
  Est hederae vis

Multa, qua crinis religata fulges;
Ridet argento domus; ara castis
Vincta verbenis avet immolato
Spargier agno;

Cuncta festinat manus, huc et illuc
Cursitant mixtae pueris puellae;
Sordidum flammae trepidant rotantes
Vertice fumum.

Ut tamen noris quibus advoceris
Gaudiis, Idus tibi sunt agendae,
Qui dies mensem Veneris marinae
Findit Aprilem,

Iure sollemnis mihi sanctiorque
Paene natali proprio, quod ex hac
Luce Maecenas meus adfluentis
Ordinat annos.

Telephum, quem tu petis, occupavit
Non tuae sortis iuvenem puella
Dives et lasciva tenetque grata
Compede vinctum.

Terret ambustus Phaethon avaras
Spes, et exemplum grave praebet ales
Pegasus terrenum equitem gravatus
Bellerophontem,

Semper ut te digna sequare et ultra
Quam licet sperare nefas putando
Disparem vites. Age iam, meorum
Finis amorum,

(Non enim posthac alia calebo
Femina) condisce modos, amanda
Voce quos reddas: minuentur atrae
  Carmine curae.

XII.

THE DELIGHTS OF SPRING.

1. **Outline of the Poem**:
   a) Spring with its birds and breezes is again at hand, 1–12;
   b) The season bids us quench our thirst with wine; but bring your contribution to the board, a box of perfume; on no other terms shalt thou share the contents of my jar, 13–24;
   c) Forget the cares of trade meanwhile, and join me in this pastime, mindful of our fleeting life, 25–28.
2. **Time**: Uncertain; between 23 and 13 B.C.
3. **Metre**: Third Asclepiadean. Introd. § 47.

Iam veris comites, quae mare temperant,
Impellunt animae lintea Thraciae;
Iam nec prata rigent nec fluvii strepunt
  Hiberna nive turgidi.

Nidum ponit, Ityn flebiliter gemens,
Infelix avis et Cecropiae domus
Aeternum opprobrium, quod male barbaras
  Regum est ulta libidines.

Dicunt in tenero gramine pinguium
Custodes ovium carmina fistula
Delectantque deum, cui pecus et nigri
  Colles Arcadiae placent.

Adduxere sitim tempora, Vergili;
Sed pressum Calibus ducere Liberum
Si gestis, iuvenum nobilium cliens,
  Nardo vina merebere.

Nardi parvos onyx eliciet cadum,
Qui nunc Sulpiciis adcubat horreis,
Spes donare novas largus amaraque
  Curarum eluere efficax.

Ad quae si properas gaudia, cum tua
Velox merce veni: non ego te meis
Immunem meditor tingere poculis,
  Plena dives ut in domo.

Verum pone moras et studium lucri
Nigrorumque memor, dum licet, ignium
Misce stultitiam consiliis brevem:
  Dulce est desipere in loco.

XIII.

RETRIBUTION.

1. Outline of the Poem:

a) Lyce, my prayers are heard; in vain thou seekest by thy meretricious arts to recall the youth that's gone forever, 1–12;

b) But Coan silks and jewels cannot restore the rosy cheek and graceful form that once inspired my heart with love, 13–22;

c) Now thou art but a target for the gibes of gay young blades, 22–28.

2. Time: Uncertain; between 23 and 13 B.C.

3. Metre: Fourth Asclepiadean. Introd. § 48.

Audivere, Lyce, di mea vota, di
Audivere, Lyce: fis anus et tamen
  Vis formosa videri
    Ludisque et bibis impudens

Et cantu tremulo pota Cupidinem
Lentum sollicitas. Ille virentis et
Doctae psallere Chiae
Pulchris excubat in genis.

Importunus enim transvolat aridas
Quercus, et refugit te, quia luridi
Dentes te, quia rugae
Turpant et capitis nives.

Nec Coae referunt iam tibi purpurae
Nec cari lapides tempora, quae semel
Notis condita fastis
Inclusit volucris dies.

Quo fugit Venus, heu, quove color? decens
Quo motus? Quid habes illius, illius,
Quae spirabat amores,
Quae me surpuerat mihi,

Felix post Cinaram notaque et artium
Gratarum facies? Sed Cinarae brevis
Annos fata dederunt,
Servatura diu parem

Cornicis vetulae temporibus Lycen,
Possent ut iuvenes visere fervidi
Multo non sine risu
Dilapsam in cineres facem.

XIV.

DRUSUS AND TIBERIUS.

1. Occasion of the Poem: Despite the defeat administered to the Raeti and Vindelici by Drusus in 15 B.C. (see introduction to Ode IV.), the Vindelici, joined by some other tribes, undertook a fresh incursion soon after. Tiberius was despatched to join Drusus, and in 14 B.C. the two brothers accomplished the complete subjugation of the invaders.

2. Outline of the Poem:

a) No praises are adequate for thy achievements, O Augustus, whose mighty hand has again been felt by our northern foes, 1–9;

b) For thine were the troops, thine the plan, thine the favoring gods, through whom Drusus and Tiberius gallantly crushed the foe, scattering them in confusion, as Auster scatters the spray, or as rolling Aufidus when he overflows the farms, 9–34;

c) 'Twas on the anniversary of the day when suppliant Alexandria opened her port to thee, 34–40;

d) All nations own thy power, from East to West, from South to North, 41–52.

3. Time: 14 B.C.

4. Metre: Alcaic. Introd. § 43.

Quae cura patrum quaeve Quiritium
Plenis honorum muneribus tuas,
Auguste, virtutes in aevom
Per titulos memoresque fastus

Aeternet, o, qua sol habitabilis
Inlustrat oras, maxime principum,
Quem legis expertes Latinae
Vindelici didicere nuper,

Quid Marte posses. Milite nam tuo
Drusus Genaunos, implacidum genus,
Breunosque velocis et arces
Alpibus impositas tremendis

Deiecit acer plus vice simplici;
Maior Neronum mox grave proelium
   Commisit immanisque Raetos
      Auspiciis pepulit secundis,

Spectandus in certamine Martio
Devota morti pectora liberae
   Quantis fatigaret ruinis,
      Indomitus prope qualis undas

Exercet Auster Pleiadum choro
Scindente nubes, impiger hostium
   Vexare turmas et frementem
      Mittere equom medios per ignes.

Sic tauriformis volvitur Aufidus,
Qui regna Dauni praefluit Apuli,
   Cum saevit horrendamque cultis
      Diluviem minitatur agris,

Ut barbarorum Claudius agmina
Ferrata vasto diruit impetu
   Primosque et extremos metendo
      Stravit humum sine clade victor,

Te copias, te consilium et tuos
Praebente divos. Nam tibi quo die
   Portus Alexandrea supplex
      Et vacuam patefecit aulam,

Fortuna lustro prospera tertio
Belli secundos reddidit exitus,
   Laudemque et optatum peractis
      Imperiis decus adrogavit.

Te Cantaber non ante domabilis
Medusque et Indus, te profugus Scythes
Miratur, o tutela praesens
Italiae dominaeque Romae.

Te, fontium qui celat origines,
Nilusque et Hister, te rapidus Tigris,
Te beluosus qui remotis
Obstrepit Oceanus Britannis,

Te non paventis fūnera Galliae
Duraeque tellus audit Hiberiae,
Te caede gaudentes Sygambri
Compositis venerantur armis.

XV.

AUGUSTUS.

1. **Outline of the Poem**:

  a) Phoebus forbids me again to sing of battles and conquered cities, 1–4;

  b) The Glory of Caesar's rule: Fertility has returned to bless our fields; the standards of Crassus have been restored; shut is Janus's temple, and the old virtues that made Rome great have been revived again; with Caesar as our guardian tranquillity is sure, 4–24;

  c) And so, in the fashion of our sires, with wine, and flute, and song, let us celebrate the glorious men of old, and Troy, Anchises, and all the famous progeny of Venus, 25–32.

2. **Time**: Probably 13 B.C.
3. **Metre**: Alcaic. Introd. § 43.

Phoebus volentem proelia me loqui
Victas et urbes increpuit lyra,
Ne parva Tyrrhenum per aequor
Vela darem. Tua, Caesar, aetas

Fruges et agris rettulit uberes
Et signa nostro restituit Iovi
Derepta Parthorum superbis
Postibus et vacuom duellis

Ianum Quirīni clausit et ordinem
Rectum evaganti frena licentiae
Iniecit emovitque culpas
Et veteres revocavit artis,

Per quas Latinum nomen et Italae
Crevere vires famaque et imperi
Porrecta maiestas ad ortus
Solis ab Hesperio cubili.

Custode rerum Caesare non furor
Civilis aut vis exiget otium,
Non ira, quae procudit enses
Et miseras inimicat urbes.

Non qui profundum Danuvium bibunt
Edicta rumpent Iulia, non Getae,
Non Seres infidive Persae,
Non Tanain prope flumen orti.

Nosque et profestis lucibus et sacris
Inter iocosi munera Liberi
Cum prole matronisque nostris,
Rite deos prius adprecati,

Virtute functos more patrum duces
Lydis remixto carmine tibiis
Troiamque et Anchisen et almae
Progeniem Veneris canemus.

CARMEN SAECULARE.

1. Occasion of the Hymn: The Valerian *gens* had from time immemorial observed the custom of offering sacrifices to the gods of the lower world upon the Tarentum, a part of the Campus Martius adjacent to the River. In the year 249 B.C., in the midst of the First Punic War, this gentile ceremonial had been converted into a national one under the name of the *Ludi Tarentini.* One hundred years later (149 B.C.), while the Third Punic War was in progress, the games had been repeated. Whether or not there existed any disposition to renew their celebration in B.C. 49 is entirely uncertain, but if there was, the troublous events of that year naturally prevented the execution of the purpose. Augustus, however, wished to revive the ancient ceremony, and secured from the *quindecimviri*, the custodians of the Sibylline books, an opinion that, according to the Etruscan reckoning of 110 years to a *saeculum*, the celebration was due in the year 17 B.C. So far as can now be determined, this decision was entirely arbitrary and was made purely for the purpose of indorsing the desire of Augustus to institute a solemn religious festival which should lend lustre to the new political order inaugurated by him.

In the programme of the festival, Augustus introduced certain new elements. The celebrations during the First and Third Punic Wars had been characterized mainly by sacrifices for the propitiation of the gods of the nether world. This feature was entirely omitted by Augustus, who now gave central prominence to Apollo and Diana. This was quite in conformity with the importance attached to the worship of Apollo by Augustus; see note on *Odes*, I. 2, 32. It is significant, too, that the direction of the saecular celebration was intrusted to the *quindecimviri*, whose official meeting place was the temple of Apollo on the Palatine; see Introd. to I. 31, 1.

The main celebration began on the evening of May 31, 17 B.C., and continued for three days, — till the night of June 3. The *Carmen Saeculare* formed a part of the third day's ceremonial, being sung in connection with a solemn sacrifice offered to Apollo upon the Palatine. The hymn was rendered by two specially chosen choruses, one of twenty-seven boys, the other of twenty-seven maidens. The members of these choruses were chosen from children whose parents were still living, and who had been joined in wedlock by *confarreatio*, the most solemn form of Roman marriage.

How the different stanzas of the hymn were distributed between the choruses can only be matter of conjecture.

2. Outline of the Hymn:

a) Give ear, O Apollo and Diana, to our prayer on the day of our holy festival, 1–8;
b) Grant thou, Apollo, that nothing more glorious than Rome may ever be, 9–12;
c) Do thou, Diana, give aid to mothers in travail, and help to rear a progeny that in after time shall renew our sacred celebration, 13–24;
d) May the Parcae, too, join prosperous destinies to those already realized, 25–28;
e) May our harvests and flocks be blest, 29–32;
f) Hear, Apollo and Diana both, the boys and maidens that invoke your favor, 33–36;
g) If Rome be your creation, grant glory and power to the Roman folk, 37–48;
h) Grant, too, the supplications of our prince, before whom now the whole world bows, and who has brought our pristine Roman virtues back again, 49–60;
i) Yes, prophetic Apollo, and gracious Diana, prolong to an ever better era the Roman State, 61–72;
j) That such is the purpose of Jove and all the gods, we have full faith, 73–76.

3. Time: 17 B.C.
4. Metre: Sapphic and Adonic. Introd. § 44.

Phoebe silvarumque potens Diana,
Lucidum caeli decus, o colendi
Semper et culti, date quae precamur
  Tempore sacro,

Quo Sibyllini monuere versus
Virgines lectas puerosque castos
Dis quibus septem placuere colles
  Dicere carmen.

Alme Sol, curru nitido diem qui
Promis et celas aliusque et idem
Nasceris, possis nihil urbe Roma
Visere maius!

Rite maturos aperire partus
Lenis, Ilithyia, tuere matres,
Sive tu Lucīna probas vocari
Seu Genitalis.

Diva, producas subolem patrumque
Prosperes decreta super iugandis
Feminis prolisque novae feraci
Lege marita,

Certus undenos deciens per annos
Orbis ut cantus referatque ludos
Ter die claro totiensque grata
Nocte frequentis.

Vosque veraces cecinisse, Parcae,
Quod semel dictum stabilisque rerum
Terminus servet, bona iam peractis
Iungite fata.

Fertilis frugum pecorisque tellus
Spicea donet Cererem corona;
Nutriant fetus et aquae salubres
Et Iovis aurae.

Condito mitis placidusque telo
Supplices audi pueros, Apollo;
Siderum regina bicornis, audi,
Luna, puellas.

Roma si vestrum est opus Iliaeque
Litus Etruscum tenuere turmae,
Iussa pars mutare Lares et urbem
  Sospite cursu,

Cui per ardentem sine fraude Troiam
Castus Aeneas patriae superstes
Liberum munivit iter, daturus
  Plura relictis :

Di, probos mores docili iuventae,
Di, senectuti placidae quietem,
Romulae genti date remque prolemque
  Et decus omne.

Quaeque vos bobus veneratur albis
Clarus Anchisae Venerisque sanguis,
Impetret, bellante prior, iacentem
  Lenis in hostem.

Iam mari terraque manus potentis
Medus Albanasque timet securis,
Iam Scythae responsa petunt superbi
  Nuper et Indi.

Iam Fides et Pax et Honor Pudorque
Priscus et neclecta redire Virtus
Audet, apparetque beata pleno
  Copia cornu.

Augur et fulgente decorus arcu
Phoebus acceptusque novem Camenis,
Qui salutari levat arte fessos
  Corporis artus,

Si Palatinas videt aequos aras,
Remque Romanam Latiumque felix
Alterum in lustrum meliusque semper
  Proroget aevom,

Quaeque Aventinum tenet Algidumque,
Quindecim Diana preces virorum
Curat et votis puerorum amicas
  Applicat auris.

Haec Iovem sentire deosque cunctos
Spem bonam certamque domum reporto
Doctus et Phoebi chorus et Dianae
  Dicere laudes.

EPODON

LIBER.

I.

FRIENDSHIP'S TRIBUTE.

1. Occasion of the Poem: Octavian and Antony had come to an open breach in the year 32 B.C. In the prosecution of the war which followed, Octavian in the spring of 31 B.C. crossed over to the coast of Epirus with his fleet and troops. But before his departure from Italy, he summoned to his headquarters at Brundisium the most influential members of the senatorial and equestrian orders, partly for consultation, partly to show by their presence the extent of his support. Among those who went was Maecenas. Horace evidently conceives his patron as setting out to share the dangers of the approaching campaign, and begs to be allowed to accompany him. This permission could not be granted. Maecenas returned to Rome and administered the civil affairs of Italy in Augustus's absence.

2. Outline of the Poem:

a) Thou goest, Maecenas, prepared to suffer every danger for the sake of Caesar; but what of me, whose life apart from thee is naught? Rather let me bear thee company in every danger, 1–14;

b) Of what avail my presence? At least 'twill save me anxious fear to be with thee, 15–22;

c) 'Tis purely for the love I bear, and not from hope of further gifts; more than enough is mine already, 23–34.

3. Time: 31 B.C.

4. Metre: Iambic Strophe. Introd. § 51.

Ibis Liburnis inter alta navium,
  Amice, propugnacula,
Paratus omne Caesaris periculum
  Subire, Maecenas, tuo.

Quid nos, quibus te vita si superstite
  Iucunda, si contra, gravis?
Utrumne iussi persequemur otium
  Non dulce ni tecum simul,
An hunc laborem mente laturi, decet
  Qua ferre non molles viros?
Feremus, et te vel per Alpium iuga
  Inhospitalem et Caucasum
Vel occidentis usque ad ultimum sinum
  Forti sequemur pectore.
Roges, tuom labore quid iuvem meo,
  Imbellis ac firmus parum?
Comes minore sum futurus in metu,
  Qui maior absentis habet:
Ut adsidens implumibus pullis avis
  Serpentium adlapsus timet
Magis relictis, non ut adsit auxili
  Latura plus praesentibus.
Libenter hoc et omne militabitur
  Bellum in tuae spem gratiae,
Non ut iuvencis inligata pluribus
  Aratra nitantur mea,
Pecusve Calabris ante sidus fervidum
  Lucana mutet pascuis,
Neque ut superni villa candens Tusculi
  Circaea tangat moenia.
Satis superque me benignitas tua
  Ditavit: haud paravero,
Quod aut avarus ut Chremes terra premam,
  Discinctus aut perdam nepos.

II.

COUNTRY JOYS.

1. Outline of the Poem:

a) 'Happy the man who dwells in peace upon his farm! He trains his vines, beholds his grazing flocks and herds, gathers his honey, or plucks the fruit and purple clusters of the vine. Ofttimes beneath some ancient oak he lies and dreams, while birds and plashing fountains lull to sleep. When winter comes, no lack of sport; he hunts the boar or hare, forgetting 'mid such joys all troublous care. With wine and olives, now and then a kid or lamb, he feasts as richly as the best, and thrills with joy to contemplate his well-fed flocks, his oxen toiling home, his many slaves gathered about the hearth,' 1–66.

b) Thus spoke the money-lender Alfius. With firm intent to lead a farmer's life he called his funds all in upon the Ides; the Calends saw them loaned again, 67–70.

2. Time: Uncertain; not after 29 B.C.

3. Metre: Iambic Strophe. Introd. § 51.

'Beatus ille qui procul negotiis,
  Ut prisca gens mortalium,
Paterna rura bobus exercet suis
  Solutus omni faenore,
Neque excitatur classico miles truci,
  Neque horret iratum mare,
Forumque vitat et superba civium
  Potentiorum limina.
Ergo aut adulta vitium propagine
  Altas maritat populos,
Aut in reducta valle mugientium
  Prospectat errantis greges,
Inutilisque falce ramos amputans
  Feliciores inserit,
Aut pressa puris mella condit amphoris,
  Aut tondet infirmas ovis;

Vel cum decorum mitibus pomis caput
Autumnus agris extulit,
Ut gaudet insitiva decerpens pira
Certantem et uvam purpurae,
Qua muneretur te, Priāpe, et te, pater
Silvāne, tutor finium.
Libet iacere modo sub antiqua ilice,
Modo in tenaci gramine.
Labuntur altis interim ripis aquae,
Queruntur in silvis aves,
Fontesque lymphis obstrepunt manantibus,
Somnos quod invitet levis.
At cum tonantis annus hibernus Iovis
Imbres nivesque comparat,
Aut trudit acris hinc et hinc multa cane
Apros in obstantis plagas,
Aut amite levi rara tendit retia,
Turdis edacibus dolos,
Pavidumque leporem et advenam laqueo gruem
Iucunda captat praemia.
Quis non malarum, quas amor curas habet,
Haec inter obliviscitur?
Quodsi pudica mulier in partem iuvet
Domum atque dulcis liberos,
Sabina qualis aut perusta solibus
Pernicis uxor Apuli,
Sacrum vetustis extruat lignis focum
Lassi sub adventum viri,
Claudensque textis cratibus laetum pecus
Distenta siccet ubera,
Et horna dulci vina promens dolio
Dapes inemptas adparet:
Non me Lucrina iuverint conchylia
Magisve rhombus aut scari,

Siquos Eois intonata fluctibus
  Hiems ad hoc vertat mare;
Non Afra avis descendat in ventrem meum,
  Non attagen Ionicus
Iucundior quam lecta de pinguissimis
  Oliva ramis arborum
Aut herba lapathi prata amantis et gravi
  Malvae salubres corpori
Vel agna festis caesa Terminalibus
  Vel haedus ereptus lupo.
Has inter epulas ut iuvat pastas oves
  Videre properantis domum,
Videre fessos vomerem inversum boves
  Collo trahentis languido
Postosque vernas, ditis examen domus,
  Circum renidentis Lares.'
Haec ubi locutus faenerator Alfius,
  Iam iam futurus rusticus,
Omnem redegit Idibus pecuniam,
  Quaerit Kalendis ponere.

III.

THAT GUILTY GARLIC!

1. Occasion of the Poem: Horace had eaten at Maecenas's table of some dish containing garlic. With delicate humor he chides his host for the unpleasant effects of the herb.

2. Outline of the Poem:

a) Let him whose impious hand has wrought a father's death be doomed to eat of garlic, — more deadly than the hemlock, 1–5;

b) Was viper's blood a part of what I ate, or had Canidia's craft been shown? Verily 'twas with such an herb Medea

anointed Jason for his task. Nor did a hotter fire e'er rage on blazing Hercules than I have felt within, 6–18;

***c*) Ill luck befall thee, if again such trick thou play me! 19–22.**

3. Time: Uncertain; not after 29 B.C.

4. Metre: Iambic Strophe. Introd. § 51.

Parentis olim siquis impia manu
  Senile guttur fregerit,
Edit cicutis allium nocentius.
  O dura messorum ilia!
Quid hoc veneni saevit in praecordiis?
  Num viperinus his cruor
Incoctus herbis me fefellit? an malas
  Canidia tractavit dapes?
Ut Argonautas praeter omnis candidum
  Medēa mirata est ducem,
Ignota tauris inligaturum iuga
  Perunxit hoc Iasonem;
Hoc delibutis ulta donis paelicem
  Serpente fugit alite.
Nec tantus umquam siderum insedit vapor
  Siticulosae Apuliae,
Nec munus umeris efficacis Herculis
  Inarsit aestuosius.
At siquid umquam tale concupiveris,
  Iocose Maecenas, precor,
Manum puella savio opponat tuo,
  Extrema et in sponda cubet.

IV.

THE UPSTART.

1. Occasion of the Poem: This epode seems to have been evoked by Horace's disgust at some slave who, having achieved first freedom and then wealth, now offensively flaunts his good luck in the public eye.

2. Outline of the Poem:

a) I hate thee as the lamb the wolf, thou whose back is seared with stripes and thy ankles with the heavy chain, 1–4;
b) Thy altered fortune cannot change thy birth, nor turn from thee the scorn of all, despite thy wealth and lands, 5–16;
c) What boots it to lead our troops against the pirate and the slave, if such as this command our legions? 17–20.

3. Time: Uncertain; not after 29 B.C.

4. Metre: Iambic Strophe. Introd. § 51.

Lupis et agnis quanta sortito obtigit,
  Tecum mihi discordia est,
Hibericis peruste funibus latus
  Et crura dura compede.
Licet superbus ambules pecunia,
  Fortuna non mutat genus.
Videsne, Sacram metiente te Viam
  Cum bis trium ulnarum toga,
Ut ora vertat huc et huc euntium
  Liberrima indignatio?
'Sectus flagellis hic triumviralibus
  Praeconis ad fastidium
Arat Falerni mille fundi iugera
  Et Appiam mannis terit
Sedilibusque magnus in primis eques
  Othone contempto sedet.
Quid attinet tot ora navium gravi
  Rostrata duci pondere
Contra latrones atque servilem manum,
  Hoc, hoc tribuno militum?'

V.

CANIDIA'S INCANTATION.

1. Occasion of the Poem: Horace wishes to express his condemnation of the practices resorted to by contemporary votaries of the black art. The sorceress Canidia and her assistants are represented as murdering by a lingering death a young lad, whom they bury in the earth up to his chin. Their purpose is to secure his dried liver for use as a love-charm.

2. Outline of the Poem:

a) The Boy: 'What means this rabble and these savage looks?' 1–10;

b) Heedless of his plaints, Canidia plies her craft. Cypresses and fig trees torn from the tombs, with blood of frog, and hoot-owl's feather, herbs, and bones snatched from the jaws of a hungry bitch, she burns in her witches' fire, 11–28;

c) Veia meanwhile was digging up the earth for their awful purpose; Folia, too, was there, whose incantations bring stars and moon from the sky, 29–46;

d) Canidia: 'O Moon and Night, lend now your help, now turn your wrath and might against my foes. Now let Subura's dogs bark and drive the aged Varus forth! Why fail my Colchian charms to work? No root or herb escaped me, and yet he sleeps unmoved. A stronger charm I'll brew, and sooner shall the heaven sink below the sea, than thou escape my purpose,' 47–82;

e) The Boy: 'Thy charms are naught to alter right and wrong. With curses I'll pursue ye all. With curving claws I'll gash your cheeks. The crowd shall drive ye forth from street to street, ye filthy hags. Your bones the wolves and birds shall scatter, a sight my parents, though not I, shall live to see,' 83–102.

3. Time: Uncertain; not after 29 B.C.

4. Metre: Iambic Strophe. Introd. § 51.

'At o deorum quicquid in caelo regit
Terras et humanum genus,
Quid iste fert tumultus et quid omnium
Voltus in unum me truces?

Per liberos te, si vocata partubus
  Lucīna veris adfuit,
Per hoc inane purpurae decus precor,
  Per improbaturum haec Iovem,
Quid ut noverca me intueris aut uti
  Petita ferro belua?'
Ut haec trementi questus ore constitit
  Insignibus raptis puer,
Impube corpus, quale posset impia
  Mollire Thracum pectora:
Canidia, brevibus implicata viperis
  Crinis et incomptum caput,
Iubet sepulcris caprificos erutas,
  Iubet cupressus funebris
Et uncta turpis ova ranae sanguine
  Plumamque nocturnae strigis
Herbasque quas Iolcos atque Hiberia
  Mittit venenorum ferax,
Et ossa ab ore rapta ieiunae canis
  Flammis aduri Colchicis.
At expedita Sagana, per totam domum
  Spargens Avernalis aquas,
Horret capillis ut marinus asperis
  Echinus aut currens aper.
Abacta nulla Veia conscientia
  Ligonibus duris humum
Exhauriebat, ingemens laboribus,
  Quo posset infossus puer
Longo die bis terque mutatae dapis
  Inemori spectaculo,
Cum promineret ore, quantum exstant aqua
  Suspensa mento corpora:
Exsecta uti medulla et aridum iecur
  Amoris esset poculum,

Interminato cum semel fixae cibo
  Intabuissent pupulae.
Non defuisse masculae libidinis
  Ariminensem Foliam
Et otiosa credidit Neapolis
  Et omne vicinum oppidum,
Quae sidera excantata voce Thessala
  Lunamque caelo deripit.
Hic inresectum saeva dente livido
  Canidia rodens pollicem
Quid dixit aut quid tacuit? 'O rebus meis
  Non infideles arbitrae,
Nox et Diana, quae silentium regis,
  Arcana cum fiunt sacra,
Nunc, nunc adeste, nunc in hostilis domos
  Iram atque numen vertite.
Formidulosis cum latent silvis ferae
  Dulci sopore languidae,
Senem, quod omnes rideant, adulterum
  Latrent Suburanae canes,
Nardo perunctum, quale non perfectius
  Meae laborarint manus.
Quid accidit? Cur dira barbarae minus
  Venena Medeae valent,
Quibus superbam fugit ulta paelicem,
  Magni Creontis filiam,
Cum palla, tabo munus imbutum, novam
  Incendio nuptam abstulit?
Atqui nec herba nec latens in asperis
  Radix fefellit me locis.
Indormit unctis omnium cubilibus
  Oblivione paelicum.
A! a! solutus ambulat veneficae
  Scientioris carmine!

Non usitatis, Vare, potionibus,
O multa fleturum caput,
Ad me recurres, nec vocata mens tua
Marsis redibit vocibus.
Maius parabo, maius infundam tibi
Fastidienti poculum,
Priusque caelum sidet inferius mari
Tellure porrecta super,
Quam non amore sic meo flagres uti
Bitumen atris ignibus.'
Sub haec puer iam non, ut ante, mollibus
Lenire verbis impias,
Sed dubius unde rumperet silentium,
Misit Thyesteas preces:
'Venena maga non fas nefasque, non valent
Convertere humanam vicem.
Diris agam vos; dira detestatio
Nulla expiatur victima.
Quin, ubi perire iussus exspiravero,
Nocturnus occurram Furor,
Petamque voltus umbra curvis unguibus,
Quae vis deorum est Manium,
Et inquietis adsidens praecordiis
Pavore somnos auferam.
Vos turba vicatim hinc et hinc saxis petens
Contundet obscenas anus;
Post insepulta membra different lupi
Et Esquilinae alites,
Neque hoc parentes, heu mihi superstites,
Effugerit spectaculum.'

VI.

THE SLANDERER.

1. Outline of the Poem: Why dost thou worry helpless strangers only, thou coward cur? Come, turn thy empty threats on me, who have no fear for thee! Like the Molossian hound. I'll track thee out. Thy howl is but a cry for food. Beware! Or else thou'lt smart as did Archilochus or Bupalus's keen foe. When I'm attacked with savage tooth, am I to play the boy and plunge in tears?

2. Time: Uncertain; not after 29 B.C.

3. Metre: Iambic Strophe. Introd. § 51.

Quid immerentis hospites vexas, canis
  Ignavos adversum lupos?
Quin huc inanis, si potes, vertis minas,
  Et me remorsurum petis?
Nam qualis aut Molossus aut fulvos Laco,
  Amica vis pastoribus,
Agam per altas aure sublata nives,
  Quaecumque praecedet fera;
Tu, cum timenda voce complesti nemus,
  Proiectum odoraris cibum.
Cave, cave: namque in malos asperrimus
  Parata tollo cornua,
Qualis Lycambae spretus infido gener
  Aut acer hostis Bupalo.
An, siquis atro dente me petiverit,
  Inultus ut flebo puer?

VII.

A THREATENED RENEWAL OF CIVIL STRIFE.

1. Occasion of the Poem: From 43 to 39 B.C. there had been incessant civil strife. In the latter year the promise of permanent peace seemed to be secured by the treaty of Misenum, negotiated with Sextus Pompeius by Octavian and Antony. The poem apparently belongs soon after this, when fresh hostilities with Pompeius were threatening.

2. Outline of the Poem:

a) Whither, whither, are ye madly rushing? Why draw again the sword once sheathed? Has not enough of Roman blood been shed on flood and field? Not that the foe might grace our triumphs, but that the city should perish by its own hand. But even wolves and lions do not slay their kind, 1–12;

b) What is the cause? Is it blind fury, or some cruel spell, or some ancient sin? This last, I ween; the curse of Romulus is ours, 13–20.

3. Time: Probably 38 B.C.

4. Metre: Iambic Strophe. Introd. § 51.

Quo, quo scelesti ruitis? Aut cur dexteris
  Aptantur enses conditi?
Parumne campis atque Neptuno super
  Fusum est Latini sanguinis?
Non ut superbas invidae Carthaginis
  Romanus arces ureret,
Intactus aut Britannus ut descenderet
  Sacra catenatus Via,
Sed ut secundum vota Parthorum sua
  Urbs haec periret dextera.
Neque hic lupis mos nec fuit leonibus,
  Numquam nisi in dispar feris.
Furorne caecus an rapit vis acrior
  An culpa? Responsum date!

Tacent, et ora pallor albus inficit,
Mentesque perculsae stupent.
Sic est: acerba fata Romanos agunt
Scelusque fraternae necis,
Ut immerentis fluxit in terram Remi
Sacer nepotibus cruor.

VIII.

The brutal coarseness of this epode leads to omission of an outline of its contents.

Rogare longo putidam te saeculo,
Vires quid enervet meas,
Cum sit tibi dens ater et rugis vetus
Frontem senectus exaret,
Hietque turpis inter aridas natis
Podex velut crudae bovis!
Sed incitat me pectus et mammae putres,
Equina quales ubera,
Venterque mollis et femur tumentibus
Exile suris additum.
Esto beata, funus atque imagines
Ducant triumphales tuom.
Nec sit marita, quae rotundioribus
Onusta bacis ambulet.
Quid quod libelli Stoici inter sericos
Iacere pulvillos amant?
Inlitterati num magis nervi rigent,
Minusve languet fascinum?
Quod ut superbo provoces ab inguine,
Ore adlaborandum est tibi.

IX.

AFTER ACTIUM.

1. **Outline of the Poem**:
   a) When, O Maecenas, shall I celebrate with thee in feast and song great Caesar's victory, as but a short time since when Neptune's favored son, Pompeius, fled, driven from the seas? 1–10;
   b) At a woman's beck our Roman troops have served, have bowed to eunuchs, and have courted Eastern ease. What wonder the Galatians turned away, and ships lay still in port? 11–20;
   c) 'Tis hard to wait to celebrate our triumph, for greater victor ne'er came back to Rome, no not from Carthage even, 21–26;
   d) In mourning garb, our foe is fleeing fast o'er unknown seas. Therefore bring beakers of the largest size and Chian, Lesbian, Caecuban. With Bacchus's gifts we'll banish all our care, 27–38.

2. **Time**: Autumn, 31 B.C.

3. **Metre**: Iambic Strophe. Introd. § 51.

Quando repostum Caecubum ad festas dapes
  Victore laetus Caesare
Tecum sub alta — sic Iovi gratum — domo,
  Beate Maecenas, bibam
Sonante mixtum tibiis carmen lyra,
  Hac Dorium, illis barbarum?
Ut nuper, actus cum freto Neptunius
  Dux fugit ustis navibus,
Minatus urbi vincla, quae detraxerat
  Servis amicus perfidis.
Romanus eheu — posteri negabitis —
  Emancipatus feminae
Fert vallum et arma miles et spadonibus
  Servire rugosis potest,

Interque signa turpe militaria
  Sol adspicit conopium.
Ad hoc frementis verterunt bis mille equos
  Galli, canentes Caesarem,
Hostiliumque navium portu latent
  Puppes sinistrorsum citae.
Io Triumphe, tu moraris aureos
  Currus et intactas boves?
Io Triumphe, nec Iugurthino parem
  Bello reportasti ducem
Neque Africanum, cui super Carthaginem
  Virtus sepulcrum condidit.
Terra marique victus hostis punico
  Lugubre mutavit sagum.
Aut ille centum nobilem Cretam urbibus,
  Ventis iturus non suis,
Exercitatas aut petit Syrtis Noto,
  Aut fertur incerto mari.
Capaciores adfer huc, puer, scyphos
  Et Chia vina aut Lesbia,
Vel quod fluentem nauseam coerceat
  Metire nobis Caecubum.
Curam metumque Caesaris rerum iuvat
  Dulci Lyaeo solvere.

X.

ILL LUCK TO MEVIUS.

1. Occasion of the Poem: Mevius and Bavius were two poetasters, who apparently had earned the contempt of all decent men. Cf. Virgil, *Ecl.* iii. 90 f.:

> Qui Bavium non odit, amet tua carmina, Mevi,
> Atque idem iungat volpes et mulgeat hircos.

2. Outline of the Poem :

a) May Auster wrench his ship with savage waves! May Eurus scatter oars and cordage! May Aquilo arise in might, nor any kindly star be seen! May he be borne on seas as wild as those that bore the band of conquering Greeks! 1–14;

b) What toil and anguish await thee and thy crew! What moans and useless prayers! If only thou become a prey to gulls, the Storms shall have a sacrifice from me, 15–24.

3. Time : Uncertain; not after 29 B.C.

4. Metre : Iambic Strophe. Introd. § 51.

Mala soluta navis exit alite,
  Ferens olentem Mevium.
Ut horridis utrumque verberes latus,
  Auster, memento, fluctibus.
Niger rudentis Eurus inverso mari
  Fractosque remos differat;
Insurgat Aquilo, quantus altis montibus
  Frangit trementis ilices.
Nec sidus atra nocte amicum appareat,
  Qua tristis Orīon cadit;
Quietiore nec feratur aequore
  Quam Graia victorum manus,
Cum Pallas usto vertit iram ab Ilio
  In impiam Aiacis ratem.
O quantus instat navitis sudor tuis
  Tibique pallor luteus
Et illa non virilis heiulatio
  Preces et aversum ad Iovem,
Ionius udo cum remugiens sinus
  Noto carinam ruperit.
Opima quodsi praeda curvo litore
  Porrecta mergos iuveris,
Libidinosus immolabitur caper
  Et agna Tempestatibus.

XI.

CUPID'S POWER.

1. **Outline of the Poem:**

a) Love seizes me again and takes away all thought of verse, 1–4;

b) 'Tis full three years since passion swayed me thus. Inachia was the last. Alas, the talk I was through all the town! When I brought my griefs to thee, vowing no more to strive against unworthy rivals, thou badst me homeward go. I went, — not homeward, but to portals that refused admittance, 5–22;

c) My love Lyciscus holds me now, from whom no friendly word or stern rebuke shall shake me free, — nothing but some fresh flame for lad or maid, 23–28.

2. **Time**: Uncertain; not after 29 B.C.

3. **Metre**: Third Archilochian. Introd. § 57.

Petti, nihil me sicut antea iuvat
  Scribere versiculos amore percussum gravi,
Amore, qui me praeter omnis expetit
  Mollibus in pueris aut in puellis urere.
Hic tertius December, ex quo destiti
  Inachia furere, silvis honorem decutit.
Heu me, per urbem, nam pudet tanti mali,
  Fabula quanta fui! Conviviorum et paenitet,
In quis amantem languor et silentium
  Arguit et latere petitus imo spiritus.
'Contrane lucrum nil valere candidum
  Pauperis ingenium!' querebar adplorans tibi,
Simul calentis inverecundus deus
  Fervidiore mero arcana promorat loco.
'Quodsi meis inaestuet praecordiis
  Libera bilis, ut haec ingrata ventis dividat
Fomenta, volnus nil malum levantia,
  Desinet imparibus certare summotus pudor.'
Ubi haec severus te palam laudaveram,
  Iussus abire domum ferebar incerto pede

Ad non amicos heu mihi postis et heu
  Limina dura, quibus lumbos et infregi latus.
Nunc gloriantis quamlibet mulierculam
  Vincere mollitia amor Lycisci me tenet;
Unde expedire non amicorum queant
  Libera consilia nec contumeliae graves,
Sed alius ardor aut puellae candidae
  Aut teretis pueri, longam renodantis comam.

XII.

The coarseness of this epode leads to omission of any outline of its contents.

Quid tibi vis, mulier nigris dignissima barris?
  Munera cur mihi quidve tabellas
Mittis, nec firmo iuveni neque naris obesae?
  Namque sagacius unus odoror,
Polypus an gravis hirsutis cubet hircus in alis,
  Quam canis acer, ubi lateat sus.
Qui sudor vietis et quam malus undique membris
  Crescit odor, cum pene soluto
Indomitam properat rabiem sedare, neque illi
  Iam manet umida creta colorque
Stercore fucatus crocodili, iamque subando
  Tenta cubilia tectaque rumpit.
Vel mea cum saevis agitat fastidia verbis:
  'Inachia langues minus ac me;
Inachiam ter nocte potes, mihi semper ad unum
  Mollis opus. Pereat male, quae te
Lesbia quaerenti taurum monstravit inertem,
  Cum mihi Cous adesset Amyntas,
Cuius in indomito constantior inguine nervos,
  Quam nova collibus arbor inhaeret.

Muricibus Tyriis iteratae vellera lanae
Cui properabantur? Tibi nempe,
Ne foret aequalis inter conviva, magis quem
Diligeret mulier sua quam te.
O ego non felix, quam tu fugis, ut pavet acris
Agna lupos capreaeque leones!'

XIII.

DEFIANCE TO THE STORM: MAKE MERRY!

1. Outline of the Poem:

a) Without, the snow is falling, and the woods are roaring with the gale, 1–3;

b) But let us, friends, enjoy our opportunity, and banish care from clouded brow! Bring out the oldest vintage! The god will soon make all things right. Therefore, with perfume sweet and music, let us free our hearts from trouble! 3–10;

c) So sang the Centaur Chiron to his foster-child, Achilles: 'O child of Thetis, goddess-born, Scamander's streams await thee, whence no power shall bring thee home again; there, with wine and song, sweet consolations, find relief for every ill!' 11–18.

2. Time: Uncertain; not after 29 B.C.

3. Metre: Second Archilochian. Introd. § 56.

Horrida tempestas caelum contraxit, et imbres
Nivesque deducunt Iovem; nunc mare, nunc siluae
Threicio Aquilone sonant. Rapiamus, amici,
Occasionem de die, dumque virent genua
Et decet, obducta solvatur fronte senectus.
Tu vina Torquāto move consule pressa meo.
Cetera mitte loqui: deus haec fortasse benigna
Reducet in sedem vice. Nunc et Achaemenio
Perfundi nardo iuvat et fide Cyllenea
Levare diris pectora sollicitudinibus,
Nobilis ut grandi cecinit Centaurus alumno:
'Invicte, mortalis dea nate puer Thetide,

Te manet Assaraci tellus, quam frigida parvi
Findunt Scamandri flumina lubricus et Simois,
Unde tibi reditum certo subtemine Parcae
Rupere, nec mater domum caerula te revehet.
Illic omne malum vino cantuque levato,
Deformis aegrimoniae dulcibus alloquiis.'

XIV.

PROMISES UNFULFILLED.

1. Outline of the Poem:

a) You weary me with asking why soft indolence has brought forgetfulness upon me, 1–5;

b). 'Tis the god, the god, that keeps me from my task; so burned Anacreon's heart, they say, for Samian Bathyllus, 6–12;

c) Thou thyself escapest not the flame; if she be fair, rejoice, 13–16.

2. Time: Uncertain; not after 29 B.C.

3. Metre: First Pythiambic. Introd. § 53.

Mollis inertia cur tantam diffuderit imis
Oblivionem sensibus,
Pocula Lethaeos ut si ducentia somnos
Arente fauce traxerim,
Candide Maecenas, occidis saepe rogando:
Deus, deus nam me vetat
Inceptos, olim promissum carmen, iambos
Ad umbilicum adducere.
Non aliter Samio dicunt arsisse Bathyllo
Anacreonta Teium,
Qui persaepe cava testudine flevit amorem
Non elaboratum ad pedem.
Ureris ipse miser: quodsi non pulchrior ignis
Accendit obsessam Ilion,
Gaude sorte tua; me libertina, nec uno
Contenta, Phryne macerat.

XV.

FAITHLESS.

1. Outline of the Poem:

a) 'Twas 'neath the smiling moon that thou didst plight thy troth, clinging to me as tightly as the ivy to the oak, and promising that while the flock should fear the wolf, while Orion stirs the wintry sea, our love should know no change, 1–10;

b) And yet, Neaera, as Horace has in him a spark of manhood, he will not suffer thee to grant thy favors to a rival, but straight will seek him out another mate, 11–16;

c) And thou, who hast supplanted me, rich though thou be in flocks and lands and gold, and in the lore of sages, thou shalt not hold the love thou now hast won. Then shall I laugh at thee, 17–24.

2. Time: Uncertain; not after 29 B.C.

3. Metre: First Pythiambic. Introd. § 53.

Nox erat et caelo fulgebat Luna sereno
  Inter minora sidera,
Cum tu, magnorum numen laesura deorum,
  In verba iurabas mea,
Artius atque hedera procera adstringitur ilex
  Lentis adhaerens bracchiis,
Dum pecori lupus et nautis infestus Orīon
  Turbaret hibernum mare,
Intonsosque agitaret Apollinis aura capillos,
  Fore hunc amorem mutuom.
O dolitura mea multum virtute Neaera!
  Nam siquid in Flacco viri est,
Non feret adsiduas potiori te dare noctes,
  Et quaeret iratus parem;
Nec semel offensi cedet constantia formae,
  Si certus intrarit dolor.
Et tu, quicumque es felicior atque meo nunc
  Superbus incedis malo,

Sis pecore et multa dives tellure licebit
  Tibique Pactōlus fluat,
Nec te Pythagorae fallant arcana renati,
  Formaque vincas Nirea,
Eheu, translatos alio maerebis amores.
  Ast ego vicissim risero.

XVI.

THE WOES OF CIVIL STRIFE.—THE ONLY HELP.

1. Occasion of the Poem: The civil strife following the assassination of Julius Caesar had not ceased with the Battle of Philippi (42 B.C.). Lucius Antonius (brother of Mark Antony) and his wife Fulvia had, in 41 B.C., incited the Perusian War, and there threatened a renewal of the dissensions that had rent the state for nearly a decade.

2. Outline of the Poem:

a) A second generation wastes away in the throes of civil war, and the city that no hostile foe could crush is perishing by forces from within. Our site shall be again a waste, and Quirinus's ashes shall be scattered to the winds by savage conquerors, 1–14;

b) Our only hope of safety is to flee, pledging each other never to return till Nature's laws be changed, 15–34;

c) Let craven hearts remain! Let all the nobler part set sail and seek the Happy Isles, where corn and wine, where fig and olive, grow untended; from hollow oaks the honey flows; the goats unbidden seek the milking-pail; the air breeds no distempers, and the king of gods dispenses showers and warmth with even hand, 35–62;

d) From gold to bronze, from bronze to iron, the ages change; yet for the righteous an escape is ready, if ye but heed my words of prophecy, 63–66.

3. Time: 41 B.C.

4. Metre: Second Pythiambic. Introd. § 54.

Altera iam teritur bellis civilibus aetas,
  Suis et ipsa Roma viribus ruit.
Quam neque finitimi valuerunt perdere Marsi
  Minacis aut Etrusca Porsenae manus,

Aemula nec virtus Capuae nec Spartacus acer
  Novisque rebus infidelis Allobrox,
Nec fera caerulea domuit Germania pube
  Parentibusque abominatus Hannibal:
Impia perdemus devoti sanguinis aetas,
  Ferisque rursus occupabitur solum.
Barbarus heu cineres insistet victor et urbem
  Eques sonante verberabit ungula,
Quaeque carent ventis et solibus ossa Quirīni,
  Nefas videre! dissipabit insolens.
Forte, quod expediat, communiter aut melior pars
  Malis carere quaeritis laboribus?
Nulla sit hac potior sententia, Phocaeorum
  Velut profugit exsecrata civitas
Agros atque lares patrios, habitandaque fana
  Apris reliquit et rapacibus lupis,
Ire, pedes quocumque ferent, quocumque per undas
  Notus vocabit aut protervos Africus.
Sic placet? an melius quis habet suadere? Secunda
  Ratem occupare quid moramur alite?
Sed iuremus in haec: simul imis saxa renarint
  Vadis levata, ne redire sit nefas;
Neu conversa domum pigeat dare lintea, quando
  Padus Matina laverit cacumina,
In mare seu celsus procurrerit Appenninus,
  Novaque monstra iunxerit libidine
Mirus amor, iuvet ut tigris subsidere cervis,
  Adulteretur et columba miluo,
Credula nec ravos timeant armenta leones,
  Ametque salsa levis hircus aequora.
Haec et quae poterunt reditus abscindere dulcis
  Eamus omnis exsecrata civitas,
Aut pars indocili melior grege; mollis et exspes
  Inominata perprimat cubilia.

Vos, quibus est virtus, muliebrem tollite luctum,
  Etrusca praeter et volate litora.
Nos manet Oceanus circumvagus; arva, beata
  Petamus arva divites et insulas,
Reddit ubi Cererem tellus inarata quotannis
  Et imputata floret usque vinea,
Germinat et numquam fallentis termes olivae,
  Suamque pulla ficus ornat arborem,
Mella cava manant ex ilice, montibus altis
  Levis crepante lympha desilit pede.
Illic iniussae veniunt ad mulctra capellae,
  Refertque tenta grex amicus ubera,
Nec vespertinus circumgemit ursus ovile,
  Neque intumescit alta viperis humus;
Pluraque felices mirabimur, ut neque largis
  Aquosus Eurus arva radat imbribus,
Pinguia nec siccis urantur semina glaebis,
  Utrumque rege temperante caelitum.
Non huc Argoo contendit remige pinus,
  Neque impudica Colchis intulit pedem;
Non huc Sidonii torserunt cornua nautae,
  Laboriosa nec cohors Ulixei.
Nulla nocent pecori contagia, nullius astri
  Gregem aestuosa torret impotentia.
Iuppiter illa piae secrevit litora genti,
  Ut inquinavit aere tempus aureum;
Aere, dehinc ferro duravit saecula, quorum
  Piis secunda vate me datur fuga.

XVII.

A MOCK RECANTATION.

1. Outline of the Poem:

a) HORACE: 'I bow at last to thy superior powers, Canidia, and beg thee, as thy suppliant, to cease thy spells, and quickly turn thy magic wheel the backward way, 1–7;

b) 'Achilles withheld not mercy from his foes, nor was Circe deaf to prayers, 8–18;

c) 'Enough and more of torture have I undergone; my youth is fled; my hair is white; thy power I own, burning with hotter flame than Aetna's; name but the penalty thou dost impose; I'll pay it; I'll sound thy praises on mendacious lute; I'll call thee pure and noble, born of glorious sire,' 19–52;

d) CANIDIA: 'My ears are deaf to all entreaty. I suffer thee unpunished to divulge my rites! To spread my name abroad throughout the town! Thy punishment is but begun; like Pelops, Tantalus, Prometheus, Sisyphus, thou shalt long for rest that may not be; thou'lt long to hurl thyself from lofty towers, to stab, to hang thyself; yet all in vain; with all my craft, shall I lament the failure of my arts on thee?' 53–81.

2. Time: Uncertain; not after 29 B.C.

3. Metre: Iambic Trimeter. Introd. § 50.

'Iam iam efficaci do manus scientiae,
Supplex et oro regna per Proserpinae,
Per et Dianae non movenda numina,
Per atque libros carminum valentium
Refixa caelo devocare sidera,
Canidia, parce vocibus tandem sacris
Citumque retro solve, solve turbinem!
Movit nepotem Telephus Nereium,
In quem superbus ordinarat agmina
Mysorum et in quem tela acuta torserat.
Unxere matres Iliae addictum feris
Alitibus atque canibus homicidam Hectorem,
Postquam relictis moenibus rex procidit

Heu pervicacis ad pedes Achillei.
Saetosa duris exuere pellibus
Laboriosi remiges Ulixei
Volente Circa membra, tunc mens et sonus
Relapsus atque notus in voltus honor.
Dedi satis superque poenarum tibi,
Amata nautis multum et institoribus.
Fugit iuventas et verecundus color
Reliquit; ossa pelle amicta lurida,
Tuis capillus albus est odoribus,
Nullum ab labore me reclinat otium;
Urget diem nox et dies noctem, neque est
Levare tenta spiritu praecordia.
Ergo negatum vincor ut credam miser,
Sabella pectus increpare carmina
Caputque Marsa dissilire nenia.
Quid amplius vis? O mare et terra, ardeo,
Quantum neque atro delibutus Hercules
Nessi cruore, nec Sicana fervida
Virens in Aetna flamma; tu, donec cinis
Iniuriosis aridus ventis ferar,
Cales venenis officina Colchicis.
Quae finis aut quod me manet stipendium?
Effare; iussas cum fide poenas luam,
Paratus expiare, seu poposceris
Centum iuvencos, sive mendaci lyra
Voles sonari: tu pudica, tu proba
Perambulabis astra sidus aureum.
Infamis Helenae Castor offensus vicem
Fraterque magni Castoris, victi prece,
Adempta vati reddidere lumina:
Et tu — potes nam — solve me dementia,
O nec paternis obsoleta sordibus
Nec in sepulcris pauperum prudens anus

Novendiales dissipare pulveres.
Tibi hospitale pectus et purae manus
Tuosque venter Pactumeius, et tuo
Cruore rubros obstetrix pannos lavit,
Utcumque fortis exsilis puerpera.'
'Quid obseratis auribus fundis preces?
Non saxa nudis surdiora navitis
Neptunus alto tundit hibernus salo.
Inultus ut tu riseris Cotytia
Volgata, sacrum liberi Cupidinis,
Et Esquilini pontifex venefici
Impune ut urbem nomine impleris meo?
Quid proderit ditasse Paelignas anus
Velociusve miscuisse toxicum?
Sed tardiora fata te votis manent;
Ingrata misero vita ducenda est in hoc,
Novis ut usque suppetas laboribus.
Optat quietem Pelopis infidi pater,
Egens benignae Tantalus semper dapis,
Optat Promētheus obligatus aliti,
Optat supremo collocare Sisyphus
In monte saxum; sed vetant leges Iovis.
Voles modo altis desilire turribus,
Modo ense pectus Norico recludere,
Frustraque vincla gutturi nectes tuo,
Fastidiosa tristis aegrimonia.
Vectàbor umeris tunc ego inimicis eques,
Meaeque terra cedet insolentiae.
An quae movere cereas imagines,
Ut ipse nosti curiosus, et polo
Deripere lunam vocibus possim meis,
Possim crematos excitare mortuos
Desiderique temperare pocula,
Plorem artis in te nil agentis exitum?'

NOTES.

ODES — BOOK I.

ODE I.

1. Maecenas: Horace's friend and patron; see Introd. § 4. **atavis . . . regibus**: *royal ancestors;* for this use of a noun in apposition with adjective force, *cf.* Virg. *Aen.* i. 273, *regina sacerdos*, 'a royal priestess'; i. 21, *populum late regem*, 'a people widely dominant.' Maecenas traced his lineage back to the old Etruscan kings.

2. O: observe the hiatus between *O* and *et;* such hiatus is regular after the interjections *o* and *a*. **praesidium, decus**: *praesidium* is used with reference to the material and moral support extended by Maecenas to the poet; *decus*, with reference to the honor which this support conferred.

3. sunt quos iuvat: *sunt qui, sunt quos* are ordinarily followed in prose by the subjunctive; yet Horace repeatedly uses the indicative; similarly, we have *est qui spernit*, line 19 below. **curriculo**: *racing chariot;* the first instance of the employment of *curriculum* in this sense. Some refer the word to a nominative *curriculus*. **pulverem Olympicum**: *i.e.* in the Olympic games. The Olympic festival was still regularly celebrated in Horace's day; it continued to be maintained without interruption until the close of the fourth century A.D.

4. collegisse: an instance of the use, common in the poets, of the perfect infinitive for the present; in this passage the use of the perfect may have been determined by metrical considerations (*cf.* *cōllēgīssĕ* with *cōllĭgĕrĕ*). **meta evitata**: grammatically, *meta* is the subject, but the logical subject is the idea of 'avoiding the turning-point' contained in *meta evitata;* *cf.* the familiar *post urbem conditam, post reges exactos*. The races in the Greek hippodrome, as in the Roman circus, were regularly run around a long low stone structure (called in Latin *spina*, 'thorn'). At each end of the *spina*, stood a detached semi-circular pier surmounted by three columns. This was the *meta*, to turn which neatly, without slackening speed (*cf. fervidis rotis*) or making too wide a sweep, required the greatest skill on the part of the driver.

5. palma: to be taken literally; in Horace's day it had long been customary at the Greek and Roman chariot races to present the victor with a palm branch. Roman sculpture abounds in illustrations of this custom. **nobilis**: here in causative sense, of that which *makes* famous.

6. terrarum dominos: *as lords of the earth; dominos* is in predicate relation to *quos*, to be supplied as the direct object of *evehit*. A similar allusion to the pride of victory in the chariot race occurs iv. 2. 17, *quos Elea* (= *Olympica*) *domum reducit palma caelestis*.

7. hunc: dependent upon *iuvat* to be supplied in thought from line 4. **mobilium, turba**: both words contain a somewhat cynical reference to the uncertainty of the popular temper. Cicero, *pro Murena*, 17. 35, speaks in a similar strain of the popular assemblies, comparing them to a sea of conflicting currents.

8. tergeminis honoribus: *to triple honors;* but *honoribus* is really ablative of means, *i.e.* exalt by conferring these honors; the triple honors are the quaestorship, the praetorship, and the consulship. The first two were a necessary preliminary to the third. **tollere**: the use of the infinitive with *certare* is chiefly poetical.

9. illum: dependent (like *hunc* in line 7) upon *iuvat* to be supplied in thought. **proprio**: note the emphasis which rests upon this word.

10. quicquid: *i.e.* the entire harvest. **Libycis**: Africa was at this time one of the main sources of the Roman grain supply. Horace repeatedly alludes to the fertility of this district, *e.g.* iii. 16. 31, *fertilis Africae; Sat.* ii. 3. 87, *frumenti quantum metit Africa.*

11. findere: note the force of this word; the clods are so hard that they have to be 'split,' as it were; yet in spite of this the man cannot be lured from his little plot of barren ground; the infinitive with *gaudere* is poetical.

12. Attalicis condicionibus: *the terms of an Attalus, i.e.* such terms as an Attalus might offer. Attalus had been the name of several kings of Pergamus in Asia Minor. Their wealth, like that of Croesus, was proverbial.

13. demoveas: lit. *turn away;* but the word is here used in the pregnant sense of 'turn from his farming and induce to,' *etc.;* one may render by *lure.* **ut secet**: *to plough;* the clause is dependent upon *demoveas*, which here takes the construction of a verb of *persuading.* **Cypria**: Cyprus was famous as a centre of shipbuilding. Note the poet's skill in adding this concrete touch to the picture; the device is repeated in verses 14 and 15 (*Myrtoum, Icariis*), and is, of course, common in all poetry.

14. Myrtoum: the Myrtoan Sea lay between the Peloponnesus and the Cyclades. It was proverbially stormy. **pavidus nauta**: *as a trembling sailor*, in predicate relation to the subject of *secet.*

15. Icariis fluctibus: the Icarian Sea was another stormy body of water; it lay off the southwest coast of Asia Minor. Legend connected it with the fall of the luckless Icarus; *fluctibus* is dative; the construction is a Grecism; see Introd. § 36, *c*, and *cf.* i. 3. 13, *decertantem Aquilonibus.*

16. otium et oppidi rura sui: *i.e.* the quiet of his native town and the peaceful fields *around* it.

18. pauperiem: simply 'narrow circumstances,' not 'poverty' as we understand the word. **pati**: dependent upon *indocilis*, a poetical construction. See Introd. § 41, *c*.

19. est qui spernit: for the indicative after *est qui*, see note on *iuvat* in line 4 above. **Massici**: understand *vini.* The Massic wine, grown on the Mons Massicus in northern Campania, was one of the famous Italian brands.

20. solido de die: the *solidus dies* was the business day, extending from the early morning to the *end* of the ninth hour, *i.e.* about 3 P.M. **demere**: the infinitive with *spernere* is a poetic construction.

21. membra: direct object of *stratus*, which is here used as a middle. B. 175. 2. *d*; A. and G. 240. *c.* N.; G. 338. N. 2. **arbuto**: the arbŭtus, or wild strawberry tree, was highly prized for its shade. In the autumn it was conspicuous for its bright red berries.

22. aquae . . . sacrae: the scholiast Porphyrio comments as follows on these words: *omnes autem fontes sacri habentur, et ideo 'caput sacrae aquae' ait.* **lene caput**: *i.e.* the gently murmuring spring. Strictly, of course, it is the spring which is sacred, and the issuing stream which gently murmurs; but the interchange of epithets needs no justification.

23. lituo: for *litui sonitu; lituo* is probably ablative; B. *L. L.*[1] § 337. The *lituus* was a curved instrument; the *tuba* was straight. The former was used in the cavalry, the latter in the infantry.

24. matribus: dative of agency, a construction occurring with some frequency, even in prose, in connection with the perfect passive participle.

25. detestata: here used passively; other instances of perfect passive participles of deponent verbs so used are i. 32. 5, *modulate*, 'tuned'; *Epod.* 16. 8, *abominatus*, 'detested.' **Iove**: here equivalent to *caelo*. Jupiter was originally the god of the sky; hence his functions as thunderer and wielder of the lightning. The root *Iov-* (Indo-European *djev-*) originally meant 'sky,' 'light.' Latin *dies*, 'day,' is the same word; *cf. Diespiter* (archaic and poetical) = *Iupiter*. B. *L. L.* 180. 4.

27. catulis: *hounds;* dative, like *matribus* above in line 24.

28. Marsus: poetical for *Marsicus*. The Marsi inhabited a mountainous district of central Italy, about fifty miles to the east of Rome. **aper**: the wild boar was highly prized by the Roman epicures, and in consequence was much hunted.

29. me: in emphatic position, introducing the climax of the ode, Horace's own aspiration. **doctarum frontium**: this is practically equivalent to 'the poet's brow'; *doctus* was applied to any one who had achieved distinction in philosophy, art, or letters. **hederae**: poetic plural; the ivy was sacred to Bacchus, one of the patron divinities of poets.

30. dis miscent: the idea is the same as that found above in line 5, *palma evehit ad deos;* for the case of *dis*, see note on line 23, *lituo*. **gelidum nemus**, *etc.*: *i.e.* the cool grove with its bands of nymphs and satyrs.

31. leves: *light-footed, lightly tripping.*

32. secernunt populo: *i.e.* distinguish from the people, raise me above the common herd. **tibias**: not the poetic plural; two *tibiae* were regularly played together; they were fastened to a single mouthpiece, one *tibia* being held in each hand.

33. Euterpe: the muse of music, including lyric poetry, which was originally composed for singing to a musical accompaniment. In works of art, Euterpe is represented with flutes in her hands. **cohibet**: *withhold.* **Polyhymnia**: another muse of poetry, often defined as 'the muse of the sublime hymn.'

---

[1] *Bennett's Latin Language.*

34. Lesboum barbiton: *i.e.* the lyre of the Lesbian poets, Sappho and Alcaeus (600 B.C.). These were Horace's chief models in the composition of his lyric poems. He imitated not merely their poetic form, but also very largely their themes and their poetic phraseology. Introd. § 18. **tendere**: *tune*, lit. *stretch* (*i.e.* the strings); the infinitive with *refugere* is poetical.

35. lyricis vatibus inseris: *i.e.* acknowledge my claim to rank as a lyric poet. The first meaning of *vates* apparently was 'seer,' 'soothsayer,' 'prophet.' Virgil and Horace, however, apply it to poets as a loftier and more honorable designation than *poeta*. Some think that *vates* originally meant 'poet,' 'bard,' and that Virgil and Horace simply revived the early usage; but this view is not well supported. Note the poetical employment of the present tense with the force of a future. The subject of *inseris* is emphatic; we should have expected *tu* to be expressed.

36. sublimi feriam sidera vertice: *i.e.* my pride and joy will be complete.

ODE II.

1. terris: the dative is best explained as equivalent to *in terras*. **nivis**: snow is not unusual in central Italy in the winter months, though it rarely lies long.

2. Pater: *i.e.* Jupiter. **rubente**: referring to the lightning.

3. sacras arces: probably the two summits of the Capitoline, on which stood temples, one sacred to Juno, the other to Jupiter, Juno, and Minerva in common.

4. terruit, terruit: such repetition of the same word without an intervening conjunction is a favorite device of Horace.

5. gentis: *i.e.* all the races of the earth. The storm had doubtless been local, but Horace conceives it as widely prevalent. **grave ne rediret**: the clause depends upon the idea of *fearing* involved in *terruit*, 'made to fear,' 'inspired with terror.' Note that in poetry words which ordinarily stand first in their clause are frequently 'postponed' (placed after); so here *ne*; *cf.* line 7, *omne cum*; line 9, *piscium et*.

6. Pyrrhae: wife of Deucalion. According to the myth, all mankind, except Deucalion and Pyrrha, had been destroyed by a flood. They renewed the human race by casting stones behind them; the stones hurled by Deucalion became men; those hurled by Pyrrha became women. **nova monstra**: explained by the following clauses.

7. **Proteus**: the prophetic 'old man of the sea'; he tended the seals of Poseidon (Neptune). **pecus**: *i.e.* the herd of seals.

8. **visere**: the use of the infinitive to denote purpose is poetical.

10. **columbis**: the *columba* did not ordinarily nest in trees; but Horace was hardly a scientific observer.

11. **superiecto**: *i.e.* spread over the surface of the earth. The emphasis of the clause rests upon this word. Note also the interlocked order of the words, *superiecto pavidae aequore dammae*, a favorite arrangement in Horace.

13. **flavom**: Horace seems to have followed the earlier spelling in *-vos*, *-vom*; *-quos*, *-quom*; *-uos*, *-uom*, *etc.* The spellings *-vus*, *-vum*; *-cus*, *-cum*; *-uus*, *-uum*, had become well established in ordinary usage before his day, but poets naturally cling tenaciously to the old style. *Cf.* B. *L. L.* § 57. 1. As applied to the Tiber, *flavom* is a poetical designation for its turbid stream.

14. **litore Etrusco**: *litus* is here used for *ripa*. The Etruscan bank is the right bank of the Tiber. Just at the city the river makes a sharp turn, so that the water, hurled on by the current (and perhaps by the wind), seemed to come directly from the bank opposite the city.

15. **deiectum**: the supine. **monumenta regis**: the 'memorial of the king' is the Regia, or official residence of the pontifex maximus, situated at the southeastern end of the Roman Forum. Some remains of its foundations have been brought to light in recent years. The building was called *monumenta regis*, because it was popularly thought to date from the time of King Numa, whose great interest in the religious ceremonials of his time is well attested in the traditions that cluster about his name. Since the Roman Forum was on low land, the Tiber not infrequently rose high enough to flood the ground on which the Regia stood. Such inundations occur periodically to-day.

16. **templaque Vestae**: probably we have not here an instance of the poetic plural. There were two temples of Vesta, one called *aedes Vestae*, the other *aedicula Vestae*. They were situated adjacent to the Regia.

17. **Iliae**: Ilia is another name for Rhea Silvia, the mother of Romulus and Remus; according to the common legend, she was thrown by Amulius's order into the Tiber, and the river god came to be looked upon as her spouse. Hence the flood is represented by the poet as intended to avenge the wrongs of Ilia. For another view, see below on *querenti*. **iactat**: *shows*; the *dum*-clause is explicative of the preceding *ire deiectum*, *i.e.* the Tiber advances to hurl down the

temples of the city in his quest of vengeance. **nimium** : to be joined with *ultorem;* the god is too eager an avenger. **querenti** : *i.e.* of her own wrongs. Others refer it to complaints at the assassination of Caesar (her descendant, according to the familiar tradition); in that case, the Tiber must be thought of as aiming to avenge the crime of Caesar's murder.

18. sinistra : *i.e.* the bank on which the greater part of the city of Rome was built.

19. ripa : *i.e.* over the bank; ablative of place. **ux-orius amnis** : the Aeolic lyric poets, whom Horace imitates, very frequently broke a word in this way at the end of the line. Horace rarely follows them in this; only two or three other instances occur in the *Odes.* *Cf.* i. 25. 11, *inter-lunia.*

21. audiet : the subject is *iuventus.* **civis acuisse ferrum** : *i.e.* against each other, in civil war.

22. Persae : a common designation in Horace for the Parthians, a warlike nation dwelling southeast of the Caspian. The poets of the Augustan age allude to them indifferently as *Parthi*, *Medi* (see line 51 below), or *Persae.* The Romans had first come into definite collision with this people in 53 B.C., the year of Crassus's disastrous defeat at Carrhae. Though subsequently twice defeated in battle (39 and 38 B.C.), the Parthians had not been crushed, and recently had gained some signal successes over the Roman arms. **melius perirent** : *had better perished*, *i.e.* it would have been better had the Parthians perished by the swords which had been drawn in civil strife; the subjunctive is used to express the conclusion of a past conditional sentence of the contrary-to-fact type, the imperfect being irregularly used for the pluperfect.

23. audiet : repetition of the verb without conjunction, as *terruit* above in line 5. **pugnas** : *i.e.* civil conflicts. **vitio** : to be taken with *rara*, which here has the force of 'thinned out,' 'decimated.' **parentum** : both *parentum* and *parentium* occur as the genitive plural of *parens.*

24. iuventus : *i.e.* our descendants, posterity.

25. Having touched upon the existing distress, and having briefly indicated its cause, the poet now proceeds to suggest the remedy : Some one of the gods must vouchsafe help. **divom** : accusative singular.

26. rebus : *in behalf of the fortunes;* dative of interest, a construction used of persons, or things personified, and only slightly less strong than *pro* with the ablative. **prece** : this word is rarely used in the singular. **qua** : for the post-position, see above on line 5. **fatigent** : *i.e.* importune.

27. virgines sanctae : *i.e.* the Vestal Virgins. **minus** = *parum.*

28. carmina : *litanies;* their prayers were couched in some traditional liturgical verse-form.

29. partis : *rôle, duty;* in this sense the word is confined to the plural.

31. candentis : *i.e.* fair white; *cf.* the Homeric φαίδιμος ὦμος; participles and adjectives in *-ns* regularly form the accusative plural in *-is* in Horace. **umeros** : object of *amictus*, which is here used as a middle; see note on i. 1. 21.

32. augur Apollo : according to Suetonius (*Aug.* 94), Augustus was declared by his mother to be the son of Apollo; and the god is said to have assisted him visibly at the battle of Actium; hence the special appropriateness of the present invocation. Even before the date of this ode, Augustus had done much to increase and extend the worship of Apollo; in 28 B.C. he had erected to him the magnificent temple on the Palatine referred to in i. 31. Apollo receives the epithet *augur* as the god of prophecy.

33. sive tu = *vel tu si.* **Erycina ridens** : *blithe Erycina, i.e.* Venus, who received this designation from the temple dedicated to her on Mt. Eryx in Sicily; she is naturally invoked here as the ancestress (*genetrix*) of the Roman people, and especially of the Julian gens.

34. quam circum : anastrophe; not uncommon with dissyllabic prepositions.

36. auctor : *our founder, i.e.* Mars, the father of Romulus.

37. heu : to be joined closely in thought with *nimis longo.* **satiate** : vocative by attraction to *auctor*, though logically in agreement with the subject of *respicis.* **ludo** : *i.e.* the sport or game of war.

38. clamor : *the battle-cry.* **leves** : *polished.*

39. acer voltus : *i.e.* the fierce glance of triumph. **Marsi** : the Marsians were among the flower of the Roman infantry; *cf.* ii. 20. 18; iii. 5. 9. There is added point in this reference to the Marsian soldiery, since their name obviously designates them as connected with the god.

41. mutata figura : *i.e.* changing thy form of god. **iuvenem imitaris** : poetic for 'assumest the form of a youth'; the poet wishes to suggest that Mercury may even now be present on earth in the person of Octavian. This conception of Octavian as a god embodied in human form was probably not original with Horace. It had doubtless existed for some time in the popular mind, as may be gathered from the utterances of contemporary poets. Horace may perhaps have been the first to suggest Mercury as the specific divinity incarnated in the emperor, though traces of the same belief are found elsewhere also. Mercury was doubtless thus chosen as being the patron deity of trade and commerce, *i.e.* the pursuits of peace such as Augustus was endeavoring to promote. The word *iuvenis* designates any one of military age (17–45), and hence is appropriate to Octavian, who at this time was thirty-five years old.

42. **ales filius**: in apposition with the subject of *imitaris*. Mercury is familiarly represented with wings upon his ankles and his cap (*petasus*).

43. **Maiae**: the mother of Mercury. **patiens vocari**: *patior* with the simple infinitive is poetical; *cf.* Virg. *Aen.* viii. 577, *patior quemvis durare laborem.* When so used, *patior* often seems to have the force of 'will gladly,' 'am eager'; *cf.* iii. 9. 15, *pro quo bis patiar mori*, 'for whom I will gladly die.'

44. **Caesaris ultor**: the punishment of the murderers of Caesar was an avowed object in the formation of the Second Triumvirate, and after the victory at Philippi, Octavian erected at Rome a temple to Mars Ultor, of which some remains are still standing.

45. **in caelum redeas**: Mercury, not Augustus, is to be thought of.

46. **laetus intersis**: *i.e.* be glad to abide.

47. **vitiis**: dative with *iniquom*, which is here used in the sense of 'hostile'; *cf.* i. 10. 15, *iniqua Troiae castra.* For the spelling, *-quom*, see on line 13, *flavom.*

48. **ocior**: the adjective has adverbial force, — *too speedily.* **aura**: with special reference to Mercury as a winged god.

49. **magnos triumphos**: in August of 29 B.C., Octavian had celebrated triumphs lasting for three days over the Pannonians, Dalmatians, and Egyptians.

50. **ames dici**: the infinitive with *amo*, a construction frequent in Horace, is confined to poetry. **pater atque princeps**: *pater* is to be understood merely as a conventional term of respect; the formal designation of *pater patriae* was not conferred upon Augustus until 2 B.C., long after the date of this ode; *princeps* is probably for *princeps senatus*, a name given under the Republic to the ranking senator, the recognized leader of the senatorial body. The title had

been conferred upon Augustus in 28 B.C., shortly before the time of this ode. The title Augustus dates from January, 27 B.C.

51. Medos: see note on *Persae*, line 22 above. **equitare**: *i.e.* on their hostile incursions.

52. Caesar: the poet here passes by way of a climax from the conception of Mercury as a god embodied in human form, and addresses the Emperor by his customary title.

ODE III.

1. Sic . . . sic, *etc.*: we should naturally expect these words to be followed by an *ut*-clause (*ut reddas serves*), instead of which, by a simple anacoluthon, the poet employs jussive subjunctives (*reddas*, *serves*), explanatory of *sic*, — 'may the goddess guide thee thus: bring Virgil unharmed to Attic shores, and save the half of my life.' **diva potens Cypri**: *the goddess who rules over Cyprus.* Venus, as sprung from the sea, was regarded as a patron goddess of sailors, and was widely worshipped in the island of Cyprus, where she had many temples.

2. fratres Helenae: Castor and Pollux, famous as the guardian divinities of seamen. **lucida sidera**: the reference is probably to the electrical phenomenon known as St. Elmo's fire. When seen double on the yards of a vessel, these fires were thought by the ancients to represent the presence of Castor and Pollux, and were regarded as a favorable sign. *Cf.* Macaulay, *Battle of Lake Regillus*, 765 ff.: —

'Safe comes the ship to harbor
Through billows and through gales,
If once the great *Twin Brethren*
Sit *shining* on her sails.'

3. ventorum pater: Aeolus.

4. aliis: here for *ceteris*, as in *Sat.* i. 4. 2. **Iāpygă**: Greek accusative; Iapyx was the northwest wind, which would be favorable for vessels sailing from Italy (Brundisium) to Greece.

6. debes Vergilium: *art responsible for Virgil*, lit. *owest Virgil* (*sc.* to me and his other friends).

7. reddas: lit. *deliver him, i.e. bring him; credere* ('entrust') and *reddere* ('pay back') are current mercantile terms, and *reddas* is doubtless here used with a touch of its technical meaning.

8. animae dimidium meae: the cordial relations existing between Horace and Virgil are abundantly attested in contemporary literature; see Introd. § 5, and *cf.*, *e.g.*, *Sat.* i. 6. 54, *optimus Vergilius;* i. 5. 40, *Varius Vergiliusque, animae quales neque candidiores terra tulit neque quīs me sit devinctior alter.*

10. fragilem truci: contrasted ideas are thus regularly put side by side when it is desired to mark the antithesis.

12. nec: the conjunction connects *commisit* and *timuit.*

13. decertantem: the *de* is intensive, 'struggling to a decisive issue'; so frequently in Horace in similar compounds, *e.g. deproelior, debello.* **Aquilonibus**: dative with a verb of *contending*, a Grecism; *cf.* i. 1. 15, *luctantem Icariis fluctibus Africum.* The plural is used to indicate the successive blasts of the wind.

14. tristis Hyadăs: the Hyades are spoken of as *tristis*, 'gloomy,' because rainy weather prevailed at the seasons when they rose and set.

16. maior: *sc. est.* **tollere seu ponere**: with *tollere* understand *seu*, and for the absence of the first *seu*, *cf.* i. 6. 19, *vacui sive quid urimur.* Notus raises the waves of the Adriatic by blowing; he quiets them (*ponere*) by subsiding. On the spelling **volt**, which was probably already archaic in Horace's day, see B. *L. L.* § 57. 1. *a.*

17. quem mortis gradum: *what form of death's approach*, lit. *what approach of death.*

19. vidit: *i.e.* had the courage to gaze.

20. Acroceraunia: lit. 'thunder heights,' a rocky promontory in Epirus running out into the Ionian Sea. They are called *infamis*, 'of evil name,' because they were the scene of frequent shipwrecks.

21. abscidit: from *abscindo* or *abscīdo?* The metre shows.

22. prudens: *with set purpose, intentionally.* **Oceano dissociabili**: *by 'the estranging sea'; dissociabilis* is here used with active force. Adjectives in *-bilis* are found in this use occasionally at all periods; *cf.* ii. 14. 6, *inlacrimabilem;* Plautus, *Mil. Glo.* 1144, *date operam adiutabilem;* Ovid, *Met.* xiii. 857, *penetrabile fulmen;* Cic. *Tusc. Disp.* i. 17. 40, 42, *spirabilis; de Nat. Deo.* iii. 12. 29, *patibilis.*

24. non tangenda: *i.e.* which the god intended should not be touched; hence the epithet *impiae.*

25. omnia: man's conquest of one element (water) has already been detailed; the poet now goes on to speak of others, *viz.* fire (Prometheus), air (Daedalus), earth (Hercules). **perpeti**: the infinitive dependent upon an adjective, as in i. 1. 18, *indocilis pauperiem pati.*

26. per vetitum nefas: *i.e.* men rush into wickedness even in the face of express prohibition.

27. Iapeti: a Titan, son of Uranus and Gaea, and father of Prometheus. **genus**: for *filius*, as frequently in the poets; *cf.* ii. 18. 37, *Tantali genus*, *i.e.* Pelops.

28. ignem . . . intulit: according to the familiar tradition, Prometheus stole fire from the gods, secreted it in a hollow reed, and so communicated it to mortals. **fraude mala**: Prometheus's treachery is spoken of as *mala*, because of the dire results which it had entailed.

29. post ignem subductum: *i.e. after the theft of fire;* for the idiom, *cf.* i. 1. 4, *meta evitata.* According to the myth, Prometheus's theft of fire was the immediate occasion of the results described in lines 30–33. As a punishment for Prometheus's impiety, Jupiter sent Pandora, from whose box escaped the various ills that afterward afflicted humanity. **aetheria domo**: *i.e.* its home in the aether, the highest heaven above the common air.

30. macies: the word properly indicates the condition which results from wasting disease; logically it is rather the result of *nova febrium cohors*, with which it is grammatically coördinated.

32. semotique prius tarda necessitas leti: *i.e.* hitherto Death had been far off and slow in coming; *prius* is to be combined in thought with both *tarda* and *semoti.*

33. corripuit gradum: *quickened its pace.*

34. vacuom: for the spelling, see note on i. 2. 13, *flavom.* **aërā̆**: the Greek accusative, as in *Iapyga*, line 4.

35. non datis: by litotes for *negatis.*

36. perrupīt Acheronta: the *-īt* probably represents, not an arbitrary lengthening, but a reminiscence of the earlier quantity of the perfect ending; perfects in *-īt* occur repeatedly in Plautus and Terence. The incident referred to in *perrupit Acheronta* is the twelfth (according to other accounts the eleventh) of Hercules's twelve labors; in this he succeeded in bringing Cerberus to the upper world. Acheron is here used to denote the lower world in general, not the river merely. **Herculeus labor**: *i.e.* the toiling Hercules; the figure is common in poetry; *cf.* iii. 21. 11, *Catonis virtus*, *i.e.* the virtuous Cato.

37. nil ardui est: lit. *there is nothing of steep*, *i.e.* nothing is too difficult.

38. neque patimur = *and prevent;* litotes.

40. ponere: in the sense of *deponere*, as frequently in the poets, and occasionally also in prose.

ODE IV.

1. Solvitur: *is breaking up.* **vice veris**: *vice* properly means the alternation of one thing with another. It is difficult to bring out this force in English; we may translate, *the coming of spring;* yet in Latin the genitive is appositional, spring itself being the substitute (*vice*) for winter. **Favoni**: the west wind or zephyr was a regular accompaniment of spring.

2. trahunt: sc. *in mare.* **siccas carinas**: *i.e.* boats that have been under shelter or out of water for the winter. With the ancients, navigation was suspended for the winter months. **machinae**: the reference is to some contrivance for launching the boats — tackle and rollers, very likely.

3. neque iam: *and no longer.*

5. Cythěrēa: so called from Cythēra, an island off the southern coast of Laconia, which was colonized at an early time by the Phoenicians. These seafaring men introduced the worship of Venus, whence doubtless arose the legend that Venus was sprung from the sea. To the Romans, Venus was preëminently the presiding deity of spring; as the goddess of love, she naturally came to typify the reproductive forces and processes of nature and to be regarded as originating and fostering (*cf. alma Venus*) the new life of the year. Note that, though the *e* of *Cythēra* is long, the corresponding *e* of *Cythěrēa* is short; so also in Greek, Κύθηρα but Κυθέρειος. **imminente luna**: *while the moon stands overhead.*

6. iunctae: *i.e. linked* (*hand in hand*) *with;* the ablative is one of association; see Introd. § 38. *a.* **Nymphis, Gratiae**: often mentioned as attendants and companions of the goddess; *cf.* 1. 30. **decentes**: *comely.*

7. alterno pede: *i.e.* in the dance. **gravis**: *mighty.* **Cyclopum**: the Cyclopes were the servants of Vulcan, employed by him in forging the thunderbolts of Jupiter; *cf.* the fine passage in Virgil, *Aen.* viii. 424 ff.

8. Volcanus: for the spelling, see B. *App.* § 57. 1. *a.* **ardens**: this epithet naturally befits the god of fire; strictly it applies to the fire itself, but is easily transferred to the god. **visit**: Vulcan naturally revisits his workshop in the spring, for at that season come the thunder-storms in which Jupiter wields the bolts forged by the Cyclopes.

9. nunc decet: *'tis fitting now.* **nitidum**: *i.e.* glistening with perfumed oils, with which the ancients commonly anointed the hair. **impedire**: poetic for *cingere* or *vincire*. **myrto**: sacred to Venus.

10. flore: used collectively. **solutae**: *i.e.* from the bondage of winter's frosts.

11. et = *etiam*. **Fauno**: the god of shepherds and farmers. The root is *fau-*, the same as seen in *faveo*; hence originally 'the propitious one.' **lucis**: in Horace, *lucus* is used only of sacred groves; otherwise *nemus* is employed.

12. agna, haedo: the ablatives depend upon some passive form of *immolo* (*sibi immolari*) to be supplied, — *whether he demand that sacrifice be made by a lamb, etc.* A similar use of the ablative is found in iii. 24. 56 f., *ludere doctior, seu Graeco iubeas* (sc. *ludere*) *trocho*.

13. pallida pulsat pede pauperum: notice the effective alliteration, a rhetorical device sparingly employed by Horace. **pallida Mors**: the epithet seems borrowed from Death's victims. **aequo**: *impartial*. **pulsat pede**: with the Romans it was apparently common to employ the foot in knocking at the door.

14. regum: *the wealthy*, a frequent meaning of *rex* in Horace; cf. ii. 14. 11, *sive reges sive inopes coloni*. **turris**: *i.e.* palaces. **beate Sesti**: *blest Sestius*; *beatus*, as the participle of the almost obsolete verb *beo*, originally meant 'blest,' 'endowed with wealth,' 'rich'; secondarily it acquired the sense of 'happy'; yet the early meaning of 'rich,' 'wealthy,' is found with some frequency both in prose and poetry. Note that a certain adversative force inheres in *beate*, 'despite thy riches, Sestius.' The Sestius referred to was probably Lucius Sestius Quirinus, son of the P. Sestius defended by Cicero in an extant speech. Sestius had been an adherent of Brutus, but after Philippi had won the favor of Augustus, who in 23 B.C. appointed him consul suffectus, *i.e.* to fill the consulship for the balance of an unexpired term.

15. vitae summa brevis: *life's brief span*. **spem incohare**: *cf.* Seneca, *Epist.* 101, *quanta dementia est spes longas incohare*.

16. iam: *soon*. **nox**: 'Death's dark night.' **fabulaeque Manes**: *the ghostly shades*; *fabulae* means that the *Manes* are unsubstantial; though placed before *Manes*, the word is logically in apposition with it. For the appositive with adjective force, cf. i. 1. 1, *atavis regibus*.

17. exilis: *cheerless*; lit. *meagre*, *poor*, *i.e.* supplied with no comfort or pleasures. **Plutonia**: the adjective with the force of a genitive, as frequently. **quo simul mearis**: *as soon as thou goest thither; simul* for *simul ac*, as not uncommonly.

18. regna vini: *i.e.* the office of presiding at the festive board. The Romans at their convivial gatherings commonly chose one of their number to act as master of ceremonies (*magister bibendi*). The choice was determined by throwing the dice. The *tali*, 'knuckle bones,' were dice with four flat sides and two rounded ones; only the flat sides had spots. **sortiere**: *i.e.* secure by lot by a throw of the dice.

19. calet: *are enamoured.*

ODE V.

1. multa in rosa: *on a bed of roses; cf.* Seneca, *Epist.* 36. 9, *in rosa iacere.*

2. urget: not 'courts,' 'woos,' but *embraces.*

3. Pyrrha: Greek Πυῤῥά, lit. 'the auburn-haired'; *cf. flavam* in the following line. **sub**: *under the arch of;* just as *pro*, lit. 'in front of,' at times means 'in the front part of' (*e.g. pro curia*, 'in the front part of the senate-house'), so *sub*, lit. 'under,' not infrequently means 'in the lower part of'; *cf. Epodes*, 9. 3, *sub alta domo.*

4. flavam: blond hair was rare, and so admired by the Romans.

5. simplex munditiis: *in simple elegance.* **fidem**: understand *mutatam* from *mutatos* in the following verse.

6. aspera nigris aequora ventis: the order of the words is that known as the 'interlocked' (*synchysis*), a very common device with the poets. Another instance is found below in line 13 f., *tabula sacer votiva paries.*

7. nigris: the epithet is transferred from the storm-clouds to the winds which they seem to send forth.

8. emirabitur: found only here; it is an intensified *mirabitur.* **insolens**: *in surprise; for insuetus, i.e.* unused to such experience.

9. aurea: in predicate relation to *te*, 'thinking thee golden,' *i.e.* true-hearted.

10. vacuam: *i.e.* of passion for another; supply in sense *te fore.*

12. miseri: *sc. sunt.*

13. me: emphatic, as shown by the position. **sacer paries**: the wall of some temple on which he has hung a votive offering.

14. indicat . . . vestimenta: *i.e.* 'I have escaped, though barely, from love's shipwreck'; *tabula votiva*, as the metre shows, is ablative; it is to be joined in thought with *indicat.*

15. suspendisse, *etc.*: those who escaped from shipwreck often suspended to Neptune a votive offering, sometimes also the garments they had worn.

16. maris: dependent upon *potenti; cf.* i. 3. 1, *diva potens Cypri.* **deo**: used figuratively; *i.e.* the god of love's tempestuous sea.

ODE VI.

1. Scribēris: *i.e.* written about, celebrated. The use of the future here is somewhat peculiar; Horace means that Agrippa will *find* in Varius the fitting poet to sing his achievements. **Vario**: *by Varius;* dative of agent with *scriberis; cf.* Prudentius, *Per.* iii. 136, *scriberis ecce mihi.* This construction, though rare with the uncompounded tenses of the passive voice, is well attested both for prose and poetry. Other instances in Horace are *Sat.* i. 6. 116, *cena ministratur pueris tribus; Epist.* i. 19. 3, *carmina quae scribuntur aquae potoribus.* Varius, an intimate and highly prized friend of Horace and Virgil, was distinguished as an epic and tragic poet. To the epic field belonged his *Panegyric* of Augustus, to the tragic his *Thyestes*, which is highly praised by Quintilian. It was Varius who, in company with Plotius, issued the *Aeneid* after Virgil's death. None of Varius's own works have come down to us. **fortis, victor**: in predicate relation to the subject of *scriberis.*

2. Maeonii: *Homeric, i.e.* epic; Maeonia was another name for Lydia, one of the reputed homes of Homer. **aliti**: *bard*, lit. 'bird'; the conception of a poet as a soaring bird is particularly common in antiquity; *cf.* ii. 20, where Horace represents himself as transformed into a swan.

3. quam cumque: for *quamcumque* (tmesis), as sometimes also in prose; as antecedent of the relative we may understand in thought *propter eam rem.* **ferox**: *bold, warlike*, not 'fierce.' **navibus**: Agrippa's naval successes had been achieved at Naulochus (defeat of Sextus Pompeius, 36 B.C.) and at Actium.

4. gesserit: future perfect.

5. nos: for *ego.* **Agrippa**: Marcus Vipsanius Agrippa (63–12 B.C.) was the intimate friend and adviser of Augustus. His brilliant military successes in many critical emergencies, along with his skilful statesmanship, greatly endeared him to the Emperor, who later (21 B.C.) gave him his daughter Julia in marriage. **dicere**: *tell of, sing of.*

6. **Pelidae**: Achilles. **Pelidae stomachum**: the *wrath of Peleus's son*, the theme of the *Iliad*; *stomachus* designated properly, not the digestive organs, but rather the region about the heart, which was naturally regarded as the seat of the emotions. **cedere nescii**: *unyielding, inexorable*; the infinitive is governed by the adjective, as in i. 1. 18, *indocilis pauperiem pati.*

7. **cursus per mare Ulixei**: the theme of the *Odyssey*. **duplicis**: *crafty*, Homer's standing epithet for Ulysses. **Ulixĕī**: poetic genitive: *cf.* i. 15. 34, *Achillĕī*. These forms go back to lost nominatives in *-ēus* (*cf.* Greek Ὀδυσσεύς, Ἀχιλλεύς) treated as though *-e-us*.

8. **saevam Pelopis domum**: *i.e.* the tragic events connected with Thyestes, Atreus, Agamemnon, Orestes, and others of this fated house. Varius had treated these in his tragedy of *Thyestes*, to which Horace here gracefully alludes.

9. **conamur**: *i.e.* I do not even attempt these subjects, much less actually succeed in them; for the *pluralis modestiae*, *cf.* ii. 13. 22, *vidimus*. **tenues grandia**: *i.e.* I, a *humble* poet, do not attempt these *lofty* themes. The antithesis is emphasized by the juxtaposition of the adjectives; *cf.* i. 15. 2, *perfidus hospitam*; ii. 4. 6, *captivae dominum*. **dum**: the *dum*-clause, in addition to its temporal character, has a slight causal force.

10. **imbellisque lyrae**: *i.e.* the lyre devoted to the harmless themes of peace, such as love, wine, *etc.*; *lyrae* is governed by *potens*; *cf.* i. 3. 1, *diva potens Cypri*; i. 5. 15, *potenti maris deo.*

11. **Caesaris**: Octavian.

13–16. This stanza seems somewhat out of relation to the rest of the ode; hence some critics have regarded it as an interpolation; if genuine, it may mean: 'I could no more do justice to Agrippa's achievements than I could rival Homer.'

13. **tunica**: here equivalent to *lorica*, 'coat of mail.'

14. **scripserit**: potential subjunctive, — *who would worthily describe?*

15. **nigrum**: *begrimed*. **Merionen**: a brave Cretan hero who assisted the Greeks in the siege of Troy.

16. **Tydīden**: *Tydeus's son*, Diomedes. **superis parem**: Diomedes, the doughtiest of the Grecian heroes after Achilles, had on one occasion, by Athena's help, wounded Mars and Venus in battle.

18. **sectis**: and so harmless; their resentment is simulated. **in iuvenes**: with *acrium*.

19. **vacui**: *i.e.* free from an attachment. **vacui sive urimur**:

for *sive vacui (sumus) sive urimur; cf.* i. 3. 16, *tollere seu ponere volt freta.* **quid urimur**: *am inspired with any passion; quid* is accusative of the 'result produced' ('internal object'); this construction occurs at times, as here, with the passive voice; with *urimur*, understand in thought *amore.*

20. non praeter solitum leves: *i.e.* with my customary lightheartedness; *leves* agrees with the subject of *cantamus.*

ODE VII.

1. Laudabunt: almost equivalent here to 'may praise'; *cf.* the same use in Virgil, *Aen.* vi. 847, *excudent alii spirantia mollius aera . . . tu regere imperio populos Romane memento*, where *tu* forms a similar contrast with *alii* to that furnished here by *me* in line 10. **alii**: contrasted with *me* in line 10; 'others may praise their favorite cities; as for me, Tibur is the fairest spot.' **claram**: *famous*, for its climate, its pleasant location, and its schools of eloquence; Catullus speaks of it as *nobilis.* **Mytilēnen**: on the island of Lesbos, famed for its patronage of art and literature; it was the home of Alcaeus.

2. Ephesum: in Horace's day, the flourishing metropolis of the Roman province of Asia, noted also for its temple of Diana, which ranked as one of the seven wonders of the world. **bimarisve**: the citadel of Corinth commanded a view of the Corinthian Gulf to the West, of the Saronic Gulf to the East.

3. moenia: there was nothing noteworthy in the walls themselves. *Corinthi moenia* is simply a phrase for the city as a whole. **Baccho**: Bacchus, according to the common tradition, was born at Thebes, of Semele, daughter of Cadmus. **Apolline**: *i.e.* for the shrine of Apollo.

4. Tempe: the wild and beautiful valley of the Penēus in northern Thessaly.

5. sunt quibus est: the indicative (instead of the subjunctive) with *sunt qui* occurs repeatedly in Horace; *cf.* i. 1. 3, *sunt quos iuvat;* i. 1. 19, *est qui nec spernit.* **quibus unum opus est**: *whose sole task it is.* **Palladis urbem**: Athens.

6. carmine perpetuo: lit. *a continuous*, and so a long, *poem.*

7. undique decerptam olivam: a difficult passage, of doubtful meaning. Apparently, by *an olive (garland) gathered from all sides,* the poet means a garland of poems on topics drawn from every corner of the mythical and legendary history of Athens. By a bold touch, this garland of poetry is spoken of as placed upon the brow of the successful poet; *oliva* is thus virtually used to cover two ideas: (*a*) the actual olive twig typical of successful poetic achievement; (*b*) the topics of poetic treatment. **praeponere**: as shown by ancient works of art, the garland placed upon the head often projected in front of the forehead; cf. Seneca, *Medea*, 70, *praecingere roseo tempora vinculo*. **olivam**: the olive was sacred to Athene, the patron goddess of Athens.

8. **plurimus**: *many a one;* unexampled in this sense, but supported by the occasional use of *multus* in this meaning, *e.g.* Lucan, *Pharsalia*, iii. 707, *multus sua volnera puppi affixit*. **Iunonis**: a prominent deity in Argive worship. Remains of her temple, the Heraeum, have recently been brought to light on the site of the ancient city of Argos.

9. **aptum equis Argos**: *aptum equis* is an evident translation of the standing Homeric epithet of Argos, ἱππόβοτον, lit. 'horse-feeding'; the level plains about the city afforded excellent pasturage. **dites Mycenas**: the wealth of Mycenae was well-nigh proverbial. Recent archaeological investigation bears abundant evidence to its ancient splendor. Homer speaks of it as πολύχρυσος ('all-golden').

10. **me**: Horace himself had a villa at Tibur. **patiens**: *hardy;* Sparta was no longer famed in Horace's day for the valor of its citizens; the poet is speaking of its ancient reputation.

11. **Larisae**: a city of Thessaly situated on the Penēus. **percussit**: *i.e.* with admiration.

12. **Albuneae resonantis**: Albunea is here the nymph conceived to inhabit the fountain of the same name, which gushed up in a grotto (*cf. domus*) at Tibur; *resonantis* is poetically transferred from *domus* to *Albuneae;* the reference is to the noisy roar of the neighboring waterfall (*praeceps Anio*).

13. **Tiburni**: one of the three mythical founders of Tibur. **lucus**: *i.e.* a sacred grove, as in i. 4. 11, and regularly in Horace. **uda**: *watered.*

14. **rivis**: these are artificial watercourses, constructed for purposes of irrigation.

15. **albus deterget Notus**: as its context and position show, *albus* (used predicatively) is emphatic; the poet means: 'Just as Notus is often a *clearing* (*albus*) wind and banishes'; note the use of *albus* as applied to the wind, instead of to the weather which the wind accompanies; it is precisely analogous to the use of *nigris* in i. 5. 7,

nigris ventis. Cf. also iii. 27. 19, *albus Iapyx;* iii. 7. 1, *candidus Favonius.*

17. sapiens: *wisely.*

18. tristitiam, labores: the special causes of Plancus's affliction are unknown.

19. molli mero: *mellow wine.* **Plance**: Lucius Munatius Plancus (born about 85 B.C.) had been consul in 42 B.C. He was a man of weak character, and in the tempestuous times following the assassination of Caesar vacillated between parties, transferring his allegiance repeatedly from one cause to another. Ultimately he became a supporter of Octavian and was the originator of the proposition to confer upon the Emperor the title of Augustus (27 B.C.). Horace's relations with Plancus are unknown.

20. tenent, tenebit: as the tenses show, Plancus is not now at Tibur, but presumably in the field.

21. Tiburis tui: these words form the connecting link between the first and second parts of the ode; the clearness of the transition is somewhat clouded by the length of the comparison introduced by *albus ut obscuro.* Plancus is said to have been born at Tibur, and may also have owned a villa there. **Teucer**: son of Telamon and half-brother of Ajax. Teucer is used as an example to enforce the poet's exhortation to Plancus; hence the emphatic position of the word at the beginning of its clause. The substance of the illustration was probably familiar to all educated Romans, from Pacuvius's tragedy of *Teucer.* **Salamina**: Greek accusative of *Salamis, Salaminis.*

22. fugeret: when Ajax and Teucer set out for the Trojan War, their father, Telamon, had enjoined upon them that each should guard the other and neither should return alone. Ajax, driven mad by Athena, had wrought havoc among the cattle in the Grecian camp, and out of shame for his conduct had taken his own life. Telamon, however, was inexorable, and upon Teucer's return banished him from home. **uda**: lit. *moist*, but here, as occasionally elsewhere, in the sense of *flushed.* **Lyaeo**: by a common metonymy for *vino.*

23. populea: the poplar was sacred to the *wandering* Hercules (*cf.* Virgil, *Buc.* 7. 61, *populus Alcidae gratissima*) and hence appropriate to Teucer's present fortunes.

24. adfatus: the perfect participle is here used as a present, denoting contemporaneous action. B. 336. 5; A. and G. 290. *b*; G. 282. N.; H. 550. N.

25. **quo . . . cumque**: tmesis, as i. 6. 3. **melior**: *i.e.* kinder. **parente** = *patre* (*meo*).

26. **ibimus**: almost with the hortatory force of *let us go.*

27. **nil desperandum**: *never despair!* **Teucro duce et auspice Teucro**: note the chiasmus; *auspice Teucro* means, *under Teucer's auspices.* With the whole expression *cf.*, for example, such phrases as *Augusti ductu et auspiciis.*

28. **certus**: *unerring*, an evident translation of the Greek νημερτής.

29. **ambiguam Salamina**: *a second Salamis*, *i.e.* one whose name, if mentioned alone, would cause uncertainty as to which of the two was meant. **tellure nova**: the new land in which the second Salamis was founded proved to be Cyprus.

30. **O fortes peioraque passi**: *cf.* the similar exhortation of Aeneas to his comrades in *Aen.* i. 199, *O passi graviora, dabit deus his quoque finem.*

32. **iterabimus aequor**: lit. *repeat* (*i.e.* resume our voyage over) *the deep*, he had just returned with his followers from Troy.

ODE VIII.

1. **Lydia**: with Horace, a typical name for a coquette.

2. **Sybarin**: the name is fictitious, but seems to be chosen with reference to the sybaritic life now pursued by the youth.

4. **campum**: the Campus Martius, which was used for athletic exercise and sports. **patiens**: with adversative force, — *though capable of enduring.*

6. **Gallica ora**: *i.e.* mouth of his Gallic steed; excellent horses came from cisalpine Gaul. **lupatis frenis**: *wolf-bit bridle*; such bridles were furnished with a peculiar kind of jagged bit.

8. **timet Tiberim tangere**: the Tiber was much frequented for swimming; *timere* with the infinitive is essentially a poetic construction in Horace's day. **flavom, olivom**: for the spelling, see note on i. 2. 13, where also the force of *flavos* is explained. **olivom**: used in anointing the body before wrestling.

9. **sanguine viperino**: mentioned in *Epodes*, 3. 6, as a deadly poison.

10. **neque iam livida gestat**, *etc.*: *and now no longer go about with arms aglow from martial exercise; livida* denotes the dark blue color of the veins swollen by exercise; *livida gestat bracchia* is literally: *carry his arms aglow*, *i.e.* move about with arms aglow.

11. disco . . . nobilis expedito: *distinguished for hurling, often the discus, often the javelin, beyond the farthest mark* (reached by others). The *discus* was a disk of stone or metal similar to the modern quoit.

13. quid: *why?* **marinae**: *sea-born.* Thetis was a Nereid.

14. filium Thetidis: Achilles. That he might escape the certain destruction which it was foretold he should meet did he join the Trojan expedition, his mother had concealed him at the court of Lycomedes on the island of Scyros. **dicunt**: *sc. latuisse.* **sub**: of time, *just before.* The interval was really ten years, but Troy's doom is poetically conceived as near at hand.

15. virilis cultus: *manly garb;* Achilles had disguised himself at Scyros by donning maiden's attire.

16. Lycias catèrvas: *Lycian troops;* the Lycians were allies of the Trojans, who are really meant.

ODE IX.

1. ut: *how*, introducing the subjunctives of indirect question, *stet, sustineant, constiterint.* **stet**: *i.e.* stands out distinctly against the sky; picturesque for *sit.*

2. Soracte: a mountain about 28 miles north of Rome, rising conspicuously from the plain to a height of 2000 feet. Its modern name is *S. Oreste.* **nec iam**: *and no longer.*

3. laborantes: lit. *toiling, straining;* we naturally use no figure, but say *bending.*

4. constiterint: *are congealed;* here Horace is giving us either an exaggeration, or (what is more probable) simply an artificial reproduction of the ode of Alcaeus of which this poem is an imitation; *cf.* the Alcaic fragment, *πεπάγασιν δ' ὐδάτων ῥοαί.* Kiessling assures us that the Tiber does not freeze over once in a century.

5. super = *high upon; cf.* the use of *sub* in i. 5. 3, with the note.

6. reponens: *re-* in composition, among various other meanings, often conveys the idea of doing something *in response to an obligation;* thus *reddere*, 'give as is due'; so here *reponens*, 'piling, as you ought'; so below, line 20, *repetantur*, 'let (the campus and squares) be sought, *as they ought to be.*' **benignius**: *i.e.* more generously than usual, — right generously.

7. deprome: *bring down, i.e.* from the wine-room; wine was often kept in store-rooms located in the second story of the dwelling; *cf.* iii. 21. 1 f., *O . . . pia testa . . . descende* (*sc. horreo*). **quadrimum Sabina merum diota**: interlocked order (synchysis), as in i. 5. 6, and frequently in poetry. **quadrimum**: *four years old*, lit. *of four winters; quadrīmus* is from **quadri-him-us*, in which *him-* is the same root as seen in *hiem-s*, Greek χειμ-ών; other compounds are *bīmus, trīmus.* **Sabina**: poetic transference of the epithet, from the wine to the jar; strictly, it is the wine which is *Sabinum.*

8. **Thaliarche**: a fictitious name, yet a suggestive one; it means 'master of festivities.'

9. **cetera**: *i.e. all else* but the moment's pleasure. **qui stravere**: the clause is illative,—*for as soon as they have quieted.* **simul**: for *simul ac*, as i. 4. 17, and not infrequently.

10. **aequore**: to be taken with *deproeliantis.*

11. **deproeliantis**: *battling, i.e.* with each other; the *de* is intensive, as in i. 3. 13, *decertantem Aquilonibus*, a passage which is otherwise similar to that before us; *deproelior* is found only here. **cupressi**: a tall, slender tree, in shape something like the Lombardy poplar, and hence particularly exposed to the action of the wind.

13. **fuge quaerere**: a poetical periphrasis for *noli quaerere;* such periphrases, while frequent in all poetry, ancient and modern, are particularly common in Horace.

14. **quem . . . cumque**: tmesis as in i. 6. 3; i. 7. 25. **dierum**: dependent upon *quemcumque.* **lucro appone**: *set down as gain*, lit. *to gain;* a mercantile figure.

15. **nec sperne**: *nec* occurs repeatedly in Horace's lyric poems, where we should normally expect *neve* (*neu*), *i.e.* in prohibitions, and in jussive and optative subjunctives, *e.g.* iii. 7. 30, *neque in vias despice; Epodes*, 10. 9, *nec sidus amicum adpareat.*

16. **puer**: *in youth.* **neque tu**: *sc. sperne;* in disjunctive sentences, the *tu* is not seldom reserved for the second member, as here; *cf. Epist.* i. 2. 63, *hunc frenis, hunc tu compesce catenis.*

17. **donec**: *while;* in this sense the word is not found before the Augustan period. **virenti**: understand in thought *tibi*,—'and while you are in the bloom of youth.'

18. **nunc**: *i.e.* in youth. **campus**: *i.e.* the Campus Martius, the place of sports and martial exercise, as indicated in Ode 8.

19. **lenes susurri**: *sc. amantium.* **sub noctem**: *at nightfall; as night is drawing on;* the use of *sub* is the same as that in i. 8. 14, *sub funera.*

20. composita hora: *at the trysting hour.* **repetantur**: for the force of the *re-*, see note on line 6, *reponens.*

21. et: *also, too.* **latentis proditor intumo puellae risus ab angulo**: the arrangement is carefully studied; the three modifiers are placed together, succeeding each other in the same order as the three nouns which they qualify, which are likewise placed together; translate, *now too the merry laugh from some secret corner which betrays the hiding girl.*

22. risus, pignus: these words also are the subject of *repetantur*, but the construction is somewhat zeugmatic, *i.e.* with *risus* and *pignus* some other idea than that of *repetere* is to be supplied; owing to the remoteness of *repetantur*, this construction, though grammatically somewhat loose, is not harsh.

23. pignus: *forfeit*; a bracelet or a ring, as shown by the following *lacertis, digito.* **lacertis, digito**: best taken as datives of separation. B. 188. 2. *d*; A. & G. 229; G. 347. 5; H. 386. 2.

24. male pertinaci: *scarcely*, or *not really, resisting*; the girl's unwillingness is only simulated; for another picture of the same sort, *cf.* i. 6. 17–18, *sectis unguibus acrium*; for this force of *male*, *cf.* Virg. *Aen.* ii. 23, *statio male fida carinis.*

ODE X.

The ode seems to have been a free imitation of a similar hymn to Mercury (Hermes) composed by Alcaeus, some fragments of which remain.

1. Mercuri: to the Roman mind Mercury was primarily the patron god of trade (*cf. merx, merc-ator*). To this conception were later added many attributes of the kindred Greek divinity Hermes, who was primarily the messenger of the gods. It is this later composite conception which lies at the basis of the present ode. **facunde**: applied to Mercury as the messenger or herald of the gods; *cf.* the Greek epithet λόγιος. In Acts xiv. 12, we are told that 'they called Paul Mercurius, because he was the chief speaker.' **nepos**: he was the son of Jupiter and Maia, Atlas's daughter.

2. feros cultus: Horace, in *Sat.* i. 3. 100, speaks of primitive man as a *mutum et turpe pecus.* The first defect (*mutum*) would naturally be remedied by the gift of language; the second (*turpe*) by the institution of graceful athletic exercises, such as those of the palaestra. **recentum**: *i.e.* just created, primitive; the genitive in *-um*, for *-ium*, is poetic.

3. **voce**: *i.e.* with speech, the gift of language. As the god of intercourse, commerce (*cf. com-merc-ium* with *Merc-urius*), and communication in general, Mercury was naturally credited with bestowing the power of communication by means of language. **catus**: this word (obsolete in Horace's day) contains the notion of wise insight, — here insight into the needs of mortals; Horace employs it again in iii. 12. 10. **decorae**: causative, — *grace-giving*.

4. **more**: *the institution.* **palaestrae**: Mercury's function as the presiding deity of athletics was recognized in the Greek epithet ἀγώνιος.

6. **curvae lyrae**: Mercury is said to have invented the lyre by stretching strings across the shell of a tortoise which he had found; *curvae*, of course, refers to the shape of the shell.

8. **condere**: *to hide;* the infinitive dependent upon an adjective, as in i. 1. 18, *indocilis pati*, and frequently in poetry. **furto**: a special instance of this propensity is mentioned in the next stanza.

9. **boves**: emphatic by position. **olim**: *once upon a time;* the word limits the sentence as a whole. **reddidisses**: practically equivalent to a subordinate clause in indirect discourse dependent upon the idea of saying involved in *minaci voce;* we may conceive Apollo as saying in direct discourse, *nisi . . . reddideris, ego te, etc.* In indirect discourse after a secondary tense (*terret* is historical present), the future perfect indicative of the direct form naturally becomes the pluperfect subjunctive, *reddidisses.*

10. **per dolum**: instead of the adverb *dolose.* **amotas**: lit. *abstracted, diverted;* semi-jocose for 'stolen.' **puerum**: Mercury is said to have played this prank on the very day of his birth.

11. **viduos**: with the force of a perfect passive participle (*privatus, spoliatus*), as often in the poets; though *viduos* is grammatically in agreement with the subject of *risit*, yet logically the idea is: 'laughed to find himself bereft.' On the orthography of *viduos*, see note on i. 3. 34, *vacuom;* Introd. § 34.

12. **risit**: aoristic, — *burst into laughter.*

13. **quin et**: *quin* is intensive, as in the frequent *quin etiam; et* here = *etiam*, 'also.' **Atridas**: Menelaus and Agamemnon.

14. **Ilio relicto**: Priam passed out of the city on his way to Achilles, in order to ransom Hector's body. See *Il.* 24. 334 f. **dives**: appositively; *laden with gifts;* alluding probably to the rich presents which Priam brought as a ransom.

15. **Thessalosque ignis**: *i.e.* the watch-fires of the Thessalian

Myrmidons of Achilles. **Troiae**: dative, dependent upon *iniqua*; cf. i. 2. 47, *nostris vitiis iniquom.*

16. fefellit: *escaped the notice of.*

17. reponis: *i.e.* put in the place where they belong, 'duly conduct'; for this force of *re-*, see note on i. 9. 6, *reponens.* The conception of Mercury as the guide of souls to the lower world was covered by the Greek epithet ψυχοπομπός.

18. sedibus laetis: *i.e.* the Elysian Fields; the case is ablative. **virga**: said to have been presented to him by Apollo in return for the lyre which Mercury had contrived. **levem**: *ghostly, unsubstantial;* the idea is the same as in *fabulae*, i. 4. 16.

19. turbam: of the shades.

20. imis: for the usual *inferis.*

ODE XI.

1. ne quaesieris: the perfect subjunctive in prohibitions is practically confined to the poets and colloquial speech. **scire nefas**: *i.e.* it is impossible to know; *cf.* i. 24. 20. The phrase is used parenthetically; understand *est.*

2. finem: sc. *vitae.* **Leuconoë**: the name is fictitious. Perhaps Horace intended it to suggest the meaning: 'of clear insight' (*i.e.* into the future), from Greek λευκός and νοῦς. **nec**: on *nec* (*neque*) for *neve* (*neu*) with imperative, optative, and jussive expressions, see note on i. 9. 15, *nec sperne.* Observe, too, that *nec* here is not disjunctive, but rather explanatory of the preceding *ne quaesieris*, *i.e.* 'do not seek by trying the calculations,' *etc.* Similarly ii. 11. 3, *remittas quaerere nec trepides.* **Babylonios numeros**: *Babylonios* is synonymous with *Chaldaeos.* The Chaldeans were typical representatives of the art of astrology; *numeros* refers to their calculations by means of tables and numbers. Beginning with Horace's day, the influence of these impostors continued for centuries at Rome. Legislation, though often directed against them, proved futile.

3. ut: exclamatory, — *how much better, etc.*; *ut* for *quanto* with a comparative, as here, is apparently a Grecism; *cf.* Plautus, *Truc.* 806, *ut facilius.* **quicquid erit**: *i.e.* whatever fate shall come.

4. plures: *i.e.* more than the present. **tribuit**: *has destined.* **Iuppiter**: the disposition of events is represented as governed now by the Fates, now by Jupiter. **ultimam**: in predicate relationship to *eam* understood, the antecedent of *quae.*

5. **oppositis debilitat,** *etc.*: the winter is represented as wearing out the sea by (= against) the cliffs (*pumicibus*), which serve as a barrier (*oppositis*) to the waves ; a rather cumbrous figure.

6. **sapias**: *i.e.* don't be foolish ! Leave the idle speculations of astrology. **vina liques**: for removing the sediment ; a common domestic operation, and so here used for performing one's customary household duties. **spatio brevi**: causal ablative, — *since the space (of our life) is short.*

7. **spem longam reseces**: *cf.* the similar thought in i. 4. 15, *vitae summa brevis spem nos vetat incohare longam.* **fugerit**: *will be gone*; the future perfect is here used, as frequently, to denote the immediate consummation of the future act. **invida**: *i.e.* time (*aetas*) which begrudges us enjoyment of life's pleasures.

8. **carpe diem**: *i.e.* reap its fruit, its pleasures ; possibly with the added notion of swiftness. Horace here must not be regarded as recommending the life of a voluptuary ; he never suggests that as an ideal. He is rather urging a wise enjoyment of life's blessings while they are present. **quam minimum**: *as little as possible*, *i.e.* not at all. **postero**: neuter, — *to the future.*

ODE XII.

1. **Quem virum aut heroa,** *etc.*: the opening lines of the ode are an imitation of the beginning of Pindar's second Olympian ode, *τίνα θεόν, τίν' ἥρωα, τίνα δ' ἄνδρα κελαδήσομεν;* **acri**: *shrill, clear-toned.*

2. **celebrare**: the infinitive is poetically used to denote purpose, as in i. 2. 8, *visere montes*; cf. especially *Epp.* i. 3. 7, *quis sibi res gestas Augusti scribere sumit?* **Clio**: the muse of history, and so appropriate for the purpose mentioned by the poet.

3. **iocosa**: *playful*; a permanent characteristic of the echo, as though endeavoring to deceive and mislead mortals.

4. **imago**: *echo*; the full phrase is *imago vocis*; yet even prose writers use the simple *imago* in this sense.

5. **Heliconis**: Mt. Helicon in Boeotia. Like Pindus and Haemus, it was a celebrated haunt of the Muses. **oris**: *borders, slopes.*

6. **super Pindo**: *i.e.* on the summit of ; *cf.* the use of *super* in i. 9. 5, *super foco.* Mt. Pindus was between Thessaly and Epirus. **gelido Haemo**: Mt. Haemus was in Thrace. It is called 'cool' because of its elevation.

7. **unde**: its antecedent is *Haemo.* **temere**: *i.e.* in confusion.

The word is the locative of an obsolete nominative *temus* (like *genus*, *-eris*) meaning 'darkness'; hence originally 'in the dark,' 'blindly,' 'in confusion.' The final *e*, often marked long in dictionaries, is really short. **insecutae**: *sc. sunt.*

8. **Orphea**: Orpheus lived in Thrace. **silvae**: even the trees are said to have yielded to the spell of Orpheus's lyre.

9. **arte materna**: *i.e.* the skill with which his mother (Calliope, the Muse) had endowed him.

11. **blandum**: limiting *Orphea.* **et**: *even.* **auritas**: *listening, attentive.* **fidibus**: with *ducere.*

12. **ducere**: the infinitive depends upon the adjective (*blandum*); *cf.* i. 1. 18, *indocilis pauperiem pati.*

13. **solitis**: *i.e.* familiar, oft-repeated; for *solitus* in this passive sense, *cf.* i. 6. 20, *praeter solitum.* **parentis**: *viz.* Jupiter. For the thought, *cf.* Virg. *Buc.* 3. 60, *ab Iove principium Musae, Iovis omnia plena.*

16. **horis**: *seasons*, a poetic sense of the word.

17. **unde** = *a quo.* The antecedent is *parentis.*

18. **nec quicquam simile aut secundum**: *cf.* Martial, xii. 8. 2, *terrarum dea Roma, cui par est nihil et nihil secundum.* **secundum, proximos**: this use of *secundus* ('next and near') and *proximus* ('next, but at a distance') occurs elsewhere, *e.g.* Cic. *Brutus*, 47. 173; *cf.* also Virgil's *proximus huic, longo sed proximus intervallo.*

19. **illi**: brachylogy for *illius honoribus.* Cf. i. 1. 23, *lituo tubae permixtus sonitus.*

21. **proeliis audax**: Pallas's prowess in battle is frequently mentioned; *cf.* Virg. *Aen.* xi. 483, *armipotens, praeses belli.*

22. **Liber**: Bacchus. **inimica virgo beluis**: the reference is to the huntress Diana.

24. **Phoebe**: preëminent for his skill in archery. On the importance attached by Augustus to the worship of Apollo and the reasons for this, see note on i. 2. 32.

25. **Alciden**: Hercules. He was the grandson of Alceus. **pueros Ledae**: Castor and Pollux; *puer* for *filius*, as in i. 32. 10, and often in poetry.

26. **hunc**: Castor. **equis**: with *superare.* **illum**: Pollux. **superare**: used absolutely; the infinitive dependent upon an adjective, as above, in line 12. **pugnis**: *with the fists, in boxing;* from *pugnus.*

27. **simul**: for *simul ac*, as often.

28. stella: *constellation* (Gemini); Castor and Pollux were the especial patrons of mariners. See i. 3. 2 and note.

29. saxis: *i.e.* the cliffs of the coast.

34. Pompili: Numa Pompilius, whose reign, according to tradition, was characterized by the cessation of war and the establishment of elaborate religious ceremonials. **superbos**: apparently here used in the complimentary sense of 'glorious,' with an allusion to the magnificent public buildings which Tarquinius erected, as well as to the generally successful course of his reign.

35. Tarquini: the second Tarquin is meant. **fasces**: the bundles containing axes, carried by the lictors as the symbols of the authority of the kings, and later of the consuls. **Catonis**: Cato Uticensis, who ended his life by suicide at Utica in 46 B.C., after Caesar's victory, was the champion *par excellence* of the Republican cause. Hence the present allusion, particularly in an ode whose climax is the praise of Augustus, has not only excited surprise, but has even led some critics (*e.g.* Bentley) to suggest an alteration of the text. But Cato had not been a personal opponent of Octavian, and the interval since his death (some twenty years) had doubtless served to obliterate recollections of the old party strife. Cato's character and motives, moreover, had been recognized by all as of singular purity and disinterestedness. Another similar allusion to Cato occurs in ii. 1. 23, *et cuncta terrarum subacta praeter atrocem animum Catonis*; *cf.* also Virgil's tribute in *Aen.* viii. 670, *secretosque pios his dantem iura Catonem.* Similar encomiums occur in other contemporary writers.

36. nobile = *clarum*, as often.

37. Regulum: said to have been put to death with cruel tortures after his return to Carthage from Rome, where he had dissuaded the Senate from making an exchange of prisoners with the Carthaginians; *cf.* iii. 5. The story, however, is probably apocryphal. **Scauros**: *i.e.* men like Scaurus; the reference is to M. Aemilius Scaurus (163–89 B.C.), who served with distinction in the Cimbrian War, and was twice consul. Valerius Maximus, v. 8. 4, calls him *lumen ac decus patriae.* **animae**: genitive with *prodigum*, which here follows the analogy of adjectives of fulness.

38. Paulum: L. Aemilius Paulus; he fell at Cannae, 216 B.C. **Poeno**: *i.e.* Hannibal; the ablative absolute here denotes time.

39. gratus: *gladly*; *i.e.* the theme is a welcome one to me. **insigni camena**: *in ennobling verse*; *camena*, lit. 'muse,' by a familiar figure is used for *carmine;* with *insignis* in the causative sense of 'making distinguished,' *cf.* i. 1. 5, *palma nobilis.*

40. Fabricium: a hero in the war with Pyrrhus (281–275 B.C.), and famous for the integrity and simplicity of his character. He has been called 'the Roman Aristides'; *cf.* Cic. *de Off.* iii. 22. 87, *Fabricio, qui talis in hac urbe qualis Aristides Athenis fuit.*

41. intonsis Curium capillis: M'. Curius Dentatus was a contemporary of Fabricius, and like him served in the war against Pyrrhus. His simplicity of life is emphasized in the words *intonsis capillis.* The first barbers at Rome are said to have come from Sicily in 300 B.C., but it was nearly a century before the custom of carefully trimming the beard and hair became general.

42. utilem: in predicate relation to *Curium.* **bello**: dative of purpose. **Camillum**: M. Furius Camillus, the hero of the Gallic invasion (390 B.C.).

43. paupertas: *poverty,* not in the sense of destitution, but simply of narrow means, like *pauperies* in i. 1. 18. **arto lare**: *narrow* (*i.e.* humble) *abode; lar,* originally the god of the hearth or household, is here used figuratively for the dwelling. With *arto lare, cf. Epp.* i. 7. 58, *lare curto;* Lucan, *Pharsalia,* v. 527, *O vitae tuta facultas pauperis angustique lares.* Horace is particularly fond of dwelling upon the simplicity of the early days, and contrasting it with the demoralizing luxury of his own age.

45. crescit occulte: *grows imperceptibly;* the Mss. read *occulto,* which editors retain, construing it with *aevo.* But this is extraordinary Latin. The text of Lucretius, i. 314, *occulte decrescit vomer in arvis,* suggests that Horace here wrote *occulte,* which later became corrupted to *occulto.*

46. Marcelli: the whole family is alluded to by implication, though only one representative of the house had ever achieved a reputation commensurate with that of the other worthies here mentioned. He was M. Claudius Marcellus, the conqueror of Syracuse. Between 222 and 208 B.C. he was five times elected consul. His aggressive tactics in the Second Punic War secured him the name of the 'Sword of Rome,' in distinction from Q. Fabius Maximus Cunctator, who was known as the 'Shield of Rome.' This allusion to the fame of the Marcelli, besides giving recognition to a famous house, is doubtless intended also as a compliment to the young Marcellus (son of Octavia and nephew of Augustus), whose marriage to Julia, Augustus's daughter, probably occurred about the time this ode was written. Such a compliment would naturally appeal to the Emperor also, who had selected Marcellus as his successor. The young man's promise of future distinction was suddenly cut short by death in 23 B.C.; *cf.* the five lines commemorating this event in Virg. *Aen.* vi. 863 f., *quis, pater, ille, virum qui sic comitatur euntem? etc.* **omnis**: *viz.* all the other Roman worthies previously mentioned.

47. **Iulium sidus**: the reference is to the comet which appeared in broad daylight after the death of Julius Caesar and continued to shine for a week. It was popularly believed to contain the soul of the murdered hero. This allusion to the Julian house, following immediately the reference to that of the Marcelli, seems to point to an approaching or already consummated union of the two houses by marriage. **ignis minores** = *stellas.*

49. **pater atque custos**: Jupiter.

51. **data**: *sc. est.* **tu secundo Caesare regnes**: the perspective of the thought is somewhat obscured; Horace's prayer is really: 'May Caesar be next to thee in majesty!'

53. **Parthos**: see note on i. 2. 22, *Persae.* **Latio imminentis**: a poetical exaggeration.

54. **iusto triumpho**: *a well-earned triumph;* to be taken with *egerit.*

55. **subiectos**: *bordering on;* the notion of 'under' disappears in certain uses of this compound. **orae**: used, much as above in line 5, in the general sense of 'region,' 'district,' but with the added notion of distance.

56. **Serăs**: Greek accusative from nominative *Serĕs. Seres* was loosely applied to the peoples living on the east of the Roman frontier in Asia, in the vicinity of the modern Bokhara. **Indos**: famed for their riches and treasures. The Romans had not yet come in contact with either *Seres* or *Indi*, but it was a natural ambition to desire to include these peoples in the Roman dominion.

57. **te, tu** (58), **tu** (59): the anaphora, coupled with the emphatic position of the pronouns at the beginning of the verse, is intended to close the ode with a due recognition of the supremacy of the god. **aequos**: for the spelling, see note on i. 2. 47.

58. **gravi curru**: Jove's thunder. **Olympum** = *caelum.*

59. **parum castis** = *incestis, i.e.* polluted by the vile orgies of the time.

60. **lucis**: the dative for *in* with the accusative as in i. 2. 1, *terris.*

ODE XIII.

1. **Telephi, Telephi**: the repetition of *Telephi* at the close of two successive verses aptly indicates how Telephus's praises are constantly on Lydia's lips.

2. **cervicem**: the singular is poetical; in prose we regularly have *cervices*. **cerea**: here *white;* so also Ovid, *ex Ponto*, i. 10. 28, *membraque sunt cera pallidiora nova.* In its natural state the wax was yellowish in color, but refining produced a white variety.

4. **difficili bile**: *with angry passion; difficilis*, like English 'angry,' is transferred from the person to the emotion. **iecur**: often conceived as the seat of anger and other emotions.

6. **manent**: the plural verb with subjects connected by *nec . . . nec* is rare; yet Cicero says (*de Fin.* iii. 21. 70), *etenim nec iustitia nec amicitia esse omnino poterunt, nisi ipsae per se expetantur.* **umor**: of tears.

7. **furtim**: *i.e.* despite all efforts at concealment.

8. **quam**: to be taken with *penitus*.

9. **uror**: *i.e.* with jealousy at your continued love for Telephus, despite his cruelty.

10. **immodicae**: strictly, the epithet belongs in thought with *mero*, *i.e.* violence resulting from excessive indulgence in wine.

11. **puer**: Telephus.

12. **memorem**: *lasting;* another instance of the causative use of the adjective, as in i. 1. 5, *palma nobilis.*

13. **satis**: *i.e.* as much as you ought. **audias**: *heed.*

14. **speres**: potential subjunctive—*you would not hope*, approaching almost the force of a prohibition. **perpetuom** *sc. futurum esse;* the epithet is transferred from some such word as *fides* to the lover himself; for the spelling of *perpetuom*, see note on i. 3. 34, *vacuom.*

15. **oscula**: here, *lips*, as in Virg. *Aen.* i. 256, *oscula libavit natae.* This meaning is rare.

16. **quinta parte**: *the quintessence;* the Pythagoreans recognized five elements or essences (*essentiae*), of which the fifth (the *quinta essentia*) was the *aether.* This aether being very pure and delicate, its name of *quinta essentia* came to be synonymous with 'purity,' 'delicacy.' Our English 'quintessence' in this sense goes back, through the mediaeval philosophers, to the ancient Pythagorean conception.

17. ter et amplius: for the usual *terque quaterque.*

19. divolsus amor: *the sundering of love; cf.* the familiar *post urbem conditam.* **querimoniis**: lit. *complaints, i.e.* arising from mutual bickerings.

20. suprema die: euphemistic for *morte.*

ODE XIV.

1. navis: the conception of the state as a ship is frequent in all literatures. **referent**: *are about to carry back.* **in mare**: *into the sea* of war. **novi fluctus**: *i.e.* new civil disturbances.

2. quid agis: a common form of reproof; *cf.* Cic. *in Cat.* i. 10, *M. Tulli, quid agis!* **fortiter occupa portum**: *i.e.* bestir yourself to reach a haven of security; *occupare* means 'get possession,' not, like English *occupy*, 'to maintain possession.' The word usually connotes the idea of anticipation; so here: 'reach the haven, before the waves take thee to sea again.'

3. ut: *how.*

4. latus: *sc. sit;* the omission of the forms of *esse* in indirect questions is extremely rare at all periods.

5. mālus: *the mast.* Note the interlocked arrangement (*synchysis*) in *malus celeri saucius Africo.* **saucius** = *sauciatus.*

6. funibus: carried lengthwise along the hull from stem to stern, to strengthen the vessel.

7. durare: *endure, withstand;* in this sense the word is first found in the Augustan poets; later it appears in the post-Augustan prose writers. **carinae**: a somewhat bold instance of the poetic plural; *cf. puppibus,* below, in line 14; Virg. *Buc.* 6. 76, *rates* (of the ship of Ulysses); *Aen.* ii. 202, *arae,* 'the altar.'

8. imperiosius: *i.e.* too violent.

10. di: statues of gods were often set up in the sterns of vessels. **quos voces**: relative clause of purpose, — *to call upon.* **iterum**: with *pressa.*

11. Pontica pinus: superior material for the construction of ships came from the forests of Pontus; *pinus* and *filia* (in line 12) are both appositives of the subject of *iactes.*

12. nobilis: with *silvae.*

13. inutile: with both *genus* and *nomen.*

14. nil fidit: *puts no trust; nil* is accusative of 'result produced.' B. 176. 2. *a.* **pictis puppibus**: vessels were often painted in bright colors; in this context, *pictis* has almost the force of 'gaudy.'

15. nisi debes ludibrium: *i.e.* unless thou wishest to furnish sport.

16. cave: *beware!* used absolutely.

17. sollicitum taedium: *an object of vexing disappointment*; *sollicitum* is causal, being transferred from the person to the thing; *cf.* i. 1. 5, *palma nobilis*. The reference is probably to the period after Philippi, when Horace was still nursing his disappointment at the failure of the republican movement headed by Brutus and Cassius. **quae**: *sc. fuisti* with *taedium*; *es* with *cura*; the verb is rarely omitted in subordinate clauses.

18. nunc: *i.e.* since Horace's reconciliation to Augustus's administration. **desiderium**: *an object of fond affection*. **non levis**: litotes for *gravissima*.

19. nitentis: explained as referring to the glistening marble quarried at Paros and elsewhere; *cf* iii. 28. 14, *fulgentis Cycladas*, with note.

20. aequora: the waters of the Aegean were difficult of navigation; the expression, however, is purely figurative,— 'beware of the rocks and shoals of civil strife!' **Cycladas**: governed by *inter* in *interfusa*; the earliest instance of the construction with this word.

ODE XV.

1. Pastor: *viz.* Paris. Before the birth of Paris, his mother, Hecuba, saw in a dream a vision of a firebrand which threatened to destroy Troy. Interpreting the vision to apply to the expected child, she exposed him at his birth upon Mt. Ida. Paris grew up among the shepherds, and was tending sheep upon Mt. Ida when appealed to by the three goddesses (Juno, Venus, Minerva) to award the golden apple to the fairest. **traheret**: the word suggests haste and eagerness.

2. Idaeis: *i.e.* made of wood from Mt. Ida. **perfidus hospitam**: the antithesis between these two ideas is heightened by their juxtaposition, as so frequently in all Latin writers; *cf.* i. 6. 9, *tenues grandia*.

3. ingrato: *i.e.* to the winds, whose nature was to keep in motion; the antithesis between the natural character of the winds (*celeris*) and the unwelcome (*ingrato*) calm is well brought out by the juxtaposition of the epithets; *cf.* note on line 2. **obruit**: the subject, *Ne-*

reus, by an unusual hyperbaton, is drawn into the dependent clause (*ut caneret*). **otio**: *with a calm.*

4. **fera** : *dire, relentless.*

5. **Nereus** : the marine deity, son of Pontus and Tellus, and father of the Nereids. His prophetic powers are mentioned by Hesiod and others ; *cf.* Hesiod, *Theog.* 235, γέρων νημερτής. **mala avi**: *under evil auspices;* the ablative is strictly one of attendant circumstance (B. 221); lit. *with evil bird.*

6. **multo milite**: *with many a warrior;* the person is treated as the means, as opposed to the agent, of the action.

7. **coniurata** : alluding, probably, to the formal oath taken by the Greek chieftains at Aulis. **rumpere**: zeugma ; *rumpere* applies strictly only to *nuptias* ; with *regnum* we should expect some such verb as *frangere ;* the infinitive without subject accusative after *coniurata* is a Grecism.

9. **quantus, quantus** : the anaphora lends emphasis. **adest** : *is looming near* (Bryce).

10. **Dardanae genti**: *against the race of Dardanus;* dative of interest ; *Dardanae* is for *Dardaniae ; cf. Carmen Saeculare,* 47, *Romula* (for *Romulea*) *gens.*

11. **aegida**: *breastplate* (not 'shield,' as given in Harpers' *Dictionary*) ; *cf.* Ovid, *Met.* vi. 78, *clipeum, hastam, galeam ; defenditur aegide pectus.*

12. **currus** : the poetic plural. **rabiem**: note the striking combination of this abstract noun with the previous concrete ones (*galeam, aegida, currus*) ; we feel the need of different verbs in our English rendering. Bryce suggests 'whets her rage.'

13. **Veneris praesidio**: Venus's support was rendered in return for Paris's award of the golden apple. **ferox** : *emboldened.*

14. **pectes caesariem**: an expression, like the following *cithara . . . divides*, for effeminate self-indulgence ; *caesaries* is essentially a poetic word, usually denoting beautiful hair. **feminis**: with *grata.*

15. **carmina divides**: *i.e.* mark off into rhythmical groups, and so, sing.

16. **thalamo**: ablative of means, with strong accessory notion of place, — *by hiding in your chamber.* Homer describes Paris when vanquished by Menelaus as brought by Venus to his bedchamber.

17. **spicula**: frequent in poetry for *sagittas.* **Cnosii**: Cnosus was the ancient capital of Crete, and the Cretan reeds furnished superior arrows.

18. vitabis: conative, — *thou shalt endeavor to escape.* **sequi**: dependent upon *celerem*; *cf.* i. 1. 18, *indocilis pauperiem pati.*

19. Aiacem: not Ajax son of Telamon, but Ajax son of Oïleus; *cf.* Hom. *Il.* xiv. 520, Αἴας Ὀιλῆος ταχὺς υἱός. **tamen**: *i.e.* in spite of thy endeavor to escape (*vitabis*). Paris was finally slain by an arrow of Philoctetes. **serus**: *i.e.* too late for the good of thy countrymen; had it been earlier thou hadst spared the lives of many heroes. **adulteros crines**: for the transfer of the epithet, *cf.* i. 5. 7.

21 f. non, non; te, te: observe the passionate energy thrown into the passage by the double anaphora; note, too, that, as an interrogative, *non* is more energetic than *nonne.* **Laërtiaden**: *i.e.* Ulysses. **Pylium Nestora**: famed as the oldest of the Greek warriors, and one of the first in counsel; Homer calls him the guardian of the Greeks; his home was 'sandy Pylos' in Elis or Messenia. **respicis**: *regard, heed*; as in i. 2. 36.

24. Teucer: brother of Ajax and son of Telamon; see note on i. 7. 21. **Sthenelus**: the charioteer of Diomedes. **sciens** = *peritus.*

25. sive: in thought join *-ve* with *auriga*, *si* with *opus est.* For this use of *sive*, *cf.* i. 2. 33.

26. non piger: litotes for *impiger.* **Merionen**: a Cretan warrior and follower of Idomeneus.

27. nosces: *i.e.* thou shalt come to know his prowess. **reperire**: dependent upon *furit*, which here takes the infinitive after the analogy of *cupio*; *cf.* Ovid, *Met.* i. 200, *saevit exstinguere* (*nomen*). **atrox**: *in his rage.*

28. Tydides: *i.e. Diomedes*, bravest of the Greeks, next to Achilles. **melior**: *i.e. even braver*; Tydeus himself was of distinguished prowess. Bryce renders, 'brave father's braver son.'

29. cervos uti: as verb, understand *fugit* from *fugies*; for the position, see note on i. 2. 5, *grave ne.* For the spelling, see note on i. 2. 13, *flavom.*

30. lupum: object of *fugit* to be supplied.

31. sublimi anhelitu: '*panting with head high in air*' (Smith); lit. *with raised panting.* The bold phrase is probably an imitation of a Greek idiom. Strictly, too, it can apply only to some four-footed animal, not to a human being. Horace evidently is thinking of a panting deer fleeing with raised head, and transfers to Paris what in strictness applies to the deer only.

32. non hoc: litotes again, — *no such thing as this, i.e.* something far different, *viz.* courage in the fight. **tuae** : *i.e.* Helen.

33. iracunda classis Achillei : note the hypallage of the adjective ; Horace means, *the fleet of the wrathful Achilles, i.e.* the wrathful Achilles and his followers. Achilles's Myrmidons naturally sided with their leader, when Achilles in his wrath temporarily withdrew from participation in the war against the Trojans. For the form of the genitive *Achillei*, see note on i. 6. 7. **diem** : almost = *the doom ; cf.* Homer's *αἴσιμον ἦμαρ.* **proferet** : lit. *shall put off*, but with very much the same shade of meaning as *laudabunt* ('may praise') in i. 7. 1 ; *i.e.* 'though the wrath of Achilles postpone the day of doom, yet,' *etc.* **Ilio** : dative of reference.

34. Phrygum : for *Troianorum*, as frequently in the poets.

35. post, *etc.* : this clause stands in adversative relation to the preceding, — *Achilles's warriors may postpone, etc., but the fire shall finally burn, etc.* **certas** : *i.e.* the number is fixed by the Fates and is unalterable. **hiemes** = *annos.* Possibly the word is chosen because Troy's fall was traditionally put in the spring.

ODE XVI.

1. O matre pulchra, *etc.* : *O daughter fairer than thy mother fair ;* no clew to her identity exists.

2. quem . . . cumque : tmesis of *quicumque*, as i. 6, 3, and frequently. **criminosis** : *abusive ;* lit. *full of charges* (*crimina*). **modum** = *finem*, as in ii. 6. 7.

3. pones : future indicative with the force of the imperative (or possibly the English 'may put' ; cf. i. 7. 1, *laudabunt*). **iambis** : among the Greeks, iambic poetry (according to the traditional account) was first cultivated by Archilochus, who employed it as the vehicle of invective and personal abuse. Hence in Latin the word *iambi* is often equivalent to 'invective.' This meaning occurs frequently in Horace, who entitled his epodes *iambi* from their frequent polemic character. **flamma, mari** : sc. *modum ponere.*

5. Dindymēne : lit. *the* (*goddess*) *of Dindymus, i.e.* Cybele ; Dindymus was a mountain in Galatia, near Pessinus, sacred to Cybele. **adytis** : *at*, or *in, his shrine.*

6. incola Pythius : the god whose home is Pytho (Delphi), lit. *the Pythian dweller ; cf.* Catullus, 64. 228, (*Athena*) *sancti incola Itoni* (Itonus in Thessaly).

7. Liber: sc. *quatit Bacchas suas* ('his Bacchanals'). **aeque**: the sentence is not completed by any word that could serve as a correlative with *aeque* (*atque*, *ac*, *et*), but the substantial force of *aeque* is taken up by *sic* (line 8), to which *ut* corresponds.

8. geminant aera: *aera* means 'the brazen cymbals,'—hence lit. *double their brazen cymbals*, poetical for *clash their pairs of cymbals;* it is the cymbals that are really double; *cf.* Lucretius, ii. 635, *cum pueri armati in numerum pulsarent aeribus aera.* **Corybantes**: priests of Cybele, whose religious ceremonial consisted in wild music and dancing. This often wrought them up to such a pitch of frenzy that they beat their breasts with their hands and gashed their bodies with knives. Since the introduction of the worship of Cybele (about 200 B.C.), it had been possible to witness these orgies at Rome itself.

9. tristes ut irae: as verb, we must supply in thought some word meaning 'rouse,' 'agitate'; this is easily understood from the context. The plural *irae* is used because separate instances are thought of. **Noricus**: Noric steel (from Noreia in Styria) was famous for its hardness.

11. saevos: for the spelling, see on i. 2. 13, *flavom.*

12. tumultu: we are not to think of any single phenomenon (thunder, lightning, hail, snow, rain, *etc.*), but of all.

13–16. This stanza apparently gives the poet's excuse,—anger is implanted in the race; none can escape it.

13. fertur: the story is found only here. **principi limo**; *the primeval clay*, *i.e.* the clay from which primeval man was formed.

14. coactus addere: *when compelled to add.* Apparently the clay did not suffice for the formation of man, and Prometheus was obliged to draw upon other sources. **undique**: *i.e.* from every creature.

15. et: *also.*

16. vim: *fury.* **stomacho**: as the seat of the emotions; see on i. 6. 6.

17. irae: emphatic by position and by the context,—*'twas wrath that laid Thyestes low.* **Thyesten**: the feud between Atreus and Thyestes led the former to kill Thyestes's sons and serve their flesh at a banquet to their father.

18. urbibus: *e.g.* Thebes. **ultimae causae**: *the ultimate* (*i.e.* original) *causes; causae* is predicate nominative with *stetere.*

19. stetere: here hardly stronger than *fuere.* **cur perirent**: an extension of the dependent deliberative as employed in substantive clauses; originally this type of subjunctive was used only where the main clause contained a negative (*e.g. nulla causa est cur negemus*), or an interrogative clause implying a negative (*e.g. quid est causae cur negemus*), but by an extension of usage, the construction sometimes occurs where the main clause is affirmative, as here.

20. imprimeret . . . aratrum: ploughing the ground of a razed city seems to have been common in antiquity. **muris**: *i.e.* fragments of the ruined walls.

21. hostile: here = *hostium*, and so logically to be joined with *exercitus*. This line lacks the usual caesura. Introd. § 43.

23. temptavit: *assailed*.

24. celeres: *impetuous*.

25. misit: *drove*. **mitibus**: ablative of association with *mutare*; see B. *App*. § 337; Introd. § 38. *a*.

26. mutare: *quaero* with the infinitive is found only in the Augustan poets and later prose writers. **tristia**: *my savage (verses)*.

28. opprobriis: *i.e.* those contained in the *iambi*. **animum**: *sc. tuum*.

ODE XVII.

1. Velox: with adverbial force; *swiftly*. **Lucretilem**: a mountain in the Sabine territory near Horace's villa, now called Monte Gennaro.

2. mutat: *mutare* is much wider in meaning than any single English word that can be used to translate it; it may mean 'to give in exchange,' or 'to take (receive) in exchange'; here it has the second meaning, lit. *chooses Lucretilis in exchange for Lycaeus*; but it is more natural in English to invert the relations and render, *changes Lycaeus for Lucretilis*. The ablative is one of association. B. *L. L.* § 337; Introd. § 38. *a*. **Lycaeo**: a mountain some forty-five hundred feet in height, situated in southwestern Arcadia; it was a favorite haunt of Pan (= Faunus). **Faunus**: see on i. 4. 11.

3. aestatem: *i.e.* the summer's heat. **capellis meis**: *from my goats*; dative of separation, a variety of the dative of reference; *cf.* Virg. *Buc.* 7. 47, *solstitium pecori defendite*.

4. usque: *always*, *i.e.* when he is here.

5. arbutos: see on i. 1. 21.

6. latentis: *i.e.* scattered here and there among the other trees. **deviae**: here simply *roaming, straying*.

7. olentis uxores mariti: a sportive circumlocution for *capellae*.

8. **viridis**: apparently used as equivalent to 'poisonous'; so *virens* in Claudian, *in Rufin.* i. 290, *virens hydra.* **metuont**: on the form, see Introd. § 34.

9. **Martialis lupos**: the aggressive character of this animal naturally associated it with the god of war; *cf.* Virg. *Aen.* ix. 566, *Martius lupus.* **haediliae**: *kids;* a diminutive from *haedus; cf. porcilia* from *porcus.* The word is not usually given in our lexicons, but is attested by old glosses, which give *αἰρίφιον* (*i.e.* *ἐρίφιον*) = *haedilia.*

10. **utcumque**: *whenever.* **Tyndari**: the name is fictitious, as though intended to designate a second Helen (daughter of Tyndareus). **fistula**: *with the Pan-pipe;* Faunus (*i.e. Pan*), lends the blessing of his presence whenever he hears the music of his own pipe; since *Pan primus calamos cera coniungere plures instituit* (Virg. *Buc.* ii. 32).

11. **Ustīcae**: some unknown eminence in the neighborhood of Horace's Sabine villa. **cubantis**: apparently in the sense of 'sloping.'

13. **di me tuentur**, *etc.*: *i.e.* this protection vouchsafed by Faunus is in return for my devotion to the gods.

14. **cordi**: (*for*) *a delight;* dative of purpose. **hic, hic** (17), **hic** (21): observe the emphasis of the anaphora.

15. **ad plenum**: *to the full.*

16. **honorum**: of the products of the farm; the word depends upon *copia.* **cornu**: ablative of separation with *manabit;* the horn of plenty is an old conception.

17. **Caniculae**: *i.e.* of the summer.

18. **Teia**: *i.e.* like that of Anacreon, who was a native of Teos, and whose muse was devoted to the praises of love and wine.

19. **laborantis**: *i.e. enamoured; cf.* i. 27. 19. **in uno**: *i.e.* Ulysses.

20. **Penelopen**: the faithful wife of Ulysses. **vitream**: *sea-green* (*cf.* iv. 2. 3, *vitreo ponto*); Circe is so called because she was a marine divinity, being the daughter of Perse, the Oceanid. Similarly, iii. 18. 10, *viridis Nereidum comas; Epodes,* 13. 16, (*Thetis*) *caerula.* **Circen**: the enchantress who changed Ulysses's companions into swine. She became enamoured of Ulysses, delaying him at her palace on the island for more than a year, and bearing him two sons, Telegonus and Agrius.

21. **innocentis**: *harmless;* further explained by the *nec-* clauses. **Lesbii**: *sc. vini.*

22. sub umbra: for the meaning of *sub*, *cf.* i. 5. 3, *sub antro*.

23. confundet: *shall join*; poetic for *miscere* or *committere*, yet with the added notion of noise and confusion. **Thyōneus**: Bacchus is so called as the son of Thyone, another name for Semele. Ultimately the word goes back to θύω, 'to rage.'

24. protervom: for the spelling, see on i. 2. 13, *flavom*.

25. suspecta: *an object of suspicion*, and so of jealousy. **Cyrum**: prolepsis (anticipation), *i.e.* the subject of the subordinate clause is first introduced as the object of the main verb. *Cyrus* is a common name of slaves and freedmen. **male dispari**: just as *bene* is used to intensify good qualities, so *male* may be used to intensify bad ones; *dispari* (agreeing with *tibi*, understood) means 'ill-mated.'

28. crinibus: (probably dative); *cf.* *Sat.* i. 10. 49, *haerentem capiti multa cum laude coronam*. **immeritam vestem**: the epithet, as often, is transferred from the person to a thing connected with the person.

ODE XVIII.

1. Vare: probably Quintilius Varus, an intimate friend of Horace and Virgil. His death, which occurred 24 B.C., is celebrated in the twenty-fourth ode of this book. **sacra**: *viz.* to Bacchus. **sēveris**: the perfect subjunctive in prohibitions is practically confined to poetry and colloquial prose. *Cf.* i. 11. 1, *tu ne quaesieris*. **arborem**: the vine was accounted 'a tree.'

2. circa mite solum Tiburis: loosely put for *in miti solo circa Tibur*. The mellow soil would naturally be suited to the vine. **Tiburis**: see i. 7. Varus evidently had a villa in the neighborhood. **moenia Catili**: Catĭlus, elsewhere called Catillus, was one of the founders of Tibur; hence, the *moenia Catili* are those of Tibur itself.

3. siccis: those who abstain from wine are often designated as *sicci*, just as *madidus*, *uvidus*, *etc.*, are used of those who indulge in it; *cf.* iv. 5. 39, where *siccus* and *uvidus* both occur. **nam**: postponed, like *enim*; see note on i. 2. 5. **dura**: in predicate relation to *omnia*, *has ordained that all shall be hard*; lit. *has set forth all things hard*. **deus**: not Bacchus, but the supreme power generally conceived.

4. aliter: *viz.* than by indulgence in wine.

5. crepat: *talks of* (loud and earnestly).

6. quis non, *etc.*: from *crepat*, some such verb as *laudat* is to be supplied. **Bacche pater**: Bacchus was essentially a Greek god, and by the Greeks was conceived of as a youth. The epithet *pater* comes from the Roman conception of Liber, with whom Bacchus early became identified.

7. ac: with adversative force, *and yet* **modici munera Liberi**: a bold expression for *modum in muneribus Liberi;* logically, it is *moderation* which is transgressed.

8. Centaurea rixa: the fight of the Centaurs and Lapithae at the marriage-feast of Pirithous. The Centaurs, invited to the wedding by Pirithous, became excited by wine, and undertook to carry off the bride, Hippodamīa. **monet . . . monet** (9): the importance of the warning is finely emphasized by the anaphora. **Lapithis**: described in the myths as a Thessalian people; Pirithous was their king.

9. debellata: for the intensive force of *de-* in compounds, *cf.* i. 3. 13, *decertantem.* **Sithoniis**: a Thracian tribe noted for their excessive indulgence in wine, and the violence which accompanied their carousals. **non levis**: litotes for *iratus;* the god is angry in consequence of their license. **Euhius**: Bacchus; the name came from the cries of his worshippers, *εὐοῖ, εὐοῖ.* Note the variety of names for the god, purposely introduced by the poet.

10. exiguo fine: *i.e.* scarcely. **libidinum**: with *avidi*, *i.e.* eager to satisfy their passions; *libido* here = 'indulgence of desire,' *cf.* iv. 12. 8.

11. non ego: *non* is to be closely joined in thought with *ego*, — *I'll not be the one to, etc.* **candide**: as being youthful and fair. **Bassareu**: another designation for Bacchus; the word is Greek (Βασσαρεύς, from βασσάρα, 'fox-skin mantle'), and was applied to Bacchus as the god whose votaries wore the fox-skin in their worship.

12. quatiam: apparently in the sense, *rouse, excite* (*cf.* i. 16. 5, *mentem quatit*); *i.e.* 'I will not profane thy divinity, as excessive indulgence in wine might tempt me to.' **variis obsita frondibus**: mystic emblems covered with leaves of various kinds (such as the vine and ivy, which were sacred to Bacchus), and carried by the worshippers in caskets, as described in Catullus, 64. 259 f. Whoever of the uninitiated gazed upon the mystic emblems was said to become mad.

13. sub divom: *to the light of day; cf.* ii. 3. 23, *sub divo.* **saeva**: the cymbals are called 'wild,' because their clashing throws the worshipper into a frenzy. **tene**: *check;* for the compound *contine.* **Berecyntio**: from Berecyntus, a mountain of Phrygia noted for the celebration of the wild rites of Cybele (see note on i. 16. 5, *Corybantes*). Hence the 'Berecyntian horn' is primarily the horn used in the Corybantian worship of Cybele; but similar horns were employed in the Bacchic orgies. In fact, there was the greatest similarity between the two cults.

15. plus nimio: lit. *more by a great deal*, *i.e.* too much, or too high, by far. This use of *nimium* (= *very much*) is colloquial and poetical. **Gloria**: here in the bad sense of boastfulness.

16. arcani Fides prodiga: *a faith lavish of secrets*, *i.e.* a faith which betrays its trust (*perfidia*). Such recreancy would be a natural result of the intemperate use of Bacchus's gift. For *prodigus* with the genitive, *cf.* i. 12. 38, *animaeque magnae prodigum Paulum*. **perlucidior vitro**: true fidelity does not permit its secret to be known, but an *arcani Fides prodiga* permits a view into its inmost recesses. The regular caesura which would come after *per-* is neglected in this line.

ODE XIX.

1. saeva: in that her power is irresistible. **Cupidinum**: this conception of several Cupids is frequent in both Greek and Roman poets.

2. iubet: Horace regularly employs the singular verb when the compound subject consists of two nouns in the singular. **Semelae puer**: Bacchus. He is often mentioned as Venus's attendant.

4. amoribus: dative.

5. Glycĕrae: this name, found repeatedly in the *Odes*, lit. means 'the sweet.'

6. Pario marmore: the marble of Paros (one of the Cyclades) was famed for its whiteness.

7. protervitas: *forwardness*.

8. lubricus: *seductive*. **aspici**: the infinitive depends upon the adjective; *cf.* iv. 2. 59, (*vitulus*) *niveus videri*.

9. tota: *with all her power*. **ruens . . . deseruit**: logically *deseruit* is the subordinate idea, — *leaving Cyprus, she rushes on me*.

10. Cyprum: one of Venus's favorite haunts.

11. versis animosum equis = *bold in retreat*; when fleeing, the Parthian horsemen often discharged their arrows with great effect upon their pursuers, whence the proverbial 'Parthian flight,' 'Parthian shot'; *cf.* ii. 13. 17.

12. dicere: *sc. me*. **quae nihil attinent**: *sc. ad amores meos*.

13. vivom = *virentem;* for the spelling, see on i. 2. 13. **caespitem**: turf for an improvised altar, as often.

14. verbenas: the name is general for all herbs or sprays of foliage used in connection with sacrifices. In a sacrifice to Venus one naturally thinks of the myrtle (sacred to her) as used for this purpose. **pueri**: *i.e.* the attendant slaves.

15. bimi meri: in sacrifices unmixed wine was always offered; it was also usually relatively new; so here *bimi* (last year's vintage), and in i. 31. 2, *novom.*

16. veniet lenior: sc. *Venus; i.e.* the goddess will be less cruel at her coming.

ODE XX.

1. modicis: *plain, common*, as in *Epist.* i. 5. 2. **Sabinum**: *sc. vinum;* it belonged to the poorer grades of wine.

2. cantharis: *tankards, drinking-pots.* Horace purposely chooses the homely name of a homely vessel. Notice the accumulation of features in the opening sentence of the ode, all designed to emphasize the simplicity of the hospitality offered;—the vintage is *vile Sabinum*, and it will be served, not in the delicate polished goblets used for the finer wines, but in tankards (*cantharis*), and even these are plain (*modicis*). **ego ipse** = *I with my own hand.*

3. conditum: *put up, stored.* **levi**: *sealed, i.e.* with wax or gypsum; from *lino.* **datus . . . plausus**: after his recovery from dangerous illness in the year 30 B.C., Maecenas was greeted with tumultuous applause by the populace upon his appearance in the theatre; the event is again alluded to in ii. 17. 25. With *datus* understand *est.* **in theatro**: the Theatre of Pompey, situated in the Campus Martius. The theatre was far too distant from the Vatican and the west bank of the Tiber to produce the echo mentioned in the second stanza. That is purely the fanciful exaggeration of the poet.

5. care Maecenas eques: *dear Maecenas, knight; cf.* ii. 20. 7, *dilecte Maecenas; Epod.* i. 2, *amice Maecenas. Care* goes only with *Maecenas.* Horace adds *eques*, in apposition with *Maecenas*, as a complimentary title; *cf.* iii. 16. 20, *Maecenas, equitum decus.* Maecenas deliberately held aloof from political ambition, and remained by preference a simple *eques* to the last. **paterni fluminis**: *viz.* the Tiber. It is called Maecenas's native river, because Maecenas was born in Etruria and descended from Etruscan kings (*cf.* i. 1. 1, *Maece-*

nas atavis edite regibus), and because the Tiber was *par excellence* the Etruscan river; *cf. Sat.* ii. 2. 32, *amnis Tusci*; Virg. *Aen.* ii. 781, *Lydius* (= 'Etruscan') *Thybris.*

6. iocosa imago: *the sportive echo*, as in i. 12. 3; see note on that passage.

7. Vāticānī: this name was applied to a part of the Janiculum on the west side of the Tiber. Later poets, *e.g.* Martial and Juvenal, treat the antepenult as long.

9. Caecubum: *sc. vinum.* The Caecuban, like the three other wines mentioned in this stanza, was one of the choicer Italian wines. It was grown in Caecubum, a marshy district in southern Latium. **prelo Caleno**: the Calenian wine was grown at Cales (modern Calvi) in southern Campania. **domitam** = *pressam*, the use of which would have involved a certain repetition, *prelum* being for *pres-lom* (root *pres-*, as in *pressus*).

10. bibas: *you may drink, i.e.* at your own home; jussive subjunctive with permissive force. **mea**: in strong contrast with *tu*, and so placed at the beginning of its clause. **Falernae vites** = *Falerna vina*, a superior variety which grew in the *ager Falernus*, a district lying in Campania at the foot of the Massic Mount.

11. temperant = *flavor;* strictly, *vinum temperare* means to 'mix the wine in due proportions.' This was ordinarily done by the admixture of water; hence *temperare* more commonly means 'to reduce the strength' of the wine. The expression *temperant vites neque pocula colles* is strikingly bold in several ways: (1) We should expect *vinum* (not *pocula*) as the object of *temperant* (one mixes the wine, not the vessel containing it); (2) we should expect some word designating a person as the subject of *temperant*; (3) *vites* and *colles* are boldly used for *vina*, so that we get the picture of wine mixing the goblets. Hence some have questioned the genuineness of the text at this point. Others, in fact, reject the entire ode. **Formiani colles** = *Formianā vina*, which grew near Formiae, in southern Latium, near the borders of Campania.

ODE XXI.

1. Dianam: note that the *i*, usually short, is here measured long; so also ii. 12. 20. **dicite**: *sing of, praise*, as often.

2. intonsum: *i.e.* with long and flowing locks; Apollo was conceived of as perpetually young, and is regularly so represented in works of art. **Cynthium**: so called from Mt. Cynthos in Delos, on which

Apollo and Diana were said to have been born. **Latonam**: Greek Λητώ, mother of Apollo and Diana.

4. penitus = *dearly*. **Iovi**: dative of agent.

5. vos: *viz. virgines*. **laetam**: *sc. deam* (*Dianam*). **fluviis et coma**: for Diana as goddess of streams and forests, *cf.* Catullus 34. 9, where she is spoken of as *montium domina silvarumque virentium saltuumque reconditorum amniumque sonantum*. For *coma* = *foliis*, *cf.* iv. 7. 2; Catullus, 4. 11, *comata silva*.

6. Algido: Mt. Algidus, in Latium, some twenty miles distant from Rome, near Tusculum and the Alban Mount; it was an ancient seat of Diana's worship.

7. nigris: referring to the sombre effect of the pines and firs; *cf.* the German *Schwarzwald* ('Black Forest'), which was originally so called from its dark evergreen trees. **Erymanthi**: a mountain of Arcadia.

8. viridis Cragi: Cragus was a mountain of Lycia, the home of Latona; the genitive depends rather upon *silvis* (to be supplied in thought) than upon *nigris silvis*.

9. vos: the boys, as shown by *mares*. **Tempe**: the wild valley of the Penēus, between Thessaly and Macedonia, and a famous seat of Apollo's worship. **totidem**: *i.e.* as many as Diana.

12. fraterna lyra: the lyre invented by Mercury, as explained in i. 10. 6, note, and given by him to Apollo. Mercury and Apollo are regarded as *fratres*, since both were sons of Jupiter.

13. bellum lacrimosum: *cf.* Homer's **πόλεμον δακρυόεντα**. By *bellum* Horace means civil war.

14. pestem = *pestilentia*, as often in poetry. **principe**: on the force of this designation, see note on i. 2. 50; and on Apollo as the special patron deity of Augustus, see on i. 2. 32.

15. Persas = *Parthos*; see note on i. 2. 22.

16. vestra: this refers to both choruses, the boys and maidens.

ODE XXII.

1. Integer vitae scelerisque purus: *the man pure in life and free from guilt*. Horace uses the genitive freely with adjectives in constructions not tolerated in classical prose. Introd. § 37. *a*. Note also the bold substantive use of the two adjectives.

2. Mauris iaculis: the javelin was a favorite weapon of the Moors.

4. Fusce: Aristius Fuscus, the poet and grammarian, an intimate and valued friend of Horace. He is elsewhere alluded to by Horace (*Sat.* i. 9. 61) as a jovial wit, — one to whom a poem like the present might especially appeal.

5. Syrtis: this word properly designates the shifting quicksands off the northern coast of Africa, but here it is applied to the sandy wastes of the adjacent shore.

7. fabulosus Hydaspes: *the storied Hydaspes;* with reference to the numerous marvellous tales (accounts of giant snakes, gold-gathering ants, *etc.*) connected with the district through which this river ran. The Hydaspes was a tributary of the Indus.

9. me: this word is emphatic, made so to heighten the humor of the mock philosophy which the poet is endeavoring to enforce. **silva in Sabina**: *i.e.* in the woods near Horace's Sabine farm, which Maecenas had presented to him in the year 33 B.C. Introd. § 4.

10. Lalagen: the name (from Greek λαλαγή, 'prattle') is appropriate to the maiden characterized later (line 24) as *dulce loquentem.* **ultra terminum**: *i.e.* beyond the boundaries of my farm.

11. curis expeditis: *with my cares laid aside.* Prose diction would have doubtless been *curis expeditus.*

12. inermem: *all unarmed though I was.* Special emphasis is given this word by its position at the very end of the sentence and the stanza.

13. quale portentum: *such a monster as.* **militaris Daunias**: *Daunias* is a poetical name for Apulia, 'the land of Daunus,' a mythical king of that country. Apulia is called *militaris*, because of the martial prowess of its people; *cf.* iii. 5. 9, where the Apulians are spoken of as the flower of the Roman army.

15. Iubae tellus: *i.e.* Mauretania and Numidia. The reference may be either to Juba I., who was defeated by Caesar at Thapsus in 46 B.C., or to his son Juba II., to whom Augustus restored part of his father's dominions.

16. arida: the epithet is boldly transferred from *tellus* to the appositive *nutrix.*

17. pone: the imperative serves logically as a protasis, = *si posueris.* **pigris campis**: *on lifeless* (*i.e.* unproductive) *plains;* the reference, as the following context shows, is to the far North. The phrase belongs logically with *pone.* **nulla arbor recreatur**: *no tree is revived*, *i.e.* there are here no trees to be brought to life, and to put forth their foliage at the advent of summer.

19. quod latus mundi, *etc.*: *(in) a region of the earth over which brood, etc.* The use of *latus* (for *pars*, *regio*) is poetical. **malus Iuppiter**: *a gloomy sky; cf.* i. 1. 25, *sub Iove frigido; malus Iuppiter* is explanatory of *nebulae*, rather than distinct from it.

20. urget: the singular verb is preferred by Horace when the subject is compound.

21. sub curru, *etc.*: *i.e.* in the tropics.

22. domibus: dative of purpose.

23, 24. dulce ridentem, dulce loquentem: *sweetly laughing, sweetly prattling.* The accusative is that of 'result produced' ('internal object'); B. 176. 2. In prose this usage is restricted to accusatives of neuter pronouns and neuter adjectives of number and amount, but in poetry it is used somewhat freely outside of these limits.

ODE XXIII.

1. hinnuleo similis: beginning with the Augustan age, the use of the dative with *similis* grows increasingly frequent. We should, however, have expected *ut hinnuleus; cf.* line 9 below, *tigris ut aspera.* **Chloë**: a Greek name derived from χλόη, 'green shoot,' and hence peculiarly appropriate to the subject of this ode.

2. pavidam: a standing epithet of the deer.

3. non sine: the litotes lends emphasis. **vano**: *i.e.* groundless.

4. siluae: by poetic license for *silvae*, as in *Epodes*, 13. 2.

5. vepris: found only here; the regular nominative singular is *vepres*, though all singular forms are very rare. **inhorruit**: lit. *has bristled up*, and so, *has rustled.*

6. ad ventos: *in the wind.*

7. dimovere: *have pushed aside*, *i.e.* with their sudden movements.

8. tremit: *sc. hinnuleus.*

9. non ego: lit. *not I*, *i.e.* I should be the last.

10. Gaetulus: Gaetulia was in northern Africa. **frangere persequor**: *seek to crush (thee)*; this meaning of *persequor* is poetic and extremely rare.

12. tempestiva viro = *since thou art ripe for a mate; cf.* Virg. *Aen.* vii. 53, *iam matura viro, plenis iam nubilis annis.*

ODE XXIV.

1. sit: deliberative subjunctive, — lit. *is there to be*, verging, however, toward the meaning 'should there be,' 'ought there to be.'

pudor, modus: *quis pudor* asks, 'Should we hesitate?' *quis modus* asks, 'What limit should there be?'

2. capitis: poetical for *hominis*. **praecipe**: *teach*. **lugubris cantus**: not *mournful song*, but *song of mourning*.

3. Melpomene: fittingly invoked as the muse of tragedy. **pater**: Jupiter; the nine muses were daughters of Jupiter and Mnemosyne.

5. ergo = *really;* this force arises as the result of some reflection present to the writer's mind, but not expressed. **Quintilium**: this is probably the Quintilius Varus to whom the eighteenth ode of this book is addressed. He was a native of Cremona, and died in 24 B.C. **perpetuos**: for the orthography, see note on i. 3. 34, *vacuom*.

6. cui: relative, and dependent upon *parem*. **Pudor**: *Honor*. **Iustitiae soror**: this epithet implies that Quintilius was also *iustus*.

7. nuda Veritas: *nuda* = *aperta*, *i.e.* 'candid'; Horace elsewhere (*Ars Poet.* 438 ff.) praises Quintilius's honesty as a literary critic.

8. inveniet: the singular verb with compound subject, as in i. 22. 20, *urget*, and regularly in Horace. **parem**: *a peer*.

10. nulli: for *nemini*, as often in poetry and always in Horace. **Vergili**: the poet.

11. tu frustra pius poscis: *in vain despite thy fond devotion dost thou ask him back; frustra* is to be taken not only with *poscis*, but also with *pius*, — *i.e.* 'vain is thy petition and vain thy devotion'; *pius* is here used in the sense of 'devoted,' a frequent signification of the word. Horace means that Virgil's affectionate attachment is incapable of restoring Quintilius again to life. **heu**: with *non ita creditum*. **non ita creditum**: *i.e.* not committed to his friends by the gods on the understanding that when dead he should be restored again; *ita* anticipates the idea involved in *poscis Quintilium deos*.

12. poscis: here = *reposcis*.

13. quid: as verb we may understand some such word as *valeat*. **si . . . moderere**: *i.e.* wert thou to strike Orpheus's lyre more persuasively than Orpheus himself; though really impossible, the case is represented not as unreal, but as a possible contingency. This reference to Orpheus may be intended as a delicate compliment to Virgil for his skilful treatment of the Orpheus myth in his fourth *Georgic*, published not long before.

14. auditam: (*once*) *heard*, *i.e.* heard and heeded. Orpheus attracted not merely the beasts, but even the trees, by the charm of his music; *cf.* i. 12. 7, *vocalem temere insecutae Orphea silvae;* 11, (*Orphea*) *blandum et auritas ducere quercus.* **arboribus**: dative of agency, frequent in Horace with the perfect passive participle; *cf.* i. 1. 24, *bella matribus detestata.* **fidem**: the singular is poetic. It occurs also in i. 17. 18, *fide Teia.*

15. **num redeat,** *etc.:* this question simply repeats in more specific form the query begun by *quid;* the same protasis (*si . . . moderere*) is to be understood. **vanae imagini**: *to the unsubstantial shade.*

16. **virga horrida**: the *virga* is characterized as *horrida* because it is the symbol of passage to the lower world. **semel**: *i.e.* once for all.

17. **precibus**: the entreaties are personified. **fata**: a bold brachylogy for *portas fatorum.* **recludere**: dependent upon *lenis;* *non* limits the complex idea contained in *lenis recludere.* For the infinitive dependent upon an adjective, *cf.* i. 10. 7, *callidus condere furto;* Introd. § 41. *c.*

18. **nigro compulerit gregi**: *has gathered to his sable flock;* dative of direction, for *ad* with the accusative; the *grex* is *grex umbrarum;* the epithet *niger* is added as characteristic of death. **Mercurius**: for Mercury as ψυχοπομπός, the guide of shades to the lower world, see i. 10. 17–20.

19. **durum**: *sc. est.*

20. **nefas**: *i.e.* forbidden, impossible.

ODE XXV.

1. **Parcius**: *i.e.* less frequently than formerly. **iunctas fenestras**: probably double shutters fastened by a wooden bar; glass windows were practically, if not entirely, unknown in Horace's day.

2. **ictibus**: of the hand.

3. **tibī**: the final *i* is long, as below in line 13, and often in poetry. This is simply a retention of the original quantity. **somnos**: note the plural; so in English, *slumbers.*

5. **multum**: with *facilis;* this use of *multum* occurs repeatedly in Horace. **facilis**: with *quae;* in this sense the word means *willing, courteous, affable,* and properly applies to persons. Here, by personification, it is transferred to the door.

7. **me tuo,** *etc.: while I thy lover,* etc. The words are a snatch of a song belonging to the class known as παρακλαυσίθυρα, *i.e.* lovers'

serenades sung at the door of one's mistress. **longas noctes**: *i.e.* to-night, as thou hast many nights before. **pereunte**: *perire*, used of the languishing of a lover, is a common term in the poets; so also i. 27. 12, *quo volnere pereat.*

9. **invicem** = *vice versa*, *vicissim.* In the past Lydia had disdained her suitors; soon they shall disdain her. Note the emphatic position of *invicem*, — *thy turn shall come.* **moechos arrogantis flebis**: *shall lament that they disdain thee; arrogantis* is predicate.

10. **solo** = *deserted.* Her admirers no longer frequent the *angiportus.* **levis** = *neglected.*

11. **Thracio**, *etc.*: the allusion to the howling wind and the moonless night is intended to heighten the picture of Lydia's loneliness. *Thracio vento* is the north wind, whose home was represented by the poets as being in Thrace; *cf. Epodes*, 13. 3, *Threicio Aquilone.* **magis**: *i.e.* more than usual. In English we should use some positive word, *e.g. fiercely.* **sub inter-lunia**: *interlunium* was the period between the old and new moons, and so the season of dark nights. Belief in the effect of the changes of the moon upon the weather has always been common. As a temporal preposition, *sub* means properly 'just before'; here it is hardly employed so precisely. For the breaking of a word at the end of a Sapphic verse, *cf.* i. 2. 19, *ux-orius amnis.*

13. **cum**: here = *dum.* **tibi**: dative of reference with *saeviet.*

14. **matres equorum**: proverbially passionate.

15. **iecur**: on the liver as the seat of the emotions, see note on i. 13. 4. **ulcerosum**: *i.e.* impassioned.

16. **non sine**: note the emphasis of the litotes; so also in i. 23. 3.

17. **laeta**: *gladsome, joyous.* **pubes**: frequent in the poets for *iuventus.* **hedera, myrto**: the fresh ivy and myrtle are types of youth, just as *aridae frondes* are typical of old age.

18. **pulla**: *dark (green).* **magis**: *sc. quam aridis frondibus.*

20. **dedicet**: note the adversative asyndeton. The word is used jocosely. **Euro**: to scatter with its blasts.

ODE XXVI.

1. **Musis amicus**: *dear to the Muses, i.e.* beloved of them. The phrase stands in causal relation to *tradam, etc.* The favor of the Muses prompts the banishment of all common cares. **metus**: the plural, because concrete fears are thought of (*quis metuatur; quid terreat*).

2. protervis = *violentis.* **mare Creticum**: the definite epithet is used simply for poetic effect, as in i. 1. 14.

3. portare: the poetic use of the infinitive to denote purpose, as in i. 2. 8, *visere montes.* **quis rex**: the allusion is probably to the Dacian king, Cotiso, who in the year 30 B.C. was threatening the northern frontier of the Roman dominions. **sub Arcto**: lit. *under the bear,* and so, *in the North.*

4. orae: used, as often (*e.g.* i. 12. 55), of some distant region. **metuatur, terreat**: these indirect questions depend upon *securus;* the two thoughts are mentioned merely as suggestive of the commotions of the day. With *metuatur* understand in thought *a nobis* (*Romanis*).

5. Tiridaten: in the year 37 B.C., Phraates, having murdered his father and brothers, secured possession of the Parthian throne. In 31 B.C. Tiridates had headed a movement against the usurper, but without success, and had accordingly fled to Augustus (in 30 B.C., the date of this ode), to implore his assistance. **unice**: *entirely.*

6. quae fontibus integris gaudes: the Muses are extensively conceived of as goddesses of springs and fountains.

7. apricos: *bright, golden.* **necte . . . necte**: note the anaphora, — *weave flowers, yea, weave them as a garland. Coronam* is used predicatively; *flores* refers figuratively to the garland of verses which Horace, with the Muses' help, is (in the present poem) weaving in honor of his friend.

8. Lamiae: either L. or Q. Aelius Lamia, two brothers, members of a distinguished family with which Horace was on terms of intimacy.

9. Pimplei: Greek vocative singular of *Pimpleïs, -eïdis,* lit. 'dweller at Pimplea,' and so 'muse'; Pimplea was a fountain in Pieria, a favorite haunt of the Muses. **te**: *sc. Musa.*

10. honores: *i.e.* the honor that I wish to bestow upon him in my verse, — *tributes.* **fidibus novis**: *in new strain;* the reference, as shown by the following *Lesbio plectro,* is to the Aeolic lyric poetry, which Horace so often prides himself upon having introduced among his countrymen; possibly, the reference is even more specific, and is to the Alcaic metre in which this ode is composed. Hence, some have thought this the earliest Alcaic ode written by Horace.

11. Lesbio plectro: the *plectrum* (Greek πλῆκτρον, lit. 'striker') was a short stick with which the player struck the strings of the lyre. **sacrare**: (= *immortalitati consecrare*) *immortalize.*

ODE XXVII.

1. **Natis** : *i.e.* intended, designed. **in usum laetitiae** : *pleasure's service ; laetitiae* is possessive genitive. **scyphis** : large beakers with two handles.

2. **pugnare** : *i.e.* by hurling the beakers. **Thracum est** : *is the way of Thracians, i.e.* it befits them and them only ; various Thracian tribes were noted for their riotous excess in the use of wine ; *cf.* i. 18. 9, *Sithoniis non levis Euhius.*

3. **verecundum** : *i.e.* Bacchus is the god of wine in the sense of the proper use of wine ; he is not the god of wanton excess ; *cf.* the burden of i. 18.

4. **prohibete** : here in the sense of 'defend,' 'protect.'

5. **vino et lucernis** : dative, as often in Horace with *discrepo, differo, etc.; cf. Epist.* ii. 2. 194, *simplex nepoti discrepet.* **Medus acinaces** : the *acinaces* was a special kind of Persian scimitar ; the epithet *Medus*, however, is intended to suggest that the presence of weapons at a banquet is fit only for *Medi* (Parthians).

6. **immane quantum** : like *mirum quantum*, this phrase, by the ellipsis of some word (*e.g.* here *discrepet*), acquires the value of a compound adverb, *vastly.* **discrepat** : *is out of keeping with.* **impium** : the uproar is thus designated as constituting an offence against the *verecundus deus.*

8. **cubito presso** : *i.e.* with elbow resting on the pillow of the *lectus*, or couch, at which the ancients reclined, not merely at dinner, but throughout the following *comissatio*, or drinking.

9. **voltis severi**, *etc.* : this dramatic monologue naturally leaves much to be supplied by the reader's imagination. Apparently, the first speaker's exhortation to refrain from noisy brawling is met by the retort that he himself neglects the pleasures of the bowl ; upon this, he answers that he is ready to drink on one condition : Megylla's brother must name his sweetheart.

10. **Falerni** : see note on i. 20. 10. **Opuntiae** : of Opus, in Locris.

11. **Megyllae** : some well-known beauty. **quo beatus volnere** : note the oxymoron ('contradiction').

12. **volnere, sagitta** : *sc. amoris.* **pereat** : *languishes ;* almost a technical term in speaking of the sufferings of lovers ; *cf.* i. 25. 7, *me pereunte.*

13. **cessat voluntas** : *does your inclination falter?* This is

addressed to the *frater Megyllae*, who at first hesitates to answer the query.

14. quae . . . cumque: the tmesis, as in i. 6. 3, and frequently in this word. **domat**: *masters.* **Venus**: *passion, attachment; cf.* Virg. *Buc.* 3. 68, *parta meae Veneri sunt munera.*

15. non erubescendis: note the emphasis resting upon these words, as shown by their position at the beginning of the clause; *non* is to be closely joined in thought with *erubescendis*, — litotes. **adurit**: *sc. te.*

16. ingenuo: *worthy.*

17. quicquid habes: *whatever wound you have; habere* is here figuratively used in the technical gladiatorial sense of *habere volnus.* **age**: *come!*

18. A: the interjection; the words *A miser* follow the confidential communication of the sweetheart's name. **tutis**: *trusty.*

21. saga, magus, deus: note the climax. **solvere**: *viz.* from thy infatuation. **Thessalis venenis**: potions brewed from certain Thessalian herbs were thought by the superstitious to be possessed of magic properties. The phrase applies only to *saga* and *magus*, not, of course, to *deus.*

23. triformi Chimaera: to be taken both with *inligatum* (as ablative of association) and with *expediet;* an instance of the construction known as ἀπὸ κοινοῦ. The Chimaera (from Greek χίμαιρα, 'goat') was a fabulous monster with the body of a goat, the head of a lion, and the tail of a serpent; *inligatum*, therefore, applies to the coils of the chimaera's tail.

24. Pegasus: the winged horse, Pegasus, destroyed the Chimaera by its hoofs.

ODE XXVIII., 1.

1. maris . . . mensorem, Archyta: Archytas of Tarentum, a friend and contemporary of Plato, was a famous Pythagorean philosopher who flourished about 400 B.C. He was eminent as a geometer and astronomer, also in the fields of war and statesmanship. **numero carentis harenae**: *the countless sand;* Archytas was apparently reputed to have made some attempt to estimate the grains of sand in the universe.

2. cohibent: *confines.* Notice the spondaic ending of the verse.

3. pulveris exigui parva munera: *a slight tribute of scanty earth; pulveris* is epexegetical (appositional) genitive, and seems to be used in the sense of *tumulus; munera* is the poetic plural. The point of the observation is that Archytas, once so renowned, is now confined within the narrow limits of the grave. **litus Matinum**: the exact locality is not known; it was probably near Tarentum, Archytas's home.

5. **temptasse**: *to have explored.* **domos**: *i.e.* abodes of the gods.

6. **polum**: *polus* (properly the pole of the axis of the heavens) is often used figuratively for the heaven itself. **morituro**: causal, and made emphatic by position, — *since thou wast destined to die;* it agrees with *tibi.*

7. **et**: *also.* **Pelopis genitor**: Tantalus. **conviva deorum**: with adversative force (like the following *remotus in auras, arcanis admissus*), *though admitted to the table of the gods.*

8. **Tithonus**: son of Laomedon. The legend concerning him takes two forms. According to the account here followed, Tithonus, in answer to the prayers of Aurora, who loved him, was translated to the skies (*remotus in auras*), but was not made immortal. According to the more usual account, he was made immortal, but as Aurora failed to ask the gods to confer upon him the boon of perpetual youth, he shrivelled away and finally changed into a grasshopper. Horace follows this latter form of the story in ii. 16. 30, *longa Tithonum minuit senectus.*

9. **Minos**: king of Crete. The laws which he gave his countrymen are said to have been suggested by Jove.

10. **Tartara**: here in the general sense of the entire lower world, not in the narrower sense of the place of torment of the wicked. **Panthoiden**: *son of Panthous, viz.* Euphorbus, a Trojan hero, who slew Patroclus. He himself fell by the hand of Menelaus, who hung up his shield on the temple wall at Argos. Pythagoras (flourished 540 B.C.), the great apostle of the doctrine of metempsychosis, or transmigration of souls, maintained that he himself, in a previous state of existence, had been this same Euphorbus, and in proof of his assertion, he is said to have entered the Argive temple and to have identified Euphorbus's shield. **iterum Orco demissum**: the first time had been when Euphorbus died; the second time was when Pythagoras himself died; he is said to have been slain at Crotona, as the result of some political uprising. *Orco* here = *ad Orcum; cf.* i. 24. 18, *nigro gregi.*

11. **quamvis concesserat**: *quamvis* with the indicative first

appears (with certainty) in the Augustan poets, Horace and Virgil; later it became common in prose. **clipeo refixo**: *by taking down the shield.*

12. ultra = *praeter.*

14. iudice te: as a Pythagorean, Archytas naturally reverenced the founder of the school. **non sordidus**: *i.e.* an eminent. **auctor**: *authority.*

15. naturae: in the sense of 'the universe.' **una nox**: euphemistic for *mors.*

16. semel: *i.e.* once for all.

17. alios: *some;* the correlative *aliis* is supplanted by *nautis; cf.* i. 7. 1 f., *Laudabunt alii . . . ; sunt quibus unum opus est.* **spectacula**: predicatively, *as a spectacle;* their death is a welcome sight to the war-god.

19. mixta: *without distinction;* the emphasis of the clause rests upon this word. **densentur**: lit. *are crowded together*, *i.e.* follow each other swiftly; *denseo* is poetic; *denso, -are*, is the commoner form.

20. saeva . . . fugit: we expect rather *saevam caput Proserpinam fugit;* the idea is essentially the same; *fūgit* is the so-called 'gnomic' perfect, used to express general truths. The allusion is to the traditional lock of hair said to be taken by Proserpina from the head of each person who died; *cf.* Virg. *Aen.* iv. 698, *nondum illi* (Dido) *flavom Proserpina vertice crinem abstulerat Stygioque caput damnaverat Orco.*

ODE XXVIII., 2.

1. Me quoque: *i.e.* me as well as many another. This opening of the ode is somewhat abrupt, but is thoroughly consistent with what follows. **devexi**: according to the Elder Pliny, the setting of Orion occurred in November, the beginning of the stormy season. **comes Orionis**: in apposition with *Notus.* On a wind as the companion of winter, *cf.* i. 25. 19, *Hiemis sodali Euro.* Note the spondaic ending of the verse.

2. Illyricis: *i.e.* of the Illyrian Sea, that part of the Adriatic which borders on southern Italy.

3. nauta: some passing mariner. **vagae malignus harenae**: *vaga harena* is 'the shifting sand'; *harenae* is governed by *malignus*, which means *grudging, withholding; cf.* the use of *benignus* with the genitive in *Sat.* ii. 3. 3, *somni vinique benignus; ne*, though belonging properly to *parce*, goes also with *malignus.* Translate: *do not with-*

hold the shifting sand and refuse to scatter a little upon my unburied bones and head. **parce dare**: *parco* with the infinitive occurs first in Livy and the Augustan poets.

4. capiti inhumato: notice the striking hiatus. No other instance occurs in the *Odes*; but in *Epodes*, 13. 3, we find *Threicio Aquilone*; *inhumato* qualifies *ossibus*, as well as *capiti*.

5. particulam dare: three handfuls (see line 36) were regarded as sufficient to meet the requirements of formal interment, and to secure rest for the waiting spirit. **sic**: *viz.* if you grant my prayer (*ne parce, etc.*). This use of *sic* to resume the substance of a previous imperative or jussive subjunctive is common in poetry. **quodcumque, fluctibus**: *quodcumque* designates the content of *minabitur*; *fluctibus* is indirect object.

6. Venusinae: evidently the home of the *nauta* is Venusia, or its neighborhood.

7. plectantur silvae te sospite: the perspective of the sentence is distorted by Horace's form of expression. Logically the emphasis rests upon *te sospite, mayst thou be safe when the Venusian woods are lashed by the gale; i.e.* may the storm be confined to the land and not visit the sea. **multa**: *i.e. rich, abundant.*

8. unde potest: *unde = a quibus*, and is explained by *ab Iove Neptunoque.* **aequo**: *propitious;* with both *Iove* and *Neptuno.*

9. Neptuno, custode: Tarentum, according to the tradition, was founded by Taras, the son of Neptune; hence the god's guardianship. **sacri Tarenti**: the famous cities of antiquity are often spoken of as sacred; *cf.* Homer's Ἴλιος ἱρή, and Hor. *Odes*, iii. 19. 4, *sacro sub Ilio.*

10. neclegis . . . committere, *etc.*; *thou think'st it a light matter to do a wrong which shall later harm thy guiltless offspring?* The shade implies that failure to comply with its petition will entail ruin upon the house of the *nauta*. *Neclegis* represents the original spelling of the word, which appears occasionally in the poets, *e.g.* also in i. 2. 35; *te* is the subject of *committere; postmodo* modifies *nocituram.*

11. fors et = *fortasse.*

12. debita iura: *iura* is here used of funeral rites (*cf.* the similar use of *iusta*); hence, literally, *due rites, i.e.* the necessity of having similar rites of interment paid to you; *i.e.* you may die and lie unburied like me. **vices superbae**: *vices* means *retribution; superbae* adds the notion of a retribution consisting in the exercise of disdain (*superbia*) toward the *nauta* on the part of the one to whom he appeals; hence, *a retribution of (like) disdain.*

13. maneant: *may await;* an instance of the extremely rare *may*-potential; ordinarily this use of the subjunctive is confined to expressions of the type *aliquis dicat, quispiam dixerit.* **non linquar**: *sc. a te.*

15. non est mora longa: *i.e.* for scattering the three handfuls of earth. **licebit curras**: *may continue on your voyage;* by the poets *curro* is often used of the mariner's course.

ODE XXIX.

1. Icci: evidently an intimate friend of the poet, though very little is known of him. He is also addressed by Horace in a letter (*Epist.* i. 12). **nunc**: *i.e.* in striking contrast with the recent past. **beatis Arabum gazis**: by hypallage for *gazis beatorum Arabum; beatus = dives*, as in i. 4. 14. The wealth of the Arabians was proverbial; *cf.* also iii. 24. 1, *intactis thesauris Arabum.* Note the poetic plural in *gazis.*

3. Sabaeae: Sabaea was a district in southern Arabia ('Arabia Felix') famous for the production of incense and spices. A prosperous trade in these articles for centuries had greatly enriched its inhabitants; *cf.* Milton, *Paradise Lost*, iv. 162,

> Sabaean odours from the spicy shore
> Of Araby the bless'd.

4. Medo: *i.e.* the Parthian; see note on i. 2. 51. The expedition as planned was to be conducted only against the Arabians. In case this should be successful, possibly an attack upon the Parthians was also meditated.

5. quae virginum barbara: *what barbarian maiden?*

6. sponso necato: *her lover slain, i.e.* by thee.

7. puer ex aula: lit. *boy from the palace*, and so *page; aula = aula regia.*

8. cyathum: the cyathus was a ladle used in mixing wine with water and also in transferring the mixture to drinking cups; hence *ad cyathum statuetur = shall be thy cup-bearer?* **unctis** = *perfumed.*

9. sagittas tendere: a bold expression, since *tendere*, 'stretch,' applies properly only to the bow; *cf.* Virg. *Aen.* v. 508, *telumque tetendit.* **Sericas**: *Seres, Sericus*, are applied loosely to the peoples of the far East; *cf.* i. 12. 56.

10. arduis montibus: dative of direction; poetic for *ad arduos montes;* note, too, the intentional juxtaposition of *arduis pronos;* *cf.* i. 6. 9, note.

11. pronos: *i.e.* naturally flowing down hill.

12. et: the *et* does not add a new idea, but simply introduces a specific illustration of the principle stated in *arduis relabi montibus.*

13. nobilis: with *libros.*

14. Panaeti: a famous Stoic philosopher. He was a Rhodian who came to Rome about 150 B.C., where he won the admiration and attachment of the younger Scipio Africanus and Laelius. As a philosopher he gave especial attention to ethics; his work on this subject was extensively used by Cicero in the *de Officiis.* **Socraticam domum**: *the School of Socrates; i.e.* the writings of the great representatives of the Socratic philosophy, particularly Plato and Xenophon. On *domus*, 'school,' *cf.* Cic. *de Div.* ii. 1. 3, *familia;* Hor. *Epist.* i. 1. 13, *Lare*, — both in the same sense.

15. loricis Hiberis: *for Spanish corselet;* Spanish steel was of recognized excellence; *loricis* (poetic plural) is ablative of association; B. *L. L.* § 337; Introd. § 38. *a.*

16. pollicitus: with adversative force, — *though thou hast given promise of better things: viz.* eminence in philosophy. **tendis**: lit. *art straining;* hence, *art bent on;* a strong word. The use of the infinitive with *tendere* is mostly poetical.

ODE XXX.

1. Cnidi Paphique: Cnidos, a Doric city of Caria, was an important seat of Venus's worship; the goddess is said to have had three sanctuaries there. Paphos was on the western coast of Cyprus.

2. sperne: here almost in the original sense of the word, *put aside, leave;* *cf.* iii. 2. 24, *spernit humum.* **Cypron**: *cf.* i. 3. 1.

3. te: dependent upon both *vocantis* and *transfer.* **Glycerae**: for the name, see on i. 19. 5.

4. aedem: as the word must mean 'temple,' it is best to conceive of some little shrine erected by Glycera, possibly in the garden.

5. fervidus puer: Cupid. **solutis zonis**: *i.e. nudae*, as in iv. 7. 5.

6. properentque: we should have expected *nymphaeque properent*, but it is characteristic of Horace to append *-que*, *-ve*, in this way, to a word belonging in common to the words logically connected, instead of to one of these words themselves; *cf.* ii. 7. 24, *quis deproperare apio coronas curatve myrto?*

7. parum comis sine te: youth without love is devoid of charm.

8. Mercurius: Mercury is mentioned as the god of speech, *i.e.* of winning discourse; similarly *Suada*, the goddess of persuasion, is elsewhere mentioned as an attendant of Venus.

ODE XXXI.

1. dedicatum Apollinem: *the consecrated* or *enshrined Apollo; i.e.* Apollo, whose shrine has just been dedicated. In Latin it is possible to say either *deum dedicare* (Cic. *de Nat. Deor.* ii. 61, *ut Fides, ut Mens, quas in Capitolio dedicatas videmus*), or *deo aliquid dedicare.* On the temple referred to, see introduction to the poem; on the attitude of Augustus toward the Apollo cult and the reasons for it, see on i. 2. 32. **poscit**: not *demand*, but *ask for* (*earnestly*), — a common force of the word.

2. vates: *viz.* Horace; on *vates* as a word for 'poet,' see note on i. 1. 35. **patera**: a shallow sacrificial bowl. **novom liquorem**: wine of the last vintage was regularly used for sacrificial purposes.

4. Sardiniae: an important source of Rome's grain supply. Cicero, *pro lege Manil.* 12. 34, mentions Sicily, Sardinia, and Africa, as *tria frumentaria subsidia rei publicae.* **feraces**: *ferax* applies properly to the land, but is here poetically transferred to the crops.

5. aestuosae Calabriae: Calabria, situated at the southern extremity of the Italian peninsula, was a sultry district. **grata**: *i.e.* pleasing; the herds lend a charm to the landscape.

6. aurum aut ebur: Horace doubtless has in mind ceilings inlaid with gold and ivory; *cf.* ii. 18. 1. **Indicum**: to be taken with both *aurum* and *ebur.*

7. Liris: this stream, the modern Garigliano, ran between the boundaries of Latium and Campania. **quieta, taciturnus** (8): *quietus* implies absence of motion, *taciturnus* absence of sound; *quieta* is ablative.

8. mordet: *i.e.* wears away.

9. premant: *prune;* the ordinary word is *amputo.* The subjunctive is jussive with permissive force. **Calena falce**: the epithet is poetically transferred from the vine to the knife with which the vine is pruned. On the quality of Calenian wine, see note on i. 20. 9.

10. dives ut: for the position of the conjunction in the second place, *cf.* i. 2. 7, *omne cum Proteus, pecus egit.* **ut . . . exsiccet**: the clause expresses a certain sarcastic humor characteristic of Horace; those who grow the choicest wines, the poet urges, do so only to bring pleasure to others, not themselves.

11. culillis: see Lexicon, under *culullus; -illus* probably represents the correct spelling.

12. vina: *viz.* Calenian wines; the trader barters his Syrian merchandise for the wine, some of which he naturally sets apart for his own use. **Syra reparata merce**: *procured in exchange for Syrian wares;* for this meaning of *reparo, cf.* i. 37. 24; *merce* is ablative of means. The wares probably consisted of spices, perfumes, incense, and other Oriental products. They are called Syrian, because shipped from Syrian ports.

13. quippe: the particle intensifies the causal force which the participle *revisens* here has.

14. anno: regular prose usage would have been *in anno.*

15. me pascunt, *etc.*: *my fare is the olive;* as shown by the context and the anaphora, *me* is here emphatic. The poet proceeds to contrast the simplicity of his own aspirations with those of others.

16. cichorea: *endive;* the plural in *olivae, cichorea,* and *malvae* is poetic. **lĕves**: lit. *light, i.e.* easy of digestion, wholesome.

17. frui: object of *dones;* a poetical construction. **paratis**: *i.e.* what is at hand, what I have, as opposed to vain desires for what is beyond my power. **et . . . et**: these conjunctions connect *valido* and *integra cum mente; frui* is followed by *degere* without any connective; *nec . . . nec* connect *turpem* and *cithara carentem.* **valido**: attracted to *mihi;* logically it belongs with the omitted subject of *frui* and *degere.*

18. Latōe: vocative singular of the adjective *Latōus,* lit. *belonging to Latona* (Λητώ, Doric Λατώ); here *son of Latona, i.e.* Apollo.

19. senectam: poetic for *senectutem.*

ODE XXXII.

1. Poscimur: *I am called upon, i.e.* for a song. **vacui**: *in leisure hour.*

2. lusimus: the word is chosen to characterize the poet's previous efforts in the field of lyric poetry. **quod**: its antecedent is the following *carmen.* **et . . . et**: here in the sense of *not merely . . . but.*

3. vivat. *to live*, subjunctive of purpose. Horace frequently gives expression to a proud confidence in the immortality of his poetry. **pluris**: *sc. in annos.* **dic**: *sing.* **Latinum carmen**: evidently some serious poem which Horace has in contemplation, full of genuine Roman sentiment, like those at the opening of Book III.

5. Lesbio civi: Alcaeus; see Introd. § 21; *Lesbio* is emphatically placed at the beginning of the verse; the word *civis* is chosen in view of Alcaeus's participation in the stirring political movements of his native city; *civi* is dative of agency; *cf.* i. 1. 24, *bella matribus detestata.* **modulate**: note the passive use of the deponent participle; *cf.* i. 1. 25, *detestata.*

6. ferox bello: Alcaeus fought against the Athenians and against the tyrants of his native city Mitylene. **tamen**: *i.e.* in spite of his martial temper (*ferox bello*) and the stirring experiences of his career.

7. sive: as correlative with this we must understand *sive* with *inter arma;* the two contrasted members are poetic equivalents of *sive terra sive mari;* for the omission of the first *sive*, *cf.* i. 3. 16, *tollere seu ponere volt freta.* **udo**: *i.e.* wave-washed.

9. Liberum et Musas Veneremque: *i.e.* 'Wein, Weib und Gesang.' **illi haerentem**: *haereo* with a dative of the person seems an innovation of Horace.

10. puerum: Cupid, the regular attendant of Venus.

11. Lycum: a favorite of Alcaeus. **nigris oculis nigroque crine**: black hair and eyes are repeatedly mentioned as characteristics of special beauty; observe that the initial syllable is long in *nig-ris*, but short in *ni-groque.*

13. decus Phoebi: see note on i. 10. 6; *decus* is in apposition with *testudo.*

15. medicum: the lyre is not merely sweet; it is also a soothing balm; *cf.* Euripides, *Bacchae*, 283, where similarly wine is spoken of as a φάρμακον πόνων. **salve**: lit. *be greeted*, *i.e.* accept my greeting = be propitious to me.

16. rite vocanti: *when I invoke thee duly*; *vocanti* agrees with *mihi* to be supplied and to be construed as an ethical dative with *salve;* *cf.* Virg. *Aen.* xi. 97, *salve aeternum mihi, maxime Palla;* also the Greek χαῖρέ μοι.

ODE XXXIII.

1. Albi: the elegiac poet Albius Tibullus (54–19 B.C.), an intimate friend of Horace. *Epist.* i. 4 is also addressed to him. **plus nimio**:

with *doleas*; for the force of *nimio*, see note on i. 18. 15. **immitis**: *cruel*, because faithless.

2. Glycerae: a fictitious name. Possibly she is identical with the faithless Nemesis mentioned in Tibullus's elegies. **miserabilis**: here in active sense, *making complaint, plaintive*; *cf.* i. 3. 22, *dissociabili*; ii. 9. 9, *flebilibus modis*.

3. decantes: *de-* has the same force here as noted in previous compounds, *e.g.* i. 3. 13, *decertantem*; hence, 'sing unceasingly.' **elegos**: this designation regularly applies to love-poetry composed in the elegiac stanza (distich), *i.e.* alternate hexameter and pentameter. **cur praeniteat**: indirect question dependent upon the notion of wondering, to be supplied in thought.

4. laesa fide: *sc. a Glycera.*

5. tenui fronte: *of low forehead*; a mark of beauty.

6. Cyri: objective genitive.

8. iungentur: with reflexive, or middle, force, —*shall mate (themselves)*. **lupis**: ablative of association.

9. adultero: here a *suitor*.

10. visum: *sc. est.* **imparis**: *ill-mated.*

13. melior: *i.e.* worthier. **Venus**: *flame, passion*, as in i. 27. 14.

14. grata compede: note the oxymoron; *compes* is but rarely employed in the singular. **Myrtale**: a common name of freedwomen.

15. Hadriae: frequently referred to by Horace as a type of boisterous fury.

16. Calabros sinus: accusative of 'result produced,' *i.e.* making a curved bay; the reference is to the Gulf of Tarentum, which is here reckoned as a part of the Adriatic.

ODE XXXIV.

1. Parcus: *i.e.* bringing but slight offerings to the altars of the gods.

2. insanientis sapientiae consultus: lit. *an adept in (a votary of) a mad philosophy*; note the oxymoron in *insanientis sapientiae*; the reference is to the Epicurean philosophy, of which system the poet represents himself as having been an adherent until his recent conversion; except in the phrase *iuris consultus*, the genitive is but rarely used with *consultus*. **dum erro**: lit. *while I was wander-*

ing (*sc.* from the true path), but with distinct adversative force, — *though aforetime I wandered, yet now.*

3. retrorsum dare: *i.e.* set sail for a return to the truth.

4. iterare: *retrace.*

5. Diespiter: *i.e. Dies pater*, the original nominative of *Jupiter*: *Jupiter* was originally a vocative, which has replaced the old nominative; *Diespiter* survives chiefly in poetry. See B. *L. L.* § 180. 4.

6. nubila dividens plerumque: the emphasis rests upon *nubila*, which stands in sharp antithesis to *per purum*, — *though 'tis usually the clouds that Jove cleaves; plerumque* is also contrasted with some temporal notion to be supplied with *egit*, *e.g. yesterday*, *recently.*

7. per purum: *sc. caelum.* It was a cardinal principle of the Epicurean faith that the gods did not direct the affairs of the world, but dwelt in a state of eternal bliss somewhere in the interstellar spaces of the universe. The poet admits that the thunderbolt from a clear sky has shattered his belief in this doctrine. He is now convinced that the gods *do* intervene.

9. quo: the relative refers to the general statement made in *egit equos.* **bruta**: *lifeless.*

10. horrida Taenari sedes: Taenarus was a promontory at the southern extremity of Laconia; on it was located the fabled entrance to the lower world by which Hercules was said to have brought Cerberus to the world above; hence the epithet *horrida*; *Taenari* is the appositional genitive.

11. Atlanteus finis: *i.e.* the end of the world, where Atlas was conceived to stand, sustaining the mass upon his shoulders.

12. concutitur: the singular verb with compound subject, as usually with Horace. **valet**: emphatic, as shown by the context and the position, — 'power *is* possessed by the gods,' — a principle which the Epicureans denied; they referred all natural phenomena to the spontaneous working of inflexible physical laws. **ima summis mutare**: *to interchange the lowest and highest;* this is the general statement, which is then more particularly set forth in the antithetical *insignem attenuat, obscura promens.*

13. insignem, obscura: note the abrupt change from the concrete to the abstract. **deus**: *i.e.* Fortuna.

14. hinc; *from one man;* contrasted with *hic.* **apicem**: lit. the piece *fitted into* (root *ap-*, 'fit,' 'fasten') the top of the flamen's cap; then the cap itself; then the tiara or diadem of Oriental monarchs; then in the transferred sense of 'crown,' 'glory,' 'power,' as here. Possibly Horace means to allude to the political vicissitudes of Tiridates; see note on i. 26. 5. **rapax**: *with sudden swoop.*

15. stridore acuto: *with noisy whirring; sc. alarum.*

16. sustulit: the so-called 'gnomic' perfect, used in the expression of general truths. **hic**: *upon another.* **posuisse**: the perfect is perhaps here used in its proper temporal sense, *i.e.* Fortuna rejoices to have succeeded in placing. For the infinitive with *gaudere*, *cf.* i. 1. 11, *gaudentem findere.*

ODE XXXV.

1. diva: *viz.* Fortuna. **gratum**: *pleasant; cf.* Cic. *ad Att.* iv. 8ᵃ, 1, *(Antio) nihil amoenius.* **Antium**: a town near the coast of Latium, containing two temples dedicated to Fortuna. It was the old capital of the Volscians.

2. praesens: here in the sense of *powerful*, and governing the infinitive.

3. mortale corpus: *our mortal frame.*

4. vertere funeribus triumphos: lit. *to change triumphs with funerals, i.e. to turn proud triumphs into funeral trains; funeribus* is ablative of association. In writing these words Horace doubtless had in mind the tragic fate of the two sons of Lucius Aemilius Paulus, one of whom died a few days before, the other a few days after, their father's triumph over Perseus.

5 f. te, te, te, te: notice the emphasis produced by the anaphora. **5. ambit**: *courts, entreats*, a figurative meaning of *ambire*, a word primarily used of going about canvassing for votes.

6. ruris colonus: *peasant.* **dominam**: in predicate relation to *te*, — *thee as mistress of the sea.* The conception of Fortune as presiding goddess of agriculture and of the sea appears also upon ancient coins, which represent the goddess with a cornucopia in one hand and a rudder in the other.

7. Bithyna carina: Bithynia in northern Asia Minor was famous for its production of ship-building materials. **lacessit**: *braves*, lit. *harasses.*

8. Carpathium pelagus: the name given to that part of the Aegean north of the island of Carpathos.

9. Dacus, *etc.*: *Dacus, Scythae, urbes, gentes, Latium*, are all subjects of *ambit* (*ambiunt*) alone; *matres* and *tyranni*, while grammatically the subjects of *metuont*, are also felt to go back to *ambit.* **profugi**: *roving.*

10. Latium ferox: *martial Latium.*

11. regum matres barbarorum: the influence of the queen mother among the Oriental peoples was often very great.

12. purpurei: *clad in purple.* **metuont** = *metuunt;* Introd. § 34.

13. iniurioso: *wanton.* **ne . . . proruas**: this clause is the logical object of *metuont; te, te* are introduced proleptically. For the position of *ne* in its clause, see note on i. 2. 5, *grave ne rediret.*

14. stantem columnam: *i.e.* public order, the pillar of the government. **populus frequens**: *i.e.* a mob. **neu concitet, frangat**: this phrase simply amplifies more specifically the general idea already enunciated in *ne . . . columnam.*

15. ad arma, ad arma: the repetition is perhaps designed to suggest the cries of an excited mob. **cessantis**: *the laggards, i.e.* those who at first hold back.

17. te . . . Necessitas: Fortuna's decrees are inevitable; hence Necessity is conceived of as one of her attendants. **saeva**: *grim, relentless.*

18. clavos, cuneos, uncus, plumbum: emblems of strength. Fortuna is depicted in ancient works accompanied by the symbolic *cunei.*

19. aëna: *aënus, -a, -um* is a collateral form of *aëneus.*

20. uncus, plumbum: in building, it was common among the Romans to fasten together huge blocks of stone with iron clamps, and run with molten lead the cavities in which the ends of the clamps were inserted. Extensive remains of this kind of building may still be seen in Rome.

21. Spes, Fides: *i.e.* Hope and, sometimes, loyal friends sustain the unfortunate. **albo velata panno**: *bound with a white cloth;* probably we are to think of the goddess's hand as thus enveloped; *cf.* Livy i. 21, where the priests of Fides are said to have offered sacrifice to her with their hands bound with a cloth, to show that the seat of faith was in the right hand, and deserved to be protected. **colit**: *cherish;* the singular verb with plural subject, as regularly in Horace.

22. nec comitem abnegat: as direct object of *abnegat,* we must understand *se; cf.* Ovid, *Ars Amat.* i. 127, *si qua repugnarat nimium comitemque negarat;* Propertius, iv. 2. 39, *professus amicum.*

23. utcumque: *whenever,* but with an added adversative force. **mutata veste,** *etc.*: *in hostile mood thou leavest the homes of the* *mighty in mourning; mutata veste* is an ablative of quality and stands in predicate relation to *domos potentis*; changed raiment was a symbol of mourning, as with us; for the expression *mutata veste* used precisely as here, *cf.* Cic. *de domo sua*, 37. 99, *omnis bonos mutata veste vidi.*

The apparent contradiction of this passage is to be thus explained: Fortuna ('Chance') may be either good or ill. Whenever good Fortune abandons one, ill Fortune takes her place, *i.e.* the same goddess, but in another phase. It is obviously the Fortuna of this second phase upon whom *Spes* and *Fides* are conceived as attending.

25. **retro cedit**: *i.e.* prove faithless.

26. **diffugiunt**: *i.e.* scatter in all directions.

27. **cum faece**: *i.e.* dregs and all; stronger than merely 'to the dregs' (*faece tenus*).

28. **ferre dolosi**: (*too*) *treacherous to bear;* on the infinitive with adjectives in Horace, *cf.* i. 1. 18, *indocilis pauperiem pati.* **iugum**: *sc.* of adversity. **pariter**: *i.e.* equally with the unfortunate.

29. **iturum Caesarem**: as early as 34 B.C. Augustus had formed the plan of invading Britain. Though revived at various times thereafter, the project was never carried into execution.

30. **iuvenum recens examen**: the reference is to the levy made for the expedition of Aelius Gallus into Arabia Felix; see introduction to i. 29.

31. **timendum**: *to be an object of dread.*

32. **partibus** = *regionibus.*

33. **cicatricum**, *etc.*: alluding to the horrors of the civil wars.

34. **fratrumque**: the sentence is left incomplete. We may supply in thought *a fratribus occisorum.*

35. **nefasti**: best taken as genitive of the whole with *quid.*

38. **pepercit aris**: *i.e.* suppliants had been denied the protection of the sanctuaries to which they had fled. **O utinam**: hiatus after the monosyllabic interjection, as in i. 1. 2, *O et.*

39. **diffingas**: a rare word, found only in two passages of Horace, and apparently used in the meaning 'reforge.' The word is here used in the pregnant sense of 'reforge and turn (against).' **retusum**: *i.e.* in the civil wars. **in Massagetas**: with *diffingas.* The Massagetae were a branch of the Scythians, and at present were in alliance with the Parthians; hence the phrase virtually means in *Parthos.*

40. **Arabas**: see note on line 30, above.

ODE XXXVI.

1. fidibus: music was customary on sacrificial occasions. **iuvat placare**: almost with the hortatory force of *placemus*; *placare* here has the meaning 'thank.'

2. debito: *i.e.* due the gods for their watchful care of Numida.

3. Numidae: nothing is known of him; his *nomen* is variously given as Plotius and Pomponius.

4. Hesperia: probably here used of Spain. Numida is thought to have accompanied Augustus in the expedition of 27–25 B.C. against the Cantabrians. **sospes**: *having returned in safety.*

5. multa oscula: in some continental countries it is customary even to-day for men to exchange kisses.

6. nulli: frequent in the poets for *nemini*. **dividit** = *distribuit*; yet with *Lamiae* we must supply in thought some such word as *donat*.

7. Lamiae: probably the Aelius Lamia of i. 26.

8. non alio = *eodem*. **rege** = *magistro*. **puertiae**: poetic syncopated form for *pueritiae*; *cf.* ii. 2. 2, *lamnae*, for *laminae*.

9. mutataeque . . . togae: *i.e.* of the fact that they changed togas together. Reference is to the assumption of the *toga virilis*. With the completion of the sixteenth year, as a rule, the Roman boy laid aside the *toga praetexta* or purple-bordered toga, and assumed the plain unbordered toga of manhood (the *toga virilis*). The formal assumption of the *toga virilis* took place at the festival of the *Liberalia*, which was celebrated annually on the 17th of March. In this ceremony all young men who had completed their sixteenth year within the preceding twelvemonth were competent to participate. It thus often happened that a youth was nearly seventeen years old before putting on the badge of manhood. This would be true, for instance, of all boys born in the last two weeks of March.

10. Cressa nota: *i.e.* with a white mark; owing to a confusion of *Creta*, 'Crete,' and *creta*, 'chalk,' the adjective *Cressa* ('Cretan') is here used with *nota*, to mean a white mark. The ancient custom of marking lucky days white and unlucky days black is well attested; *cf.* Catullus, 107. 6, *o lucem candidiore nota.*

11. promptae modus amphorae: *i.e.* limit to indulgence in the jar that has been brought out; *amphorae* is here genitive; *promptae* is the participle.

12. morem in Salium: *Salium* is genitive plural. The Salii were a college of priests dating from the days of Numa and Tullius Hostilius. They guarded the sacred shields (*ancilia*), and annually, in the month of March, performed a sacred dance, carrying the shields and weapons in procession.

13. multi meri: *i.e.* capable of drinking much wine, — a hard drinker. **Damalis**: the name is Greek, and literally means 'heifer.'

14. Bassum: evidently a moderate drinker; here he is exhorted to rise to the occasion, and not permit himself to be outdone even by Damalis. **Threicia amystide**: the amystis (Greek ἄμυστις) was a long draught drunk without taking breath. On the indulgence of the Thracians in wine, see i. 18. 9, *Sithoniis*.

15 f. No feast was complete without flowers for the garlands of the banqueters.

17. putris: here apparently in the sense of 'languishing.'

18. deponent: *shall cast.* **novo adultero**: *from her new lover, viz.* Numida; for this force of *adultero*, *cf.* i. 33. 9.

20. lascivis hederis: like a fond lover, the ivy flings its arms, so to speak, about the tree. **ambitiosior**: here following the literal sense of *ambire* — 'go around' — and so *more clinging; cf. Epodes* 15. 5, for a similar characterization of the ivy.

ODE XXXVII.

1. Nunc, nunc, nunc: note the anaphora. The purpose of the poet is to emphasize the fact that no previous time had been suited for celebrating the victory over Cleopatra. After Actium any celebration would have been premature, for Antony and Cleopatra, though defeated, were still in arms, and still constituted a menace to the Roman state. It was only *now*, after the complete overthrow and death of both, that such rejoicings were fitting. This explains the use of *erat* in line 4 — 'now was the time,' not a year ago after Actium, as had been urged by many then; *cf. Ars Poetica*, 19, *sea nunc non erat his locus.* **Nunc est bibendum**: *now is the time to drink;* these opening words of the ode are a translation of Alcaeus, νῦν χρὴ μεθύσθην καὶ χθόνα πρὸς βίαν παίην ἐπειδὴ κάτθανε Μύρσιλος. Myrsilos was a tyrant of Mitylene, in whose overthrow Alcaeus himself had assisted. **pede libero**: *i.e.* feet that give themselves up to dancing without restraint.

2. Saliaribus dapibus: the banquets of the Salii, like those of the pontiffs, were proverbial for their sumptuousness.

3. pulvinar: the singular for the plural; the *pulvinaria* were cushioned couches, on which were set images of the gods, while viands were placed before them; the ceremony was designated a *lectisternium* ('couch spreading').

5. antehac: *i.e.* before the complete annihilation of Antony and Cleopatra; to be read as a dissyllable by synizesis. **nefas**: *sc. fuit.* The caesura after *nefas* is unusual for the Alcaic metre. See Introd. § 43. **Caecubum**: *sc. vinum;* see note on i. 20. 9.

6. avitis: the epithet is transferred from the wine to the store-rooms. **dum . . . parabat**: *dum* with the imperfect indicative occurs only here in Horace; we should naturally have expected the present. **Capitolio regina**: the abomination of a *regina* menacing the central sanctuary of Rome is finely emphasized by the juxtaposition of the two contrasted ideas. Such juxtaposition is a common rhetorical device, in prose as well as in poetry; another fine example is found in iii. 5. 9, *sub rege Medo Marsus et Apulus.* To the Romans, the very names *rex* and *regina* had been odious since the days of the Tarquins. Horace, also, doubtless means to suggest that Cleopatra, as an Oriental sovereign, contemplated supplanting the worship of the Capitoline deities (Jupiter, Juno, and Minerva) by introducing native Egyptian rites. She was, at all events, reputed to have made frequent boasts that she would issue her sovereign decrees from the Capitol.

7. dementis ruinas: bold transfer of the epithet from *regina* to *ruinas.*

8. funus et: for *et* in the second place, *cf.* i. 2. 9, *piscium et summa;* the order is frequent in the poets.

9. contaminato grege: the allusion is to the eunuchs of Cleopatra's court, sarcastically alluded to as *viri.*

10. morbo: with *turpium,* — *foul with disease.* **quidlibet**: any scheme of glory and conquest, however visionary. **impotens sperare**: *mad enough to hope;* the infinitive as in i. 1. 18, *indocilis pauperiem pati.*

13. vix una sospes navis ab ignibus: the grammatical subject of *minuit* is *navis,* but the logical subject is the idea contained in the whole phrase, = *the rescue of scarcely a single ship from the flames; cf.* i. 15. 33, *iracunda classis Achillei,* with note; ii. 4. 10, *ademptus Hector.* The poet is referring to the Battle of Actium; fire broke out among the ships of Antony and Cleopatra, and many of them were destroyed. Horace, however, exaggerates the facts, for Cleopatra escaped with sixty vessels.

14. **lymphatam, veros timores**: *lymphatus* properly means 'bereft of reason,' and so: 'filled with wild delusions and hallucinations,' those already hinted at in the words *quidlibet sperare impotens*; with *lymphatus* (lit. 'crazed by the nymphs,' *lympha* being a collateral form of *nympha*), *cf.* the Greek νυμφόληπτος. Horace's meaning is that Caesar turned these *unsubstantial visions* (*cf. lymphatam*) to the *reality of fear* (*veros timores*); the antithesis, therefore, which the poet aims to bring out, is between the reality of Cleopatra's terror and the unreality, *i.e.* impossibility, of the dreams of empire in which she indulged. **Mareotico**: *sc. vino*. The Mareotic wine was grown around Lake Marea, near Alexandria. It was a sweet wine with a high bouquet.

16. **ab Italia**: really from Actium; but the poet evidently wishes to emphasize the fact that, whereas Cleopatra's purpose was to proceed *in Italiam*, she was, on the contrary, forced to flee in the opposite direction. Note that the *I* of *Italia*, which is historically short, is often arbitrarily lengthened in poetry, *metri gratia*. **volantem**: *reginam* is easily understood from the context.

17. **remis adurgens**: the pursuit was not immediate, as would naturally be understood from these words. Octavian wintered at Samos, and did not push on to Egypt till the following spring (30 B.C.).

19. **nivalis**: Thessaly was not always covered with snow. The epithet is here added because the hare was usually hunted in winter, when the snow lay upon the ground.

20. **Haemoniae**: the old name for Thessaly. **daret**: *consign*.

21. **fatale monstrum**: Cleopatra. **quae**: *but she*; the feminine, despite the occurrence of *monstrum* just before. **generosius**: *i.e.* more nobly than Octavian intended she should; his secret purpose was to allow her first to grace his triumphal procession, then to put her to death.

22. **perire**: the infinitive with *quaero* is poetic; *cf.* iii. 4. 39, *finire quaerentem*. **muliebriter**: *i.e.* in womanish terror.

23. **expavit ensem**: according to Plutarch, Cleopatra first attempted suicide by the sword, but was prevented by Proculeius from executing her intention. **latentis . . . oras**: the meaning of *reparavit* here is uncertain. It seems to mean *seek in exchange*, *i.e.* she did not seek distant coasts in exchange for, or in place of, her throne as queen of Egypt; *cf.* i. 31. 12, *vina Syra reparata merce*. Cleopatra was reported to have cherished at one time the plan of

transporting such galleys as she had left, across the Isthmus of Suez and of reëstablishing her ruined fortunes somewhere on the coast of the Red Sea.

25. iacentem regiam: *iacentem* is used in the figurative sense of *ruined;* it is the opposite of *stantem* in i. 35. 14 (*stantem columnam*).

26. voltu sereno: the queen is said to have concealed her chagrin at the defeat of her troops and even to have exhibited a merry demeanor in the presence of her guards.

27. tractare: the infinitive, as above in line 11. **serpentes**: according to the traditional account, she met her death from the bite of an asp, which she had secreted in her bosom. **atrum**: as bringing death; black is the color belonging to death and to all things associated with it.

29. deliberata morte ferocior: '*emboldened by a stern resolve to die*' (Bryce).

30. saevis Liburnis: the *Liburnae* (*sc. naves*) were swift galleys patterned after those of the Liburnians, a people dwelling on the eastern coast of the Adriatic in the modern Albania. The *Liburnae* had rendered special service in the fight at Actium. They are *saevae* to Cleopatra. *Liburnis* is ablative of means with *deduci*. **scilicet**: the word has here none of the ironical force so common to it.

31. privata: *a queen no longer;* in predicate construction. **deduci**: *invidens* governing the infinitive without subject accusative is a Grecism. **superbo triumpho**: dative of purpose with *deduci*.

32. non humilis mulier: emphatic, — *no craven woman, she.*

ODE XXXVIII.

1. Persicos apparatus: *Persicos* is used generically for 'oriental.' Oriental luxury, even a generation before Horace's day, had already made great inroads in the social life of Rome. **puer**: *i.e.* slave, as often.

2. nexae philyra coronae: garlands made by fastening flowers on a wisp of linden bast (*philyra*); such *coronae* were specially made by professional craftsmen and were of great elegance. Horace, however, pleads for plain myrtle wreaths, such as can easily be plaited by himself.

3. mitte sectari: a poetic periphrasis for a prohibition. **rosa**: roses were highly prized, and great pains were often taken to force them before the season. Sometimes they were even imported from Egypt and other warm countries. **quo locorum** : *in which of its haunts.*

4. **sera** : predicatively, — *lingers late.*

5. **simplici** : *i.e.* as opposed to the luxury of costlier garlands. **nihil adlabores** : *adlaboro* is found only in two passages of Horace, here and *Epodes* 8. 20 ; it seems to mean, 'take the trouble to add' ; *nihil* goes logically with *cura*, with which it makes a prohibition,— *strive not;* for the subjunctive without *ut* in a substantive clause developed from the jussive, see B. 295. 5 ; 8.

7. **arta** : *dense.*

BOOK II.

ODE I.

1. **Motum civicum** : *i.e.* the civil wars ; *civicus* in good prose is found only in the phrase *corona civica ; cf. hosticus* (as against *hostilis*) in iii. 2. 6. **ex Metello consule** : *beginning with Metellus's consulship ;* the phrase is a modifier of *Motum.* The Metellus referred to is Quintus Caecilius Metellus Celer, whose consulship belongs to the year 60 B.C., the time of the formation of the First Triumvirate by Caesar, Pompey, and Crassus. This coalition is regarded as marking the real beginning of the civil commotions that, with few interruptions, continued for the next thirty years. Actual hostilities, however, did not commence till 49 B.C., when Caesar returned from Gaul and crossed the Rubicon.

2. **causas** : *e.g.* the death of Crassus on his ill-starred expedition against the Parthians, the death of Julia (Caesar's daughter), whom Pompey had married, the rivalry of Pompey and Caesar, *etc.* **vitia** : especially the errors of Caesar, Pompey, and their partisans. **modos** : *phases, i.e.* the general way in which the war was waged.

3. **gravis** : the *amicitiae* are styled *gravis*, because the league of the triumvirs was so portentous in its bearings on the fortunes of the Roman state.

4. **principum amicitias** : *i.e.* the league of the triumvirs.

5. **nondum expiatis cruoribus** : the same sentiment as in i. 2. 29, *Cui dabit partis scelus expiandi ?* **uncta** : *i.e. polluta.* **cruoribus** : the plural suggests the many times and places at which Roman blood had been shed ; so in Greek, *αἵματα.*

6. periculosae: *i.e.* there was danger in such a work of giving offence to the surviving partisans. **aleae**: *hazard*, — a common figure.

7. incedis per ignes, *etc.*: *per* is inexact; *super* would have been the correct word. The picture is of one walking over ashes under which slumber the treacherous embers of a recent conflagration.

9. paulum: emphatic, — *let it be only for a little that the stage is deprived of your energies.* **Musa tragoediae desit**: Pollio's reputation as a tragic poet is well attested; *cf.* Virg. *Buc.* 8. 10, *solo Sophocleo tua carmina digna coturno;* Hor. *Sat.* i. 10. 42, *Pollio regum facta canit pede ter percusso.* Yet no fragments of Pollio's tragic writings have come down to us. Note the force of *desit*, which implies that the absence is felt.

10. mox = *sed mox.* **publicas res ordinaris**: *ordinare* is here used with the force of *componere*, *i.e.* 'compose,' in the literary sense; under *publicas res* understand the events of the civil wars.

11. grande munus: *viz.* of writing tragedy.

12. Cecropio coturno: *in Attic buskin; coturnus*, properly the high shoe worn by the tragic actors to add dignity to their appearance, is used figuratively for tragedy. Tragedy is called Cecropian, *i.e.* Attic (from Cecrops, a mythical king of Attica), because it was on Attic soil that tragedy originated and developed. **repetes**: *resume;* the future has the force of an imperative, standing in adversative relation (see note on *mox*, line 10, above) to the foregoing *desit.*

13. praesidium reis: Pollio was famous as a lawyer also, especially in the defence of criminal cases.

14. consulenti: here in the sense of *deliberanti.* **Pollio**: the final *o*, regularly long, is here used as short. This shortening is relatively rare in the Augustan period, but later became quite general. **curiae**: properly the building in which the senate regularly held its deliberations; here used for the senate itself.

16. Delmatico triumpho: in 39 B.C. Pollio had achieved a notable victory over the Parthini, an Illyrian people dwelling near Dalmatia, and had also taken the Dalmatian town of Salonae.

17. iam nunc: *i.e.* the poet in anticipation conceives himself as already listening to the recital of the stirring events of Pollio's history.

21. audire duces: *i.e.* to hear them issuing their commands to their troops; with *cuncta . . . subacta*, *audire* means 'hear of.'

23. cuncta terrarum: a neuter plural adjective used substantively and followed by a genitive of the whole is found only in the poets and later prose writers; another instance in the *Odes* is iv. 12. 19, *amara curarum*. **subacta**: *sc. a Caesare.*

24. atrocem . . . Catonis: his spirit was shown in his indomitable adherence to conviction. The Cato referred to is M. Porcius Cato. At the time of the strife between Caesar and the senatorial party, Cato figured as an uncompromising defender of the constitution. He took up arms against Caesar, and committed suicide at Utica rather than fall into Caesar's hands. From the place of his death he received the name *Uticensis*. For another tribute to his memory, *cf.* i. 12. 35, *Catonis nobile letum.*

25. Iuno, *etc.*: Juno had been the patron deity of Carthage, the metropolis of Africa.

26. cesserat: the notion is that the gods had abandoned Africa when they found themselves no longer able to afford it their protection, precisely as the gods are represented as abandoning Troy, in *Aen.* ii. 351, *excessere omnes, adytis arisque relictis, di quibus imperium hoc steterat.* **impotens**: here *powerless, helpless.*

27. victorum nepotes: the reference is to the descendants of the Romans who had conquered Jugurtha. Many of these fell at the Battle of Thapsus, fought in 46 B.C.

28. rettulit: *i.e.* offered in return. **inferias**: *as a funeral offering*; used predicatively. **Iugurthae**: the Numidian king who long outgeneralled the Roman commanders sent against him, but was finally defeated in 106 B.C.

29. Latino sanguine: *Latinus*, as being less usual than *Romanus*, is more poetical. **pinguior**: not logically comparative here, but rather *enriched, drenched.*

31. auditum Medis: hyperbole; *Medis* is dative of agency. On *Medis* for *Parthis*, see i. 2. 51. As enemies of Rome the Parthians would naturally rejoice at her disasters.

32. Hesperiae: here used as an adjective, — *Italian.* The word properly means 'western,' 'land of the west,' and applies sometimes to Italy, sometimes to Spain. **sonitum ruinae**: the fall of the state is thought of as that of some huge structure.

34. ignara belli: *i.e.* do not bear traces of the conflict. **Dauniae**: properly 'Apulian' (from Daunus, a mythical king of Apulia), but here in the general sense of 'Italian,' 'Roman.'

37. relictis iocis: *i.e.* abandoning sportive themes, such as Horace was wont to treat.

38. Ceae . . . munera neniae: lit. *essay again the offices of the*

Cean dirge, *i.e.* revive the solemn style of Simonides of Ceos; *neniae* is appositional genitive.

39. **Dionaeo sub antro**: *i.e.* in love's haunt; *Dionaeo*, 'belonging to Dione (the mother of Venus),' is the equivalent of *Veneris*; on *sub antro*, see i. 5. 3.

40. **leviore plectro**: *of a lighter strain*; on the first meaning of *plectro*, see on i. 26. 11. The characteristic of the poem itself is transferred to the instrument.

ODE II.

1. **Nullus color**: *no lustre*; *i.e.* no worth. **avaris terris**: the epithet is boldly transferred from the persons who hide treasure in the earth to the earth itself.

2. **abdito**: *i.e.* laid away in a hoard. **lamnae**: syncopated for *laminae*. The word properly means a plate or bar of metal, wood, marble, *etc.*, and so comes to be used for metal in general, or, as here, for precious metal, money.

3. **Crispe Sallusti**: his full name was Gaius Sallustius Crispus. The inversion of *nomen* and *cognomen*, as here, occurs even in prose (beginning with Cicero), when the *praenomen* is omitted; *cf.* ii. 11. 2, *Hirpine Quincti*. The Sallust here referred to was a grand-nephew of the historian, and inherited the latter's vast wealth, including the famous *horti Sallustiani*, situated on the northern slope of the Quirinal. He was celebrated for his generosity. **nisi splendeat**: to be joined closely with *inimice lamnae*; the subjunctive is employed because of the implied indirect discourse; Sallust's own thought, as represented by Horace, is *lamnae inimicus sum, nisi usu splendet*. **temperato usu**: *i.e.* by avoiding prodigality on the one hand, and meanness on the other.

5. **extento aevo**: *through long ages*; ablative of duration of time. **Proculeius**: C. Proculeius Varro, son of A. Terentius Varro. When his two brothers lost their property in the civil war, Proculeius gave each a third of his fortune. He stood high in the favor of Augustus, who at one time even thought of giving him his daughter in marriage.

6. **animi paterni**: *known as a man of fatherly affection* (for his brothers); predicate genitive of quality after *notus*, limiting *Proculeius*.

7. **aget**: here used in the sense of *tollet*. **metuente solvi**:

(*pinions*) *that refuse to droop*, *i.e.* tireless; *timeo* and *metuo* are not infrequently used by the poets in the sense of *nolo; cf.* iv. 5. 20, *culpari metuit fides.*

8. superstes: *i.e.* Proculeius's fame shall survive his death.

9. regnes: the second person is here indefinite. **avidum spiritum**: *the spirit of greed.*

10. Libyam Gadibus: *i.e.* Africa to Europe.

11. iungas: *i.e.* as owner. **et** = *and so.* **uterque Poenus**: *i.e.* the Phoenicians in northern Africa and in Spain. In Horace's day there were Phoenician settlements in both countries.

12. uni: *sc. tibi.*

13. crescit, *etc.*: the poet means to institute a comparison between dropsy and avarice; the latter, like the former, he claims, grows by indulgence; help can come only by banishing the *cause* of each disease; *crescit* is emphatic by position.

14. sitim: an unquenchable thirst is one of the symptoms of the disease. **pellit**: as subject, we must understand the sufferer from the disease.

15. fugerit venis: this is pathologically correct. The disease is the result of a separation of the water in the blood; *fugerit* is future perfect; the tense emphasizes the importance of the prior fulfilment of the condition. **aquosus languor**: *i.e.* the weakness resulting from an excess of water in the system. **albo corpore**: the skin of a dropsical person is abnormally white.

17. redditum Phraaten: Phraates, king of Parthia, had been driven from his throne by the machinations of his rival, Tiridates, but had secured his restoration through the help of the Scythians in 27 B.C. *Redditum* is put first in the strophe, for the purpose of emphasizing the antithesis; though he has been *restored*, yet Virtue will not allow that he should be reckoned as being truly *happy.* **Cyri solio**: Arsaces, the founder of the Parthian dynasty of the Arsacidae, claimed descent from Cyrus, the founder of the Persian empire.

18. dissidens: *i.e.* dissenting in its views. **plebi**: *from the vulgar crowd;* Horace is particularly fond of using the dative with verbs of *differing, etc.* Introd. § 36. *c.* **beatorum**: *i.e.* happy in the full sense of the word. According to the Stoic view, which Horace has here in mind, only the upright are happy; the final *-um* is elided before the initial vowel of the following line; the phenomenon is called synapheia. *Cf.* ii. 3. 27.

19. eximit: lit. *excepts from*, *i.e.* refuses to admit to, to reckon among; *cf.* iii. 2. 32, *deseruit*, 'fail to overtake.' **Virtus**: the personification of the lofty Stoic ideal of rectitude. **falsis vocibus**: *wrong names*, *e.g.* the title *beatus* as applied to Phraates; only the upright man, urges the poet, deserves this name.

21. diadema, laurum: added as more specific explanations of *regnum*.

22. propriam: *lasting*, and so real, as opposed to the fleeting nature of the ordinary laurels of victory.

23. inretorto: *i.e.* without casting longing glances behind; *inretortus* is a new word, coined by Horace.

24. acervos: *sc.* of treasure.

ODE III.

1. Aequam . . . mentem: the figure in the Latin calls for a *level* spirit when circumstances are *steep*. This trope cannot be reproduced in English.

2. non secus: (*and*) *likewise;* asyndeton and litotes. **in bonis**: the figure begun in *arduis* is here abandoned.

3. temperatam: agreeing with *mentem* understood.

4. laetitia: *i.e.* manifestation of joy. **moriture**: *destined, doomed, to die.* In prose of the Ciceronian period, the future active participle is regularly restricted to combination with the forms of *esse;* poets and the later prose writers freely use the participle alone. **Delli**: an unprincipled character who had played a somewhat conspicuous part in the recent political history of Rome. He had successively supported and deserted Dolabella, Cassius, and Mark Antony. Just prior to the Battle of Actium, he had attached himself to Octavian; but the ode suggests that at present he was out of favor with the Emperor.

5. seu vixeris, *etc.:* to be joined closely with *moriture; cf.* ii. 2. 2, *inimice lamnae nisi splendeat.* **omni tempore**: ablative of duration of time.

6. in remoto gramine: *i.e.* in some retired grassy nook.

8. interiore nota Falerni: *with some old Falernian vintage;* lit. *with some inner label of Falernian; nota* is the mark or label attached to the wine jar, giving the date of the vintage (*cf.* iii. 21. 1, *O* (*testa*) *nata mecum consule Manlio*). Wine of the oldest vintages would naturally be kept in the remoter part (*interiore*) of the storeroom. Concerning the Falernian wine, see note on i. 20. 10.

9. quo: the adverb; (lit. *whither*) *for what purpose*, *i.e.* unless we enjoy these delights. **alba**: alluding to the silvery leaves of the poplar.

10. umbram . . . ramis: *i.e.* join their branches in inviting shade; in the Latin, *umbram* is an accusative of 'result produced' ('internal object'), — 'produce (by joining) an inviting shade.'

11. quid: used in the same sense as *quo* above. **obliquo**: *zigzag*, *winding*. **laborat**: the winding course of the stream hinders the progress of the brook; hence, the water is represented as exerting itself to hurry on.

13. huc: *i.e.* to the imaginary sylvan retreat pictured in lines 9–12. **et . . . et**: note the emphasis of the polysyndeton; so in line 15.

14. flores: for garlands. **ferre iube**: *have brought*; as subject of *ferre*, supply in thought *pueros*, 'slaves,' or some such word.

15. res: *i.e.* your fortunes. **aetas**: *youth*. **sororum trium**; *viz.* the Fates, — Clotho, Lachesis, and Atropos.

16. atra: a natural epithet of *fila*, since the Fates themselves are *atrae*.

17. cedes, *etc.*: *i.e.* you will sooner or later be forced to leave these things. **saltibus**: woodland pastures for cattle. Vast tracts of these were held by wealthy Romans, particularly in the region of southern Italy. **et . . . que**: *et* connects *saltibus* on the one hand to *domo* and *villa* on the other. **domo villaque**: *domus* is the palace; *villa* covers the entire estate.

18. flavos: as in i. 2. 13. **lavit**: poetic instead of *lavat* (from *lavare*), which is used in a literal sense.

19. cedes: the anaphora gives the force of 'yes, you must leave them.'

21. divesne, *etc.*: lit. *it makes no difference whether you linger beneath the skies rich (and) descended from ancient Inachus, or, etc.* The adjectives are predicate modifiers of the subject of *moreris*. **natus**: note the asyndeton. **Inacho**: the earliest Argive king, and so suggesting ancient lineage.

23. sub divo moreris: a poetic equivalent of *vivas*.

24. victima (*sc. es*): the apodosis of the protasis logically involved in lines 21–23.

25. eodem: *viz.* to the realm of Orcus. **cogimur**: *we are being gathered* (lit. *herded*); the figure is drawn from pastoral life; *cogo* is the technical term for gathering a scattered flock; *cf.* Virg. *Buc.* iii. 20, *Tityre, coge pecus.* **omnium**: for the purpose of an effective anaphora, Horace here uses *omnium* instead of *cuiusque*, which would be the accurate word.

26. versatur urnā: *cf.* iii. 1. 16, *omne capax movet urna nomen.* **serius ocius**: *sooner or later;* disjunctive asyndeton; the words modify *exitura.*

27. exitura, impositura: see note on line 4, *moriture.* **aeternum**: an hypermeter verse, like ii. 2. 18.

28. exsilium: *sc. mortis.* **cumbae**: *sc. Charonis.*

ODE IV.

1. ancillae: *sc. tuae.* **pudori**: dative of purpose.

2. Xanthiā Phoceu: Greek vocative of *Xanthias Phoceus;* the name *Xanthias* ('the yellow-haired') suggests that Horace may here be giving a Greek paraphrase of the name of some Roman *Flavius.* **prius**: *i.e.* before this. **insolentem**: *high-spirited; cf. Ars Poet.* 122, *iura neget* (*sc. Achilles*) *sibi nata, nihil non adroget armis.*

3. Brisēis: a captive maiden of whom Achilles was enamoured; see *Iliad* i. **colore**: *skin, complexion.*

5. Aiacem Telamone natum: *Ajax the son of Telamon,* as opposed to Ajax the son of Oileus. The former ranked next to Achilles in prowess.

6. captivae dominum: the juxtaposition of the two words emphasizes the difference of social station; though a captive, and so a slave, Tecmessa inspired her master with love. **Tĕcmessae**: the initial syllable is short; *cm* in Greek words is sometimes treated like a mute + a liquid.

7. arsit: *i.e.* with love. **Atrides**: Agamemnon. **medio in triumpho**: *i.e.* at the fall of Troy.

8. virgine rapta: the reference is to Cassandra, who at the sack of Troy was first seized by Ajax, the son of Oileus, and was then taken from him by Agamemnon.

9. barbarae: *i.e.* of the Trojans. **turmae**: properly the word refers to troops of cavalry; it is here used of troops in general.

10. Thessalo victore: *i.e.* Achilles, whose victory over Hector was the decisive event of the war; the ablative is best taken as one of instrument with *cecidere*, which is here equivalent to a passive. We should naturally have expected *a victore;* but Horace seems to be thinking of the victory as the means of Troy's overthrow. **ademptus Hector**: *the loss of Hector;* lit. *Hector removed.*

11. fessis: namely, with the long siege. **leviora tolli**: *easier to be destroyed;* for the infinitive, see on i. 1. 18, *indocilis pati.*

13. The vein of delicate irony pervading the whole ode is particularly prominent in this and the following stanza. **nescias an**, *etc.*: *one can't tell but that, etc.* *Nescias* is an instance of the rare 'can-' potential, a use restricted to the indefinite second person singular present of verbs of *thinking, knowing, seeing*, and the like. Similarly we find *videas*, 'one can see'; *intellegas*, 'one can observe.' By omission of the first alternative of the double question, the *an*- clause here stands alone; *cf.* the similar *haud scio an.* **beati**: *rich.*

15. regium: *sc. est.* **penatis iniquos**: the household gods are called cruel, as having permitted the decay of the house.

17. crede = *be sure.* **non illam**, *etc.*: *that she whom you love belongs not to the common herd; non* is emphatic; *tibi* is a dative of agency; the phrase *de plebe* depends upon *esse* to be supplied in thought; *scelesta* is used to indicate a permanent quality; *cf.* ii. 16. 39, *malignum volgus.*

19. lucro: ablative.

20. pudenda: the context shows that this refers to birth, not to character.

21. teretis: *shapely.*

22. integer: *i.e.* free from passion for the maiden. **fuge suspicari** = *noli suspicari;* see note on i. 9. 13, *fuge quaerere.*

23. cuius: (*a man*) *whose;* its antecedent is *eum*, the omitted object of *suspicari.* **octavom lustrum**: *i.e.* the fortieth year. **trepidavit** = *properavit.*

ODE V.

1. subacta: *sc. ab amore.* **valet**: as subject, understand in thought the name of the maiden referred to in line 4 f. as *tuae iuvencae*, and later (line 16) mentioned as *Lalage.* For *valet* with infinitive, *cf.* i. 34. 12.

2. cervice: poetic for *cervicibus.* **munia comparis aequare**: '*match the labors of a mate*' (Page).

5. circa est: *i.e.* is set upon.

6. campos, fluviis, cum vitulis: under these figurative references the poet means that the object of his friend's attachment is still but a child, at play with her mates in field and wood.

7. solantis = *levantis.*

10. immitis uvae: an abrupt transition to another figure. **iam**: *presently.* **tibi**: ethical dative. **lividos distinguet racemos**: *shall tinge the clusters purple, i.e.* shall ripen them; *lividos* is used proleptically.

12. purpureo varius colore: *gay with crimson;* the colors of autumn foliage and fruits are poetically attributed to autumn itself.

13 f. te sequetur proterva fronte: the poet here returns to the earlier figure of the *iuvenca.* **currit . . . aetas**: *time runs madly on; ferox* is a poetic exaggeration for *velox.*

14. illi . . . annos: *i.e.* she shall mature as you pass on from middle life; the friend addressed by the poet has reached a time of life when each passing year is felt as taking away (*dempserit*) from life's allotted span; with Lalage, who has not yet reached mature maidenhood, time is conceived as adding something; *cf. Ars Poet.* 175, *anni venientes . . . recedentes.*

16. maritum: *i.e.* thee, who wilt then be her mate.

17 f. Pholoe, Chloris, Gyges: earlier flames.

17. Fugax: *coy.*

21. si insereres . . . falleret: the form of the conditional sentence is peculiar; we should naturally expect the present subjunctive.

22. mire: with *falleret.* **hospites**: *strangers.*

23. discrimen: *i.e.* the difference between him and a maiden; *cf. ambiguo* in line 24. **obscurum**: here equivalent to *obscuratum;* hence the following ablatives.

ODE VI.

1. Septimi: very likely the Septimius mentioned in *Epp.* i. 9. 13 as *fortem bonumque.* **Gadis**: a town in southern Spain, and so in the extreme west of the Roman dominions; *Gadis* and *Cantabrum* are the direct object of *aditure;* at all periods, *adire* is occasionally used transitively. **aditure**: *i.e.* ready to go; said of a loyal friend. For the participle, see on ii. 3. 4, *moriture.*

2. Cantabrum: singular for plural; the Cantabrians were a tribe of northern Spain who had recently been defeated by the Romans, in 29 B.C. At the time this ode was written, they were apparently in revolt. Agrippa finally subdued them in 19 B.C. **iuga**: poetic plural. **nostra** = *Romana.*

3. Syrtis: here of the treacherous sands off the northern coast of Africa; in i. 22. 5, it was used of the adjacent desert. **Maura**: the wave is called Moorish from Mauretania, though this district was really somewhat farther west than the Syrtes.

5. Tibur: see on i. 7. 12. **Argeo colono**: Tibur is said to have been founded by three Argive brothers, Catilus, Coras, and Tiburnus (or Tiburtus); *Argeo* is poetic for *Argivo;* the dative is one of agent. **positum** = *conditum*.

6. senectae: poetic for *senectuti*.

7. modus: here equivalent to *finis*, 'resting-place.' **lasso**: *sc. mihi*. **maris, viarum, militiae**: the genitive is poetic. Introd. § 37. *a*. *Cf.* Virg. *Aen.* i. 178, *fessi rerum*.

9. unde: for *inde, viz.* from Tibur. For the sentiment of the entire strophe, *cf. Epp.* i. 7. 44, *mihi iam non regia Roma, Sed vacuum Tibur placet aut imbelle Tarentum.* **prohibent**: the present sometimes occurs (particularly in poetry) where logical exactness leads us to expect the future. **iniquae**: used here not as a standing epithet, but rather with adverbial force, — *cruelly*.

10. dulce pellitis ovibus: the river is spoken of as sweet to its skin-covered sheep, because they love to roam along its banks and drink its waters; *pellitis* refers to the custom of protecting the wool of the finer sheep by means of skins tied about them. The custom is still in vogue. **Galaesi**: appositional genitive with *flumen;* the *Galaesus* was a small river near Tarentum.

11. regnata . . . Phalantho: *the district* (*once*) *governed by Spartan Phalanthus, viz.* Tarentum, which was a Spartan colony founded by Phalanthus, 708 B.C.; *regno* is here transitive, a usage confined to poetry and post-Augustan prose. *Phalantho* is dative of agent. For the feminine caesura after *regnata*, see Introd. § 44.

13. omnis: *sc. omnis alios angulos.*

14. ridĕt: *has a charm;* the *ĕ* is a reminiscence of the original quantity of the termination; *cf.* ii. 13. 16, *timēt*. **Hymetto**: *i.e.* to the honey of Hymettus; 'compendiary comparison' (*cf.* i. 1. 23, *lituo*), a license which would best be retained in translation. So below, *Venafro*. Hymettus was a mountain near Athens famous for the excellence of its honey.

15. viridi Venafro: Venafrum was a Samnian town near the border of Latium, famous for its verdant olive-orchards; Pliny, *N. H.* xv. 2. 8, says Venafran oil is the best. For the dative with *certare*, *cf.* i. 3. 13, *decertantem Aquilonibus*.

16. baca: lit. *berry*, *i.e.* the olive.

17. ver longum tepidasque brumas: chiasmus. **ubi**: for the position of the introductory relative, *cf.* i. 2. 7, ***omne cum . . . egit.*** Note the ī in *ubi*, a reminiscence of the original quantity.

18. amicus Aulon Baccho: Aulon (evidently some locality, hill or vale, near Tarentum) is spoken of as dear to fertile Bacchus, since the god brings rich harvests to its vineyards; for this use of *amicus*, 'dear to,' 'beloved,' *cf.* i. 26. 1, *Musis amicus.*

19. fertili: *i.e.* productive, bringing increase. **minimum**: *by no means.* **Falernis uvis**: for the Falernian wine, see on i. 20. 10.

22. postulant: *i.e.* summon, invite. **arces**: *i.e.* heights, hill-tops, as in i. 2. 3. **calentem**: *i.e.* from the funeral pyre.

23. debita: *i.e.* due his memory.

24. vatis amici: *of thy poet friend, viz.* Horace.

ODE VII.

1. O: for the separation of the interjection from its vocative, *cf.* i. 26. 6, *O . . . Pimplei.* **saepe**: Brutus and his forces had held the field for two years before the decisive battle of Philippi, and several minor engagements had occurred during this period. **tempus in ultimum**: *into extremest peril.*

2. Bruto duce: ablative absolute with temporal force. **militiae**: with *duce*; Horace refers to the campaign of Brutus and Cassius against Octavian and Antony, in 43–42 B.C.

3. quis: Octavian, after Actium, had extended amnesty to all who had been in arms against him. **redonavit**: a word coined by Horace, and used only by him. **Quiritem**: predicate accusative with *te*. In the singular, this word is extremely rare, being confined to poetry. It designates a citizen in the fullest and highest sense of the term, also a citizen as opposed to a soldier; hence here, one who has abandoned military service and has been restored to full civic rights and privileges, — a citizen full and free.

4. patriis: *of thy country.* **Italoque**: the *I* was originally short, as here, and is always so used in prose. But the poets, from metrical exigencies, more commonly use it as long.

5. Pompei: it is not known with certainty what his full name was. The word is here dissyllabic by synizesis. **prime**: probably combining both notions: *earliest* and *dearest.*

6. cum quo: Horace always avoids *quocum* and *quibuscum.* **morantem**: *i.e.* tedious, slowly passing.

7. fregi: *i.e.* whiled away. **coronatus**: the passive here has the force of a middle; hence *capillos* is direct object; see on i. 1. 21, *membra sub arbuto stratus.*

8. **malobathro**: to be taken with *nitentis.* **Syrio**: the malobathrum was prepared from an Indian shrub; it is here called Syrian, because shipped from Syria, the great emporium of eastern products.

9. **Philippos**: the battle was fought in Nov. 42 B.C. **celerem fugam**: the partisans of Brutus and Cassius were defeated and fled.

10. **sensi**: *i.e.* experienced, went through; *sentire* is often thus used of unpleasant experiences. **relicta parmula**: Horace's reference to the loss of his shield is doubtless a literary fiction in imitation of Archilochus and other Greek poets who recount similar experiences. **non bene**: *ingloriously.*

11. **fracta**: *sc. est.* **et minaces**, *etc.*: *i.e.* 'and threatening spirits ignobly bit the dust'; a humorous reference by Horace to the large hopes and small performance of himself and his party. Indirectly the poet also intends a compliment to the Emperor.

13. **sed**: the earlier experiences of Horace and his friend had been the same; later fate had separated their paths; *sed* brings out the contrast. **me**: in strong antithesis with *te* in line 15; Horace proceeds to contrast Pompey's experience since the war with his own. **Mercurius**: as *curvae lyrae parens* (i. 10. 5), Mercury was naturally the patron god of poets, who are accordingly, in ii. 17. 29, called *Mercuriales viri.* **celer**: with adverbial force.

14. **denso aere**: *i.e.* in a cloud, the conventional Homeric way in which defeated combatants were rescued.

16. **fretis tulit aestuosis**: *i.e.* Pompey had been engaged in the stormy events of the thirteen years since Philippi. Probably he joined those who after Philippi took service under Sextus Pompeius.

17. **ergo**: *i.e.* since you are safely restored to your home. **obligatam** = *pledged; obligatus*, strictly applicable only to the person, is here transferred to the thing. **redde**: *i.e.* give in return for your preservation. **dapem**: properly of a sacrificial feast, as here.

18. **latus** = *membra.*

19. **nec**: common in poetry instead of *neu;* see on i. 9. 15.

21. **oblivioso**: *i.e.* which brings forgetfulness, 'care-dispelling.' **levia** = *polished; cf.* i. 2. 38, *galeaeque leves.* **Massico**: concerning this wine, see on i. 1. 19.

22. **ciboria**: *ciboria proprie sunt folia colocasiorum, in quorum similitudinem pocula facta eodem nomine appellantur* (Porphyrio). **exple**: *i.e.* fill to the brim.

23. quis: *sc. puer.* **udo**: *pliant;* the word seems to be used in imitation of the Greek ὑγρός, lit. 'moist,' but also 'pliant,' 'twining.'

24. deproperare: *i.e.* hurriedly weave.

25. curatve myrto: for *myrtove curat;* for the position of the enclitic, *cf.* ii. 19. 28, *pacis eras mediusque belli;* 32, *ore pedes tetigitque crura.* **quem**: *i.e.* of our company. **Venus**: *the Venus-throw*, the name given to the highest throw of the dice, or *tali.* These were numbered only on four sides: I, III, IIII, VI. In the Venus-throw all these four numbers appeared. **arbitrum bibendi**: called also the *magister bibendi;* the person chosen to act as master of ceremonies and regulate the drinking; *arbitrum* is predicate accusative with *quem.*

26. dicet: *appoint; cf.* the technical expression for appointing a dictator, *dictatorem dicere.* **non sanius**: litotes for *insanius*, 'more wildly than.'

27. Edonis: a Thracian tribe famed for the license of their carousals. **recepto** = *recuperato.*

28. furere: the word suggests a wild enthusiasm, but it almost defies translation into adequate English.

ODE VIII.

1. Ulla: emphatic by position. **iuris peierati**: *i.e.* for violation of thy oath; *iuris* for *iuris iurandi.*

2. Barine: the name is not elsewhere found, and has consequently been suspected by critics. Perhaps it is derived from *Barium*, a town on the coast of Apulia; hence 'maid of Barium.' Horace visited this town on the journey described in *Sat.* i. 5.

3. dente . . . ungui: *uno* ('a single') and *nigro* are to be taken with both *dente and ungui; i.e.* Barine, despite her violation of every pledge, does not become uglier in the least, not by so much as a single tooth or finger-nail. The Greeks and Romans believed that the gods visited the perjured with such physical inflictions as are here alluded to. **fieres**: the imperfect implies 'if it were your custom to become.'

5. crederem: *sc. tibi.* Horace declares that he *would* believe Barine, did the gods but punish her; for then she would respect her pledges. **tu**: emphatic, suggesting that Barine stands in contrast with all others. **simul**: for *simul ac*, as often in poetry, *e.g.* i. 12. 27. **obligasti . . . caput**: *i.e.* pledged yourself in vows; *caput* here is equivalent to a reflexive *te.*

7. prodis publica cura: *i.e.* when you appear you are a *publica cura*; *cura* here means 'object of affection'; *publica* is equivalent to *omnium*.

9. expedit: *i.e.* thou not only dost this with impunity, but actually reapest advantage by false swearing, for thou art more beautiful than ever; the strophe is a fuller development of the thought contained in *enitescis pulchrior multo*. **matris cineres**, *etc.*: it was common to swear by the ashes of some near relative, *e.g.* Cic. *pro Quinct.* 97, *obsecravit per fratris sui mortui cinerem*; Prop. ii. 20. 15, *ossa tibi iuro per matris et ossa parentis*; so also by the stars, *e.g.* Virg. *Aen.* vi. 458, *per sidera iuro*. **opertos**: *i.e. sepultos*.

10. fallere: *to swear falsely by*; *cf.* Virg. *Aen.* vi. 324, (*Styx*) *di cuius iurare timent et fallere numen*.

12. carentis: *exempt from*.

13. ridet, rident: the position and the anaphora both lend emphasis to these words; for the thought, *cf.* Tibull. iii. 6. 49, *periuria ridet amantum Iuppiter*; Shakspere, *Romeo and Juliet*, ii. 2, *At lovers' perjuries they say Jove laughs*. **inquam** = *upon my word, actually*. **Venus ipsa**: *even Venus*, who as the goddess of love might be expected to respect the sanctity of lovers' vows.

14. simplices: *artless*. **et**: for the position, *cf.* ii. 1. 9, *piscium et*.

15. ardentis: the epithet is transferred from the enkindled heart to the arrows of the god.

16. cruenta: by anticipation of the destruction to be wrought by the arrows, the epithet is applied to the stone on which they are sharpened.

17. tibi crescit: *i.e.* are growing up to be your victims; *tibi* is emphatic, — *for you alone*.

18. servitus nova: *i.e.* a new company of devoted slaves. **priores**: *sc. amatores*.

19. relinquont: for the spelling, see Introd. § 34.

20. minati: *viz.* to leave thy roof; *cf.* Tibull. ii. 6. 13. *iuravi quotiens rediturum ad limina numquam! Cum bene iuravi, pes tamen ipse redit*.

21 f. te, te, tua: note the effect of the anaphora. **metuont**: for the spelling, see Introd. § 34. **iuvencis**: for *iuvencus* and *iuvenca* applied to youths and maidens, *cf.* ii. 5. 6; note that *metuo*, which may govern either an accusative of direct object or a dative of interest, here irregularly unites both constructions.

22. parci: *parcus* is a standing epithet of the old man; *cf. Ars Poet.* 170, *quaerit et inventis miser abstinet ac timet uti;* such old men would naturally fear that their sons might squander their wealth upon an adventuress like Barine.

23. nuptae: *brides.* **retardet**: *i.e.* detain, make them linger.

24. aura: *radiance*, as in Virg. *Aen.* vi. 204, *auri aura*, 'the lustre of the gold.'

ODE IX.

1. Non semper: placed at the beginning of the sentence for emphasis. **hispidos**: *i.e.* the fields whose grain has been cut and which are thus left rough and stubbly at the end of harvest time, the season when the fall rains naturally begin.

2. mare Caspium: Pomponius Mela, the geographer of the early empire, speaks of the Caspian as *atrox, saevum, sine portubus, procellis undique expositum.*

3. inaequales: *i.e.* blasts which make the surface uneven; so *rough, boisterous.*

4. usque: synonymous with *semper.* **Armeniis in oris**: the reference is to the distant slopes of Mt. Taurus; for *orae* = 'mountain slopes,' *cf.* i. 12. 5.

5. Valgi: C. Valgius Rufus, a poet of some note, belonging to the literary circle which clustered about Maecenas; he was the author of love-poems, epigrams, and also of some grammatical and rhetorical works.

6. Aquilonibus: ablative of means with *laborant*, which here has the force of 'are harassed'; the plural, as in i. 3. 13.

7. Gargani: a well-wooded mountain in eastern Apulia, close to the Adriatic and exposed to the winds on all sides; it rises to the height of some five thousand feet. **laborant**: as in i. 9. 3.

9. tu: in sharp contrast with Nature herself in the phases just enumerated. **urges**: *dwellest upon.* **flebilibus modis**: *i.e.* in elegies.

10. Mysten: probably a favorite slave of Valgius. **Vespero . . . solem**: *i.e.* neither at evening nor morning; *surgente* is somewhat loosely used of the appearance of the evening star in the western sky at the time of year when it sets *after* the sun; in strictness, the same star when it rose *before* the sun, was designated as *Lucifer.*

11. amores: *i.e.* thy expressions of affection; hence the plural; *cf.* i. 16. 9, *irae.*

12. rapidum = *celerem, i.e.* swiftly moving through the heavens.

13. ter aevo functus senex : *viz.* Nestor ; *cf.* Cic. *de Sen.* 10. 31, *tertiam iam enim aetatem hominum videbat ; aevum* is here used in the sense of *aetas.* **amabilem** : here equivalent to *amatum.*

14. Antilochum : the son of Nestor and favorite of Achilles ; slain at Troy by Memnon, son of Aurora.

16. Troilon : the youthful son of Priam ; he was slain by Achilles ; *cf.* Virg. *Aen.* i. 475, *infelix puer atque impar congressus Achilli.* **Phrygiae** : *i.e.* Trojan. The Troad was a part of Phrygia.

17. mollium : *i.e.* effeminate, unmanly.

18. tandem : expressive of impatience. **querellarum** : *from complaints ;* the construction is a Grecism ; *cf.* iii. 27. 69, *abstineto irarum.* Introd. § 37. *b.*

19. cantemus : *i.e.* in verse. **tropaea** : just what victories are here alluded to is uncertain.

20. rigidum Niphaten : Niphates was a mountain of eastern Armenia ; *rigidum* here apparently means 'ice-bound' ; the name *Niphates* suggests the meaning 'snow-capped.'

21. Medumque flumen : the Euphrates ; for the form of the adjective, *cf.* i. 27. 5, *Medus acinaces ; Ars Poet.* 18, *Rhenum flumen.*

22. minores volvere vertices : *i.e.* in token of the subjugation of the tribes bordering upon its banks ; observe the change from the accusative to the infinitive after *cantemus.*

23. praescriptum : *sc. a Romanis.* **Gelonos** : a Scythian tribe who lived along the upper course of the Don, famed as bowmen (*cf.* iii. 4. 35, *pharetratos Gelonos*) and fearless riders ; in ii. 20. 18, they are spoken of as *ultimi Geloni.*

24. exiguis campis : repeating the idea of *intraque praescriptum.*

ODE X.

1. Licini : probably L. Licinius Murena, son of the Murena defended by Cicero. Through his adoption by A. Terentius Varro, he became the brother of Proculeius (see ii. 2), and of Terentia, the wife of Maecenas. The warning given by Horace in the third stanza of the ode was almost prophetic, for in 23 B.C. Licinius, who was consul for the year, engaged in a conspiracy against Augustus, was condemned, and executed. **altum** : *sc. mare ; i.e.* the deep sea. Horace is fond of comparing life with a voyage.

2. dum . . . horrescis : the clause stands in a causal relation to *premendo*, — *for fear of, etc.* **procellas** : *horresco* with the accusative is poetical ; *cf.* ii. 13. 14, *Bosphorum perhorrescit.*

3. **nimium premendo** : *by hugging too closely.*

4. **iniquom** : *i.e.* on account of reefs and shallows.

5. **auream mediocritatem** : *the golden mean ;* for *aureus* used in this sense, *cf.* i. 5. 9, *qui nunc te fruitur credulus aurea.*

6. **caret, caret** : *escapes, avoids,* as in ii. 14. 13 ; the asyndeton and anaphora emphasize the antithesis of the two members.

7. **invidenda** : *i.e.* a palace which arouses the envy of others ; *cf.* iii. 1. 45, *invidendis postibus.*

8. **sobrius** : *prudently.*

9. **saepius** : *i.e.* oftener than the lower trees, *etc.* **ingens, celsae, summos montis** : the emphasis of the passage rests upon these words, — *'tis the tall pine, etc.*

11. **summos montis** : *the tops of the mountains,* as regularly in this order ; *mons summus* means 'highest mountain.'

13. **sperat, metuit** : as the position indicates, the emphasis of the passage rests upon these two verbs. **infestis, secundis** : *for adversity, for prosperity ;* the words are equivalent to *rebus infestis, rebus secundis ;* dative of interest ; *cf.* Sall. *Cat.* 40. 2, *exitum tantis malis sperare ;* 40. 3, *miseriis suis mortem exspectare.*

14. **alteram sortem** : with *sperat* the *altera sors* is prosperity, with *metuit,* adversity.

15. **informis** : *unlovely ;* from *forma,* in the figurative sense of 'beauty.' **reducit** : *i.e.* from year to year ; *reducit,* though grammatically coördinate with *summovet,* is yet logically subordinate, — *though he brings back, yet he takes away.*

16. **idem** : *likewise.*

17. **si male** : *sc. est.* **et** : *also.* **olim** : *by and by,* as in Virg. *Aen.* i. 203, *forsan et haec olim meminisse iuvabit.*

18. **sic** : *viz. male.* **quondam** : *at times.* **cithara . . . Musam** : *i.e.* plays the lyre as a prelude to singing ; *Musam* is used by metonymy for *carmen.*

19. **arcum tendit** : *i.e.* in hostile mood, as *e.g.* in *Iliad,* i., where the shafts of the god bring pestilence upon the Greek hosts.

21. **rebus angustis** : *in time of stress ;* ablative absolute ; *angustis* here = *quae angunt.* **animosus, fortis** : *animosus* designates the inner resolution, *fortis,* aggressive physical resistance ; the two words are combined also in Cic. *de Sen.* 20. 72, *ex quo fit, ut animosior etiam senectus quam adulescentia sit et fortior.*

22. appare: *show thyself;* the student should beware of confounding this word in meaning with *videri*, 'appear.' **idem** = *on the other hand.*

23. contrahes: with imperative force, parallel with the preceding *appare.* Note the somewhat abrupt return to the nautical figure with which the ode opened. **vento**: ablative of means with *turgida*, which here has the force of a perfect participle.

ODE XI.

1. Cantaber et Scythes: chosen as dwelling on the extreme western and northern frontiers of the empire; concerning the Cantabrians, see on ii. 6. 2. Though only the Cantabrians are here referred to as *bellicosus* and only the Scythians as remote (*Hadria divisus obiecto*), the context naturally suggests that both tribes are warlike and both are separated from Rome by intervening seas. Horace wishes to rally his friend on his unnecessary concern about what is occurring on the far frontier.

2. Hirpine Quincti: for the transposition of *nomen* and *cognomen*, *cf.* ii. 2. 3, *Crispe Sallusti.* **cogitet**: *i.e.* is planning, plotting; the singular verb with compound subject, as regularly in Horace. **Hadria divisus obiecto**: there is a touch of humor in this phrase, as though Hirpinus were in fear lest the Scythians should sweep down through Illyria, cross the Adriatic, and descend upon Rome itself.

3. remittas quaerere: Horace is particularly fond of such periphrastic forms of prohibitions; *cf.* i. 9. 13, *fuge quaerere.*

4. nec trepides: *and be not anxious; nec*, at all periods of the language, is used much more commonly than *neve* (*neu*) to introduce a prohibition or negative wish after a previous imperative or subjunctive; *cf.* i. 9. 15, *lucro appone nec dulcis amores sperne puer.* **in usum aevi**: *for the needs of life; aevum* is here used in the sense of *vitae.*

5. poscentis pauca: these words contain the reason for the injunction *nec trepides, etc.*, — *since it demands but little, viz.* the things enumerated in strophes 4 and 5. **fugit retro**: *i.e.* youth and beauty are disappearing behind us, while our own lives travel forward.

6. lēvis: apparently intended to suggest the soft, smooth skin of youth as compared with the dry and wrinkled (*arida*) features of old age (*canitie*); *cf.* iv. 6. 28, *levis Agyieu* (of Apollo); Tibull. i. 8. 31, *carior est auro iuvenis, cui levia fulgent ora.*

8. canitie = *senectute.* **facilem** : *i.e.* soft, pleasant.

9. honor : *i.e.* beauty, glory ; the flowers do not retain their beauty, but wither soon.

10. vernis : not that the spring flowers were more ephemeral than others, but because coming after the long winter they were of special interest. **neque uno** : *sc. uno et eodem ; i.e.* the moon waxes and wanes.

11. aeternis consiliis : *i.e.* with thoughts of matters which belong to the remote future and for which we need feel no present concern ; *consiliis* is ablative of means with *fatigas*, but must be supplied in thought as an ablative of comparison with *minorem.* **minorem** : *unequal to them, i.e.* to their contemplation.

13. platano : a spreading shade tree extensively planted by the Romans. **hac** : to be taken with both *platano* and *pinu.* As in ii. 3, the poet evidently imagines himself already reclining in some shady retreat.

14. sic temere : *i.e.* carelessly as we are. **rosa odorati** : *i.e.* having garlanded our brows with fragrant roses ; *odorati* is used as a middle ; hence the accusative, *capillos ; cf.* i. 1. 21, *membra sub arbuto stratus.*

15. canos : *cf.* line 8, which suggests that *canities* is already pressing on Horace and his friend.

16. Assyriaque : *nardo* is here feminine ; elsewhere Horace uses the word as neuter ; *Assyria* = *Syria* in the sense noted on ii. 7. 8, *malobathro Syrio.*

17. Euhius : *i.e.* Bacchus ; see on i. 18. 9.

18. curas edacis : *cf.* i. 18. 4, *mordaces sollicitudines.* **puer** : *i.e.* slave, as in i. 38. 1. **ocius** : *right quickly.*

19. restinguet : *i.e.* temper by mingling water with it. **Falerni** : concerning this wine, see on i. 20. 10.

21. devium : *shy.*

22. eburna : *i.e.* ornamented with ivory. **dic age** : *come, bid her ; age* is interjectional.

23. maturet : *sc. venire ;* the subjunctive depends upon *dic* used as a verb of *bidding ;* a substantive clause without *ut* developed from the jussive. **incomptam** : *simple, careless ;* further explained by *nodo.*

24. comam religata : the accusative depends upon the middle participle, as in line 15, *odorati capillos.*

ODE XII.

1. Nolis: *no one would wish;* indefinite second singular. **longa ferae bella Numantiae**: the reference is to the war of 143–133 B.C. The epithet *ferae* is justified not only by the stubborn resistance of the Numantines, but also by the resolution with which many chose death rather than surrender to a Roman conqueror. Note the interlocked order of the words (synchysis).

2. durum Hannibalem: Hannibal is characterized as *durus*, in view of his prowess as an antagonist; *cf.* Virg. *Georg.* ii. 170, *Scipiadas duros bello.* **Siculum mare**: referring to the First Punic War (264–241 B.C.), and more particularly to the sea-fights of Mylae (260 B.C.) and of the Aegates (241 B.C.). Note that the three great wars alluded to are enumerated in reverse chronological order.

3. mollibus: contrasted with *ferae, durum, purpureum sanguine.*

4. aptari: here in the sense of *necti*, 'to be linked with.' **modis**: ablative of association with *aptari; cf.* iv. 9. 4, *verba socianda chordis.*

5. saevos Lapithas: for the fight of the Centaurs and the Lapithae at the wedding feast of Pirithous, see on i. 18. 8, *Centaurea cum Lapithis rixa.* **nimium**: *excited; cf.* Tac. *Hist.* iv. 23, *rebus secundis nimii.*

6. Hylaeum: the name (from Greek ὕλη, 'wood'; hence 'Ranger') is appropriate for a roving Centaur. Virgil (*Georg.* ii. 457) mentions Hylaeus as *magno Lapithis cratere minantem.* **domitos . . . manu**: Tellus, according to the legend, had ensured her offspring (the giants) against destruction by the gods, but had not taken the same precaution to protect them against mortal assault; hence Hercules was enabled to compass their ruin. **Herculea**: the adjective with the force of a genitive, as in i. 3. 36, *Herculeus labor.*

7. Telluris iuvenes: the giants. **unde** = *a quibus*, as not infrequently. **periculum**: object of *contremuit*, which is here used as the equivalent of *pertimuit; cf.* Virg. *Aen.* iii. 648, *vocemque tremesco;* Hor. *Odes*, ii. 13. 14, *Bosphorum perhorrescit.*

8. fulgens: as situated in the shining *aether; cf.* iii. 3. 33, *lucidas sedes deorum.* **domus**: here in double meaning: (1) literally, as indicated by *fulgens;* (2) in the sense of household, for all the Olympian gods were threatened; *cf.* i. 6. 8, *saeva Pelopis domus.*

9. veteris = *senis; cf.* Virg. *Aen.* vii. 180. **tuque pedestribus melius**: emphasis rests upon both *tu* and *pedestribus*, *i.e.* 'twill be better for you to describe Augustus's exploits than for me to attempt it, and 'twill be better to describe them in prose (*pedestribus historiis*) than in verse. Horace was the first to introduce the word *pedester* in this sense, in imitation of the Greek πεζὸς λόγος. There is no evidence that Maecenas ever complied with the suggestion here offered by Horace.

11. ducta per vias: *i.e.* led in triumph through the streets of the city, and particularly along the Sacra Via, through the Forum, up to the temple of Capitoline Jupiter.

12. colla: *i.e.* bound with chains; *cf.* Ovid, *Ars Amat.* i. 215, speaking of a triumph, *ibunt ante duces, onerati colla catenis.* **minacium**: *i.e.* before their subjugation.

13. me: in emphatic contrast with *tu.* **dulcīs**: with *cantus.* **dominae Licymniae**. the reference is probably to Maecenas's newly wedded wife Terentia, daughter of Aulus Terentius Varro. She is here designated by the pseudonym *Licymnia*, in accordance with a practice common among the Roman poets, whereby fictitious Greek names were substituted for the actual Latin ones; but the number and quantity of the syllables were scrupulously observed. Thus here *Lĭcȳmnĭă* = *Tĕrēntĭă.* Similarly Catullus called Clodia, Lesbia; Tibullus gave the name Delia to Plania; Propertius, the name Cynthia to Hostia. The name Licymnia is thought by some to have been chosen from its easy suggestion of λιγύς, ὑμνός ('the sweet singer'); *cf.* line 13 f., *dulcis cantus.*

14. cantus: object of *dicere* ('sing of'); musical accomplishments were a part of the education of the women of Horace's day. **lucidum fulgentis**: *brightly gleaming;* for this poetic use of the accusative, *cf.* i. 22. 24, *dulce loquentem.*

15. bene: in the sense of *valde, probe* (*cf.* French *bien*); to be taken with *fidum.*

17. nec dedecuit: litotes for *et valde decuit.* **ferre pedem**: poetic for *saltare.*

18. certare ioco: evidently referring to sallies of wit in social intercourse, *e.g.* at *convivia*, which the women of Horace's day sometimes attended. **dare bracchia**: this refers to the dance, in which joining of hands naturally formed an important feature.

19. ludentem: *i.e.* participating in the ceremonial observance. **nitidis**: *i.e.* in festal array. **virginibus**: with *dare.* **sacro die**: *i.e.* the day of some recurring festival.

20. celebris: *thronged;* the epithet is here transferred from the temple to the goddess herself; *cf.* Tibull. iv. 4. 23, *Phoebe, iam celeber, iam laetus eris.*

21. dives Achaemenes: mythical founder of the Persian royal house of the *Achaemenidae.* The wealth of the Persian kings was proverbial; *cf.* iii. 9. 4, *Persarum vigui rege beatior.*

22. Phrygiae opes: the richness of Phrygia in various products is often referred to. **Mygdonias**: derived from the name of Mygdon, an early Phrygian king.

23. permutare: *muto* and its compounds cover a wider range of meaning than our English 'change'; they may mean either 'give in exchange' or 'take in exchange'; *permutare* here has the latter meaning; *cf.* i. 16. 26; i. 17. 2. **crine**: ablative of association with *permutare.* B. *App.* § 337; Introd. § 38. *a.*

24. plenas aut Arabum domos: for the position of the conjunction, see on i. 2. 5; on the proverbial wealth of the Arabians, *cf.* i. 29. 1, *beatis Arabum gazis;* iii. 24. 1.

25 f. cum flagrantia, *etc.:* three situations are enumerated: (1) Sometimes Licymnia bends down her neck to receive Maecenas's kisses; (2) sometimes in teasing playfulness (*facili saevitia*) she refuses, since she prefers to have them snatched from her (*magis gaudeat eripi*); (3) sometimes she even takes the initiative (*occupat*) and snatches them herself from Maecenas. The diaeresis which we should naturally expect in the middle of the verse (Introd. § 47) is here neglected; *cf.* i. 18. 16. **detorquet**: *i.e.* turns aside from its position; *de* in composition frequently has the force of 'from where some one or something naturally belongs.'

26. cervicem: the poetic singular, as in i. 13. 2; Horace never employs the plural form. **facili saevitia**: lit. *with an easy (graceful, winsome) cruelty,* a good example of oxymoron.

27. quae . . . gaudeat: *since she delights more;* the clause explains why Licymnia at times refuses the kisses; the antecedent of *quae* is the subject of *negat;* the subjunctive is one of characteristic with the accessory notion of cause, — 'as being one who delights.' **poscente magis**: *more than he who asks them* (*sc. oscula*).

28. occupat: parallel with *detorquet* and *negat;* note the disjunctive asyndeton; we should have expected *aut* before *interdum.*

ODE XIII.

1. Ille, illum (line 5), **ille** (line 8): observe the emphasis of the anaphora. **et**: correlative with *et* in line 2. **posuit**: *i.e.* planted.

2. quicumque: *sc. te posuit.* **primum**: *i.e.* originally.

3. produxit: *reared;* properly used of children, though somewhat rare in this sense.

4. opprobrium pagi: *the scandal of the neighborhood;* the district (*pagus*) in which Horace's Sabine farm was situated was Mandēla.

5. et: *even, actually.* **crediderim**: potential subjunctive.

6. fregisse cervicem: *strangled;* for *cervicem*, see note on ii. 12. 26. **penetralia**: properly an adjective; here used substantively in the sense of 'hearthstone,' the inner part of the house, where the images of the Penates were set up.

7. nocturno: *i.e.* shed at night, when the stranger would be expected to be sleeping securely in the house of his host.

8. venena Colcha: *i.e.* such potions as were brewed by Medea, the famous mythical sorceress, whose home was Colchis; on *Colcha* for *Colchica*, *cf.* ii. 9. 21, *Medum flumen*, with note. Ovid, *Met.* xiii. 20, has *Colcha carina.*

9. quicquid nefas: *quisquis* is occasionally used as an adjective in early Latin and in the poets; *cf. Sat.* ii. 1. 60, *quisquis color.* **concipitur**: *is conceived of.*

10. tractavit: zeugma; with *venena* the word means 'has handled,' with *nefas*, 'has engaged in.' **agro meo**: the Sabine farm; see Introd. § 4.

11. triste lignum: *thou wretched stump; lignum* is contemptuous for *arbos.* **caducum**: here in the sense of *casurum*, 'destined to fall'; *cf.* Virg. *Aen.* x. 622, *caduco iuveni.*

13. quid vitet: *what to shun;* deliberative subjunctive in indirect question. **numquam homini,** *etc.*: *man never takes sufficient heed from hour to hour; homini* is dative of agent with *cautum est*, which is here gnomic.

14. navita Poenus, *etc.*: introducing an illustration of the general truth just enunciated; *Poenus* ('Punic') is introduced merely for the sake of greater vividness; see on i. 1. 13; *trabe Cypria; navita*, for *nauta*, is archaic and poetic. **Bosphorum**: the Thracian Bosphorus, noted for its tempestuous weather; *cf.* iii. 4. 30, *insanientem Bosphorum.*

15. ultra . . . fata: *hidden fates* (= death) *from other quarters beyond*, *i.e.* after passing the obvious and well-known dangers of the Bosphorus itself.

16. caeca = *occulta.* **timēt**: for the quantity of the *e*, see on ii. 6. 14, *ridēt.*

17. miles (*sc. Romanus*), *etc.*: another illustration. **sagittas et celerem fugam**: object of *perhorrescit; cf.* ii. 10. 2, *procellas horrescis.* The reference is to the Parthian custom of wheeling in flight and discharging arrows upon the pursuing enemy; *cf.* Virg. *Georg.* iii. 31, *fidentemque fuga Parthum versisque sagittis.*

18. catenas: by metonymy for captivity; supply in thought *Italas* from *Italum robur.* **Italum robur**: *i.e.* the flower of the Italian soldiery, *e.g.* Marsian and Apulian (*cf.* iii. 5. 9); for this use of *robur, cf.* Cic. *in Cat.* ii. 11, *florem totius Italiae ac robur educite.* For the quantity of the *I*, see on ii. 7. 4, *Italoque.*

19. sed improvisa: the emphasis of the sentence rests on *improvisa;* the dangers that men fear, says Horace, are obvious and visible ones (*Bosphorum, sagittas, fugam, catenas, Italum robur*), but the violence that ravages and shall ravage the generations of men is something they do not see and do not anticipate, just as in the case of the falling tree which had so nearly destroyed the poet himself.

20. rapuit rapietque: similarly *Epp.* i. 2. 43, *labitur et labetur;* i. 7. 21, *tulit et feret.*

21. quam paene vidimus: *how narrowly I escaped seeing!* *vidimus* is a *plurale modestiae; cf.* i. 6. 9, *nos conamur.* **furvae**: the epithet is transferred from the *regna* to the goddess who presides over them. **Prŏserpinae**: here with ŏ; but ō in i. 28. 20; *Sat.* ii. 5. 110.

22. iudicantem Aeacum: Aeacus, Minos, and Rhadamanthus are frequently mentioned as performing the functions of judges in the lower world.

23. discriptas: *i.e.* set apart from the abodes of the wicked.

24. Aeoliis fidibus: the epithet 'Aeolian' is applied to the lyre, since Sappho lived in Lesbos (an Aeolic Island) and wrote in the Aeolic dialect. **querentem Sappho,** *etc.*: Sappho's strongly masculine, ardent nature naturally complained of the cold, unsympathetic attitude of her townswomen, who failed to requite her affection. *Sappho* is accusative.

26. sonantem: *i.e.* playing and singing; the verb is here used transitively; its object is *dura.* **plenius**: *i.e.* the subjects of Alcaeus's song (battles, exile, *etc.*) are richer than the purely erotic song of Sappho. **aureo plectro**: for the *plectrum*, see note on i. 26. 11, *Lesbio plectro.*

27. Alcaee: the most famous of the Greek melic poets. See Introd. § 21. **dura, dura, dura**: note the effective anaphora; the hardships were those of Alcaeus's personal experience on land and sea.

28. mala: editors sometimes join this with *dura belli;* but the hardships of exile (*fugae*) were beyond question more terrible to the ancient mind than those of war.

29. utrumque, *etc.:* lit. *marvel that both utter, etc.;* but the evident idea is: *marvel at both* (Sappho and Alcaeus) *as they utter.* **sacro silentio**: *i.e.* such silence as was observed at sacrifices and other sacred ceremonials; *cf.* iii. 1. 2, *favete linguis.*

30. magis pugnas, *etc.: i.e.* prefer to listen to descriptions of battles and the expulsion of tyrants, rather than to the complaints of Sappho.

31. exactos tyrannos: Alcaeus had been active in securing the banishment of Myrtilus, tyrant of Mitylene; for *exactos tyrannos* 'the expulsion of tyrants,' *cf.* the common *post reges exactos.*

32. densum umeris: lit. *dense with their shoulders, i.e.* packed shoulder to shoulder. **bibit aure**: *cf.* Propertius, iv. 6. 8, *suspensis auribus ista bibam;* Ovid, *Tristia,* iii. 5. 14, *auribus illa bibi.* **volgus**: *sc. umbrarum.*

33. quid mirum: *sc. est,* — *what wonder?* **ubi**: lit. *when,* but with decided causal force. **stupens**: *charmed, beguiled.*

34. belua centiceps: *viz.* Cerberus; elsewhere he is usually represented as having but three heads.

36. recreantur: here with reflexive meaning, *refresh themselves, stop for rest;* ordinarily the serpents twined in the hairs of the Furies were in a state of restless motion; but the sweet strains of Alcaeus's lyre lull them to rest.

37. quin et: merely a stronger *quin,* — *yea also,* as in i. 10. 13. **Prometheus**: this is the only passage in Latin literature which alludes to Prometheus as undergoing punishment in Hades. The ordinary account represents him as expiating his offence on Mt. Caucasus. For the offence itself, see i. 3. 27. **Pelopis parens**: Tantalus.

38. laborum decipitur: *are beguiled of their sufferings;* the genitive here is a Grecism; *cf.* iii. 27. 69, *abstineto irarum.* For the singular verb with compound subject, *cf.* ii. 11. 2.

39. Orion: famed as a hunter.

40. timidos: not 'timid,' but *wary, shy.* The lynx usually hunted its prey at night, retiring by day to its lair, which was difficult for the hunter to discover. Elsewhere the word is usually feminine, but Priscian (500 A.D.) expressly mentions its use as masculine in this passage.

ODE XIV.

1. Eheu denotes profound feeling. **fugaces**: predicatively with *anni*, — *the years glide swiftly by*. **Postume, Postume**: note the impressive repetition of the name; as i. 13. 1, *Cum tu, Lydia, Telephi cervicem roseam, cerea Telephi laudas bracchia*, and frequently in Horace. Postumus's identity is uncertain.

2. pietas: apparently here used in the broadest sense, covering all human responsibility, to the gods and to one's fellow-men.

3. senectae: poetic for *senectuti*.

4. indomitae = *indomabili*.

5. trecenis: *three hundred, i.e.* three hecatombs; 'three hundred' is not infrequent for a large round number. **quotquot eunt dies** = *cottidie*.

6. inlacrimabilem: the verb here has active force; *cf.* the Greek ἄκλαυστος, and *Odes*, i. 3. 22, *dissociabili*.

7. tauris: the most expensive victim offered in sacrifice. **ter amplum Geryonen**: Geryon was a mythical monster with three bodies. His abode was Spain, where he was the possessor of a herd of magnificent cattle. Hercules succeeded in killing Geryon, and thus secured the cattle. With *ter amplum*, *cf.* Virg. *Aen.* vi. 289, *forma tricorporis umbrae*.

8. Tityon: son of Terra; he attempted to ravish Latona, but was slain by the darts of her children, Apollo and Diana. He is represented in Tartarus as covering nine acres with his vast frame; *cf.* Virg. *Aen.* vi. 596. The inexorableness of Pluto is well brought out by reference to the fact that even Geryon and Tityos were unable to escape his grasp.

9. unda: *sc. Stygia*. **scilicet**: *with certainty*. **omnibus**: with *enaviganda*.

11. enaviganda: *viz.* in Charon's skiff; as a transitive verb, *enavigare* is found first in Horace. **reges**: *princes*, in the sense of men of wealth; *cf.* i. 4. 14, *regumque turris*.

12. coloni: *peasants*, the original meaning of the word (from *colo*, 'cultivate').

13. carebimus: *i.e.* avoid, evade; *cf.* ii. 10. 6. Note that logically *carebimus* stands in adversative relation to the following *visendus, linquenda*, — 'though we escape, yet we must visit, must leave, *etc.*'

14. fractis rauci fluctibus Hadriae: note the interlocked arrangement (synchysis); *fractis fluctibus* means 'breakers.'

15. per autumnos nocentem: autumn was the sickly season at Rome; *cf. Sat.* ii. 6. 19, *Autumnusque gravis, Libitinae quaestus acerbae.*

16. corporibus may be taken with either *nocentem* or *metuemus.* **Austrum**: the south wind, which prevailed in autumn, is conceived as bringing the seeds of disease.

17. visendus: like *linquenda* in line 21, this word is strongly emphatic.

18. Cocytos: Greek Κωκυτός, from κωκύω, *i.e.* the river of lamentation; *cf.* Milton, *Paradise Lost*, ii. 579, *Cocytus named of lamentation loud.* **Danai genus infame**: the fifty daughters of Danaus, the Danaids, had (with the exception of one, Hypermnestra) slain their husbands on the wedding night. As a penalty for their crime, they are represented in the lower world as endlessly pouring water into perforated vessels. On *genus*, 'offspring,' 'daughters,' *cf.* i. 3. 27, *Iapeti genus*, 'son of Iapetus.'

20. Sisyphus Aeolides: in the lower world he is said to have been punished by rolling up hill a huge stone, which, so soon as it reached the summit, again rolled down. His special crime is variously stated. **laboris**: with verbs of 'condemning,' the genitive is regularly used to denote the charge; to denote the penalty the ablative is commonly used; B. 208. 2. *b*; the genitive of the penalty, as here, is poetic.

21. linquenda tellus, *etc.*: *cf.* Lucretius, iii. 894, *iam iam non domus accipiet te laeta, neque uxor optima nec dulces occurrent oscula nati praeripere.*

23. invisas cupressos: the cypress was emblematical of death, and hence was frequently planted about the tombs of the dead and places where bodies were burned.

24. brevem: *short-lived; cf.* ii. 3. 13, *nimium brevis flores.*

25. Caecuba: *sc. vina;* for the Caecuban wine, see on i. 20. 9. **dignior**: the heir is characterized as worthier because he uses what Postumus jealously guards (*servata centum clavibus*) and refuses to enjoy.

26. mero tinguet pavimentum: hyperbole, for the purpose of giving a vivid picture of the reckless abandon with which the heir enters into his new possessions; *cf.* Cic. *Phil.* ii. 41. 105, *natabant pavimenta vino, madebant parietes.* The floors of the Roman dwelling were regularly paved with marble, the central space often consisting of elaborate mosaic patterns.

27. superbis pontificum potiore cenis: *i.e.* a wine better than that used at the splendid banquets of the priests; compendiary comparison. The feasts of the priestly colleges were proverbial for their magnificence; *cf.* i. 37. 2, *Saliaribus dapibus.*

ODE XV.

1. Iam: *presently, soon;* as in i. 4. 16. **pauca**: *i.e.* only a few. **regiae moles**: *princely piles; regiae* here equals *regales.* An era of magnificent building began in the peaceful times following the civil wars. Wealthy men vied with each other in laying out vast country estates on the grandest and most luxurious scale. Horace frequently enters his protest against the evils of such lavish expenditure.

3. Lucrino lacu: the Lucrine lake was near Naples. While it was not large, yet its size would be great for a fish-pond.

4. stagna: artificial ponds or lakes, for the breeding of fish. **platanus caelebs**: *the lonely plane tree;* the tree is characterized as *caelebs* because it was primarily a shade tree and was not adapted to the training of the vine, as was the elm, for example, which, in consequence, is sometimes spoken of as *married to* the vine.

5. evincet: *shall supplant.*

6. myrtus: here of the fourth declension, and, as the metre helps to show, nominative plural. **omnis copia narium**: a bold poetic expression for 'every kind of sweet perfume.'

7. olivetis: *i.e.* in places where olive orchards had previously stood; Horace's prophecy implies the disappearance of the *oliveta.*

9. spissa: *i.e.* densely planted; the laurel itself was not a dense shrub. **laurea**: *sc. arbor; the laurel.*

10. ictus: *i.e.* the beating rays of the sun.

11. intonsi Catonis: Cato Major (234–149 B.C.), often cited as typical of the old-fashioned sturdy simplicity. On the early mode of wearing the hair, see on i. 12. 41.

12. auspiciis: *i.e.* under the rule, guidance.

13. census: lit. *assessment*, and so *property.*

14. commune: *i.e.* the common weal. **decempedis**: the porticoes of the present day, it is implied, are so large that the unit of their measurement is not the foot, but ten feet.

15. metata: for the perfect passive participle of deponents used passively, *cf.* i. 1. 25, *detestata.* **privatis**: best taken as dative of interest with *metata*, — 'for private individuals'; *privatis* implies, what is known to be true, that the temples and other *public* buildings of the early days were often constructed on a large and costly plan. **opacam Arcton**: *i.e.* the shady north side.

16. **excipiebat**: lit. *caught*, *received*, *i.e.* lay open to.

17. **fortuitum caespitem**: the reference is obviously to the use of turf in constructing the simple homes of the early days; *cf.* Virg. *Buc.* i. 68, *tuguri congestum caespite culmen; fortuitum = forte oblatum*, *i.e.* which chance everywhere offered.

18. **leges**: sumptuary laws, which were intended to enforce simplicity of living. **publico sumptu**: referring to both towns and temples.

20. **novo saxo**: the reference is to marble, which was a novelty in the early days, and hence expensive; in Horace's time, its use had become well-nigh universal. With the thought of the closing stanza, *cf.* what Sallust, *Cat.* 9, says of the early Romans: *in suppliciis deorum magnifici erant, domi parci erant;* and contrast the words of the younger Cato speaking of the closing days of the Republic (Sall. *Cat.* 52): *habemus luxuriam et avaritiam, publice egestatem, privatim opulentiam.*

ODE XVI.

1. **Otium, otium** (line 5), **otium** (line 6): observe the emphasis of the anaphora and the initial position in the verse. *Otium* is used in the sense of the Greek ἀταραξία, *i.e.* freedom from care and trouble.

2. **prensus** = *deprehensus*, the regular nautical term; *prensus* is here used substantively, 'the mariner overtaken.' **Aegaeo**: *sc. mari.* **simul**: for *simul atque*, as in i. 9. 9, and frequently in the poets.

3. **certa**: to be taken predicatively, —*shine sure.*

4. **sidera**: as the ancients had not discovered the magnetic needle, they were dependent upon the stars when navigating at night.

5. **bello furiosa Thrace**: *cf.* Virg. *Aen.* iii. 13, *terra Mavortia, Thraces arant.*

6. **Medi pharetra decori**: the Parthians, distinguished for their skill with the bow; see on i. 2. 22, *Persae.*

7. **Grosphe**: probably Pompeius Grosphus, who, in *Epp.* i. 12. 23, is commended by Horace to his friend Iccius, then in Sicily, as a man who *nil nisi verum orabit et aequum.* **purpura**: *i.e.* purple vestments, coverings, and hangings; all stuffs dyed with purple were rich and costly. **ve-nale**: with *neque*, *which cannot be bought;* for

the division of the word between two successive lines, *cf.* i. 2. 19, *uxorius amnis.*

8. **neque auro**: Horace nowhere else admits elision in the fourth verse of the Sapphic stanza.

9. **non**: emphatic, — *'tis not riches nor the consul's lictor that banishes.* **enim**: justifying the statement in lines 7 and 8. With the thought of the strophe, *cf.* Lucretius, ii. 37–52, where the same idea is developed with fuller illustration. **consularis lictor**: lit. *the consul's lictor*, but logically, 'the consul with his lictors,' which is a figurative expression for the highest power.

10. **summovet**: *summovere* was the technical term for clearing the crowd from the streets by the lictors; *cf.* Livy, iii. 48, *i, lictor, summovere turbam.*

11. **laqueata tecta**: *fretted ceilings;* see on ii. 18. 1.

13. **vivitur**: lit. *it is lived* (*by one*), *i.e.* one lives. The sentence is in adversative relation to the previous strophe, — wealth and power cannot banish care, *but* he lives happily (*i.e.* without care), who, *etc.* **parvo**: *upon a little.* **bene** = *beate.* **cui**: dative of reference, — *on whose frugal board glistens;* its antecedent is (*ab*) *eo* to be supplied in thought with *vivitur; cui* extends also to *aufert.* **paternum salinum**: it was customary among the Romans to offer a sacrifice of salted meal to the household gods at the beginning of each meal; hence the *salinum* was an indispensable article of table furniture, and as such was naturally handed down from generation to generation as an heirloom.

15. **levis somnos**: *soft slumbers; levis* is opposed to *gravis; cf.* ii. 11. 8, *facilem somnum.* **timor**: *viz.* of loss, robbery, *etc.* **cupido**: in the sense of *greed, avarice;* the word is always masculine in Horace.

17. **quid**: *why?* **fortes**: with adverbial force, — *eagerly.* **iaculamur**: *aim at, strive for.* **aevo** = *aetate.*

18. **multa**: *i.e.* many possessions. **terras alio calentis sole**: *i.e.* foreign climes.

19. **mutamus**: *i.e.* seek in exchange (for our own); on the broad meaning of *mutare* as compared with English 'change,' *cf.* i. 17. 2; for the sentiment, *cf. Epp.* i. 11. 27, *caelum, non animum, mutant qui trans mare currunt.* **patriae**: as the position and context show, *patriae* is emphatic, and is contrasted with *se;* the construction of the genitive with *exsul* is after the analogy of the genitive with *expers.*

20. fugit: *i.e.* ever escaped; note the poetic use of the simple verb in the sense of the compound *effugere*.

21. scandit, *etc.*: for the thought, *cf.* iii. 1. 37 ff. **aeratas navis**: *i.e.* triremes with brazen prows.

22. relinquit: here in the sense of 'fail to overtake'; *cf.* the similar use of *deserere* in iii. 2. 32.

25. laetus in praesens: the injunction in *oderit* and *temperet* extends also to *laetus*, *i.e.* let the soul be joyful in the present and refuse, *etc.* **quod ultra est**: *i.e.* the future.

26. oderit: *let it disdain;* the infinitive with *odi* is poetical. **lento**: *quiet*, *i.e.* a smile of quiet resignation.

27. ab omni parte: *in every respect, altogether.*

29. Two illustrations are given of the truth just enunciated, one drawn from the career of Achilles, whose life was brief, but glorious, the other from that of Tithonus, whose life was long, but wretched. **abstulit clarum minuit senectus**; note the poet's art as seen in the juxtaposition of the contrasted ideas; Achilles was cut off (*abstulit*) despite his glory (*clarum*); Tithonus, despite his length of days (*senectus*), wasted away (*minuit*). This should be borne in mind by the student in translating. **cita**: in the sense of *early, untimely.*

30. Tithonum: see on i. 28. 8.

31. mihī: the original quantity of the final *i* is here retained, as often in poetry. **forsan**: at this period of the language, the word is poetic only. **negarit**: future perfect.

32. hora: *i.e.* the passing hour.

33. te, tibi, te: emphatic by position and anaphora. **greges Siculaeque vaccae**: *a hundred herds of Sicilian kine;* hendiadys. Grosphus's estate was in Sicily. **circum**: when prepositions suffer anastrophe, they usually stand immediately after the governed word, but *cf.* i. 2. 34, *quam Iocus circum.*

34. tibi: *for you.* **tollit hinnitum**: *whinnies;* the final *-um* is elided before the initial vowel of the following verse, thus producing an hypermeter line; *cf.* ii. 2. 18; Introd. § 44.

35. apta quadrigis equa: for racing, mares were preferred by the Romans. **bis tinctae**: Greek δίβαφοι. **Afro murice**: the coast of Gaetulia was famed for the choice quality of the purple dye yielded by its shell-fish (*murex*).

37. mihi: as contrasted with *te.* **parva rura**: the Sabine farm.

38. spiritum tenuem: *the fine inspiration;* the phrase is logically in adversative relation to *parva rura*, *i.e.* though Fate has not given me an extensive estate like yours, yet she has given me the priceless gift of song. **Graiae Camenae**: *i.e.* Greek poetry, particularly Greek lyric poetry. *Camena* is the native Latin word corresponding to the Greek Μοῦσα.

39. non mendax: of the Fate whose decrees are unerring; *cf. Carm. Saec.* 25, *veraces cecinisse Parcae;* possibly also Horace may be thinking of the Fate that has not belied his own hopes and aspirations for poetic fame. **malignum volgus**: *the envious crowd*, *viz.* of those who, failing in appreciation of Horace's art, begrudged him his poetic fame and his social status as the friend of Maecenas, Augustus, and the other chief men of the day.

40. spernere; coördinate with *spiritum* as object of *dedit;* the infinitive with *dare* is poetical; *cf.* i. 31. 17, *frui dones.*

ODE XVII.

1. querellis exanimas: *i.e.* crush me by thy forebodings of ill. Maecenas evidently despaired of recovering from his illness.

2. prius: *i.e.* before me. Introd. § 6.

4. decus columenque rerum: *cf.* i. 1. 2, *praesidium et dulce decus meum; rerum* is here almost equivalent to 'existence.'

5. te meae: the contrasted ideas are juxtaposed, as regularly. **partem animae**: *the half of my life; pars* is here used in the same sense as *dimidium* in i. 3. 8, *animae dimidium meae.* **rapit**: in colloquial language and in poetry, the present is not infrequently used where in standard prose the future would be employed.

6. maturior vis: *i.e.* some untimely blow; the comparative here has the force of a strengthened positive. **altera**: *sc pars.*

7. carus: *i.e.* to myself and others. **nec superstes integer**: *nor surviving entire; i.e.* Horace feels himself so much a part of his friend that Maecenas's death will destroy the completeness of his own self; *superstes* is here employed with the value of the missing participle of *superesse; integer* is thus used predicatively.

8. ille dies: *i.e.* the day of thy death. **utramque ruinam**: *the doom of both of us;* for *utriusque ruinam.*

9. non: to be joined with *perfidum.*

10. dixi sacramentum: *sacramentum dicere* was the technical military term for swearing allegiance to one's commander; so here Horace represents himself as having made a solemn pledge of devotion to his friend. **ibimus, ibimus**: such emphatic repetitions are characteristic of Horace; *cf.* iii. 3. 18, *Iliŏn*, *Ilion;* iv. 4. 70, *occidit*, *occid't*. The 'we' in *ibimus* does not refer to Horace alone, as shown by *comites* in v. 12; the poet means that they shall both go on their final journey whenever Maecenas leads the way. As a matter of fact, the poet survived his friend and patron only a few weeks, though both lived for many years after the date of this poem.

12. carpere iter: a poetic expression for 'travel'; *cf. Sat.* ii. 6. 93, *carpe viam.*

13. Chimaerae: see on i. 27. 23.

14. si resurgat, centimanus Gyas: Gyas was one of the hundred-handed monsters who were overthrown in their assault upon the Olympian deities. The myth represented them as confined under Mt. Aetna and other volcanic mountains; hence the addition, *si resurgat.*

15. divellet: *sc. a te.*

16. placitumque: *-que* is irregularly joined to *placitum* instead of to *Parcis;* see on i. 30. 6.

17. seu Libra seu me Scorpios, *etc.: lit. whether Libra or dread Scorpio gazes on me as the predominant constellation of my natal hour, etc., i.e.* whether Libra or Scorpio or Capricorn is the constellation on which hangs my destiny. Some particular star was popularly believed to be predominant in the life of each individual. The present, *adspicit* (instead of *adspexit*), is used because the influence is conceived of as permanent. *Pars* (through *adspicit*) is in predicate relation to the subjects *Libra*, *Scorpios*, *Capricornus; adspicere* and *pars* (in the sense of 'sign of the zodiac') are both technical terms of ancient astrology.

Horace's utterances in i. 11 imply that he lacked faith in astrology. Such was probably his real attitude. The allusions in this poem need not be interpreted as more than a poet's free application of popular belief.

19. tyrannus . . . undae: the rising of Capricorn was supposed to bring tempestuous weather.

21. utrumque nostrum astrum: for *utriusque nostrum astrum; utrumque* agrees directly with *astrum; nostrum* is best taken as genitive plural.

22. consentit: *i.e.* indicate the same destiny. **te**: the sentence introduces the reasons for the statement just made. **Iovis tutela; impio Saturno**: in astrology the influence of the planet Jupiter was regarded as favorable, that of Saturn as malign; *cf.* the English 'jovial,' 'saturnine.'

23. refulgens: *re-* (as in *resisto*) seems to suggest that the benign influence of Jupiter counteracts the baleful influence of Saturn.

24. eripuit: the reference is to Maecenas's recovery from illness in 30 B.C. **volucris Fati**: Fate is thus characterized, since it comes swiftly.

25. cum populus . . . crepuit: the temporal clause is, of course, inexact; Maecenas's illness was prior to the occasion here referred to. It was on his reappearance in public that the people manifested their joy at his recovery. For another reference to the same occurrence, see i. 20. 5 f.

26. crepuit sonum: the accusative is of 'result produced'; *crepare* rarely takes an object; *cf.* Prop. iv. 9. 4, *et manibus faustos ter crepuere sonos.*

27. truncus inlapsus, *etc.*: the incident is described more fully in ii. 13. **cerebro**: poetic for *capiti.*

28. sustulerat: *sustulisset* would ordinarily have been used here; the indicative expresses the thought with greater vividness, representing the result as one all but consummated; for this form of conditional sentence, *cf.* iii. 16. 3, *tristes excubiae munierant satis, si non Iuppiter et Venus risissent.* **Faunus**: from the root *fav-*; hence literally 'the favorable god,' particularly the patron god of shepherds, and sometimes also, as here, the patron god of poets. As seen by i. 17, Horace cherished the thought that this god loved to abide upon his estate.

29. Mercurialium virorum: *i.e.* men under the protection of Mercury, the inventor of the lyre, and so the tutelary patron of poets.

30. reddere: *i.e.* to give in return for, or in recognition of, the favor of the gods; for the infinitive with *memento*, *cf.* ii. 3. 1, *aequam memento servare.*

32. humilem: *i.e.* a simple offering as opposed to the more costly one of Maecenas.

ODE XVIII.

1. ebur neque aureum lacunar: *i.e.* panelled ceilings decorated with ivory and gold. Such ceilings were coming into vogue in Horace's day.

3. trabes Hymettiae: *i.e.* beams of Hymettian marble; *trabs* may refer not only to beams of wood, but also, as here, to the marble architrave resting upon columns; the Hymettian marble was quarried on Mt. Hymettus near Athens. Its color was white, marked with delicate bluish-grey veining.

4. **ultima recisas Africa**: the reference is probably to the Numidian marble, a highly prized variety with rich dark veins of yellow and purple (the *giallo antico*); *ultima* does not here have superlative force, but merely designates Africa (Numidia) as relatively remote from Rome.

5. **Attali regiam occupavi**: *occupo* regularly (like Greek φθάνω) involves the notion of anticipation, of doing something before some one else, or unexpectedly to one's self; so here, 'I have not come suddenly, unexpectedly, into possession of the palace of an Attalus,' as did the Roman people in 133 B.C., when Attalus III., King of Pergamus, at his death bequeathed his kingdom to the Roman people. This idea is further emphasized by the words *ignotus heres*, *i.e.* 'not knowing I was an heir'; *ignotus* is here used actively.

7. **Laconicas purpuras**: *i.e.* vestments dyed with Laconian purple. The coast of Laconia furnished the shells of the *murex*, which when ground formed the basis of a most splendid and costly dye, second only to that prepared on the coast of Phoenicia. Enormous shell-heaps near Gytheum on the southern Laconian coast are said to testify to the extent of the ancient industry.

8. **trahunt**: here *trail; cf. Ars Poet.* 215, *tibicen traxitque vagus per pulpita vestem.* **honestae clientae** = *high-born dames.*

9. **fides**: *i.e.* loyalty and devotion to my friends, particularly to my patron Maecenas. **ingeni**: in allusion to Horace's poetic gifts; *cf.* ii. 16. 38, *spiritum Graiae tenuem Camenae.*

10. **benigna**: *generous.* **est**: *sc. mihi.* **pauperem**: the adjective has adversative force. **dives**: probably to be taken generally, — *i.e.* many a rich man.

11. **nihil deos lacesso**: *lacesso* here takes the construction of verbs of *demanding*, like *flagito* below; *cf.* the similar use of *veneror* in *Car. Saec.* 49. **supra**: here an adverb.

12. **potentem amicum**: *viz.* Horace's patron, Maecenas.

13. **largiora**: *i.e.* more liberal bounty.

14. **unicis Sabinis**: *with my cherished Sabine farm*; *Sabinis* is the ablative of *Sabini*, lit. 'Sabines'; but by the Roman idiom names of peoples were freely used to designate estates situated among a people; thus *mei Sabini* = 'my Sabine estate'; *mei Tusci*, 'my Tuscan estate'; no substantive is to be supplied in this usage; for *unicus*, 'unexampled,' 'precious,' *cf.* iii. 14. 5, *unico gaudens mulier marito.*

15. truditur dies die: *'day treads upon the heel of day.'*

16. pergunt: *haste.* **interire**: *i.e.* to wane.

17. tu: some imaginary rich man, addressed as representative of the class. **secanda marmora locas**: *let contracts for sawing marble;* the Romans of Horace's day seldom built structures of solid marble, but ordinarily attached a thin veneer of marble slabs to walls of brick, tufa, or concrete; such slabs were also used for pavements; *secanda* refers to cutting or sawing the marble into these slabs. This process was difficult and slow; hence the significance of the following words, *sub ipsum funus.* For the grammatical usage in *secanda marmora*, see B. 337. 7. *b*. 2.

18. sub ipsum funus: *on the very verge of the grave.*

20. Bais: for *Bāīis* (*i.e. Bājis*), as frequently in words of this type. The ablative is one of place. Baiae was a famous seaside resort at the northern extremity of the Bay of Naples, attractive not only for its delightful climate, but also for its warm springs, which were utilized for baths. **urges summovere litora**: *art eager to push out the shore;* the infinitive with *urges* is poetical and rare; *summovere* is used for *promovere.* In Horace's day the fashion had become prevalent of building houses out over the edge of the water, massive piles of masonry being laid under the water for the purpose; *cf.* iii. 1. 33 f., *contracta pisces aequora iactis in altum molibus.*

22. parum locuples: lit. *too little rich, i.e.* not contented; hence the following ablative. **continente ripa**: *the mainland; cf.* Livy, xliv. 28, *continenti litori; ripa* is used for *litore* in order to avoid the repetition of *litus* in two successive lines; participles used as adjectives more commonly have -ī in the ablative, but many exceptions occur both in prose and poetry.

23. quid quod, *etc.*: lit. *what (of the fact) that? i.e.* consider the enormity! As Lucian Müller observes, the expression *quid est quod* is seldom found in poetry of a high order; it belongs rather to oratorical prose. **usque proximos revellis agri terminos**: *usque* means 'straight on,' 'continuously'; in sense it is here joined closely with *proximos*, *i.e.* you tear down the boundary stones of the adjoining estate, one set after another; boundary stones were regarded by the ancients as something sacred, being under the special tutelage of the god Terminus; *cf.* the annual festival of the *Terminalia*: *proximos*, while grammatically limiting *terminos*, is logically to be taken with *agri.*

25. clientium: the obligations of the *patronus* to his *cliens* were most strict; the Laws of the Twelve Tables declared, 'Whoever wrongs his client, shall be accursed.'

26. salīs: as the quantity shows, from the verb *salio.* The bold word suggests the contemptuous attitude of the rich lord.

28. sordidos: our 'ragged' is the nearest equivalent in English; there is no reference to squalor.

29. certior: predicatively with *manet;* hence, *more certainly.*

30. rapacis Orci fine destinata: *than the destined limit of rapacious Orcus;* the genitive is appositional, *i.e.* the limit where Orcus is; *cf.* i. 34. 11, *Atlanteus finis,* 'the limit where Atlas is'; there is a certain sarcasm in the poet's suggestion that there is one *finis* not to be treated with contempt, however lightly the rich man may ignore the *fines* of his clients. For the gender of *finis* (regularly masculine), *cf. Epod.* 17. 36; Lucretius also regularly uses the word as feminine.

32. erum: this word (lit. *master* of slaves) suggests that the rich man, by casting aside all justice, is no longer a protecting *patronus* towards his *clientes*, but a mere slave-master. **ultra tendis**: *i.e.* strive for more, for more lands and grander houses. **aequa**: with adverbial force, *impartially; cf.* i. 4. 13, *pallida Mors aequo pulsat pede.*

34. regumque pueris: *reges* in the sense of 'the rich,' as often; *cf.* i. 4. 14, *regumque turris; pueris = filiis.* Note that in the second foot of the verse the long of the iambus is resolved into two shorts (*pŭ-ĕr-is*). This is the only instance of such resolution in the entire poem. **satelles Orci**: Orcus is here the god; the *satelles* is Charon.

35. callidum Promethea, *etc.:* the story alluded to is unknown; the negative (*nec*) is to be taken with *auro captus*, as well as with *revexit; captus* is used in the sense of *corruptus*, 'bribed.'

36. hic: referring to Orcus.

37. Tantalum: *cf.* i. 28 (1). 7. **Tantali genus**: the reference is to Pelops; *genus* for *filius*, as in i. 3. 27, *Iapeti genus.* Tantalus and Pelops are cited as types of rich men. The possessions of the former were traditionally described as extending a ten days' journey.

38. levare: depending upon *vocatus*, — a poetic usage. Introd. § 41. *d.*

40. vocatus atque non vocatus: *i.e.* death comes relentlessly, whether desired or not. **audit**: used absolutely, — *gives ear.*

ODE XIX.

1. Bacchum: the theme of the ode is emphasized by the position of the word. **remotis**: *i.e.* in some lonely retired spot. **carmina**: hymns in honor of the god.

3. nymphas: the nymphs had nursed Bacchus when an infant, and are often represented as in his train.

4. capripedum: the classic poets represent the satyrs as having the heads and bodies of human beings, with the legs of goats. **acutas**: lit. *pointed*, as the ears of the satyrs were regularly conceived, but here with the added notion of 'attentive.'

5. euhoe: Greek εὐοῖ, the cry of the Bacchic worshippers; hence the god is called *Euhius; cf.* i. 18. 9. **recenti metu**: *i.e.* the awe with which the spectacle inspired him is still fresh in his mind.

6. pleno pectore: ablative absolute with causal force. For the sentiment, *cf.* iii. 25. 1, *quo me, Bacche, rapis tui plenum?* **turbidum laetatur**: *rejoices tumultuously; turbidum* is an accusative of the result produced; *cf.* i. 22. 23, *dulce ridentem;* ii. 12. 14, *lucidum fulgentis oculos.* Introd. § 35. *b.*

7. parce, parce: emphatic repetition, as in ii. 17. 10, *ibimus, ibimus.* **Liber**: see on i. 12. 22.

8. gravi thyrso: *gravi* means *mighty, potent;* the *thyrsus* was the staff carried by the worshippers of Bacchus; it was wound about with fillets and foliage, and was tipped with a pine-cone. Those touched by it were supposed to come under the spell of the god, and involuntarily to join in the excited celebration of his festival.

9. fas est: *i.e.* in view of the vision already vouchsafed. **pervicacis Thyiadas**: *tireless Thyads* (Greek θύειν, 'rave'; *cf. Maenades*, from μαίνομαι); only women and maidens shared in these celebrations; "waving their thyrsi and torches, with serpents in their flying hair, to the music of tambourines and shrill flutes, they shouted and raved, danced and roved through wood and over mountains" (Küster).

10. vini fontem, *etc.*: Bacchus is the god of productivity and fertility; hence at the touch of his thyrsus streams of wine and milk and honey are conceived as bursting forth. **et**: postponed, as often in the poets.

12. iterare: lit. *repeat*, and so *re-produce* in narrative, *describe.*

13. et: *also.* **beatae coniugis**: lit. *of his blessed, = of his* *deified, consort* (Ariadne); *beatae* is the participle of *beo*, a verb which in Horace's day had become well-nigh obsolete.

14. honorem: the reference is to the crown of Ariadne, made by Vulcan for her wedding gift, and which was afterwards placed among the stars; the accusative depends upon some such word as *dicere*, to be supplied in thought from *iterare*. **Penthĕī**: *Pentheus*, of the third declension in Greek, is here declined as of the second. Pentheus was king of Thebes. His hostility toward the celebration of the worship of Bacchus brought upon him the vengeance of the god; his palace fell in ruins, while a band of frenzied Bacchanals, his own mother and sisters at their head, fell upon him and tore him to pieces. The legend is vividly depicted in Euripides's *Bacchae*.

15. non leni = *gravissima*.

16. et: as above, in line 10. **Lycurgi**: a Thracian king, who was visited with blindness in punishment for his hostility to the god.

17. tu, tu: notice the emphasis lent by the frequent repetition of the pronoun in this and the following lines. **flectis amnes**: apparently an allusion to the occasion when Bacchus, in his triumphal progress through the Orient, dried up at a touch of his thyrsus the rivers Orontes and Hydaspes, over which he and his followers then passed dry-shod. **mare barbarum**: probably the Indian Ocean, which, as the legend goes, Bacchus also visited.

18. separatis: a synonym of *remotus* in the sense noted above (line 1). **uvidus**: *i.e.* flushed with wine; *cf.* i. 7. 22, *uda Lyaeo tempora*.

19. nodo coerces, *etc.*: *i.e. bindest with harmless knot of serpents the hair of the Bistonian women*; *fraus* in this sense is confined to the phrases *sine fraude* and *fraudi esse*. The Bistonians were a Thracian tribe devoted to the Bacchic orgies. Elsewhere the Bacchanals are represented as themselves twining serpents in their hair.

21. parentis: *sc. tui*, *viz.* Jove. **per arduom**: *i.e.* up the ascent to Olympus.

22. scanderet: here with conative force, corresponding to the conative use of the imperfect indicative *scandebat*. The allusion is to the war of the giants upon the gods.

23. Rhoetum: one of the giants. **leonis**: with *mala*, as well as with *unguibus*; Bacchus on this occasion assumed the form of a lion.

25. aptior: in predicative agreement (through *dictus*) with *tu* understood.

27. ferebaris: *thou wast reputed.*

28. pacis eras medius, *etc.*: *i.e.* thou didst share in peace and war: the emphasis, as the context shows, rests upon *belli*, — *in war as well as peace;* on *mediusque belli* for *medius bellique*, *cf.* ii. 7. 25; the meaning here attached to *medius*, 'sharing in,' is nowhere else attested.

29. te vidit: Bacchus had descended to Hades to bring back Semele, his mother. **insons**: with adverbial force, — *without offering harm.* **aureo cornu decorum**: *cornu* is best taken as referring to the golden drinking horn, filled presumably with wine, carried by the god. **atterens**: *sc. tibi.*

31. recedentis: dependent upon the genitive involved in *tuos* (*pedes*) understood. **trilingui ore tetigitque**: *i.e.* fawned upon thee; *trilingui ore* for *linguis trium capitum;* for the position of *-que*, see above on line 28.

ODE XX.

1. tenui: *i.e.* slight, feeble.

2. biformis: in that he changes his human form for that of a swan.

4. longius: for *diutius*, as in Nepos, *Att.* ii. 4; Caes. *B. G.* iv. 1. **invidia maior**: *i.e.* superior to envy, beyond its reach. During his lifetime, Horace had been a mark for malignant criticism; *cf. Sat.* i. 6. 46, *quem rodunt omnes libertino patre natum.*

5. pauperum sanguis parentum: for Horace's humble parentage, see Introd. § 1, and *cf.* iii. 30. 12, *ex humili potens.*

6. quem vocas: *whom you so call*, *i.e.* my real self shall not die.

9. residunt: *are gathering.* **cruribus**: best taken as dative of reference. **asperae pelles**: *i.e.* the wrinkled skin of the swan.

10. album in alitem: *i.e.* into a swan.

11. superne: with short final *e*, as in Lucretius, vi. 544. **lĕves**: note the quantity of the first *e*.

13. tutior: *i.e.* he is to escape any such disaster as befell Icarus.

15. canorus ales: the ancients popularly attributed the gift of song to the swan.

16. Hyperboreos campos: the Hyperboreans were a mythical folk, conceived as dwelling in the far North (hence the name). They were represented as passing an idyllic existence in a sunny land, in the midst of plenty, and uncontaminated by the vices of civilization.

17. Colchus: Colchis was in the remote East, at the extremity of the Black Sea. **qui dissimulat metum, Dacus** : *i.e.* the Dacian, who feigns not to fear.

18. Marsae cohortis : the Marsians, here, as elsewhere (*cf.* i. 2. 39; iii. 5. 9), are cited as typical of Roman prowess; they were famous as infantrymen.

19. Geloni : a Scythian tribe, dwelling in what is now southwestern Russia. **peritus Hiber** : no one has yet fathomed the significance of this reference to the 'learned Spaniard'; very probably the text is corrupt.

20. Rhodani potor : *i.e.* the Gaul.

21. With this closing stanza of the ode, we may compare Ennius:

> Nemo me dacrumis decoret neque funera fletu
> Faxit. Cur? Volito vivo' per ora virum.

inani funere : Horace characterizes his death as *inani*, because it is unreal; his real self, as he has already asserted, will live on. **neniae** : the dirges of the *praeficae* (hired mourners).

22. turpes : *unseemly;* alluding to the customary frantic manifestations of grief at funerals, such as tearing the hair, beating the breast, *etc.*

23. sepulcri honores : *i.e.* the honor of erecting a tomb to my memory; *sepulcri* is appositional genitive.

24. mitte : *dispense with.*

BOOK III.

ODE I.

1–4. Though incorporated in the first ode by nearly all editors, this opening stanza is really introductory to the entire series of the six following odes.

1. 'Odi profanum volgus,' *etc.:* properly the language of the priest in conducting some solemn ceremony whose sanctity would be polluted by the presence of those not properly qualified to participate in the rite, *e.g.* foreigners, slaves, and in some cases women. As Page observes, *profanus* literally means 'outside the shrine,' and so 'forbidden to enter.' The phrase *profanum volgus* defies English translation, owing to the absence of the corresponding institution in our modern civilization; neither Page's 'unhallowed throng' nor Smith's 'uninitiate herd' gives a just rendering. As priest of the muses,

Horace here makes the conventional priestly warning his own, bidding none approach but those who have full right, and enjoining upon these to keep a reverent silence (*favete linguis*). With *odi profanum volgus et arceo*, *cf.* Virg. *Aen.* vi. 258, *procul O, procul este, profani;* and with *favete linguis*, *cf.* the Greek εὐφημεῖτε, similarly employed in Hellenic ritual.

2. **carmina non prius audita**: the reference is probably solely to the serious content of the following six odes.

4. **virginibus puerisque**: *i.e.* for the rising generation, the future hope of the state.

5. **regum . . . Iovis**: both words are made emphatic by position and chiasmus; the power of *kings* is over their own subjects; but *Jove's* power is over the kings themselves; this double statement is intended merely to prepare the way for the more general and important one in lines 14 f. **greges**: apparently a reminiscence of the Homeric conception by which the king was the 'shepherd of his people,' ποιμὴν λαῶν.

7. **Giganteo triumpho**: *cf.* ii. 12. 7; 19. 21 f. *Giganteo* has the force of an objective genitive.

8. **supercilio**: *i.e.* with the nod of his brow; *cf.* the familiar passage, *Il.* i. 528, ἦ, καὶ κυανέῃσιν ἐπ' ὀφρύσι νεῦσε Κρονίων. **moventis**: *controlling, determining.*

9. **est ut**, *etc.*: the clauses in lines 9–14 stand logically in an adversative relation to *sortitur*, *movet*, — 'though men differ individually in power and wealth and rank, yet inexorable Destiny with impartial hand pronounces the doom of high and low alike.' **est ut ordinet, descendat, contendat, sit**: lit. *it is that, etc.*, — merely a poetic periphrasis for *ordinat*, *descendit*, *contendit*, *est*. **viro vir latius**: *i.e.* one man more extensively than another.

10. **arbusta**: vineyards and olive groves, important sources of wealth among the Romans, as among the modern Italians. **sulcis**: *i.e.* the regular diagonal lines (arranged *in quincuncem*) in which the vines were planted. **hic generosior descendat, contendat**: the logical perspective of these clauses is somewhat obscured to our English sense by the apparent prominence of these two verbs. The verbs are really very subordinate elements in the situations which the poet is aiming to depict; the emphasis rests upon *generosior* and *moribus melior;* lit. *one man comes down to the Campus a candidate of higher birth, another competes better in character and repute;* *i.e.* one candidate who comes down to the Campus is nobler born, another

contestant is of higher character (while yet a third has a larger body of supporters); logically, therefore, *descendat* and *contendat* are not limited each to its grammatical subject, for both the candidates referred to *come down* to the Campus, and both *contest* for the high office; the verbs merely give color and detail to the general picture. **hic, hic, illi**: *one, another, yet a third.*

11. descendat: *i.e.* from the hills on which Rome was built. The *Campus* was on low, level ground. **Campum**: *i.e.* the Campus Martius; it was here that the Comitia Centuriata assembled for the election of the chief Roman magistrates. **petitor**: in predicate relation to *hic.*

12. meliorque fama: *i.e. famaque melior; cf.* ii. 19. 28; 32.

13. clientium: the original relation of *patronus* and *cliens* had fundamentally changed by Horace's time. In his day the *clientes* were often *cives*, who for a definite consideration (commonly a dole of food) served as the visible supporters and partisans of some political leader desirous of thus emphasizing his public importance. Horace's opinion of such methods seems indicated by the word *turba.*

14. aequa lege Necessitas, *etc.*: *Necessitas* here is Death; a different conception is seen in i. 35. 17, where *Necessitas* is the handmaiden of *Fortuna;* the thought is a commonplace with Horace; *cf.* i. 4. 13; ii. 18. 32.

15. sortitur: *pronounces the doom.* **insignis et imos**: *cf.* i. 34. 13.

16. omne capax movet urna: for the thought, *cf.* ii. 3. 25, where is found the same conception of the constant movement of the lots in the urn of Fate.

17 f. The connection of thought between this and the preceding stanzas seems to be this: In view of the futility of all earthly power, and wealth, and glory, let us be content with a humble lot, and cease to strive for the vanities which can never bring peace. **destrictus ensis**, *etc.*: an allusion to the familiar story of the 'sword of Damocles.' Damocles was "a Syracusan, one of the companions and flatterers of the elder Dionysius. When Damocles extolled the great felicity of Dionysius on account of his wealth and power, the tyrant invited him to try what his happiness really was, and placed him at a magnificent banquet, in the midst of which Damocles saw a naked sword suspended over his head by a single horse-hair, — a sight which quickly dispelled all his visions of happiness" (Smith's *Classical Dictionary*). Cicero, *Tusc. Disp.* v. 61 f., gives the story in fuller detail. **cui**: its antecedent is *illi* to be supplied in thought with *elaborabunt.*

18. cervice: poetic for *cervicibus; cf.* i. 13. 2; ii. 5. 2. **Siculae dapes**: alluding to the banquet placed before Damocles by the Sicilian tyrant Dionysius; Sicilian luxury, however, was proverbial.

19. elaborabunt: the word is nicely chosen, involving, as it does, the notion of producing by the application of effort; so here, with the negative, — 'by no amount of effort will such viands be made to produce,' *etc.*

21. agrestium virorum: *of peasants;* the genitive is best taken with *domos.*

24. Tempe: *a Tempe;* the famous valley in northern Thessaly through which flowed the river Penēus. It was in reality a wild but beautiful gorge, though Horace here seems to use the word in the generic sense of 'vale.'

25. desiderantem quod satis est: *i.e.* desiring *only* what he needs. In view of the length of the sentence beginning with *desiderantem*, it is better in translating to change the structure of the sentence, — *the man who desires . . . is troubled not by . . . nor by, etc.*

27. Arcturi cadentis impetus, *etc.*: the autumnal storms were conceived as caused by the setting of Arcturus (end of October) and the rising of Haedus (beginning of October).

29. verberatae vineae: *i.e.* the lashing of one's vineyards; for this use of the participle, *cf.* ii. 4. 10, *ademptus Hector tradidit Pergama.*

30. arbore culpante: the ablative absolute here gives the justification of the epithet *mendax* just applied to *fundus*, — 'yes, treacherous, for the trees complain at one time of too much rain,' *etc.*

31. torrentia sidera: *i.e.* the dog star.

32. iniquas: *i.e.* cruel, bitter.

33 f. The poet turns somewhat abruptly to a condemnation of the lavish expenditure in building characteristic of the day. **contracta**: in predicate relation to *aequora*, and made emphatic by position. The extravagant hyperbole of the statement here made is hardly in keeping with Horace's usual taste.

34. iactis in altum molibus: referring to foundations for palatial residences built out over the water at Baiae and elsewhere; *cf.* ii. 18. 20. Orelli says *iacere* ('lay') was a technical term in Roman building. **huc**: *i.e. in altum.* **frequens redemptor cum famulis**: *i.e.* the contractor with his throng of laborers.

35. caementa: the *moles* of line 34.

36. terrae: with *fastidiosus;* the owner disdains the land, and builds out into the sea; *cf.* ii. 18. 22, *parum locuples continente ripa.*

39 f. A repetition in form and content of ii. 16. 21 f. **triremi**: here a private galley kept for pleasure purposes.

41. dolentem: agreeing with an indefinite pronoun ('one') to be supplied in thought. The reference is to distress of mind, not of body. **Phrygius lapis**: the marble quarried at Synnada in Phrygia, variously described as reddish with blue tints, and white with reddish tints.

42. purpurarum usus: a periphrasis for *purpurae*, purple rugs, coverlets, or vestments. **clarior**: to our sense, somewhat unnaturally combined with *usus.*

43. Falerna vitis: *vitis* for *vinum*, as often. On the Falernian wine, see i. 20. 10.

44. Achaemeniumque costum: the spikenard is called 'Achaemenian' from the ancient Persian dynasty of the Achaemenidae (*cf.* ii. 12. 21). It was in reality an Indian product, and is here called Persian either because brought from Persian emporiums or because widely used in Persia.

45. invidendis: as in ii. 10. 7, *invidenda aula.* **postibus**: *i.e.* marble columns. **et novo ritu**: there is a slight inconcinnity here in the two members connected by *et; invidendis postibus* is an ablative of quality; *novo ritu* of accordance. By *novo*, we are hardly to understand anything specific; the allusion is rather to the generally luxurious standards of the time.

46. sublime: in predicate relation to *atrium*, — *rear aloft.* **atrium**: properly the main room of the Roman house, but here used by synecdoche for the whole edifice; *cf.* English 'hall.'

47. valle permutem divitias: for the double meaning possible with *muto* and its compounds, see i. 17. 2; *valle* is an ablative of association. The *vallis Sabina* is Horace's Sabine farm, presented to him by Maecenas about 33 B.C. For the poet's satisfaction with this estate, *cf.* ii. 18. 14, *satis beatus unicis Sabinis.*

ODE II.

1. Angustam pauperiem: *trying privation.* **amice**: *with patience.*

2. robustus: almost with the participial force of 'hardened'; *cf.*

Cic. *in Cat.* ii. 9. 20, *genus exercitatione robustum.* **puer**: the military age was only seventeen.

3. **Parthos**: see on i. 2. 22.

4. **eques**: predicatively, *as a horseman;* as the Parthian strength was mainly in the cavalry, the Roman youth are urged to seek excellence in the same arm of the service.

5. **sub divo**: *i.e.* under the open sky; so also, ii. 3. 23; *cf.* i. 1. 25, *sub Iove.* **trepidis in rebus**: *i.e.* in dangers; *trepidis* is transferred from the person experiencing the emotion to the circumstances causing the emotion.

6. **illum**: emphatic; *i.e.* let *him* be such a one that, at sight of him, *etc.* **hosticis** = *hostilibus* (*i.e. hostium*); *cf.* ii. 1. 1, *motum civicum,* where *civicum* = *civilem* (*i.e. civium*). **ex moenibus prospiciens**: such 'views from the walls' are a repeated feature in ancient writers; *e.g.* see *Iliad*, iii. 148 f.

7. **matrona** = *uxor.*

9. **suspiret**: for the singular verb with compound subject, a construction specially frequent in Horace, *cf.* ii. 13. 38, *decipitur.* **rudis** = *inscius;* hence the genitive.

10. **sponsus regius**: *i.e.* some youth of royal blood, betrothed to the maiden watching with her mother from the wall. **asperum tactu leonem**: *i.e.* the Roman, referred to above in *illum.*

13. **dulce et decorum,** *etc.*: evidently modelled on Tyrtaeus (Frag. 10), τεθνάμεναι γὰρ καλὸν ἐπὶ προμάχοισι πεσόντα ἄνδρ' ἀγαθὸν περὶ ᾗ πατρίδι μαρνάμενον.

14. **et**: *too;* with *fugacem virum.* **persequitur**: here apparently in the sense of *consequitur,* 'overtakes'; properly it conveys only the notion of persistent pursuit, — 'dogs the steps of.' For the sentiment, *cf.* Simonides (Frag. 65), ὁ δ' αὖ θάνατος κίχε καὶ τὸν φυγόμαχον.

15. **iuventae**: poetic for *iuventutis;* *cf. senecta* for *senectus.*

17. **Virtus**: *i.e.* true manhood, true worth. **repulsae nescia sordidae**: *i.e.* admitting no disgrace (the emphasis on *sordidae*) in temporary defeat or disappointment; *repulsa* is the technical term for defeat at the polls. In the popular mind such a political defeat would be associated with a certain lack of prestige, — hence, *sordidae.* Horace, however, is employing *repulsa* figuratively in a wide sense, to cover every rebuff of fortune or society for which the individual character is not primarily responsible. The possessor of true worth, he asserts, is so far superior to such rebuffs, that they merely bring him fresh glory.

18. intaminatis: the word is rare and chiefly poetic.

19. ponit: for *deponit*, as in i. 3. 40, *ponere fulmina*, and often. **securis**: the axes of the lictors, symbolic of the consular authority; here the meaning is not specially restricted to *consular* authority, but covers the conception of authority in general.

20. arbitrio popularis aurae: *at the dictates of popular favor; aura*, lit. 'breeze,' often has the figurative meaning here noted, *e.g.* Cic. *de Harusp. Responso*, 20. 43; *cf.* also *pro Cluéntio*, 130, *ventus popularis.*

21. Virtus: emphatic continuance of the thought begun in line 17.

22. negata: *i.e.* denied to others.

23. udam humum: figurative for all grovelling pursuits and ambitions.

25. et: *also; i.e.* fidelity to a trust has its sure reward, as well as *Virtus.* For the sentiment of this verse, *cf.* Simonides (Frag. 66), ἔστι καὶ σιγᾶς ἀκίνδυνον γέρας. **fideli silentio**: logically, rather *fidei silenti,* since fidelity is the quality really in the mind of the poet. A special instance of *fides* is cited, — by way of greater concreteness, — as suggesting the quality in general. *Fides* is repeatedly emphasized by Horace as of cardinal importance; *cf.* i. 24. 6, where *Fides* is styled *Iustitiae soror;* i. 18. 16, where the poet censures *arcani fides prodiga;* i. 35. 25, where the *infidum volgus* desert the victim of adversity. As a goddess, Fides was worshipped in a temple on the Capitoline, whose foundation was attributed to Numa.

26. vetabo sit, solvat: a peculiar construction not elsewhere found; the subjunctive in *sit* and *solvat* is probably to be explained as following the analogy of the subjunctive with *iubeo; iubeo*, while ordinarily construed with the infinitive, is also, at most periods, occasionally construed with the subjunctive either with or without *ut;* it is a noticeable feature of linguistic development that words of opposite meaning mutually influence each other's construction; so here *vetabo sit* seems to be modelled on some such expression as *iubebo sit.* **Cereris sacrum**: the Eleusinian mysteries of Demeter (Roman *Ceres*), one of the most conspicuous Hellenic rituals, had been transplanted to Italy, where they likewise came to be of great importance. The secrets of the mysteries were supposed to be faithfully guarded by those initiated into them.

27. volgarit: subjunctive by attraction.

28. trabibus: *roof-tree.*

29. solvat: *loose* from its moorings; *launch.* **phaselon**: originally a long, slender bean (Greek φάσηλος), whence figuratively 'skiff,' 'bark'; *cf.* English 'shell.' Horace retains the Greek inflection of the word. **Diespiter**: for the etymology and original force of the word, see on i. 34. 5; i. 1. 25.

30. neclectus: *when outraged* · the spelling *nec-* is archaic. **incesto addidit integrum**: *i.e* has involved the innocent with the guilty, *viz.* in inflicting punishment.

31. antecedentem: with adversative force, *i.e.* even though the guilty man may gain the start of Vengeance.

32. deseruit: *fails to overtake;* the perfect is gnomic; for the force of *desero*, 'fail to overtake,' *cf. Cat.* ii. 3, *qui exercitum deseruerunt*, 'who have failed to join the army.' **pede Poena claudo**: the ablative of quality has adversative force, — 'Vengeance, though lame of foot.'

ODE III.

1. Iustum et tenacem propositi: *i.e.* tenacious of purpose in a righteous cause.

3. instantis: *threatening.*

4. mente: ablative of separation; *quatit* here has the force of *excutit.*

5. dux . . . Hadriae: *cf.* i. 3. 15 (*Noti*), *quo non arbiter Hadriae maior.*

7. si fractus inlabatur orbis: *i.e.* if the vault of heaven should break and fall.

8. impavidum: in predicate relation to the omitted object of *ferient;* note, too, the emphatic position. **ferient**: the indicative here in the apodosis gives greater vividness.

9. hac arte: *i.e.* by the quality or virtue covered by *iustum et tenacem propositi.* Note again the emphasis of the position, ''twas by such virtue that,' *etc.; arte* depends upon *enisus*, which involves the notion of strenuous effort. **Pollux**, **Hercules**: mortals whose achievements raised them to the gods. In *Epp.* ii. 1. 5, Horace mentions them, in connection with Romulus and Bacchus (as here), as great benefactors of mankind. **vagus**: *viz.* in the performance of his famous labors.

10. arces igneas: *i.e.* the starry citadels of heaven.

11. quos inter: anastrophe, as not infrequently with many dissyllabic prepositions.

12. purpureo ore: *with ruddy lips; purpureo* is merely a more picturesque word for *pulchro*. **bibet**: *i.e.* when he, like Pollux and Hercules, shall be deified and admitted to the company of the gods.

13. hac: *sc. arte;* to be joined closely in thought with *merentem*, which is here used absolutely. Bacchus was fabled to have travelled in triumphal progress through the Orient, introducing the arts of civilized life, particularly the culture of the vine. **merentem**; in causal relation to *vexere*. **tuae vexere tigres**: the Greek legend represented Bacchus as passing in triumph through India upon a chariot drawn by panthers. In Roman literature, tigers take the place of panthers. But the present passage hardly alludes to Bacchus's Indian progress; we are rather to think of the tigers as conveying Bacchus to the skies; *cf.* Prop. iv. 17. 8, *lyncibus ad caelum vecta Ariadna tuis;* Ovid, *Trist.* i. 3. 19, (*Bacche*) *ipse quoque aetherias meritis invectus es arces.*

15. Quirinus: Romulus.

16. Martis: the father of Romulus. **Acheronta fugit**: *i.e.* was raised to the skies; in *Acheronta*, Horace follows the Greek inflection; *fugit* is for *effugit*.

17. gratum elocuta . . . Iunone, *etc.*: the ablative absolute here expresses time, — *at the time when Juno uttered the words, welcome to the gods met in council.* Juno's utterance is characterized as *gratum*, since Juno alone of the gods cherished a hostility for the Roman race. **consiliantibus**: *i.e.* deliberating whether or not Romulus should be admitted to the company of the gods.

18. Ilion, Ilion: for the repetition, *cf.* ii. 17. 10, *ibimus, ibimus.*

19. fatalis iudex: Paris, who awarded the golden apple to Venus as fairest of the goddesses; with *fatalis*, *cf.* the Greek Δύσπαρις, 'luckless Paris'; also Horace's *fatale monstrum* (Cleopatra), i. 37. 21.

20. mulier peregrina: Helen. **vertit**: the singular verb with compound subject, as frequently in Horace.

21. ex quo . . . destituit: to be joined closely with *damnatum*, which goes back to *Ilion* (here neuter; *cf.* i. 10. 14, *Ilio relicto*); *ex quo* is equivalent to *ex quo tempore; destituit* here has the force of *deprived, cheated;* hence the ablative.

22. mercede pacta: *the covenanted reward;* Poseidon and Apollo had erected the walls of Troy for Laomedon, king of that city; upon the completion of the work, Laomedon not merely refused the gods the promised reward, but rudely expelled them from his dominions; with *pacta*, used passively, *cf.* i. 1. 25, *detestata.* **mihi . . . damnatum**: *i.e.* handed over for punishment to me.

23. castae Minervae : *i.e.* the virgin goddess, Ἀθήνη παρθένος.

24. duce : Laomedon.

25. iam nec : *and no longer.* **Lacaenae adulterae** : Helen, wife of Menelaus, King of Sparta; the case is probably dative. **splendet** : lit. *shines*, and so, with *adulterae* (dative of reference), *dazzles his Spartan paramour; cf.* i. 5. 13, *quibus intemptata nites.*

26. famosus hospes : Paris; *cf.* i. 15. 1, *pastor perfidus.* **domus periura** : an allusion to the broken promise of Laomedon, the taint of which clung to his descendants.

28. Hectoreis : the adjective takes the place of a possessive genitive; *cf.* i. 3. 36, *Herculeus labor.* **opibus** : for *ope.*

29. nostris : *viz.* of all the gods. **ductum** = *tractum, prolonged.* **seditionibus** : *dissensions;* the gods had espoused different sides in the struggle between Troy and Greece.

30. protinus : *from this time forth.* In the previous verse the implication is that the Trojan War has but just ended; the poet's imagination represents the death of Romulus as contemporaneous with that event.

31. iras et nepotem redonabo : zeugma; with *iras, redonabo* has the force of 'relinquish,' with *nepotem*, of 'give up.' **nepotem** : Romulus, son of Mars, who was the son of Juno.

32. Troica sacerdos : Rhea Silvia; she is called *Troica*, because of Trojan descent, being the daughter of Numitor, who was descended from Aeneas.

33. Marti : *i.e.* the goddess gives up Romulus to Mars, that the god may fulfil his own pleasure as regards his son. **lucidas sedes** : *the shining abodes* of the gods.

34. ducere : *to quaff.* **nectaris sucos** : the genitive is appositional.

35. adscribi : a technical term for enrolling any one as citizen, soldier, colonist, *etc.;* hence here of formal admittance to the company of the immortals.

37. dum saeviat, *etc.:* an allusion to the plan attributed to Julius Caesar of rebuilding Troy upon its ancient site; Augustus is thought to have revived consideration of this project.

40. busto : *i.e.* the spot where the bodies of Paris and Priam were burned; the case is dative. The severity of the conditions imposed by Juno is to be judged in the light of the great sanctity attached by the Romans to the places where the remains of the dead were deposited.

42. celent : *sc.* on the same spot.

43. fulgens: *resplendent;* in predicate relation to *Capitolium*. The *Capitolium* was the temple on the Capitoline Hill dedicated jointly to Jupiter, Juno, and Minerva. Its roof was richly decorated with gilded tiles. **triumphatis Medis**: *triumpho*, regularly intransitive, is here used as transitive — *conquered ; Medis* for *Parthis*, as frequently in Horace ; *cf.* i. 2. 51.

45. late: with *horrenda.*

46. medius liquor: *i.e.* the Strait of Gibraltar.

47. ab Afro: poetic variation for *ab Africa.*

48. tumidus: *viz.* with its annual overflow.

49. aurum inrepertum . . . fortior, *etc.:* lit. *braver to spurn, etc.;* but the comparative idea belongs rather with the whole clause than with the quality contained in *fortior* itself, — *conspicuous rather for spurning the gold which as yet is undiscovered, etc., than for gathering, etc.*

50. cum celat: *cum* causal with the indicative; this was the regular construction in early Latin, and appears occasionally in the classical poets. **spernere fortior**: for the poetic use of the infinitive with adjectives, *cf.* i. 1. 18, *indocilis pauperiem pati.*

51. quam cogere, *etc.:* it had not always been Rome's glory to live up to the lofty ideal proclaimed in these lines; in the last decades of the Republic, Roman provincial governors had exhibited a shocking disregard of the rights of subject provinces, and had pursued a plan of systematic plundering. A better era began with the imperial régime. Horace, apparently, is pleading for a higher standard of official honesty. Küster suggests that we have here an implicit reference to the disaster to Crassus at Carrhae in 53 B.C. It seems indisputable that Crassus undertook his eastern expedition with the hope of increasing his already enormous wealth. To this purpose, all else was apparently subordinated. The resulting demoralization of his troops made a Parthian victory over the Romans an easy matter.

53. mundo obstitit: *i.e.* bounds the world; *obstitit* is the perfect of *obsisto.*

55. debacchentur ignes, nebulae: zeugma; with *ignes* (the tropic heats), *debacchentur* has the force of *rage;* with *nebulae*, the notion of *prevail.*

56. pluviique rores: poetic for 'dripping rain.'

57. Quiritibus: ordinarily applied to the Romans in their capacity as peaceful citizens, not, as here, in their capacity as warriors.

58. hac lege: *on these conditions.* **ne velint**: *viz. let them* *not cherish the desire;* an instance of the so-called 'stipulative subjunctive,' a jussive development; the clause is explanatory of *hac lege.* The reference is to the proposition, made about the time of this ode, for rebuilding Troy upon its ancient site; see above on line 37. **nimium pii**: *i.e.* in an excess of devotion to the memory of their Trojan ancestors.

61. Troiae renascens alite lugubri: condensed for 'if the fortunes of Troy revive again (it shall be) under evil auspices'; *renascens,* though belonging grammatically with *fortuna,* logically limits *Troiae; alite* is used poetically for *auspiciis; cf.* i. 15. 5, *mala avi.*

62. iterabitur: its subject is grammatically *fortuna,* but *fortuna* in a different sense from that in which the word is employed with *renascens;* Horace means that its evil fortune or doom shall be repeated.

64. coniuge me Iovis et sorore: *cf.* Virg. *Aen.* i. 46, *ast ego, quae divom incedo regina Iovisque et soror et coniunx.*

65. ter: emphatic by position. **aëneus**: predicatively; *i.e.* even should it *be* of bronze.

66. auctore Phoebo: *auctor* in the sense of 'builder,' as in Virg. *Georg.* iii. 36, *Troiae Cynthius* (= *Apollo*) *auctor.*

67. Argivis: dative of agency; *cf.* i. 1. 24, *matribus detestata.* The word *Argivi* is here chosen as a designation of the Greeks in general, since the worship of Juno was specially cherished among the Argives; at Argos itself she had a magnificent temple, remains of which have been recently brought to light by excavations.

69. iocosae lyrae: *iocosa,* as applying to Horace's muse, must be accepted with reservations; see Introd. § 21 f. **non conveniet**: *i.e.* if I continue in the present strain; for the sentiment, *cf.* ii. 1. 37, *sed ne relictis, Musa, procax iocis Ceae retractes munera neniae.*

70. pervicax: *cf.* ii. 1. 37, *procax.*

72. modis parvis: *i.e.* in lyric, as opposed to heroic verse.

ODE IV.

1. dic age: in this interjectional use, *age, agite* ('come!'), more commonly precede the imperative with which they are connected, *e.g.* i. 32. 3, *age dic Latinum carmen;* but, as here, ii. 11. 22, *dic age, maturet.*

2. regina Calliope: Calliope was properly the muse of epic poetry; here she is invoked rather as muse of poetry in general.

Horace does not always conceive of the Muses as each confined to a single narrow province, but often invokes now one, now another, at random,— Polyhymnia, Calliope, Euterpe, Clio, Melpomene. Calliope is here called 'queen' (*regina*) as a presiding deity of song.

3. **seu voce mavis**: *i.e. vel voce, si mavis; cf.* i. 2. 33, *sive tu mavis = vel tu, si vis.* **acuta**: *i.e. clear, sweet.*

4. **fidibus citharaque Phoebi**: *on the strings of Phoebus's lyre; cf.* Virg. *Aen.* vi. 120, *fretus cithara fidibusque canoris.*

5. **auditis**: the poet addresses his companions; as object of *auditis* and of *audire* (line 6), we are to supply in thought *Musam.* **ludit amabilis insania**: *does some fond illusion mock me?*

6. **pios lucos**: *i.e.* spots hallowed by the presence of the divinities; *lucus* is properly a sacred grove; for groves as the favorite haunts of poets, *cf.* i. 1. 30, *me gelidum nemus, etc.*

9. **fabulosae palumbes**: *i.e.* the doves of story and legend; thus they were said to bring ambrosia to Zeus; to have suggested the founding of the oracle at Dodona; to be attendants of Venus, *etc.* **Volture in avio**: *on trackless Vultur;* Mt. Vultur (Horace here uses the earlier form *Voltur*) was near the poet's birthplace, Venusia in Apulia.

10. **nutricis Ăpuliae**: for a country figuratively conceived as *nutrix, cf.* i. 22. 15, *Iubae tellus leonum arida nutrix.* The ordinary quantity of the first syllable of *Apuliae* is here violated; but such changes in proper names are not infrequent in poetry; *cf., e.g.,* i. 20. 7, *Vātĭcani* (elsewhere *Vātī-*). **extra limen**: Mt. Vultur was just beyond the Apulian border.

11. **ludo fatigatumque somno**: *worn out with play and overcome with drowsiness;* zeugma; for the position of *-que, cf.* i. 30. 6; ii. 19. 28.

12. **fronde nova texere**: similar marvels were told of the youth of other famous poets; thus the Muses are said to have revealed themselves to the youthful Hesiod as he grazed his flocks on the slopes of Helicon; bees were said to have touched the lips of Pindar, as a presage of the sweetness of his song; *cf.* also the legends of Arion, Stesichorus, and others.

13. **mirum quod foret omnibus**: *that all might marvel;* a relative clause of purpose.

14. **nidum Acherontiae**: so called because it nestled high up among the rocks on a spur of Mt. Vultur; *cf.* Macaulay, *Horatius at the Bridge*, 22 ff.:—

From many a lonely hamlet,
Which, hid by beech and pine,
Like an eagle's nest, hangs on the crest
Of purple Apennine.

15. **Bantinos**: of Bantia, an old Oscan town.

16. **humilis Forenti**: Forentum lay in the valley south of Venusia.

17. **ut dormirem, ut premerer**: indirect questions dependent upon *mirum*, — *how I slept, how I was covered.* **atris**: probably referring to the venom of the vipers; *cf.* i. 37. 28, *atrum venenum.*

18. **sacra lauro . . . myrto**: *sacra* agrees with both nouns; the bay was sacred to Apollo, the myrtle to Bacchus and Venus; the two shrubs, therefore, suggest the spheres of poetry in which Horace was destined to excel.

19. **conlataque myrto**: for *myrtoque conlata; cf.* line 11, *fatigatumque somno.*

20. **non sine dis**: *i.e.* the gods must surely have always lent him their protection. **animosus**: *courageous, fearless.*

21. **vester, vester**: emphasis is gained by initial position and repetition (*cf.* iii. 3. 18, *Ilion, Ilion*); lit. *yours, yours, O Muses, I ascend to my lofty Sabine farm, i.e.* as the object of your care, and devoted to your service. **in arduos Sabinos**: for *Sabini*, the name of the people used to designate an estate, see ii. 18. 14, *unicis Sabinis.*

22. **tollor**: with middle force; *I mount.* **seu mihi,** *etc.*: the expression is elliptical; from the preceding context we must supply in thought some such sentiment as *vester sum semper.* **frigidum Praeneste**: Praeneste, in Latium about twenty miles east of Rome, was situated on a high elevation some 2500 feet above the level of the sea; it was a favorite resort in the summer season.

23. **Tibur supinum**: Tibur is so called because situated on a sloping hillside; *cf.* Juvenal, iii. 192, *proni Tiburis arce.*

24. **liquidae Baiae**: *serene Baiae;* the allusion is probably to the clear air of the region, which is still a noticeable climatic feature to-day; for *liquidus* in this sense, *cf.* Virg. *Georg.* iv. 59, *per aestatem liquidam.* **placuere**: *i.e.* have temporarily drawn him thither.

25. **vestris**: the emphasis of line 21 is continued. **amicum**: the adjective has causal force; the poet's devotion to the springs of the Muses and to the dancing bands of nymphs and satyrs that frequent them, is given as the cause of the protection vouchsafed him on land and sea.

26. Philippis versa acies: Horace had fought under Brutus against Octavian in the Battle of Philippi, 42 B.C.; see Introd. § 3; *Odes*, ii. 7. 9, *tecum Philippos et celerem fugam sensi; Philippis* is ablative of separation with *versa*. In ii. 7, Horace with the poet's license attributes his rescue to the interposition of Mercury.

27. devota arbor: see ii. 13, *Ille et nefasto te posuit die, etc.* In ii. 17. 28, the poet's rescue is attributed to Faunus; in iii. 8 to Bacchus; here to the Muses.

28. nec Sicula Palinurus unda: Palinurus was a promontory on the western coast of Lucania, off which Horace seems at some time narrowly to have escaped death by drowning. The name was derived from that of Aeneas's pilot, who is said to have been drowned off this headland; see Virg. *Aen.* v. 836 ff.

29. utcumque: *whenever;* as in ii. 17. 11, *utcumque praecedes.*

30. insanientem Bosphorum: *cf.* ii. 13. 14, *navita Bosphorum Poenus perhorrescit.*

32. litoris Assyrii: *of the Syrian strand; Assyrius* for *Syrius* is not infrequent in the poets; *cf.* ii. 11. 16.

33. Britannos hospitibus feros: Tacitus *Ann.* xiv. 30, tells us that the Britons were wont to sacrifice their captives to the gods.

34. laetum . . . Concanum: the Concani were a Spanish tribe said to drink the blood of horses.

35. Gelonos: a Scythian tribe mentioned also in ii. 9. 23; 20. 19.

36. Scythicum amnem: the Tanais, the modern Don.

37. vos: emphatic, like *vester*, above, in line 20, and *vestris* in line 25. **altum**: *noble, august.*

38. fessas cohortes addidit oppidis: after Actium, Augustus gave allotments of land to some 120,000 veteran soldiers; later, other soldiers (300,000 in all) received similar allotments.

39. finire quaerentem: the infinitive with *quaero* is poetic and (in prose) post-Augustan; *cf.* i. 37. 22, *perire quaerens.* **labores**: *viz.* the efforts by dint of which he restored order to the Roman state.

40. Pierio recreatis antro: Augustus was himself sincerely and profoundly interested in literature, and even made some attempts at verse; *Pierio antro* is simply figurative for cultivated retirement.

41. lene consilium = *moderationem et clementiam* (Orelli), qualities for which Octavian was conspicuous after his defeat of Antony; note that *consilium* is here trisyllabic, the second *i* becoming consonantal; *cf.* iii. 6. 6, *principium.* **et dato** (*sc. consilio*) **gaudetis**: *i.e.* and give it gladly, because it is heeded.

42. ut: *how.*

43. Titanas immanemque turbam: with the poet's license, Horace here and below represents as contemporaneous at least four different assaults made upon Jupiter and the Olympian gods: (1) the attack of the Titans; (2) the attack of the giants; (3) the attack of the two brothers, Otus and Ephialtes (the Aloïdae); (4) the attack of Typhōeus. The giants, the Aloïdae, and Typhōeus, therefore, are all embraced under *immanem turbam.*

44. fulmine caduco: the epithet *caducus* occurs with *fulmen* only here.

45. qui temperat: *viz.* Jupiter; the antecedent of *qui* is the subject of *sustulerit.* **terram inertem**: *the lifeless earth; cf.* i. 34. 9, *bruta tellus.*

46. regna tristia: the lower world.

50. fidens iuventus: *insolent crew; fidens* (as often *confidens*) is here used *in malam partem.* **horrida bracchiis**: an allusion to the hundred hands of the Uranids: Aegaeon, Gyas, and Cotta. They were properly distinct from the giants, though often, as here, confounded with them.

51. fratres: Otus and Ephialtes, sons of Alōeus; in their impious assault upon heaven they piled Mt. Ossa upon Olympus, and Pelion upon Ossa, but were struck down by the bolts of Jupiter.

53. Typhōeus: a hundred-headed fire-breathing monster, subdued by the bolts of Jove. The name is kindred with τυφώς, 'whirlwind.' **Mimas, Porphyrion, Rhoetus, Enceladus**: various giants.

55. evolsis truncis: ablative of means with *iaculator*, which here takes the same construction as *iaculari; cf.* i. 2. 3, *dextera iaculatus.*

57. sonantem: *i.e.* with the missiles hurled against it. **Palladis**: as the goddess of wisdom, Pallas is significantly contrasted with the giants, whose only weapon is brute force. **aegida**: see on i. 15. 11.

58. possent: deliberative subjunctive. **hinc, hinc**: *on this side, on that.* **avidus**: merely as the god of fire.

60. positurus = *depositurus;* so i. 3. 40, *ponere fulmina.*

61. rore = *aqua.* **Castaliae**: a sacred spring on Mt. Parnassus, near Delphi. **lavit**: in the *Odes*, Horace prefers the forms of the third conjugation, which are mainly archaic.

62. Lyciae: an important seat of the Apollo cult.

63. natalem silvam: *viz.* on Mt. Cynthus, in the island of Delos.

64. Patareus: a designation of the god derived from Patara, a town of Lycia, celebrated for its shrine and oracle of Apollo. Concerning the new importance lent to the worship of Apollo by Augustus, see the note on i. 2. 32.

65 f. The central thought of the ode is contained in this strophe: Brute force comes to naught, but might wisely controlled is blessed of the gods.

69. testis mearum centimanus Gyas, *etc.*: a pompous prosaic passage, unworthy of Horace; hence some editors reject the entire strophe (lines 69–72). On *Gyas*, see ii. 17. 14.

71. temptator Orion: Orion, having attempted to violate Diana, was slain by the arrows of the enraged goddess; *temptator* is a word newly coined by Horace.

72. virginea = *virginis, viz. Dianae.*

73. iniecta monstris Terra: according to the legend, the giants were buried under various volcanic mountains.

74. partus: poetic plural. **luridum**: here, *pale.*

75. nec peredit, nec reliquit: *i.e.* the fire *has* not as yet eaten through; and the vulture *has* not as yet once left; the perfect is more effective than the present would have been.

77. incontinentis Tityi: for his attempted rape of Latona, he was consigned to Tartarus; *cf.* ii. 14. 8.

78. ales: the vulture that gnawed continually at his liver. **nequitiae**: abstract for the concrete; = *libidinoso.*

79. amatorem Pirithoum: Pirithous, king of the Lapithae, had endeavored to steal Proserpina from Hades and bring her to the upper world; foiled in this purpose, he was put in chains by Pluto.

The conclusion is almost irresistible that under the allusion to the giants and other reckless monsters Horace intends to suggest Antony and his recent alliance with Cleopatra against the Roman state, while on the other hand Jupiter, Pallas, and the Olympian gods are meant to be typical of Augustus.

ODE V.

1. caelo: to be taken grammatically with *regnare*, not with *tonantem.* As shown by its position, the word is emphatic, being strongly contrasted with *praesens*, *i.e.* 'we believe Jove to be lord *in the sky*, but Augustus shall be held to be a god *on earth.*' **tonantem**: with causal force, *because of his thunders.* **credidimus** : *i.e.* have long believed in the past and believe now.

3. **Augustus** : at the time this ode was written, the title Augustus had been but just conferred. Horace's use of the new designation was intended to be complimentary. **adiectis Britannis**, *etc.*: with causal force, balancing *tonantem* in line 1; Horace anticipates the subjugation of the Britons and Parthians as something already accomplished. The project of invading Britain, though often mooted during Augustus's reign, was not carried out. For *gravibus Persis*, *cf.* i. 2. 22.

5. **milesne Crassi**, *etc.*: the mention of the Parthians suggests the various reverses to the Roman arms experienced in fighting that people, and so serves as a transition to the real theme of the ode, — the importance of courage in the Roman soldiery. The reference in the two succeeding stanzas is to the disgraceful defeat of Crassus by the Parthians at the Battle of Carrhae in 53 B.C. In this engagement the Roman troops had tamely surrendered, and many of them were said subsequently to have taken service under Parthian leaders and even to have wedded Parthian women. *Miles* is here used collectively. **coniuge barbara**: ablative of association with *maritus*, 'wedded,' which here follows the analogy of the verb *marito*; *cf.* Ovid, *Heroides*, 4. 134, *fratre marita soror*. See B. *L. L.* § 337.

6. **turpis**: with adverbial force. **maritus** : in predicate relation to *miles*. **hostium socerorum** : *hostile fathers-in-law;* Smith suggests translating : *in the service of the foe whose daughter he has wedded;* for *hostium* with the force of an adjective, *cf.* i. 1. 1, *atavis regibus*, 'royal ancestors.'

7. **pro**: the interjection. **curia** : the Senate House ; here mentioned as symbolic of Roman power and dominion.

8. **consenuit** : the disaster of Carrhae had occurred nearly thirty years before the time of this ode.

9. **rege Medo, Marsus et Apulus** : *Medo*, as frequently in Horace, is used for *Partho;* the Marsians and Apulians were the flower of the Roman soldiery. By the juxtaposition of the words, *Medo Marsus et Apulus*, Horace aims to emphasize the disgraceful conduct of the Roman legions. The effect is further heightened by the use of *rege*, always a hated name to the free Roman.

10. **anciliorum**: the sacred shields kept in the custody of the Salii. One was said to have fallen from heaven in the reign of Numa. To protect this from theft, Numa is said to have ordered eleven

others to be made after the pattern of the original. **nominis**: *viz. Romanus.* **togae**: the distinctive badge of Roman citizenship; *cf.* Virg. *Aen.* i. 282, *gentemque togatam.* With the whole passage, *cf.* Florus, iv. ii. 3, *Antonius, patriae, nominis, togae, fascium oblitus.*

12. Iove: *i.e.* the temple of Jupiter (Juno and Minerva) on the Capitol, the most important of all Roman temples, and typical of Rome's greatness.

13. hoc: *i.e.* the decay of martial courage as exemplified by the troops of Crassus. **Reguli**: hero of the First Punic War. The date of his capture was put in 255 B.C., that of his embassy in 251.

14. condicionibus, exemplo: *from the terms, and from a precedent.* The *condiciones* were that the Romans who had surrendered should be ransomed from the Carthaginians. The words are in the dative with *dissentientis*, by a poetical construction. Introd. § 36. *c.*

15. trahenti: *entailing.*

16. veniens in aevom: *for future ages.*

17. perirĕt: the original quantity of the final vowel is here retained. It was regularly short in Horace's day. **immiserabilis**: *unpitied;* used predicatively.

18. signa: *sc. nostra.* **ego**: emphatic, — '*with my own eyes.*

19. adfixa: *i.e.* suspended upon the walls.

21. vidi ego: emphatic chiastic repetition of the preceding *ego vidi.* **civium**: special stress rests upon this word; the picture of a *civis Romanus* with his arms pinioned behind his back was to the true Roman the climax of humiliation.

22. libero: grammatically with *tergo*, but logically with *civium*, — 'the arms of free citizens pinioned behind their backs.'

23. portas: *sc. Carthaginis.* **non clausas**: by litotes for *apertas*, — *wide open*, in token of confident security.

24. Marte: by metonymy for *bello.* **coli**: *i.e.* again in a state of tillage. **populata**: here used as the passive of the rare *populo*; ordinarily the verb is deponent (*populor*).

25. auro: there is scorn in the word; Regulus revolts at the thought of ransoming men who had forfeited all claims to the name of Roman. **scilicet**: in bitter irony; to be taken closely with *acrior*, which is used predicatively.

26. flagitio additis damnum: *to disgrace you are adding loss.* Regulus means that the proposed ransom would be thrown away, and gives his reasons.

27. amissos colores: *viz.* its pure white.

28. refert: *regains.*

30. curat reponi deterioribus: *cares not to be restored to degenerate (hearts)*; *i.e.* would not, even if it could.

31. si pugnat, . . . erit, . . . proteret: a stronger form of expression for *nisi pugnat . . . non erit . . . non proteret.* The deer of course does not fight, when freed from the toils.

33. perfidis se credidit hostibus: there is a grim sarcasm in the combination *perfidis credidit; se credere*, though not elsewhere found, suggests putting oneself with trustful confidence in the hands of some one else. To do this to a faithless foe, such as the Carthaginians were traditionally regarded (*cf.* the proverbial *Punica fides*), evokes the scorn of Regulus.

36. sensit timuitque: a hysteron-proteron; the fearing was prior to feeling the thongs and was the cause of it, not subsequent and the result of it.

37. hic: *i.e.* he and all who had basely surrendered. **unde vitam sumeret inscius**: lit. *ignorant whence to take life*, *i.e.* not knowing that the way to secure life was by his own right hand; *sumeret* is a dependent deliberative.

38. pacem duello miscuit: *confounded peace with war*, *i.e.* thought war was peace, and acted accordingly. For the ablative of association, *cf.* above, line 5, *coniuge maritus.* B. *L. L.* § 337. The form *duello* is archaic for *bello.* This archaic touch is especially appropriate in the mouth of Regulus.

39. probrosis altior Italiae ruinis: *the more exalted from the shame of Italia's downfall.* The logical emphasis, as indicated by the context and word-order, is upon *probrosis; ruinis* is ablative of means.

41. fertur: *sc. Regulus.*

42. ut capitis minor: *as one bereft of civil rights. Caput* is often used in the sense of one's political rights or status; on Horace's free use of the genitive with adjectives, *cf.* i. 22. 1, *integer vitae.*

44. humi: in poetry the locative is sometimes used, as here, to denote not place where, but the direction of motion.

45. donec firmaret, properaret: *till he should strengthen, etc.* **consilio numquam alias dato**: *i.e.* by advice such as had never before been given; Regulus was urging a policy that involved his own destruction.

46. auctor: lit. *as advocate*, *i.e.* by his influence.

48. egregius exsul: a fine oxymoron.

49. quae sibi tortor pararet: legend had it that Regulus returned to Carthage in accordance with the promise given his captors, and was put to death with shocking tortures. Modern historical scholars regard the story as apocryphal.

51. obstantis: *blocking his path.*

52. reditus: poetic plural. **morantem**: with conative force.

53. clientum: poetic form for *clientium.* **longa**: *long-continued, tedious.*

55. Venafranos in agros: Venafrum, in Samnium near the borders of Latium, famous for its olive-orchards. **Lacedaemonium Tarentum**: Tarentum was a Spartan colony. Both Tarentum and Venafrum were holiday resorts in Horace's time. Their charm for him may be gathered from ii. 6.

ODE VI.

1. Delicta maiorum: the reference is probably to the civil war of Marius and Sulla, 88 B.C.

2. Romane: the singular, for the plural, is more impressive; similarly Virg. *Aen.* vi. 851, *tu regere imperio populos, Romane, memento.* **donec templa refeceris**: as a result of the recent civil disturbances, the shrines of the gods had fallen into neglect. It was the policy of Augustus, here endorsed by Horace, to restore and rebuild them.

4. foeda fumo: either as the result of neglect or of actual conflagration.

5. minorem: *less than*, and so *dependent upon.* **quod**: *in that.*

6. hinc = *a deis.* **principium**: for the sententious omission of the verb, *cf.* such expressions as *hinc illae lacrumae; lupus in fabula; principium* is here trisyllabic; *cf.* iii. 4. 41, *consilium.* **huc** = *ad deos.* **exitum** = *felicem exitum*, 'happy outcome,' 'success.'

7. di neclecti: logically, *the neglect of the gods;* for the archaic form *neclecti, cf.* i. 28 (2). 10.

8. Hesperiae: poetic for *Italiae.* **luctuosae**: proleptic; Italy was in sorrow as a result of her sufferings. These are explained in the following stanzas.

9. iam bis Monaeses et Pacori manus: the Romans had in reality suffered three signal defeats at the hands of the Parthians: that of Crassus at Carrhae in 53 B.C.; that of Decidius Saxa, a lieutenant of Antony, in 40 B.C.; and that of Antony himself in 36 B.C. It is probably the last two that Horace has here in mind. Pacorus, son of King Orodes, had inflicted the first of these two defeats; Monaeses, a distinguished Parthian leader, the second.

10. contudit, renidet: the singular verb with a compound subject is the rule in Horace.

11. adiecisse: the infinitive depends upon *renidet*, lit. 'gleams,' here used in the transferred sense of *beams with joy;* hence the infinitive, after the analogy of *gaudet*.

12. torquibus exiguis: the Parthians wore golden neck-chains; these are called *exiguis*, as compared with the rich booty secured by the Parthians from the Romans.

13. paene delevit Dacus et Aethiops: this statement is somewhat exaggerated; yet, at the time of the struggle between Antony and Octavian, the Dacians had allied themselves with the former and had for a time added a new element of danger; *cf.* *Sat.* ii. 6. 53, *numquid de Dacis audisti?* *Aethiops* is here used poetically for *Aegyptii*, the subjects of Cleopatra. The fact that peoples like the Dacians and Aegyptians had furnished a real menace to Rome, is intended to suggest the lamentable condition into which the Roman state had fallen. **occupatam seditionibus**: the reference is to the strife between Antony and Octavian.

15. hic classe formidatus: the Aegyptian fleet comprised two hundred sail.

16. melior = *praestantior*.

17. culpae: *fecundus* takes the genitive after the analogy of *plenus*. **saecula**: *the times*.

18. genus = *progeniem*.

19. hoc fonte: *viz.* the decay of the home. **clades**: in the general sense of 'disaster.'

20. in patriam populumque fluxit: starting in the home, disaster has pervaded the entire country and nation.

21. motus Ionicos: Ionic dances were characterized by their wantonness.

22. matura: *prematurely;* *cf.* ii. 17. 6, *maturior*. **fingitur artibus**: *i.e.* trains herself in the arts of coquetry; *fingitur* is used as a middle; *artibus* is ablative.

23. iam nunc: *i.e.* while still young.

24. de tenero ungui: *with her whole soul;* a Latin translation of the Greek ἐξ ἁπαλῶν ὀνύχων; *cf.* the English 'to her finger-tips.'

25. mox: *viz.* when married. **iuniores adulteros**: *her young paramours; iuniores* hardly has any special comparative force.

26. inter mariti vina: the presence of women at the convivial gatherings of men was in itself a serious lapse from the practice of earlier generations. **eligit**: she does not choose an object of her affection, but surrenders herself to the first comer.

27. cui donet: not merely an indirect question, but also a deliberative subjunctive; in direct form, *cui donem?* **raptim**: *hurriedly.*

29. iussa: *at the bidding* of her paramour. **coram**: *i.e.* in the presence of all; to be joined with *iussa.* **non sine conscio marito**: *with her husband's full complicity.*

30. institor, navis magister: so Canidia, in *Epod.* 17. 20, is scornfully characterized as beloved of pedlers and sailors, *amata nautis multum et institoribus.*

32. dedecorum: *i.e.* disgraceful pleasures. **pretiosus**: *i.e.* paying liberally for the favors he receives.

Kiessling calls attention to the studied antitheses of the foregoing picture. The woman does not choose the objects of her favors (*eligit*), but comes at call (*iussa*) of men of the lowest class, pedlers and sailors; nor are her favors gifts (*donet*), but she sells them for a price (*emptor*); she does not act stealthily (*impermissa*), but with the full knowledge and collusion of her husband (*conscio marito*); not hurriedly (*raptim*), but rising deliberately for the purpose (*surgit*); not in the dark (*luminibus remotis*), but openly in the eyes of all (*coram*).

33. non his parentibus: the emphasis of the sentence rests upon these words, — *not such the parents of whom were born the men that dyed the sea with Punic blood.*

34. infecit . . . Punico: the reference is to the First Punic War, more particularly to Duilius's victory at Mylae, 260 B.C.

35. Pyrrhum: defeated by M'. Curius in 275 B.C. **cecīdit**: *overthrew;* here used as the causative of *cado.*

36. Antiochum, Hannibalem: the former, often called Antiochus the Great (*cf. ingentem*), was defeated at Magnesia in 190 B.C.; Hannibal was overthrown at Zama in 202 B.C.

37. rusticorum mascula militum proles: note the interlocked order (synchysis). **mascula**: as contrasted with the effeminacy of the later Romans.

38. Sabellis = *Sabinis;* the stern simplicity of the Sabines is often alluded to in Latin literature. **docta** = *assueta.*

40. recisos fustis: firewood.

41. ubi mutaret: subjunctive of iterative action; the indicative is the regular mood for denoting iterative action in Ciceronian prose; but the subjunctive begins to be found in the Augustan poets, and becomes common in Livy and post-Augustan writers.

42. mutaret umbras: *shifted the shadows;* strictly this might apply to any period of the day, but the reference is evidently to evening.

43. amicum: *welcome, sc. bobus.*

44. agens = *adducens.*

46. peior avis: compendiary comparison for *aetate avorum peior.*

47. nequiores: *sc. quam parentes.* **daturos** = *edituros.*

48. vitiosiorem: *sc. quam nos.* Four generations are aptly characterized in three successive lines.

ODE VII.

1. Quid fles Gygen: *why weepest thou for Gyges?* **Asterie**: the name (from ἀστήρ) suggests 'as radiant as the stars.' **candidi**: *i.e.* bringing fair weather; *cf.* i. 7. 15, *albus Notus.*

2. Favonii: the zephyrs are the harbingers of spring; *cf.* i. 4. 1, *vice veris et Favoni.*

3. Thyna = *Bithyna; cf.* i. 35. 7. **beatum**: *enriched, richly laden.*

4. fide: genitive; Julius Caesar, in his *de Analogia*, gave the preference to this form even in prose.

5. Notis actus ad Oricum: the stormy southeast winds have forced Gyges to abandon temporarily the voyage eastward and have led him to take refuge at Oricus, a harbor on the coast of Epirus.

6. insana Caprae sidera: the stormy weather brought by the rising of this constellation. The goat was a part of the same constellation as the kids (*haedi; cf.* iii. 1. 28); its evening rising occurred about October 1st. The time is therefore autumn.

9. atqui: *and yet, i.e.* despite Gyges's devotion to Asterie. **sollicitae nuntius hospitae**: *the messenger of his enamoured hostess.*

10. Chloen: the *hospita.* **tuis ignibus**: *thy lover*, lit. *thy flame; cf.* Ovid, *Amores*, iii. 9. 56, *dum tuus ignis eram.*

13. ut: *how.* **Proetum mulier perfida**, *etc.*: according to Homer (*Iliad*, vi. 155 f.), the *mulier perfida* was Antēa; according to later accounts, Sthenoboea. Proetus was her husband. Sthenoboea had fallen in love with Bellerophon, who rejected her advances, whereupon she accused him to her husband of having made improper proposals to her. Proetus, unwilling to kill Bellerophon himself, despatched him to Iobates, king of Lycia, with a letter requesting the latter to put him to death. Iobates thought to comply by sending Bellerophon to fight the dreaded Chimaera.

14. nimis casto : *i.e.* too upright for his own safety.

16. maturare : *i.e.* bring swiftly ; the infinitive with *impello* is a poetic usage.

17. paene datum Pelea, *etc.:* Hippolyte, wife of the Thessalian king Acastus, had fallen in love with Peleus. When her advances had been rejected, she brought accusations of improper conduct against Peleus, and endeavored, though without success, to compass his destruction.

20. historias movet: *suggests tales.*

21. scopulis surdior : *i.e.* more deaf to her entreaties than the cliffs to the sound of the waves. **Icari** : *Icaros*, an islet near Samos; it was ordinarily known as Icaria.

25. quamvis conspicitur, denatat: riding and swimming are often alluded to as important athletic accomplishments, *e.g.* i. 8. 6, 8 ; iii. 12. 10 f. ; for *quamvis* with the indicative, *cf.* i. 28 (1). 13, *quamvis concesserat*, and see Introd. § 41. *a.*

26. aeque: with *sciens.* **gramine Martio**: *on the grass of the Campus Martius.*

28. Tusco alveo : *i.e.* the Tiber's channel. The Tiber is often called 'the Tuscan stream' ; *cf.* i. 20. 5, *paterni fluminis ripae.* The ablative is one of 'the way by which.'

29. neque : *neque, nec*, instead of *neve*, are often used in the poets with the imperative and with the jussive and optative subjunctives ; *cf.* ii. 7. 19, *nec parce ; Epod.* 10. 9, *nec sidus amicum appareat.*

30. sub cantu : *at (the sound of) the music; cantus* may be the music either of voice or of instrument ; *cf. tibia canere.* **querulae** : *i.e.* voicing the lover's plaint.

31. vocanti: with adversative force, — *though he call thee cruel ;* the dative depends on *difficilis; cf.* iii. 10. 11, *Penelopen difficilem procis.*

32. difficilis: *unyielding.*

ODE VIII.

1. Martiis caelebs, *etc.:* the first of March was the Matronalia, or Feast of Matrons, on which married women brought sacrifice to Juno, and their husbands offered prayers for a happy continuance of their wedlock. Hence, Maecenas might naturally wonder why the bachelor Horace should be making festival on that day.

2. velint: *mean.*

3. carbo: on which to burn incense.

4. caespite vivo: *vivus* for *virens* ('green'), as in i. 19. 13; the fresh turf serves as altar.

5. docte sermones utriusque linguae: lit. *taught the lore*, *i.e.* learned in the lore of both tongues (Latin and Greek), familiar with the traditions and traditional observances of both peoples.

6. voveram: *i.e.* prior to these preparations; hence the pluperfect. **album caprum**: white offerings were sacrificed to the gods of the upper world, black ones to those of the world below.

7. Libero: Horace here by implication attributes his preservation to Bacchus, the patron god of poets; in ii. 17. 28, with a poet's license, he attributes it to Faunus. **funeratus**: elsewhere the word regularly means 'buried,' 'interred.'

8. arboris ictu: see ii. 13.

10. corticem adstrictum pice: the mouth of the wine jar was closed with a cork stopper and was sealed with pitch; *cortex*, lit. 'bark,' is here used *par excellence* for the bark of the Spanish oak (*suber*), from which cork was, and still is, prepared. **demovebit**: *de-* here, as often, means from the place where anything properly belongs.

11. fumum bibere institutae: wine jars were regularly set in an upper room, where they were exposed to the smoke from the fireplace below. The smoke was thought to favor an early 'aging' of the wine.

12. consule Tullo: there were two consuls of this name, to either of whom Horace may be here referring. The elder was consul in 66 B.C., the younger in 33. Probably the latter is meant, as in that year Horace received the gift of the Sabine farm from Maecenas. By this interpretation, the poet is made to pay a graceful compliment to Maecenas. His first Sabine vintage is to be reserved for an appropriate annual commemoration of the day.

13. sume: of course at Horace's house. **amici sospitis**: *i.e.*

in commemoration of your friend's preservation; lit. *of your friend safe.*

14. centum: hospitable exaggeration. The cyathus was one-twelfth of a pint.

15. perfer = *patere.* **in lucem**: *till daybreak.* **procul omnis esto,** *etc.*: not a command to Maecenas, but rather an assurance that there shall be no noisy guests, as often at convivial meetings.

17. mitte: *leave.* **civilis super urbe curas**: the expression is somewhat redundant, meaning only 'cares of state'; *super*, in the sense of *de*, is poetic; after Horace it appears also in prose.

18. Daci Cotisonis: Cotiso, a Dacian leader, had been in league with Antony (see note in iii. 6. 13). Crassus defeated him overwhelmingly in 29 B.C., just before the time of this ode.

19. Medus: for *Parthus*, as often. **sibi**: with *luctuosis.*

20. dissidet armis: *i.e.* is engaged in armed dissensions. The reference is to the strife between Tiridates and Phraates for the Parthian throne, lasting from 31 to 27 B.C.

21. servit: used absolutely, — *is our subject.*

22. Cantaber: the Cantabrians were defeated early in 29 B.C. by Statilius Taurus. They were not, however, completely subdued till 19 B.C.

23. Scythae: the Geloni, a Scythian tribe, were subdued in the year 29 B.C.; *cf.* ii. 9. 23. **laxo**: *unstrung.*

24. campis: the steppes of southwestern Russia.

25. neclegens: agreeing with the subject of *parce*, and so sharing the imperative force; hence equivalent to *neclegens esto*, 'be free from care'; *neclegens* here = *securus*; for the spelling *nec-*, *cf.* i. 28 (2). 10. **nequa populus laboret**: *lest the people suffer in any way;* the clause depends upon *cavere.*

26. parce cavere: a choicer form of expression in place of the ordinary *noli cavere; cf.* i. 9. 13, *fuge quaerere.* **privatus**: like *neclegens* (above, line 25), *privatus* shares the imperative force of *parce*, *i.e.* 'be for the nonce a private citizen.'

ODE IX.

1. Donec: in this sense of 'while,' 'as long as,' *donec* does not appear until the Augustan era; so also i. 9. 17.

2. quisquam: here used adjectively in the sense of *ullus.* **potior**: *i.e.* 'more favored rival.'

3. **cervici**: for *cervicibus;* in best prose the word is regularly a *plurale tantum*. **dabat** = *circumdabat*.

4. **Persarum rege**: proverbial for great wealth and power; *cf.* ii. 12. 21, *dives Achaemenes*.

5. **alia**: with *arsisti*, 'to be inflamed with passion for'; *cf.* ii. 4. 7, *arsit Atrides virgine rapta*. Similarly, *tepere* takes the ablative in i. 4. 19.

6. **erat Lydia** = *eram ego*. **post Chloen**: *i.e.* in less esteem than Chloe.

7. **multi nominis**: genitive of quality, here appended directly to a proper name, at variance with ordinary usage, in which some such word as *mulier* would have been added. **Lydia**: in opposition with the subject of *vigui*.

8. **Ilia**: the bride of Mars and mother of Romulus and Remus.

9. **me**: note the emphasis.

10. **modos** = *carmina*. **citharae**: *sciens* takes the genitive after the analogy of *peritus* and similar adjectives; so also i. 15. 24, *sciens pugnae*.

12. **animae**: *i.e.* the light of my life, my love. **superstiti**: proleptic, — *and suffer her to live*.

13. **me**: as in line 9.

14. **Thurini**: of Thurii in southern Italy.

15. **patiar mori**: the construction of the simple infinitive with *patior* is poetic. In this use *patior* often has the force, not of 'endure,' but of 'be right willing'; *cf.* i. 2. 43 (*patiens vocari Caesaris ultor*), and note.

17 f. **redit, cogit,** *etc.*: in poetry the present indicative is often used instead of the future to give greater vividness.

22. **levior cortice**: *i.e.* fickle. **cortice**: *cork;* see note on iii. 8. 10. **improbo**: *tempestuous*.

24. **vivere amem**: for this poetic use of the infinitive, *cf.* i. 2. 50, *hic ames dici pater atque princeps*.

A special feature of the exquisite art that characterizes this ode is seen in the way Lydia outbids her lover in her successive responses. Thus she caps *gratus eram* in 1, with *arsisti*, 'madly infatuated,' in 6; so in 13, *torret* is much stronger than *regit* in 9; the lover speaks of Thracian Chloe in 9, only to be met with an imposing *Thurini Calais filius Ornyti* in 14; while the *non metuam mori* of 11 is answered by the *bis patiar mori* of 15, in which the special force of *patiar* must be borne in mind.

ODE X.

1. **Tanain**: The Don, in Scythia. The word follows the Greek declension. **si biberes**: the condition is, of course, unreal, *i.e.* if thou wert a Scythian woman instead of a Roman. Drinking the waters of a stream is a common poetic periphrasis for dwelling on its bank; *cf.* ii. 20. 20, *Rhodani potor.*

2. **saevo nupta viro**: *wedded to some strict husband;* for the high standards of domestic virtue among these northern nomads, *cf.* iii. 24. 19 f. **asperas**: *cruel;* the doors are personified.

3. **porrectum**: the suppliant is conceived as lying at full length before the threshold. **obicere**: the infinitive depends upon *plorares*, a stronger *nolles*, — a bold poetic use. **incolis Aquilonibus**: *i.e.* your native blasts; Scythia is conceived as the home of the north wind.

5. **ianua**: as verb supply in thought from *remugiat* some such word as *crepet.* **quo (nemus)**: *sc. strepitu.*

6. **inter tecta**: the trees are planted in the inner courtyard of the house. **satum**: for *consitum.*

7. **ventis**: ablative of cause. **ut**: *how.*

8. **puro numine**: '*in cloudless majesty*' (Smith). **Iuppiter**: as god of the sky.

9. **pone**: for *depone*, as often both in prose and poetry; *cf.* i. 3. 40, *ponere fulmina.*

10. **ne currente retro funis eat rota**: lit. *lest the rope run back as the wheel revolves, i.e.* lest thou be suddenly checked in thy present course. The figure is evidently drawn from some familiar mechanical operation, in which a rope runs over a pulley; control is lost, and the rope moves swiftly back in the wrong direction; *retro* is best taken with *eat* only; *currente rota* is ablative absolute.

11. **non te Penelopen,** *etc.*: the negative extends not merely to the words *te Penelopen*, but also to *Tyrrhenus genuit parens, i.e.* 'thou art no Penelope, nor did a Tuscan father beget thee.' Penelope is often cited as a type of wifely constancy; *Tyrrhenus* is equivalent to *clarus*, the Tuscans being noted for their wealth and luxury; *Penelopen* is a predicate accusative. **difficilem procis**: for *difficilis*, 'unyielding,' with the dative, *cf.* iii. 7. 31, *vocanti difficilis.*

13. **quamvis curvat**: for *quamvis* with the indicative, *cf.* i. 28. (1) 13; Introd. § 41. *a.*

14. **tinctus viola**: the reference is to the yellow, not the purple, violet.

15. nec vir Pieria paelice saucius : *nor the fact that thy husband is smitten with love for a Thessalian paramour;* he tries to influence Lyce by urging her husband's infidelity. *Pieria*, lit. *Pierian* (Mt. Pieros in Thessaly), is here used for *Thessala.*

16. curvat : lit. *bends thee*, *i.e.* to pity.

19. hoc latus : *hoc* = *meum ; latus* = *corpus*, as in ii. 7. 18; the lover is pictured as lying at Lyce's threshhold. **aquae caelestis** : *the rain;* this reference to the rain is inconsistent with *puro numine*, line 8. Possibly the lover does not mean that it is raining now, but that he has often endured the rain before, while vainly waiting for admission.

ODE XI.

1. nam : introducing the reason for the invocation. **te docilis magistro** : equivalent to *a te magistro doctus; te magistro* is ablative absolute; the emphasis rests on *te.*

2. movit Amphion lapides : the walls of Thebes are said to have risen to the music of Amphion's lyre. **canendo** : of a musical instrument, as often.

3. testudo : Mercury was fabled to have attached strings to a tortoise-shell, thus inventing the lyre; *cf.* i. 10. 6, *curvae lyrae parentem.* **resonare** : for the infinitive, *cf.* i. 10. 7, *callidus condere*, and see Introd. § 41. *c.*

4. nervis : ablative.

5. nec olim : *i.e.* before the chords were strung to the shell by Mercury. **loquax** : here equivalent to *canora*, 'tuneful.' **grata** : to gods or men.

6. templis : the music of the lyre was a frequent accompaniment of religious ritual.

7. quibus adplicet, *etc.* : *to which Lyde shall lend her ears;* a 'jussive characterizing clause'; its jussive nature is seen in the fact that it is equivalent to an independent 'and let Lyde lend'; its characterizing force is seen in the fact that the clause as a whole is an adjective modifier of *modos.* This 'jussive characterizing clause' is not to be confounded with the 'clause of characteristic,' which is another variety of characterizing clause, being developed from the potential. **obstinatas** : *i.e.* stubborn as yet.

10. exsultim : found only here.

11. adhuc protervo cruda marito : *not ready as yet for an eager mate.*

13. tu: *sc. lyra.* **tigris, silvas ducere,** *etc.*: *viz.* in the hands of Orpheus; *cf.* i. 12. 7. **comites**: in predicate relation to both *tigris* and *silvas*; for the position of *-que*, *cf.* i. 30. 6, *Gratiae properentque Nymphae*, for *Gratiae Nymphaeque properent*; so often in the poets.

15. cessit ianitor: Cerberus permitted Orpheus to bring back Eurydice to the upper world. **tibi blandienti**: *i.e.* to thy persuasive strains.

17. furiale: *i.e.* his head is conceived as twined about with serpents, like those of the Furies.

19. mānet: from *mano.*

20. ore trilingui: the description is inaccurate, as in ii. 19. 31; Cerberus was conceived as having three heads, not one head and three tongues.

21. Ixīon: Ixīon, king of the Lapithae, attempted to ravish Juno, and was punished in Tartarus by being fastened to a revolving wheel. **Tityos**: for his crime and punishment, see note on ii. 14. 8. **voltu risit invito**: *smiled through their anguish*; for the singular verb with compound subject, see Introd. § 39.

22. urna: for *urnae* (each maiden had one), the vessels of the Danaids, into which they were condemned perpetually to pour water.

23. puellas = *filias.*

25 f. The reference to the Danaids serves as an excuse for the following digression. **audiat**: *i.e.* let her hear and take timely warning. **notas**: this limits *scelus* as well as *poenas*; *cf.* i. 31. 6, *non aurum aut ebur Indicum.*

26. virginum: the Danaids. **inane lymphae**: *empty of water*; *inane* takes the case of its opposite *plenus*, — a poetic construction; Introd. § 37. *a.*

27. fundo: ablative of the 'way by which.' **pereuntis**: here in the literal sense of 'going through,' 'flowing through.'

28. seraque fata quae manent: *i.e.* though postponed, they are sure. **sub Orco.** Orcus is here the person, not the place.

30. impiae, impiae: note the emphatic repetition. **quid potuere maius**: *what greater crime could they* (*conceive*)!

31. sponsos: the fifty sons of Aegyptus, to whom the fifty Danaids were wedded. **potuere**: *they had the heart.* **duro ferro**: *with the ruthless steel.*

33. una: *one only, viz.* Hypermnestra. **face nuptiali**: by metonymy for *nuptiis*; torches were carried in the bridal procession.

34. **periurum**: Danaus had pretended to offer his daughters in good faith to the sons of Aegyptus.

35. **splendide mendax**: a striking oxymoron. **virgo**: in apposition with *una*.

37. **iuveni marito**: *cf.* i. 1. 1, *atavis regibus.*

38. **longus somnus**: *sc. mortis.* **unde non times**: *i.e.* from my father or sisters; as antecedent of *unde* we may supply in thought *ab eis.*

40. **falle**: *elude, escape.*

42. **lacerant**: Hypermnestra conceives the murders to be now in progress.

45. **me**: emphatic, — 'as for me (I care not what befalls); let my father,' *etc.*

47. **vel**: intensive, — *even.* **Numidarum agros**: the country of savage beasts and poisonous serpents.

48. **classe**: *by ship, by sea;* we expect *nave.*

49. **pedes quo te rapiunt et aurae**: *i.e.* by land and sea.

51. **nostri memorem**: *commemorative of me.* **sepulcro**: probably a cenotaph.

52. **querellam**: *i.e.* an epitaph.

ODE XII.

1. **Miserarum**: strong emphasis rests upon this word, — 'hapless the maids who may not . . . or (if they do) must live half dead with terror' (*exanimari*), *etc.* **dare ludum** = *indulgere; cf.* the English 'give play.'

2. **lavere** = *eluere*, 'drown.'

3. **patruae**: for the traditionally cruel uncle, *cf. Sat.* ii. 3. 88, *ne sis patruus mihi.*

4. **tibi**: Neobule addresses herself. **Cythereae puer ales**: Cupid. **telas**: poetic plural.

5. **operosae Minervae**: Minerva was the goddess of weaving, spinning, *etc.;* the epithet *operosus* is transferred from the craftswomen to Minerva herself.

6. **Liparaei**: *from Lipara*, an island north of Sicily.

7. **simul** = *simul ac*, as often in the poets. **lavit**: as subject understand *Hebrus.* For swimming and riding as typical forms of exercise among Roman youth, *cf.* iii. 7. 25 f.

8. **Bellerophonte**: the rider of Pegasus; note the -$\bar{e}$; Horace fol-

lows the first declension. The nominative *Bellerophon*, in fact, is unknown in Latin poetry.

9. segni: with *pugno* as well as with *pede*.

10. agitato: *sc. a canibus.*

11. grege: *sc. cervorum.* **iaculari**: for the infinitive with *catus*, see Introd. § 41. *c.* and *cf.* iii. 11. 3, *resonare callida.*

12. excipere: *sc. venabulo;* the infinitive as in 11; *cf.* i. 15. 18, *celerem sequi.*

ODE XIII.

1. Bandusiae: probably some fountain near Venusia, Horace's birthplace. A Greek town, Πανδοσιά, was not far distant. The genitive is apparently appositional; *cf.* ii. 6. 10, *Galaesi flumen.* **splendidior vitro**: *splendidus* means 'shining,' not 'transparent'; Horace therefore is probably thinking of the iridescent Etruscan glass.

2. non sine = *cum.* **floribus**: at the festival of the Fontanalia it was customary to deck the springs with garlands.

3. haedo: *i.e.* the sacrifice of a kid.

4. cui: dative of reference, — *whose brow just budding, etc.*

5. proelia: *viz.* with his rivals. **destinat**: *foretoken.*

6. tibi: ethical dative.

8. suboles gregis: the *haedus* of line 3.

9. hora: *season.*

10. nescit = *non potest.* **frigus**: the cool shade of the trees about the spring.

13. nobilium fontium: predicate 'genitive of the whole.' **tu quoque**: *i.e.* Bandusia shall rank with Arethūsa and Hippocrēne.

14. me dicente: ablative absolute with causal force; *dico* here, as often, means 'to sing,' 'to celebrate.'

15. Note the fine suiting of sound to sense in the repetition of *l* in *loquaces, lymphae, desiliunt.*

ODE XIV.

1. Herculis ritu: *i.e.* just as Hercules had undergone toil and danger in the performance of his labors, one of which, the securing of Geryon's cattle, had taken him to Spain, the scene of Augustus's recent exploits. **modo**: *i.e.* in the recent past. Augustus had gone to Spain in 27 B.C. (nearly three years before the time of this ode) to direct in person the military operations against certain Spanish tribes.

2. morte venalem: Augustus had actually been ill in Spain, and even a rumor of his death had reached the city. **laurum** = *victoriam.*

3. Caesar: Augustus.

4. victor: he had not permanently subjugated the Spanish peninsula; this was not effected until 19 B.C.

5. unico: lit. *unique*, *unexampled*, and so, *peerless*. **mulier**: here for *uxor*, *viz.* Livia.

6. iustis divis: the justice of the gods is seen in their vouchsafing Augustus's safe return.

7. soror: Octavia. **decorae**: here for *decoratae*.

8. supplice vitta: fillets were bound about the heads of persons engaging in any formal religious ceremonial. The present ceremonial is one of thanksgiving; hence, *with the fillet of thanksgiving.*

9. nuper: *viz.* by the successes of the Spanish campaign.

10. sospitum = *conservatorum.*

11. maleominatis parcite verbis. *refrain from ill-omened words; cf.* iii. 1. 2, *favete linguis.*

13. hic dies: the day of Augustus's return. **vere**: with *festus.*

14. tumultum: used especially of civil disturbances.

15. mori: the infinitive with *metuam* in this sense is unusual; the regular construction would have been *ne moriar*; such expressions as iii. 11. 10, *metuit tangi*, are not like the present passage; in them, *metuo* is a stronger *nolo*. **tenente Caesare**: for the sentiment, *cf.* iv. 15. 17, *custode rerum Caesare non furor civilis exiget otium.*

18. Marsi duelli: the Social War of 91–89 B.C. For the form *duelli* (= *belli*), *cf.* iii. 5. 38.

19. Spartacum: leader of the slave insurrection of 73–71 B.C. His followers naturally plundered whatever they could lay hands upon. **siqua**: *if anywhere.* **vagantem**: Spartacus's roving bands laid waste large parts of Italy.

20. fallere: *escape.* **testa** = *cadus.*

21. argutae Neaerae: *clear-voiced Neaera.* **properet**: substantive clause developed from the jussive, used as object of *dic*; *ut* is absent, as frequently in clauses of this type.

22. murreum: probably *chestnut.*

23. ianitorem: *viz.* of Neaera's house.

24. abito: *i.e.* do not wait.

25. animos: *my high spirit*; poetic plural.

26. litium et rixae cupidos: *i.e.* formerly and naturally. In

Epp. i. 20. 25, Horace speaks of himself as naturally hot tempered, —*irasci celerem.*

27. non ego hoc ferrem: the imperfect for the pluperfect, *tulissem.*

28. consule Planco: Munatius Plancus (see i. 7) was consul in 42 B.C., the year of Philippi, when Horace was fighting with Brutus against Octavian; Introd. § 3. In admitting his hot-headedness at that period, Horace probably designs indirectly to confess his error in opposing Octavian.

ODE XV.

1. pauperis Ibyci: the poverty of the husband suggests that her help is needed at home.

2. nequitiae = *libidini.* **fige**: stronger than *pone;* it implies fixing the end irrevocably.

3. famosis: *disreputable.* **laboribus**: *i.e.* arts of coquetry; the word suggests that the woman's conduct involves an effort, and is not spontaneous.

4. maturo: *i.e.* death would not be premature; the creature is *old* enough already. **propior**: not really comparative; merely an intensive positive.

5. inter . . . virgines: for the separation, *cf.* iii. 27. 51, *inter errem leones.*

6. nebulam spargere: *i.e.* by thy presence.

7. siquid: *sc. decet.* **Pholoën**: daughter of Chloris.

8. rectius: *more fittingly.*

10. pulso tympano: the beating of tambourines was a regular accompaniment of the orgiastic worship of Bacchus.

11. cogit: *i.e.* with Pholoë the passion is real; her feelings force her to engage in these mad frolics; with her mother such conduct is a mere affectation.

12. similem capreae: for *ut capream; cf.* i. 23. 1.

13. lanae: *i.e.* wool working, — spinning, weaving, and the like. **nobilem Luceriam**: Luceria was an Apulian town famous for the superior fleeces of its sheep.

16. vetulam: in apposition with *te*, and giving the reason why wine and roses no longer befit Chloris. The separation of the word from *te* and its reservation till the final line of the stanza produce a climax.

ODE XVI.

1. Danaën: an oracle had declared to Acrisius that his daughter would bear a son who should kill his grandfather. To prevent the fulfilment of this prophecy, Acrisius immured Danaë in a brazen tower.

2. robustae: *of oak* (*robur*).

3. tristes: *strict*. **munierant**: more vivid than *muniissent*; *cf.* ii. 17. 28, *sustulerat nisi levasset*, with note.

4. adulteris: *adventurers*.

7. risissent: *i.e.* scorned, and so thwarted, his precautions; "Love laughs at locksmiths." **fore**: depending upon the idea of thinking or knowing implied in the context,—*for they* (*Venus and Jupiter*) *knew*.

8. converso in pretium: according to the myth, Jupiter visited Danaë in a shower of gold. Horace's use of *pretium* suggests that he interpreted the shower of gold as pointing to the bribery of Danaë's guards. **deo**: dative.

9. aurum: *converso in pretium*, in line 8, naturally suggests some general reflections upon the power of gold. **satellites**: probably *courtiers*.

10. perrumpere: for the poetic use of the infinitive with *amo*, *cf.* ii. 3. 10, *pinus albaque populus umbram consociare amant.* **saxa**: the walls of fortresses; *cf.* the story of Tarpeia.

11. auguris Argivi domus: the *augur Argivus* is Amphiarāus; under promise of a golden necklace, his wife Eriphȳle was persuaded by Polynīces to induce her husband to share in the expedition of the Seven against Thebes, where in the midst of the fighting he was swallowed up in a chasm of the earth that suddenly opened. As a punishment for Eriphyle's cupidity, her son Alcmaeon slew his mother, for which deed he was driven mad by the Furies. The whole household (*domus*) of Amphiaraus, therefore, was ruined by Eriphyle's covetousness (*ob lucrum*); *demersa*, though made by Horace to apply to the entire *domus*, seems suggested primarily by the special fate of Amphiaraus himself; for *domus* in the sense of 'household,' 'family,' *cf.* i. 6. 8, *saevam Pelopis domum*.

13. diffidit urbium portas vir Macedo: the allusion is to Philip of Macedon; among the cities that yielded to his bribery were Olynthus, Potidaea, Amphipolis. Philip was wont to say that any fortress could be taken into which an ass laden with gold could be led. (Cic. *ad Att.* i. 16. 12); *vir Macedo* is meant to convey contempt.

14. aemulos reges: *e.g.* Pausanias, Arrhybas.

15. muneribus; **munera**: note the emphasis of the asyndetic repetition of the same word; under *muneribus* we must understand bribes paid to the generals of Philip's rivals. **navium duces**: *admirals.*

16. saevos = *timendos:* the word is in adversative relation to *munera inlaqueant,* — despite the terror they inspire, they succumb to gold.

17. crescentem: in strongly adversative relation to *sequitur,* — 'your hoard may grow; yet care follows and constant greed for more.'

18. maiorum: neuter, in the sense of *maiorum opum.* **iure perhorrui**: explicative asyndeton, — *and so I have with reason shrunk from, etc.*

19. conspicuom: in predicate relation to *verticem*, and with proleptic force. **tollere**: for the poetic use of the infinitive with *perhorrui, cf.* ii. 2. 7, *pinna metuente solvi*, and see Introd. § 41 *e.*

20. Maecenas, equitum decus: Horace seems to refer to Maecenas's steadfast preference for remaining in the equestrian order, instead of aspiring to senatorial honors; the poet also intimates that his own restraint receives sanction from Maecenas's modesty.

21. For the sentiment, *cf.* ii. 2. 9, *latius regnes avidum domando spiritum quam si Libyam remotis Gadibus iungas.*

22. plura: the correlative *tanto* is lacking, but is easily supplied in thought. **feret** = *accipiet.*

23. castra, transfuga, partis: all military terms.

24. partis: *the party, the side.* **gestio**: a strong word, — *am eager, am anxious.*

25. contemptae rei: *i.e.* of the wealth that I scorn.

26. quidquid arāt Apulus: *i.e.* the produce of all the broad acres of Apulia; for the archaic reminiscence in *arāt, cf.* ii. 6. 14, *ridēt.*

28. inops: *needy*, as I should really be in such case.

29. purae rivos aquae: the Digentia, which flowed through Horace's Sabine farm.

31. fulgentem imperio, *etc.:* lit. (*my brook and woods and trusty patch of ground*) *escape him shining with* (= endowed with) *the imperium over fertile Africa as being happier* (bringing more joy) *than his allotment; i.e.* the governor of rich Africa fails to see that my humble possessions bring more joy than his allotment. *Africae* limits *imperio*, but is to be understood also with *sorte; imperio* is to be taken in its technical sense of the *imperium*, with which the provincial governors (proconsuls, praetors) were formally invested; *sorte* is also used in its technical meaning, — not 'lot' in general, but the regular assignment by lot of the provincial administrations; *beatior* stands in predicate relation to the subjects of *fallit; fallit* in this sense is a Grecism corresponding to a λανθάνει ὀλβιωτέρα οὖσα. The Latin necessarily dispenses with the present participle of *esse*. For the singular verb with compound subject, see Introd. § 39.

33. Calabrae apes: for the high repute of the Calabrian honey, *cf.* ii. 6. 14.

34. Laestrygonia amphora: the reference is to Formian wine (for which see note on i. 20. 11). Formiae was identified with the Homeric Laestrygonia. **Bacchus** = *vinum*.

35. languescit = *mitescit*, 'is mellowing,' *i.e.* in the store-room (*apotheca*). **pinguia**: *thick, heavy*. **Gallicis pascuis**: *i.e.* in the pastures of cisalpine Gaul, particularly along the Po.

38. tu: Maecenas.

39. contracto porrigam: *i.e.* I *lengthen* my purse by *shortening* my desires. The antithesis between *contracto* and *porrigam* is artistically heightened by putting one word at the beginning, the other at the end, of the clause; a similar antithesis is found in the English: "The nation that shortens its sword lengthens its boundaries."

41. Mygdoniis campis: *i.e.* Phrygia; see ii. 12. 22; *campis* is probably ablative of association with *continuem*, lit. 'make continuous with'. Introd. § 38. *a*; B. *App.* § 337. **regnum Alyattei**: Lydia; Alyattes was the father of Croesus. For the form of the genitive, *cf.* i. 6. 7, *Ulixei; Epod.* 17. 14, *Achillei*. **multa petentibus desunt multa**: note the rhetorical effect of the chiasmus. The clause as a whole stands in adversative relation to what precedes, — *yet they who seek much, etc.*

43. bene est: *sc. illi*.

44. quod satis est: *i.e.* just enough and nothing more; *cf.* iii. 1. 25, *desiderantem quod satis est*.

ODE XVII.

1. Aeli: Aelius Lamia; see i. 26. **vetusto nobilis ab Lamo**: *illustrious scion of ancient Lamus;* this is a mock compliment, for Lamus was the cannibal king of the Laestrygonians. The Romans of Horace's day were fond of referring their ancestry to the famous worthies of the heroic age; thus Virg. *Aen.* v. 117 f. derives the Memmii from Mnestheus, the Sergii from Sergestus. Horace humorously satirizes this tendency, at the expense of his friend.

2. **priores**: *i.e.* the original, the early Lamiae. **hinc**: *viz. ab Lamo.*

4. **per memores fastos**: *i.e.* through all recorded history; note the gentle banter of this grandiloquence; the *fasti* are here personified, and characterized as themselves endowed with memory.

5. **auctore ab illo**: *from him as founder* (*of your house*); for this meaning of *auctor*, *cf.* i. 2. 36.

7. **princeps** = *primus.* **innantem Maricae litòribus Lirim**: lit. *the Liris flooding Marica's shores*, *i.e.* the shores along the mouth of the Liris, near Minturnae. Marica was a nymph, the consort of Faunus, and mother of Latinus, according to Virgil, *Aen.* vii. 47. She had a sacred grove near the mouth of the Liris, which is characterized as *innatans*, because at its mouth it spread out over wide marshes. For the Liris, see note on i. 31. 7.

9. **late**: *tyrannus* is virtually equivalent to *regens;* hence the adverbial modifier; *cf.* Virg. *Aen.* i. 21, *populum late regem.* **nemus**: *i.e.* the ground beneath the trees.

11. **demissa ab Euro**: *cf. Epodes*, 16. 54.

12. **aquae**: *of rain.*

13. **annosa**: the longevity of the crow was proverbial; Hesiod put its age at nine generations of men. **dum potes**: *i.e.* before the storm.

14. **Genium**: the presiding divinity of each man, conceived of as born and dying with him.

15. **curabis**: with imperative force. **bimenstri**: the young pigs were withdrawn from the mother at two months, and were then suitable for sacrificial purposes.

16. **operum**: *from their tasks;* for this use of the genitive (a Grecism), *cf.* ii. 13. 38, *laborum decipitur;* ii. 9. 17, *desine querellarum.*

ODE XVIII.

1. **Faune**: the god of shepherds and farmers. **Nympharum amator**: Faunus, originally an indigenous Italic divinity, ultimately took on in the popular mind many of the attributes of the Greek Pan; thus he is here conceived as seeking the company of the nymphs, who

take to flight to escape his advances. **fugientum**: for this poetic form of the genitive plural, *cf.* iii. 27. 10, *imminentum.*

2. **meos finis et rura**: *i.e.* the Sabine farm.

3. **lenis incedas abeasque aequos**: the emphasis rests not upon the verbs, but upon the adjectives, *i.e.* 'be propitious at thy coming and thy going!' Note the chiasmus. **parvis alumnis**: *i.e.* the young of the flocks. *Alumnis* depends only upon *aequos.*

5. **pleno anno**: *i.e.* at the year's end, *viz.* at the Faunalia, on December 5th (*Nonae Decembres*, line 10); *pleno* is here used in the sense of *exacto;* the construction is the ablative absolute. **cadit**: *i.e.* as a sacrifice.

6. **larga nec** = *nec larga.* **Veneris sodali**: in apposition with *craterae;* wine and love are natural companions.

7. **vetus ara fumat**: asyndeton; *vetus* suggests that Faunus's worship has long been maintained on the estate.

9. **herboso campo**: in central Italy the grass is still green in December.

10. **nonae Decembres**: the Lupercalia, the regular annual festival in honor of Faunus, fell on February 13th. The festival to which Horace here alludes is not elsewhere mentioned; possibly it was a purely local celebration.

11. **festus**: *i.e.* in holiday garb and holiday spirits.

12. **pagus**: *i.e.* the population of the district, Mandēla by name.

13. **audaces**: the emphasis of the sentence rests upon this word, — 'the lambs have no fear when the wolf roams among them.' Faunus was identical with Lupercus, 'the wolf-repeller'; hence his presence gives courage to the flocks.

14. **spargit agrestis frondes**: *its woodland foliage;* in Italy the deciduous trees lose their leaves in December. **tibi**: *for thee, in thy honor.*

15. **invisam**: since it is the occasion of his toil. **pepulisse**: for the perfect infinitive with *gaudet*, *cf.* i. 34. 16, *posuisse gaudet.*

16. **ter**: *i.e.* in triple time.

ODE XIX.

1. **Quantum distet . . . narras**: *i.e.* you indulge in learned antiquarian discussion: *quantum distet* means 'how far distant (in time)'; *narro* is used here, as often, of long and tedious description. **Inacho**: the earliest king of Argos.

2. Codrus: the last king of Athens. An oracle had declared that the Dorians should be successful in their invasion of Attica, if the life of the Attic king were spared. Codrus thereupon determined to sacrifice his life for his country. Entering the Dorian camp in disguise, he engaged in a brawl with some soldiers and was thus killed. **timidus mori**: for the infinitive, *cf.* i. 1. 18, *indocilis pati;* Introd. § 41. *c.*

3. genus Aeaci: the line of Peleus, Achilles, Neoptolemus on one side, of Telamon and Ajax on the other.

4. sacro Ilio: Homer's Ἴλιος ἱρή.

5. Chium cadum: *i.e. cadum vini Chii.*

6. mercemur, temperet, caream: the subjunctives are not only indirect questions, but are also dependent deliberatives. **aquam temperet**: *i.e.* temper its coldness, and so warm it for brewing some cheering beverage, such as the *calda*, a kind of punch.

7. quo praebente domum: *i.e.* at whose house? **quota**: *sc. hora, — at what hour?*

8. Paelignis frigoribus: the district of the Paeligni lay among the highlands of the Apennines, and so was noticeably colder than most other portions of Italy; hence *Paeligna frigora* is proverbial for severe cold. Note the poetical plural in *frigoribus.*

9. da lunae novae, noctis mediae, Murenae: *i.e.* a health to the day (the first of the month), to the hour (midnight), and to our host (Murena). The poet in fancy conceives the revel as already begun. The genitives depend upon some such word as *cyathos*, to be supplied in thought; *cf.* iii. 8. 13, *sume, Maecenas, cyathos amici sospitis centum.*

10. puer: the attendant slave. **auguris Murenae**: apparently, the gathering is to celebrate Murena's recent election to the augurship. Concerning Murena, see note on ii. 10. 1.

11. tribus aut novem cyathis commodis: *with three or nine cyathi, as may be fitting; commodis* has adverbial force, and is explained by what follows. The *cyathus* was one-twelfth of the *sextarius* (a pint). Hence the three *cyathi* of wine are to be conceived as mixed with nine *cyathi* of water to make up the *poculum;* while similarly the nine *cyathi* of wine are mixed with three of water.

14. ternos ter: *i.e.* the nine Muses call for nine *cyathi.* **attonitus**: *rapt, inspired.*

15. vates: *poet.* **tris supra**: by anastrophe for *supra tris;*

the three Graces forbid their votaries to exceed three *cyathi*. **prohibet**: here in the less usual sense of 'forbid.'

17. iuncta sororibus: the Graces are regularly represented as inseparable; see note on iii. 21. 22. The ablative is one of association; Introd. § 38. *a; B. L. L.* § 337.

18. insanire: *to join mad revel.* **Berecyntiae tibiae**: *i.e.* such flutes as were used in the wildly orgiastic worship of Cybele, as celebrated on Mt. Berecyntus in Phrygia.

19. cessant: here, not *cease*, but *wait*.

20. tacitā: grammatically in agreement with *lyra*, but to be understood in thought also with *fistula*.

21. parcentis dexteras: *i.e.* hands slow to perform the various hospitable duties of the occasion.

22. audiat invidus, *etc.*: *i.e.* let the din be so mad and loud that Lycus shall hear and envy.

24. vicina: apparently either a young wife or some maiden whom Lycus courts. **non habilis**: *not suited;* she is young, and Lycus old.

26. puro vespero: lit. *the cloudless evening-star*, *i.e.* the evening-star in cloudless skies; *cf.* iii. 10. 8, *puro numine*.

27. tempestiva Rhode: *ripe Rosa*. Here we have the climax of the ode: Rosa is far better than archaeology (*cf.* line 1 f.).

28. lentus: *i.e. slow*, *consuming*.

ODE XX.

1. Non vides: *non*, for *nonne*, indicates a higher degree of emotion. **moveas**: *disturb*.

2. catulos leaenae: Nearchus's jealous admirer is likened to a furious beast, and Nearchus is conceived as one of her whelps. The figure is maintained consistently to line 10, where it is abruptly abandoned.

3. inaudax: newly coined by Horace, and not found later.

4. raptor: Pyrrhus has stolen the youth away.

5. obstantis iuvenum catervas: the bands of hunters (figuratively).

6. insignem = *pulchrum*.

7. grande certamen: in loose apposition with the statement preceding. **cedat**: *sc. utrum*.

8. maior an illa: understand *sit*, — *or whether she* (Nearchus's admirer) *shall be victorious*.

10. haec dentes acuit: understand *et*. Horace inaccurately attributes to the lion a habit attributed by Homer to the boar and said to be peculiar to that animal.

11. arbiter pugnae: Nearchus; he is called *arbiter*, because it lies in his power to settle the dispute by indicating his own preference. **posuisse sub pede**: *i.e.* in scornful indifference.

12. palmam: the token of victory.

13. recreare: note the change of tense; *i.e.* he is said *to have* trampled on the palm of victory, and now *to be* cooling his shoulders, *etc.*

15. Nireus: characterized by Homer as the fairest of all the Greeks who came to Troy; *Il.* ii. 673.

16. raptus ab Ida: Ganymedes, the son of Tros, one of the early kings of Troy. Attracted by the surpassing beauty of the youth, Jove carried him away from Ida to Olympus to be his cup-bearer.

ODE XXI.

1. nata: the jar is addressed as born in Manlius's consulship; *i.e.* the wine it contains was made in that year. **Manlio**: L. Manlius Torquatus was consul in 65 B.C., the year of the poet's birth.

2. querellas: lovers' plaints. **geris**: lit. *carriest*, *i.e.* containest (potentially). **iocos**: *mirth.*

3. rixam: between the revellers.

4. facilem: *soft*, *sweet*, as in ii. 11. 8. **pia testa**: *thou goodly jar*, as fulfilling the beneficent functions enumerated below (lines 13–20).

5. quocumque lectum nomine Massicum: *i.e.* for whatever purpose (of those just mentioned) the Massic was gathered that thou holdest; *quocumque nomine* is used here in the sense of *quacumque causa; lectum*, strictly applicable to the grapes of which the wine was made, is here applied to the wine itself.

6. moveri = *demoveri*, *i.e.* to be brought down from the store-room (*horreum*). In the poets and post-Augustan prose-writers, *dignus* is often construed with the infinitive.

7. descende: the store-room was usually in an upper story; see note on iii. 8. 11. **Corvino**: M. Valerius Messalla Corvinus, distinguished as the patron of the poet Tibullus, was also a friend of Horace. Like Horace, he had supported the fortunes of Brutus and Cassius in the campaign of Philippi, and like him he had later given his support to the new régime of Augustus. He was of noble birth, and was one of the ablest orators of his day.

8. **languidiora** : *i.e.* mellower than usual ; *cf.* iii. 16. 35, *languescit.*

9. **Socraticis** : *i.e.* pertaining to philosophy. **madet** : so we speak of 'being saturated' with a subject, or 'steeped in' it. But the word is here nicely chosen by the poet to suggest that Corvinus is also not unwilling *vino madere.*

10. **sermonibus** : *lore,* as in iii. 8. 5, *docte sermones utriusque linguae.* **horridus** : *austerely.*

11. Cato is here characterized as habitually abstemious ; yet in the *de Senectute* (14. 46), Cicero represents him as describing with enthusiasm the convivial delights which he enjoyed with his friends and neighbors on his Sabine estate. **Catonis virtus** : *the virtuous Cato ; cf. Sat.* ii. 1. 72, *virtus Scipiadae et mitis sapientia Laeli, i.e.* the heroic Scipio and the wise Laelius. The reference, as shown by *prisci,* is to Cato the Censor (234–149 B.C.).

13. **lene tormentum** : 'pleasant compulsion,' an evident imitation of Bacchylides's characterization of wine as a γλυκεῖ' ἀνάγκα. Note the effective oxymoron.

14. **plerumque** : *usually ;* with *duro.* **duro** : *dull ;* lit. *hard, i.e.* unresponsive. **sapientium . . . Lyaeo** : in contrast with *duro ;* the witless are stimulated to thought ; the minds of the wise are unlocked, and they reveal their secret thoughts under the spell of the god (*Lyaeo* is ablative).

17. **anxiis** : *distressed.*

18. **cornua** : the horn in Roman, as in Hebrew, literature is the symbol of power and confidence ; *cf. Psalms,* cxlviii. 14, *He exalteth the horn of his people ;* Ovid, *Ars Amat.* i. 239, *tum* (after wine) *pauper cornua sumit.*

19. **post te** : *i.e.* after enjoying thy beneficent influence. **trementi** : here transitive ; *cf.* ii. 12. 8, *periculum contremuit.* **iratos regum apices** : the epithet (by hypallage) agrees with *apices* instead of *regum ;* for *apices* (= *coronas*), see note on i. 34. 14.

21. **et si laeta,** *etc.* : *i.e.* 'and Venus, if she lend her gracious presence.'

22. **segnes nodum solvere** : *i.e.* who never break their bond ; for the description, *cf.* iii. 19. 17, *Gratia nudis iuncta sororibus.* For the infinitive with *solvere, cf.* i. 1. 18, *indocilis pauperiem pati ; nodum* is, of course, the bond that unites the sisters, who are often represented in ancient works of art with their arms entwined about one another.

23. vivae lucernae: *the burning lamps; cf.* iii. 8. 14, *vigiles lucernae.* **producent**: the object is properly *te* (the *testa*) but is transferred to the occasion itself.

24. fugat: a more vivid picture than had Horace written *fugaverit*, which would have been the usual tense.

ODE XXII.

2. laborantis puellas: young mothers in travail. **ter vocata**: this triple repetition is a common feature of ancient rituals.

3. audis: Diana, as well as Juno, was supposed to assist women in childbirth.

4. diva triformis: Diana on earth, Luna in heaven, and Hecate in the lower world.

5. villae: the dwelling-house on the poet's Sabine farm. **tua pinus esto**: *thine be the pine;* the emphasis of the line rests on *tua;* the poet prays that the tree may belong to the goddess, in the sense that it is to be under her protection.

6. quam: referring to the tree, to which, as blest by the goddess, the poet proposes to sacrifice, instead of directly to the goddess herself. **per exactos annos**: *i.e.* at each year's end; *per* is distributive.

7. obliquom meditantis ictum: *that practises sidelong thrusts*, a characteristic of the boar.

8. donem: subjunctive in a relative clause of purpose; the goddess is asked to bless the tree, that Horace may in turn make sacrifice for the favor.

ODE XXIII.

1. Caelo: *heavenward;* dative of direction of motion. **supinas**: *i.e.* with palms upward, the customary way of holding the hands in Roman supplication; *cf.* Virg. *Aen.* i. 93, *duplices tendens ad sidera palmas.* **tuleris**: for *sustuleris.*

2. nascente luna: *i.e.* when the moon is new. A monthly sacrifice at the time of the new moon was apparently customary; *cf.* iii. 19. 9, *da lunae novae.* **Phidyle**: evidently formed from the root of the Greek φείδομαι, 'spare'; hence 'the frugal one,' a fitting name for a country lass.

3. placarīs: for the long *i*, *cf.* iv. 7. 20, 21, *dederīs, occiderīs.*

5. Africum: the sirocco, which withered vegetation.

6. fecunda = *fertilis.* **sterilem**: here active, — *blighting.*

7. **alumni**: the young lambs, calves, and kids, born the preceding spring.

8. **grave tempus**: *the sickly season; cf. Sat.* ii. 6. 19, *autumnus gravis.* **pomifero anno**: ablative of time; for *annus* in this sense ('season'), *cf. Epod.* 2. 29, *annus hibernus*, 'the winter season.'

9. **nam quae,** *etc.*: *nam* introduces the justification of the general idea previously enunciated, *viz.*: for thee, a simple sacrifice suffices; no costly victim is necessary. **nivali**: *snow-capped.* **Algido**: Mt. Algidus, on the eastern edge of the Alban Hills, some twenty miles southeast of Rome.

10. **devota**: *i.e.* destined for the altar. **quercus inter**: *i.e.* feeding on acorns; for the anastrophe of the preposition, *cf.* iii. 3. 11.

11. **Albanis in herbis**: the pasturage in the vicinity of Mt. Alba.

12. **victima**: used regularly of some larger and costly animal, such as a steer, or a full-grown sheep. **pontificum securis tinguet**: the emphasis is on *pontificum*; *i.e.* is destined for the imposing ceremonial of the priests.

13. **cervice**: here used for *sanguine.* **te**: as contrasted with the *pontifices.*

14. **temptare**: *to importune;* as object understand *deos* from *parvos deos*, the object of *coronantem.* **bidentium**: according to Hyginus, a *bidens* is a victim having two teeth more prominent than the rest, which indicate that the animal has reached maturity.

15. **coronantem**: with conditional force, — 'it is not necessary for you to offer costly victims if you only garland,' *etc.*; *i.e.* 'it is not necessary . . . and it suffices to garland.' **parvos deos**: the small images of the gods.

16. **fragili**: *brittle*, not flexible like the willow, for instance.

17. **immunis**: here in the sense (not elsewhere authenticated) of *pura*, 'innocent.' The word is emphatic and contains the climax of the ode.

18. **non sumptuosa blandior hostia**: *not (made) more persuasive by a costly sacrifice; blandior* agrees with *manus.*

19. **mollivit**: *it* (*sc. ea*, the hand) *has appeased.* **aversos**: *estranged.* **Penatis**: *cf.* line 4, *Lares.* Any original distinction that may have existed between these two words had long since disappeared in Horace's day; he uses them interchangeably.

20. **farre et mica** = *salted meal*, a regular accompaniment of sacrifices. **saliente**: lit. *dancing*, *i.e.* crackling. The greater the crackling when the salted meal was cast upon the flame, the better the omen.

ODE XXIV.

In general character and spirit, this ode closely resembles the first three odes of this book.

1. intactis: *i.e.* as yet untouched by the Romans; *cf.* i. 29. 1, *Icci, beatis nunc Arabum invides gazis.* **opulentior thesauris Arabum**: poetically free for *quam Arabes intactis thesauris.*

2. divitis Indiae: India was a proverbially rich land; it furnished spices, precious stones, ivory, metals, metal work, ceramic wares, *etc.*

3. caementis: *i.e.* with buildings; *cf.* iii. 1. 33 ff. **licet**: *though.*

4. Tyrrhenum omne et mare Apulicum: *i.e.* all the western and eastern coast of Italy. As a matter of fact, there was little or no building on the eastern coast, of the sort mentioned in iii. 1. 33 ff. Horace, with the characteristic of a poet, merely states a hypothetical case. For the quantity *Ăpulicum*, *cf.* iii. 4. 10, *Ăpuliae.*

5. figīt: the long *i* is not here a reminiscence of an earlier quantity, as in i. 3. 36, *perrupīt*, or in ii. 6. 14, *ridēt*, but is probably an analogical extension after such models. On the present with future force, *cf.* i. 1. 35, *inseris.*

6. summis verticibus: *thy topmost roof;* the case is ablative.

7. clavos: *cf.* i. 35. 18, where *cunei*, *unci*, and *liquidum plumbum* are also mentioned as symbols of the might of *Necessitas.*

9. campestres Scythae: the Scythians who dwell on the vast steppes of the North. **melius**: *i.e.* better than we Romans with our effeminate luxury and false ideals of life.

10. quorum: with *domos.* **vagas domos**: the Scythians were nomads. **rite**: *as is their custom.*

11. rigidi: *stern, strict.* **Getae**: they dwelt to the north of the Danube, near the Black Sea.

12. liberas: *i.e.* not the property of any master, but belonging in common to the tribe.

14. nec cultura longior annuā: Caesar, *B.G.* iv. 1, gives a similar account of the German Suebi.

15. defunctumque: *having finished; -que* has adversative force.

16. aequali sorte: *i.e.* the successor (*vicarius*) is likewise to till the assigned plot for a single season and is then to relinquish it to some one else; *sorte* is an ablative of quality. **recreat**: *relieves.*

17. illic: *i.e.* among these simple northern tribes.

18. mulier: not the traditional Roman *noverca.* **temperat**: *spares.* **innocens**: in predicate construction with adverbial force,

— *without harming them.* Note the retention of the primitive force of *in-nocens;* so also in i. 17. 21, *innocentis Lesbii.*

19. dotata coniunx: at Rome, the richly dowered wife often indulged in the greatest liberty of conduct; hence she is spoken of as 'ruling her husband,' instead of yielding a becoming obedience to his authority. For the decay of social purity in contemporary Roman society, *cf.* iii. 6. 17 f.

20. nitido adultero: *the dashing paramour.*

21. dos: *viz.* among the Scythians and Getae. **magna**: with *dos.*

22. metuens: *that shrinks from;* for the genitive, *cf.* iii. 19. 16, *rixarum metuens.* **alterius**: *another* (than her husband); *alīus* is practically unknown in Latin.

23. certo foedere: *of steadfast devotion;* ablative of quality.

24. aut: *or* (if the sin is committed). **pretium**: *the penalty.*

The foregoing idealization of the northern races is thoroughly characteristic of ancient literature. Tacitus, in his *Germania*, depicts the Germans in similar fashion. *Cf.* also the note on ii. 20. 16, *Hyperboreos.*

25. quisquis volet, *etc.*: a complimentary allusion to the endeavors of Octavian to improve the standards of social life.

26. rabiem civicam: the frenzy of civil strife. On *civicam*, *cf.* ii. 1. 1 and note.

27. quaeret subscribi: for *quaeret* with the infinitive, *cf.* i. 37. 22, *perire quaerens.* **'pater urbium'**: subject of *subscribi.*

28. subscribi: *i.e.* inscribed on the base (*sub*) of the statue.

29. refrenare licentiam: in iv. 15. 9 f., Horace credits Augustus with accomplishing this very object, *ordinem rectum evaganti frena licentiae iniecit.*

30. clarus: *i.e.* destined to be glorious. **postgenitis**: *in the eyes of posterity;* dative of 'the person judging,' a variety of the dative of reference; B. 188. 2. *c.* **quatenus**: *inasmuch as*, introducing the reason why the true patriot must look to posterity for appreciation.

31. virtutem incolumem odimus: *i.e.* we show despite for true worth while its possessor is still alive.

32. invidi: *through envy;* with both *odimus* and *quaerimus.*

33. quid: *sc. proficiunt,* — *of what avail?* **querimoniae**: laments over our present evil plight.

35. sine moribus: *i.e.* without morals; the phrase is to be joined closely with *vanae.* For the thought, *cf.* the strikingly similar passage in Tacitus, *Germania*, 19, *plus ibi boni mores valent quam alibi bonae leges*.

36. fervidis pars inclusa caloribus: the torrid zone.

38. latus: *region*, as in i. 22. 19.

39. duratae solo: *i.e.* lying frozen on the ground.

40. mercatorem abigunt: *i.e.* prevent the trader from seeking gain. The restless spirit of greed, according to Horace, is the ultimate cause of the existing social demoralization.

41. vincunt, iubet: note the effect of the asyndeton.

42. magnum opprobrium: (in apposition with *pauperies*) *i.e.* interpreted as a reproach; for *pauperies*, 'narrow means,' not 'poverty,' *cf.* i. 1. 19.

43. quidvis: with *facere*, 'any crime whatsoever'; with *pati*, 'any disgrace'; as subject of the infinitives, *nos* is to be understood.

44. deserit: an abrupt change of construction; we should have expected *deserere* dependent upon *iubet*. **arduae**: in agreement with *virtutis*, instead of *viam*; hypallage.

45. in Capitolium vel in mare: *i.e.* either let us offer to the gods, or throw into the sea, the cause of our offending (*summi materiem mali*). *Capitolium* suggests the altar of the Capitoline temple.

46. quo clamor vocat, *etc.*: lit. *whither the shouts now summon us*; but logically the clause refers to an attendant circumstance of the proposed act, 'to the plaudits of the shouting crowd,' as though in a triumphal procession; *faventium* illustrates the substantive use of the present participle as a noun of agency (here, *fautor*); *faveo* often has this meaning of 'applaud,' *i.e.* show favor by applause; note the hendiadys in *clamor et turba*.

47. mare proximum: *i.e.* the nearer, the better, for the act cannot be too quickly consummated.

48. lapides: *i.e.* precious stones; synonymous with *gemmas*. **inutile**: here, not *useless*, but *baneful*, by a kind of litotes (properly, 'softening' of the expression).

49. summi mali: in English (with change of figure) we should naturally say, 'our deep depravity.'

50. mittamus: zeugma; the word is strictly appropriate only with *in mare proximum*, not with *in Capitolium*, which calls for *feramus*, or some such word. **bene**: *i.e.* sincerely.

52. elementa: *the seeds*, *the causes*.

53. asperioribus studiis: *sterner pursuits*, *e.g.* swimming, running, leaping, boxing, *etc.*; *cf.* i. 8.

54. nescit, timet: he lacks both the skill and courage that should characterize a manly lad. **equo haerere**: he cannot even keep his seat, — much less ride with skill and grace.

55. ingenuos: for the nominative *ingenuos*, see Introd. § 34.

56. ludere doctior: the infinitive dependent upon an adjective, as i. 1. 18, *indocilis pauperiem pati.*

57. seu . . . seu = *vel si . . . vel si.* **Graeco trocho**: there is scorn in the word *Graeco*; the young man is so lost to sentiments of patriotism that he seeks amusement in foreign sports. The better sentiment among the Romans, particularly in the earlier and nobler days of their history, steadfastly opposed the introduction of all foreign ways and ideas. The *trochus* was a hoop, to the circumference of which were attached rings that rattled as the hoop was trundled. **iubeas, malis**: subjunctive, because of the indefinite second singular in a subordinate clause.

58. vetita legibus alea: gambling was always a serious vice among the Romans, and severe penalties were prescribed against it.

59. cum fallat et properet: the *cum*-clause is circumstantial rather than strictly temporal, — *while his father's perfidy, etc.* **periura fides** = *perfidia.*

60. consortem socium: *his business partner.* **hospites**: to violate the obligations of guest-friendship was impious.

61. indigno heredi: the effeminate son just described.

62. properet: *i.e.* hurriedly amass; *cf.* ii. 7. 24, *deproperare coronas.* **improbae divitiae**: *ill-gotten wealth*; the epithet is transferred from the owner to his riches.

63. tamen curtae nescio quid, *etc.*: *i.e.* despite his accumulations, the man feels that his possessions are scanty (*curtae*) and something is ever lacking to make up the desired fortune. Thus Horace returns to the sentiment enunciated earlier in the ode: Insatiable greed is the root of all our misery. Note that in *nescio quis*, when used as an indefinite pronoun, the *o* is always short.

ODE XXV

1. tui plenum: *cf.* ii. 19. 6, *plenoque Bacchi pectore turbidum laetatur.*

2. nemora: like *specus* governed by *in.*

3. mente nova: *in my fresh inspiration.*

5. meditans, *etc.*: lit. *planning*, *i.e.* engaged in composing the verses that shall immortalize his glory.

6. stellis inserere, *etc.* : *i.e.* to immortalize ; *cf.* iii. 3. 10, *arcis attigit igneas.*

7. insigne : *a glorious deed;* the reference is apparently to some great achievement, most probably the victory of Actium.

9. exsomnis : *i.e.* tireless in celebrating the orgies of the god.

10. nive candidam : the allusion is probably to the snow-capped mountains of Thrace.

11. pede barbaro lustratam : *i.e.* traversed by the feet of Thracian Bacchanals.

12. Rhodopen . a lofty mountain of Thrace. **ut** : *than ; ac* would have been the usual conjunction after *secus.*

13. vacuom : for the spelling, see Introd. § 34.

14. potens : *lord.*

15. valentium . . . fraxinos : *i.e.* in their inspired frenzy. **vertere** = *evertere*, 'to tear up by the roots' ; for the infinitive with *valere*, *cf.* i. 34. 12, *valet ima summis mutare.*

18. nil mortale : *i.e.* nothing common or usual ; 'my song shall be divine.' **loquar** = *dicam.*

19. Lenaee : lit. *thou (god) of the wine-press ;* one of the many names of Bacchus.

20. cingentem : agreeing with the subject of *sequi* (*me*), not with *deum.*

ODE XXVI.

1. duellis = *bellis*, *i.e.* the lists of love ; for the form, see the note on iii. 5. 38.

2. militavi : often thus used of campaigns in Love's service.

3. arma : the weapons of Love, as enumerated in line 7.

4. hic paries : a niche in the wall of Venus's shrine.

5. marinae Veneris : *i.e.* Venus, who sprang from the sea ; her statue, of course, is meant. For a rationalizing interpretation of the legend of Venus's birth from the sea, see note on i. 4. 5.

6. ponite : *i.e.* lay as votive offerings ; the words are addressed to the poet's attendants, who are conceived as bearing the offerings.

7 funalia, vectes, arcus : the equipment of the lover in his nocturnal roamings ; the *funalia* light his way ; the *vectes* are used in forcing the doors of his reluctant mistress ; *arcus* is obscure and doubtless corrupt ; *ascias* (*i.e. ascyas*, by 'hardening'), 'axes,' has been suggested as the true reading.

8. oppositis : *i.e.* barred against the lover's entrance. **fori-**

bus: dative with *minacis*. **minacis**: *i.e.* threatening to destroy them.

9. **beatam**: *rich*. **diva regina**: *O queenly goddess;* for the adjective force of *regina*, *cf.* i. 1. 1, *atavis regibus* with note. **Cyprum**: concerning this seat of Venus's worship, see note on i. 3. 1.

10. **Memphin**: in Egypt. **Sithonia** = *Thracia;* the Sithonii were a Thracian tribe.

11. **sublimi**: *uplifted*.

12. **Chloen**: mentioned also in i. 23. 1, and repeatedly in Book iii. **semel**: with *tange; just once;* a single blow of the goddess's lash will suffice to break the maiden's pride.

ODE XXVII.

1. **Impios ducat, rumpat**: though standing prominently at the opening of the poem, these clauses are logically subordinate to *prece suscitabo; i.e.* 'I shall entreat the gods to bestow good omens on my friends, while willing that evil omens may befall the wicked.'

2. **praegnas**: collateral form of *praegnans*.

4. **feta**: *that has just brought forth*.

5. **rumpat** = *interrumpat*.

6. **si**: here in the temporal sense of *when*, a meaning of *si* found occasionally throughout the entire period of the language. **per obliquom**: *athwart their path;* dependent upon the idea of motion involved in *similis sagittae*. **similis sagittae**: *i.e.* with a sudden darting movement.

7. **ego cui timebo**: the evident antithesis between this phrase and *impios* shows that by *ego cui timebo* Horace means the good.

9. **stantis repetat paludes**: this was said to prognosticate rain.

10. **imbrium divina**: *prophetic of showers:* the raven (*corvus*, *cornix*) by its croaking was thought to foretell the coming rain; *cf.* iii. 17. 12. For the genitive with *divinus*, *cf. Ars Poet.* 218, *divina futuri*.

11. **oscinem**: *i.e.* giving auguries by its notes. **prece suscitabo**: *i.e.* will invoke.

12. **solis ab ortu**: with the ancients, favorable omens came from the East.

13. **sis licet felix**: it seems best, following Page, to take *licet* as parenthetical and to regard *sis*, like *vivas*, as an optative subjunctive; *licet* then has the force of 'so far as I am concerned,' *i.e.* the poet will interpose no obstacle to Galatea's departure, if she is bent on going.

15. laevos picus: the Romans faced the south when they sacrificed or took the auspices; hence omens appearing on their left (toward the east) were favorable. But with the Greeks, who faced the north in their ceremonial observances, the left side was unfavorable, and we occasionally find the poets, as here, following the Greek conceptions.

16. vaga: *i.e.* flying to water (the *stantes paludes* of line 9), and so giving prophecy of rain.

17. sed vides: introducing a caution against setting out at present; for though the omens are favorable, the season is unpropitious.

18. pronus Orion: *setting Orion;* this constellation set early in November. **ego**: emphatic, —*from my own experience I know.* **quid sit**: *i.e.* what mischief it can bring.

19. Hadriae: appositional genitive; the *sinus* is the Hadria itself. **albus**: *i.e.* even though clear; *cf.* i. 7. 15, *albus Notus.*

23. trementis verbere: *quivering with the shock.*

24. ripas: for *litora*, as in ii. 18. 22.

25. sic: with the same courage as thou now. But remember her fate! **et**: *too.* **Europe**: according to the common tradition, daughter of Agenor, king of Phoenicia. **doloso tauro**: Jove, in the guise of a bull, had mingled with a herd of cattle grazing near the spot where Europa and her attendants were engaged in sport. Attracted by the gentleness of the animal, Europa ventured to mount its back, whereupon it rushed into the sea and carried her to Crete.

27. medias fraudes: *the dangers of mid sea.* For the accusative with *palluit*, *cf.* iii. 21. 19, *iratos trementi apices.*

28. audax: *i.e.* she who just now had so boldly trusted the bull.

29. nuper: *but now;* to be construed with *studiosa.*

31. astra praeter: for the anastrophe, *cf.* iii. 23. 10, *quercus inter.*

32. vidit: *i.e.* while being borne on the bull's back.

33. simul = *simul atque.* **centum potentem oppidis**: the Homeric ἑκατόμπολις.

35. filiae: appositional genitive with *nomen.*

36. victa: with *pietas.*

37. unde quo veni: *i.e.* what a contrast between the home I left and the spot to which I have come. **levis**: *i.e.* too slight a penalty. **una mors**: *a single death;* Europa means that a girl should die many times in order fitly to atone for such a fault.

38. vigilans: the emphasis of the first member rests on this word.

41. porta eburna: *cf.* Virg. *Aen.* vi. 894, *sunt geminae Somni* *portae, quarum altera fertur cornea, qua veris facilis datur exitus umbris, altera candenti perfecta nitens elephanto, sed falsa ad caelum mittunt insomnia Manes.*

46. iratae: *in my anger.*

47. modo: *but now.* **multum** = *magnopere.* **amati**: Europa had garlanded its horns with flowers and stroked it with her hands.

49. impudens, impudens: the repetition and position lend special emphasis, — 'shameless my abandonment of home, shameless my continued existence.' **patrios Penates**: with the poet's license, Horace attributes a purely Roman conception to the Phoenician Europa.

54. malas: here for *genas.* **sucus**: *i.e.* my fresh life's blood.

55. praedae = *mihi;* she conceives herself the destined prey of some wild beast. **speciosa**: *while still beautiful.*

56. pascere: for the infinitive, *cf.* iii. 24. 27, *si quaeret subscribi.*

58. hac (ab orno): *i.e.* the first at hand.

59. pendulum laedere collum: lit. *destroy your hanging neck, i.e. hang thyself.* **zona**: *by the girdle.* **bene secuta**: *which has happily followed thee, i.e.* which thou hast fortunately brought with thee (for the purpose).

61. acuta leto: lit. *sharp for death, i.e.* with a sharpness suited for death or that invites to death.

62. age: purely interjectional, — *come!*

63. erile carpere pensum: *carpere pensum* is properly 'to card the wool,' a menial task, as it involved little skill; *erilis* is to be conceived as derived from *era*, not *erus.*

65. regius sanguis: *a king's daughter.* **dominae tradi barbarae paelex**: *i.e.* the master's wife will wreak vengeance on his favorite.

67. perfidum ridens: the smile was perfidious, since the goddess, while feigning sympathy for the wronged maiden, secretly delighted in what had happened. **remisso**: inasmuch the bow's work was accomplished.

68. filius: Cupid.

69. ubī: for the ī, *cf.* ii. 6. 17. **lusit**: the subject is *Venus* understood.

70. irarum: *from wrath.* For this Grecism, see Introd. § 37. *b.*

73. esse nescis: *thou knowest not that thou art;* a Grecism for *te esse nescis.*

74. mitte: *cease! abandon!* **bene**: as becomes the wife of the king of gods.

75. sectus orbis: *viz.* Europe.

76. nomina: for this striking poetic plural, *cf.* iv. 2. 3, *daturus nomina ponto* (of Icarus). **ducet** = *accipiet.*

ODE XXVIII.

1. quid potius: *i.e.* what rather than what I now suggest (*viz. prome Caecubum*). **die Neptuni**: *i.e.* of the Neptunalia, which fell on the 23d of July.

3. strenua: with adverbial force.

4. munitae adhibe vim sapientiae: *i.e.* a truce to serious thoughts!

5. inclinare: *i.e.* toward the west; ordinarily, the expression is *dies* (not *meridies*) *inclinare.*

6. stet: *stood still.*

7. parcis: *hesitate;* for the infinitive, *cf.* i. 28 (2). 3. **deripere**: the verb suggests haste. **horreo**: see note on iii. 8. 11.

8. cessantem: *i.e.* the jar lingers too long; it ought already to be here. **Bibuli consulis amphoram**: Bibulus was the colleague of Julius Caesar in 59 B.C.

9. nos: here for *ego*, as shown by the contrasted *tu.* **invicem**: *i.e.* on my part.

10. viridis comas: the hair of the Nereids is often described as *caeruleus* or *viridis*, like the color of the sea.

11. curva: see note on i. 10. 6. **recines**: *i.e.* thou shalt sing in response to my song of Neptune and the Nereids.

12. Cynthiae: Diana; so called from Mt. Cynthus, her birthplace, on the isle of Delos.

13. summo = *extremo.* **quae Cnidon,** *etc.*: Venus.

14. fulgentis: *i.e.* whence the shining marble comes; *cf.* i. 14. 19, *nitentis Cycladas;* so Virg. *Aen.* iii. 126, calls Paros *nivea*, in consequence of the snow-white marble quarried there.

16. merita: since Night favors lovers. **nenia**: here not 'dirge,' but simply *lay, song.*

ODE XXIX.

1. Tyrrhena regum progenies: *cf.* i. 1. 1, *atavis edite regibus* *Tyrrhena* by hypallage for *Tyrrhenorum.* **tibi**: *for thee;* depend ent upon *est.*

2. non verso: lit. *not turned, tipped*, and so *untouched.* **cado** ablative of place.

4. balanus: the nut of an Arabian plant from which a fragrant oil was expressed.

6. semper: with *contempleris*. **udum Tibur**: *cf.* i. 7. 13. **Aefulae**: a town in Latium near Praeneste.

7. contempleris: *i.e.* do not be content with continual contemplation of these spots from your lofty city palace, but come visit them! All the places mentioned are visible from the highest point of the city.

8. Telegoni iuga: Tusculum, founded by Telegonus, the son of Ulysses and Circe. **parricidae**: Telegonus, sent by Circe to find his father, came to Ithaca and unwittingly slew Ulysses.

9. fastidiosam: that brings weariness and satiety.

10. molem . . . arduis: exaggerated description of Maecenas's palace on the Esquiline.

11. beatae: *wealthy.*

13. plerumque: *many a time.* **vices**: *i.e.* from luxury to simplicity.

14. lare = *tecto*; hence *sub.*

16. explicuere: aorist, like i. 34. 16, *sustulit.*

17. clarus: *bright.* **occultum**: *i.e.* till recently. **pater**: Cepheus.

18. ostendit ignem: used of the rising of the constellation. As a matter of fact, this constellation is always visible in the latitude of Rome. Possibly Horace was following the calendar of the Alexandrian astronomers, in whose latitude the evening rising of the constellation fell, according to Kiessling, on the 23d of July.

19. vesani: so called, because of the intense heat accompanying its rising.

20. dies siccos: the dog-days of midsummer. **referente**: *i.e.* bringing around in its annual course.

21. iam: *viz.* in the summer.

23. caret ripa, *etc.*: a picture of the profound stillness of midsummer.

25. tu curas: *i.e.* instead of giving yourself up to the demands of the season and the delights of the country. Maecenas had lent Octavian much assistance in establishing public order at the close of civil strife, and seems to have continued his sense of responsibility even after permanent tranquillity was assured.

27. Serĕs, Bactra, Tanais: all far distant from Rome. Horace means to urge the needlessness of Maecenas's concern for what is happening in these remote quarters. *Serĕs* follows the Greek inflection;

cf. i. 12. 56, *Serăs.* *Bactra* is for *Parthi; cf.* i. 2. 22 and note. **regnata** : *once ruled;* for this transitive use of the word, *cf.* ii. 6. 11, *regnata rura.* **Cyro** : Cyrus the Elder is meant ; the case is dative ; *cf.* ii. 6. 11, *regnata Phalantho.*

28. **parent** : *i.e.* are planning. **Tanais discors** : the Tanais is the River Don ; by *Tanais discors*, Horace means the Scythians living on the banks of the Tanais, who were agitated by constant dissensions.

29. **prudens** : *i.e.* purposely. **futuri temporis** : with *exitum.*

30. **premit** : *veils.*

31. **ultra fas trepidat** : *i.e.* is unduly anxious.

32. **quod adest memento componere aequos** : *i.e.* to adjust the present with composed spirit ; *aequos* (nominative) is equivalent to *aequo animo;* for *memento* with the infinitive, *cf.* ii. 3. 1, *aequam memento rebus in arduis servare mentem.*

33. **fluminis ritu** : *like a river.*

35. **Etruscum** : the final syllable is elided before the initial vowel of the following line ; *cf.* ii. 3. 27.

36. **adesos** : *polished, smooth.*

37. **stirpes raptas** : trunks of trees torn from the banks by the torrent. **-que, et, et** : note the emphasis of the polysyndeton.

38. **una** = *secum.*

40. **quietos** : *i.e.* ordinarily peaceful.

41. **potens sui** : *master of himself.*

42. **in diem** : *day by day ;* at each day's end.

43. **vixi** : *i.e.* 'I have truly lived.'

44. **pater** = *Juppiter.*

46. **quodcumque retro est** : *i.e.* whatever of good has been thus far enjoyed.

47. **diffinget infectumque reddet** : '*alter and undo*' (Bryce) ; not greatly different from the idea contained in *irritum efficiet*, '*render vain.*'

48. **vexit** = *advexit.*

50. **ludum ludere** : *ludum* is cognate accusative; on *ludere*, *cf.* i. 1. 19, *indocilis pauperiem pati.*

53. **manentem** : *while she stays.* **celeris quatit pinnas** : *i.e.* preparatory to taking her flight.

55. **virtute** : as though a garment.

56. **Pauperiem** : personified. **quaero** : *sc. uxorem* ('as a bride').

57. **non est meum** : *'tis not my wont.*

59. decurrere: *to have recourse.*

60. ne addant: a substantive clause used as the object of *pacisci.* **Cypriae Tyriaeque merces**: the cargo of the ship.

61. addant divitias: *i.e.* by the loss of the vessel.

62. tum: in token of the god's approval of his attitude. **biremis scaphae**: *my two-oared skiff.*

63. Aegaeos: *i.e.* of the Aegean Sea.

64. aura: *i.e.* the favoring breeze. **geminus Pollux**: *i.e.* Castor and Pollux, the patron gods of mariners; *cf.* i. 3. 2.

ODE XXX.

1. monumentum: Books i.–iii. of the *Odes*, published in 23 B.C. **aere**: the word suggests either bronze tablets containing inscriptions, or bronze statues.

2. regali situ: *majestic pile;* this meaning of *situs* is not elsewhere found, but seems necessary here.

3. impotens: *i.e. impotens sui*, and so *ungovernable.*

4. possit: subjunctive of characteristic.

5. fuga temporum: *flight of the seasons.*

6. omnis: *entirely.* **multaque**: *-que* is adversative.

7. Libitinam: the death goddess, and so *death.* **usque**: *on and on*, *continuously;* the word modifies *crescam.* **postera laude**: *i.e.* the glory that posterity shall bestow; the words are to be closely joined with *recens* ('fresh').

8. dum . . . pontifex: an allusion to a ceremony of prayer for the welfare of the state, said to have been celebrated annually on the Ides of March. **Capitolium**: here the hill on the summit of which was the temple of the same name.

9. tacita virgine: probably a priestess, who, keeping a reverent silence, joined the priest in the ceremony above referred to.

10. dicar: *I shall be celebrated.* **qua obstrepit**, *etc.*: the *qua*-clauses limit *dicar;* Horace means that his fame shall flourish in his native Apulia. Similar sentiments are found in other Roman poets. **violens**: rare and poetical for *violentus.* **Aufidus**: a river of Apulia.

11. pauper aquae Daunus: lit. *Daunus poor in water*, *i.e.* Daunus, king of a parched land. The expression is almost incredibly bold, however, and extremely unlike Horace. Daunus was an early king of Apulia. For the genitive with *pauper*, see Introd. § 37. *a.*

12. regnavit: *i.e.* once ruled. **populorum**: the genitive is a Grecism; *cf.* iii. 27. 69, *abstineto irarum.* **ex humili potens**: *exalted from low estate*, *i.e.* by the fame of my song.

13. princeps deduxisse: *as the first who adapted; deduxisse* is governed directly by *dicar; princeps* is nearly equivalent to *primus* in the sense of 'the first who'; it involves, however, the notion of leadership, which *primus* lacks. Horace's statement is not strictly accurate. Catullus, some years before Horace, had introduced the Sapphic and Glyconic metres. **Aeolium carmen**: *i.e.* the forms of the Aeolian poetry of Sappho and Alcaeus. **Italos**: the *I* is here long.

14. deduxisse = *transtulisse.* **modos**: *measures, poetry.* **sume superbiam**: apparently, *take the proud honor.*

15. quaesitam: lit. *sought*, but here with the implication of *won.* **mihi**: ethical dative. **Delphica**: the bay was sacred to Apollo, the god of Delphi.

16. volens: *graciously.* **Melpomene**: strictly the Muse of tragedy, but here, in accordance with Horace's usage, muse in general; see note on iii. 4. 2, *Calliope.*

The proud confidence in his literary immortality to which Horace here gives expression is paralleled not merely by the concluding ode of Book II., but by many similar utterances of Latin poets from Ennius to Martial. To Roman taste such prophecies apparently gave no offence.

BOOK IV.[1]

ODE I.

2. precor, precor: for the repetition, *cf.* ii. 17. 10, *ibimus, ibimus*, with note.

3. non sum qualis eram: *i.e.* not so capable of responding to the behests of the goddess. **bonae Cinarae**: *kindly Cinara.* In *Epist.* i. 14. 33, Horace speaks of her unselfish devotion.

4. dulcium . . . Cupidinum: *imperious mother of sweet Cupids;* for the conception of several Cupids attendant upon the goddess, see note on i. 19. 1, where this same line occurs.

6. circa lustra decem: the prepositional phrase serves as an adjective modifier of the omitted object of *flectere;* this object is gram-

---

[1] On Book iv., see Introd. § 9.

matically indefinite ('one'), but refers to Horace; *durum* also agrees with it. If this ode falls in the year 13 B.C., as is probable, Horace had already exceeded his ten *lustra* by more than a year. **mollibus iam durum imperiis**: *already unresponsive to thy soft commands;* for this use of *mollis*, *cf.* the English 'soft impeachment.'

8. revocant = *vocant.*

9. tempestivius: *sc.* than to my abode. **in domum comissabere**: 'haste in joyous revelry to the home'; the Latin *comissari* is from the Greek κωμάζειν, which, in turn, is derived from κῶμος, 'band of revellers'; here the conception is of Venus with her train of Cupids hastening to the house of Paulus.

10. Pauli Maximi: Paulus Fabius Maximus, born in 43 B.C., and consul in 11 B.C., two years after the date of this ode. He was a friend of Ovid and was connected by marriage with Augustus. **purpureis ales oloribus**: *on thy winged chariot of purple swans;* lit. *winged with purple swans; purpureus* is used here, as often elsewhere, not in its literal sense, but merely as a poetic word for *pulcher*.

12. torrere quaeris: for the infinitive with *quaero*, *cf.* i. 37. 22, *perire quaerens.* **iecur**: on the liver as the seat of the emotions, *cf.* i. 13. 4.

13. et, et, et, et: note the cumulative effect of the polysyndeton.

14. sollicitis reis: *cf.* ii. 1. 13, *maestis reis.* **non tacitus**: *i.e.* an eloquent defender.

15. puer: the word is loosely used. Paulus was already thirty. **artium**: *accomplishments.*

16. militiae: Horace reverts to the figure with which the ode begins.

17. quandoque = *quando*, as in iv. 2. 34; *Ars Poet.* 359. **potentior muneribus aemuli**: *i.e.* triumphing over some free-handed rival; *muneribus* is ablative of comparison. Paulus, too, is wealthy (*cf.* lines 19, 20), but his birth and figure and eloquence, along with his other accomplishments, are to assure his triumph in the lists of love, without recourse to gifts.

18. riserit: *i.e.* in triumph.

19. Albanos lacus: besides the Alban Lake itself, there were three other smaller lakes lying near it. Paulus probably had a country seat in the neighborhood, which is still one of the most attractive localities of all Italy. **te marmoream ponet**: *shall set up thy marble statue.*

20. sub trabe citrea: *i.e.* under the roof of a chapel or temple built of citron wood; *trabe* for *trabibus.* The *citrus* was the African cedar, the fragrant wood of which was much sought and very costly.

21. naribus duces: *shalt inhale.*

22. Berecyntiae: see on i. 18. 13.

24. carminibus: here in the sense of 'strains.' **fistula**: the shepherd's pipe.

25. bis die: at morning and evening.

26. tuom: for the spelling, see Introd. § 34.

28. morem Salium: see on i. 36. 12. **ter**: as in iii. 18. 16.

29. me: in strong contrast with Paulus. **femina, puer, spes**: subjects of *iuvat.*

30. spes animi credula mutui: *trustful hope of requited affection;* note the interlocked order (synchysis).

31. certare mero, vincire tempora: *i.e.* the pleasures of drinking-bouts.

33. sed cur heu, Ligurine, *etc.*: one of the few notes of genuine passion to be found in Horace's lyrics; see Introd. §§ 25, 33.

34. rara: '*now and then*' (Bryce). Though he endeavors to repress the tears, they now and then steal forth.

35. facunda: with *lingua.* **parum decoro**: *unbecoming.* The line is an hypermeter, the final *o* of *decoro* suffering elision before the initial vowel of the following line; *cf.* iii. 29. 35.

36. cadit lingua: (*why*) *does my tongue falter?*

37. nocturnis . . . teneo: *now in visions of the night I hold thee captive.*

38. iam . . . iam = *modo . . . modo.* **volucrem**: *i.e.* flying before me.

40. dure: *thou hard of heart.*

ODE II.

1. Pindarum: the greatest of the Greek lyric poets (ca. 522–442 B.C.). Of the various kinds of poetry here mentioned by Horace (dithyrambs, hymns, odes, and elegies), the triumphal odes alone have come down to us. **aemulari**: *rival, emulate.* In this sense the verb governs the accusative. In the meaning 'be envious of' it governs the dative.

2. Iule: *Julus*, a dissyllabic form of the Virgilian *Iulus.* **ceratis . . . pinnis**: *i.e.* he is likely to meet the fate of Icarus. The expression, of course, is purely figurative. *Ceratis*, lit. *waxed*, here means *fastened with wax.*

3. daturus nomina : *destined to give his name*, just as the Icarian Sea was named from Icarus. For this free use of the future participle, see note on ii. 3. 4. For the poetic plural in *nomina*, *cf.* iii. 27. 76.

5. monte decurrens velut : for the post-position of *velut*, see note on i. 2. 5, *grave ne rediret*.

6. notas ripas : *its wonted banks*. **aluere** : *have raised*, the original meaning of *alo* ; *cf. altus*, 'high,' originally 'raised up.'

7. fervet, ruit : the seething and dashing of the torrent are figuratively applied to Pindar's impassioned utterance. **immensus** : *i.e.* brooking no restraint. This use of the word is almost Pindarically bold, as is the whole figure of which it forms a part. Note the feminine cæsura of this verse ; Introd. § 44. **profundo ore** : *with sonorous voice*, — an abrupt abandonment of the figure begun in line 5 and continued as far as *ruit*.

9. laurea : *sc. fronde* or *corona* ; the badge of excellence. **donandus** : *worthy to be crowned*. **Apollinari** : *i.e.* sacred to Apollo ; *cf.* iii. 30. 15, *Delphica lauro*.

10. audacis dithyrambos : the dithyramb was an impassioned hymn in honor of Bacchus, suggesting, in its wild freedom, the license of the Bacchic orgies. Samples of the type may be seen in Horace, ii. 19 and iii. 25. These, however, probably fall far short of Pindar's dithyrambs in their freedom. The name is derived from an epithet of the god. **nova verba** : words newly coined, — often bold compounds.

11. devolvit, *etc.* : Horace returns to the figure of the rushing stream. **numeris . . . solutis** : the untrammelled metrical structure was another feature of the bold license characteristic of the Greek dithyramb.

13. deos regesve canit : an allusion to Pindar's hymns and paeans. By *reges*, as shown by the following context, we are to understand the kings of the heroic age, such as Theseus, Peleus, Pirithous.

14. sanguinem : as in ii. 20. 6. **cecidere, cecidit** : *were overthrown* ; used as the passive of *caedo*, as in ii. 4. 9. **iusta morte** : one of the Centaurs had carried off Hippodamīa, the bride of Pirithous.

15. tremendae flamma Chimaerae : *i.e.* the Chimaera with its dread fire. Concerning the Chimaera, see note on i. 27. 23.

17. sive quos Elea, *etc.* : the victors in the games at Olympia in Elis, the most celebrated of all the Greek games. With the sentiment of this passage, *cf.* i. 1. 5, *palmaque nobilis terrarum dominos evehit ad deos*. Horace here refers to those celebrated in Pindar's triumphal odes.

18. caelestis: in predicate relation to *quos*, — *leads home exalted to the skies.* **pugilem, equom**: boxing and chariot racing, as the most important events in the Greek festivals, are here cited as typical of the others, such as the foot-race, hurling the discus, *etc.* *Equom* naturally suggests the victorious owner, as well as the horse.

19. dicit: *sings, celebrates*, as often. **signis**: *statues;* the ablative of comparison is here peculiar; we should have expected *quam* with the ablative.

20. munere: *viz.* the ode composed in honor of the victor.

21. flebili sponsae iuvenemve: *-ve* (introducing *plorat*) is equivalent to *sive*, and is here boldly postponed to a relatively remote point of the sentence. For such postponement in general, see note on i. 2. 5. *Flebilis*, 'weeping, tearful,' is here used actively; *cf. Ars Poet.* 123, *flebilis Ino;* ii. 9. 9, *flebilibus modis. Sponsae* is dative of separation; the word is here used in the sense of 'bride,' 'wife.' **iuvenem raptum plorat**: an allusion to Pindar's elegies or dirges (θρῆνοι)..

22. viris animumque moresque: for the cumulative effect of the polysyndeton, *cf.* iii. 29. 37; iv. 1. 13. The verse is hypermetric.

23. aureos: *i.e.* pure as gold and as worthy of admiration. **nigroque**: *-que* is elided, as at the end of the preceding verse, thus giving us two successive hypermetric lines.

24. invidet Orco: *i.e.* he begrudges Orcus the possession of the dead hero's noble qualities, and so endeavors to rescue them from oblivion and to make them immortal in his verse.

25. multa aura: *a strong breeze:* figuratively for the genius of Pindar. **Dircaeum cycnum**: Pindar. For the swan as typical of poets, *cf.* ii. 20. Pindar is called Dircaean ('Theban') from the fountain of Dirce situated near Thebes.

26. in altos tractus: typical of the lofty flights of his song.

27. ego: in strong contrast with Pindar, just mentioned, and (by anticipation) with Antonius, mentioned later (33 ff.). **apis Matinae**: the *mons Matinus* was a spur of Mt. Gargānus on the eastern coast of Apulia. Southern Italy was famous for its bees and honey; *cf.* iii. 16. 33.

29. per laborem plurimum: *industriously.*

30. uvidi Tiburis: *cf.* i. 7. 13; iii. 29. 6, *udum Tibur.*

31. ripas: of the Anio. **operosa**: the emphasis of the clause rests upon this word. Horace (inconsistently with his utterances elsewhere) disclaims any signal gifts of song, and insists that his verse is but the product of plodding industry, like the honey gathered by the toiling bee. Cumulative effect is given to the assertion by the immediate addition of *parvos*, which is designed to emphasize the slightness of his poetic inspiration. **parvos**: nominative, — *a humble bard*, *i.e.* of small gifts.

33. maiore poeta plectro: *poeta* is in apposition with the omitted subject of *concines*, *viz. tu*, referring to Antonius; *plectro* is ablative of quality. On *plectrum* as the equivalent of *carmen*, *cf.* i. 26. 11.

34. quandoque: in the sense of *quando*, as in iv. 1. 17. **trahet**: *i.e.* in triumphal procession. **ferocis**: in iv. 14. 51, the Sygambri are characterized as *caede gaudentes*.

35. per sacrum clivom: the *Sacer Clivus* was the name given to that part of the Sacred Way which extended from the vicinity of the later Arch of Titus down towards the Forum. **decorus**: in the sense of *decoratus*, as in iii. 14. 7.

36. fronde: *viz.* of laurel, the badge of victory. **Sygambros**: see 'Occasion of the Poem.'

39. in aurum: *i.e.* to the Golden Age.

41. -que, et: poetical for *et . . . et*.

42. publicum ludum: imposing spectacles, such as gladiatorial and other contests, were regular accompaniments of triumphal celebrations. **super**: *in celebration of*. **impetrato**: suggesting that the return of the Emperor was vouchsafed by the gods in answer to the prayers of his people.

43. forum litibus orbum: on festal occasions all public business, especially that of the courts, was regularly suspended; *orbum* is here for *vacuum*.

45. meae . . . pars: *i.e.* Horace promises to add some slight composition of his own to the larger performance of Antonius. **siquid loquar**, *etc.*: *i.e.* 'if I have any fitting inspiration'; *loquar* for *canam*.

46. bona: here for *magna*. **Sol** = *dies*.

49. tu: *tu* is the triumphal procession, here addressed as though a person; *cf. Epodes*, 9. 21, *Io triumphe, tu moraris aureos currus*.

51. civitas: in apposition with the subject of *dicemus*.

53. te: Horace abruptly returns from his apostrophe of the triumph to Antonius. **tauri, vitulus**: Antonius is to offer a costly sacrifice, Horace a humble one, proportionate to his means; *cf.* ii. 17. 30 ff.

54. solvet: *i.e.* shall release me from my vow; he had vowed the bullock when praying for the safe return of Augustus. **relicta matre** : *i.e.* the bullock is only just weaned.

56. in mea vota : *for the fulfilment of my vows; i.e.* to enable me to fulfil them by sacrifice.

57. fronte : *i.e.* with its budding horns. **imitatus** : the perfect participle here denotes contemporary action ; *cf.* i. 7. 24, *adfatus.* **curvatos ignis**, *etc.* : *i.e.* the crescent moon when entering upon its third day, the first occasion on which the new moon is visible.

59. qua duxit, *etc.* : *where it has (got) a mark;* the clause limits *niveus.* **notam** : *sc. album.* **niveus videri** : for the infinitive with *niveus*, see Introd. § 41. c.

60. cetera : *i.e.* elsewhere ; synecdochical (or Greek) accusative.

ODE III.

1. Melpomene : strictly the muse of tragedy, but invoked here simply as muse in general ; so often in Horace ; *cf.* iii. 4. 2, *Calliope; Melpomene*, as here, iii. 30. 16.

2. placido lumine : *with serene* (*i.e.* kindly) *gaze.*

3. labor Isthmius : *i.e.* exertion in the contests of the Isthmian festival.

4. clarabit pugilem : *i.e.* 'shall make a famous boxer' ; *pugilem* is predicate accusative. As in the previous ode (2. 18), boxing and chariot racing are mentioned as typical of all the contests embraced in the Greek national games.

5. curru ducet : *i.e.* in the race. **Achaico** : best taken as referring generally to all the Greek games. After the capture of Corinth in 146 B.C., the name Achaia was given to the province into which Greece was erected ; hence *Achaicus* = 'Greek.'

6. res bellica : *some martial deed.* **Deliis foliis** : the 'Delian leaves' are the leaves of the bay or laurel, sacred to Apollo, the god born at Delos.

8. quod contuderit : *for having crushed; contuderit* is subjunctive, and gives the reason supposed to be present in the minds of the Romans when celebrating the triumph.

9. ostendet Capitolio : an allusion to a triumphal procession ; see note on iv. 2. 35.

10. Tibur : see on i. 7. 13. **aquae, comae** : on springs and groves as lending inspiration to the poet, see i. 1. 30. **praefluont** :

here for *praeterfluont*, as not infrequently even in prose. On the termination *-ont*, see Introd. § 34.

12. **fingent** = *reddent.*

13. **principis urbium**: *queen of cities.*

14. **dignatur**: *deems it fitting.* **amabilis**: since poets are dear to all.

16. **iam minus**: *i.e.* less than formerly. **dente mordeor invido**: *I am gnawed by Envy's tooth.* In *Sat.* i. 6. 45 f., Horace speaks of himself as envied because of Maecenas's friendship for him.

17. **testudinis aureae**: see on i. 10. 6.

18. **dulcem quae strepitum**, *etc.*: *that modulatest the sweet tones, etc.*; *strepitus* for *sonitus*, as in *Epp.* i. 2. 31. **Pieri**: Greek vocative of *Pieris*, 'maid of Pieria,' 'muse'; *cf.* i. 26. 9, *Pimplei*, where also there is a similar separation of the vocative from its interjection (*O*).

19. **quoque**: *even*, a sense of the word already beginning to appear in Horace, and becoming common later. Another instance in Horace is *Epp.* ii. 2. 36.

20. **donatura**: *that wouldst lend*; for the free use of the future participle in Horace, see on ii. 3. 4. **cycni sonum**: for the misconception of the ancients concerning the music of the swan, see note on ii. 20. 15.

21. **totum muneris**, *etc.*: *this is all thy gift*, lit. *of thy gift* (predicate genitive).

22. **quod monstror fidicen**, *etc.*: *that I am pointed out as the minstrel of the Roman lyre*; explanatory of *hoc*. For the sentiment, *cf.* iii. 30. 13.

24. **spiro**: *i.e.* 'am inspired with the gift of song.' **si placeo**: *i.e.* 'if I really do.' **tuom**: Introd. § 34.

ODE IV.

On this ode in general, see Introd. § 9, end.

1. **Qualem**, *etc.*: *like the lightning's winged servant, to whom, etc.* The correlative of *qualem* is *talem*, to be supplied in thought with *videre Drusum* in line 18. **ministrum fulminis alitem**: the eagle, which was conceived as guarding the bolts of Jove and supplying them to the god when needed. Horace's characterization suggests the eagle in general, but, as lines 5 ff. clearly show, he is really thinking

of a single young eagle. Note that *ministrum*, the appositive of *alitem*, precedes it. This order is found occasionally in the poets.

2. regnum in avis: *dominion over the birds.*

3. expertus fidelem in Ganymēde: *having found it faithful in the case of Ganymedes.* The eagle had carried Ganymedes to the skies to be the cup-bearer of Zeus (Jupiter).

5 ff. olim, iam, mox, nunc: introducing the different stages in the growing powers of the young eagle; *olim* here means, *at first.* **iuventas**: poetic for *iuventus*, as in ii. 11. 6.

7. verni . . . venti: Horace's description does not tally exactly with the facts. The young eagles were not ready to fly till summer; but see on i. 2. 10, *columbis.*

9. paventem: *i.e.* timid at first.

10. hostem: predicatively, — *as a foe.*

11. dracones = *serpentes.*

13. qualemve laetis caprea, *etc.*: *or like a lion just weaned of which a roe has caught a glimpse, etc.* We should have expected an earlier introduction of the word *leonem*; but the initial picture of the roe peacefully grazing in abundant pasturage gives greater emphasis to the prowess of the young lion. *Pascuis* is dative, dependent upon *intenta.*

14. ubere: *rich*; here used as an adjective, limiting *lacte.*

16. dente novo: *i.e.* his teeth are as yet unused to the prey; the roe is his first victim. **peritura**: *destined to die*; see on ii. 3. 4.

17. videre, *etc.*: *such was Drusus, as the Vindelici beheld him, etc.* See note on line 1, *qualem.* **Raetis**: here used as an adjective for *Raeticis*; *cf.* i. 1. 28, *Marsus*, for *Marsicus.*

18 Vindelici: they lived in the modern Tyrol. **quibus mos unde,** *etc.*: *but whence was derived their custom of shielding the right arm, etc.*; *quibus* is the relative and is the dative of reference; *unde*, interrogative, limiting *deductus*, introduces the indirect question.

The whole parenthesis is quite in the manner of Pindar's triumphal odes. Yet the effect is extremely awkward, and aptly illustrates what Horace himself says in iv. 2. 1 ff. of the dangers that beset those who strive to imitate Pindar's style.

19. mos: Horace boldly represents the custom as arming these northern warriors with the Amazonian axe.

20. Amazonia securi: represented in ancient works of art as a two-edged axe.

21. obarmet: a word newly coined by Horace. **quaerere**

distuli: *I have forborne to seek;* the infinitive with *differo* is poetical, but is found also in Livy.

22. nec fas est: *nor is it vouchsafed*, as in i. 11. 1. **sed**: *i.e.* 'but, however that may be.' **diu victrices**: *though long victorious.*

23. late: '*on many a field*' (Bryce). **catervae**: *hordes;* used contemptuously of barbarians.

24. iuvenis: *viz.* Drusus. **revictae**: *re-* implies that the hordes were vanquished in return for the defeats they had inflicted upon the Romans.

25. sensere: *i.e.* were made to see and feel. **mens, indoles**: *head, heart.* **rite**: with *nutrita;* the hyperbaton lends emphasis.

26. nutrita: with *mens* as well as *indoles.* **faustis sub penetralibus**: '*beneath an auspicious roof*' (Page). Both *faustis* and *penetralibus* are ceremonial terms, and as such are designedly chosen to magnify the influence of the imperial household; *penetralia* is used in the transferred sense of the whole dwelling; hence *sub.*

27. paternus: *fatherly.* Augustus is credited with caring for his step-sons as though they were his own children.

28. pueros Nerones: *the youthful Neros*, Drusus and his brother Tiberius. For the substantive with adjective force, *cf.* i. 1. 1, *atavis regibus.* Drusus was the son of T. Claudius Nero and Livia, who, after being divorced from her husband, became the wife of Augustus.

29. fortes creantur fortibus et bonis: the chief emphasis of the clause rests upon the last three words, — *'tis only from the sturdy and the good that sturdy youths are born.* The reference is to Drusus's ancestors; the Nero family of the Claudian *gens* was highly distinguished in Roman annals; see below, line 37 ff.

30. patrum virtus: *the merits of their sires.*

31. imbellem feroces: the juxtaposition heightens the antithesis; *cf.* i. 6. 9, *tenues grandia.*

33 ff. The strophe emphasizes the indebtedness of Drusus and his brother to the wise and fostering care of Augustus. Their inherited worth might easily have come to naught, implies the poet, had it not been for Augustus's careful nurture.

33. doctrina sed: *doctrina* here means *training;* for the postposition of *sed*, see on i. 2. 5. **vim insitam**: *inborn worth.* **promovet**: *increases*, lit. *advances.*

35. utcumque: *whenever*, as in ii. 17. 11.

36. bene nata: *i.e.* even good endowments.

37 ff. Horace here returns to the glory of the Nero family, and devotes the remainder of the ode to a celebration of its illustrious achievements.

38. testis: *sc. est.* **Metaurum flumen**: *i.e.* the battle of the Metaurus (207 B.C.), in which Hasdrubal was defeated and slain. C. Claudius Nero, one of the consuls, though not in chief command, rendered important service in the engagement. The Metaurus was a small stream in Umbria, flowing into the Adriatic. The word is here used adjectively, limiting *flumen*; *cf. Ars Poet.* 18, *flumen Rhenum.* **Hasdrubal devictus**: *the utter defeat of Hasdrubal*; *cf.* ii. 4. 10, *ademptus Hector*; for the special force of *de* in composition, see note on i. 3. 13, *decertantem.*

39. pulcher: *glorious.*

40. ille dies: the day of the Metaurus. **Latio**: probably best taken as ablative with *fugatis.* **tenebris**: *i.e.* the gloom resulting from their previous disasters, particularly the defeat at Cannae.

41. qui primus, *etc.*: *that was the first to smile.* **adorea**: probably not from *ador* ('spelt'), as stated in Harper's *Dictionary*, but from *adoro* ('address'); hence 1) 'an address to victorious troops'; 2) as here, 'victory.'

42. dirus Afer ut: to be joined closely with *primus risit*, — *the first to smile since the dire Carthaginian*; for *ut* in this sense, *cf. Epodes*, 7. 19, *ut fluxit*; for the late postponement of *ut* in the sentence, *cf.* iv. 2. 21, *iuvenemve.* The *dirus Afer* is Hannibal.

43. taedas: *i.e.* a forest of pines.

44. equitavit: *i.e.* began to ride on his hostile raids; for this meaning of *equitare*, *cf.* i. 2. 51. The verb is here used by zeugma with *flamma* and *Eurus*, with which we may understand in thought some such verb as *furit.*

45. post hoc: *i.e.* after the battle of the Metaurus. **usque**: *continuously*; to be taken with *secundis.*

46. pubes: *i.e.* young warriors. **crevit**: *viz.* in courage and prowess.

47. tumultu: *havoc*; designedly used as a stronger word than *bellum.*

48. deos: *i.e.* the statues of the gods. **rectos**: *set up again*; the simple verb is here used for the compound, *erigo*; *rectos* is in predicate relation to *deos.*

49. perfidus: the standing epithet of Hannibal in Roman writers, though the name probably does him great injustice.

50. luporum : the word is doubtless intended to suggest that the wolf's brood (Romulus and Remus) transmitted the wolf spirit to their posterity.

51. ultro: *i.e.* gratuitously, and so, needlessly. **opimus triumphus**: boldly modelled on the familiar *spolia opima*.

53. cremato fortis ab Ilio: *sturdy (still) after Ilium's destruction.*

54. sacra: the images of their gods.

57. ut ilex tonsa: *i.e.* like an oak, shorn of its boughs and leaves. Such oaks often put forth new shoots; similarly with the defeated Romans.

58. nigrae feraci frondis: *rich in dark leafage;* for the genitive, see Introd. § 37. *a.* **Algido**: a mountain on the eastern edge of the Alban hills.

60. ducit opes animumque: *draws help and heart.*

61. non hydra, *etc.*: *not the hydra, when its body was hewn, grew mightier against Hercules, unwilling to submit; firmior* is used predicatively. The reference is to Hercules's contest with the Lernaean hydra, one of the famous twelve labors.

63. monstrumve: the reference is to the earth-born heroes who sprang from the dragon's teeth sown by Jason at Colchis and by Cadmus at Thebes. **submisere**: *sent up.* **Colchi**: the name of the people instead of the name of the place.

64. Echionaeve Thebae: Thebes is called Echionian from Echion, one of those who sprang from the dragon's teeth sown by Cadmus, king of Thebes.

65. merses, luctere: jussives, with the force of protases, — *drown it in the depths, it comes forth fairer; wrestle with it, etc.*

66. integrum victorem: *i.e.* a fresh antagonist, flushed with victory.

68. coniugibus: dative of agency. **loquenda**: *to be sung, celebrated.*

69. iam: limiting the combined ideas contained in *non mittam.* **nuntios superbos**: such as had been sent to Carthage after Cannae.

70. occidit, occidit, *etc.*: *perished, perished all our hope, etc.;* for the sententious repetition, *cf.* ii. 17. 10, 11, *ibimus, ibimus.*

73. nil Claudiae non, *etc.*: *there is nothing the Claudian might shall not achieve.*

75. curae sagaces: *viz.* of Augustus.

76. expediunt: *guide.* **acuta**: *the crises.*

ODE V.

1. Divis orte bonis: *sprung from the blessed gods.* For the conception, *cf. Carm. Saec.* 50, where Augustus is spoken of as *Veneris sanguis.* **Romulae**: for *Romuleae*, as in *Carm. Saec.* 47.

2. abes: *thou art absent.*

3. patrum: *i.e.* the senators.

4. sancto concilio: with *pollicitus.* This complimentary designation of the senate could hardly have failed to evoke the appreciation of Augustus, since he had recently made earnest endeavors to reform that body by purging it of unworthy members, and to restore the ancient respect in which the people at large had held it.

5. lucem: figuratively for hope and confidence. **dux bone**: with reference to Augustus's present function as commander of the Roman armies in the field.

6. tuos: nominative; Introd. § 34.

7. it: *passes.*

8. melius nitent: *i.e.* shine with a kindlier radiance.

9. iuvenem: for *filium.* **Notus**: the south wind prevents a voyage to the westward.

10. Carpathii maris: that part of the Aegean which was near the island of Carpathos, off the southwest coast of Asia Minor. **aequora**: here in the original sense of 'level surface.'

11. longius: for *diutius*, as in ii. 20. 4.

13. ominibus: *i.e.* consulting the omens. With *votis ominibusque et precibus*, *cf.* the close of Livy's Preface to Book i., *cum bonis potius ominibus votisque et precationibus deorum dearumque libentius inciperemus.*

15. desideriis: poetic plural.

16. quaerit: here in the sense of *requirit*, *yearn for.* **Caesarem**: emphatic variation instead of *te.*

17 ff. Kiessling calls attention to the fact that in Horace's enumeration of the blessings of Augustus's rule we have an asyndetic series of clauses, each occupying a single line.

17. tutus bos, *etc.*: *i.e.* all these blessings are the result of thy rule. In the first clause the emphasis rests upon *tutus*, which here has adverbial force. **rura, rura**: designedly repeated, to emphasize the prosperity of the peasants under Augustus's régime. After the desolation of the civil wars, Augustus had displayed the liveliest interest in reviving prosperous agricultural conditions throughout Italy.

18. nutrit: *i.e.* makes them fertile. **Faustitas** = *Felicitas;* the word is newly coined by Horace, and is not elsewhere found. It naturally partakes of the solemn ceremonial connotation of *faustus;* see on iv. 4. 26.

19. pacatum: the emphatic word of the clause. The reference is to the extermination of the pirates that had formerly infested the Mediterranean. Suetonius, in his life of Augustus, 98, tells us that as the emperor was once sailing past Puteoli the passengers and crew of an Alexandrian ship hailed him as the source of their freedom and prosperity. In the *Monumentum Ancyranum* (the famous account of Augustus's reign prepared by himself), he says *mare pacavi a praedonibus* (Tablet iii. 2. 6).

20. culpari metuit fides: *i.e.* shrinks from incurring blame. For this meaning and construction of *metuo, cf.* ii. 2. 7, *penna metuente solvi.* Under *fides* Horace probably means to suggest commercial honor; *cf.* his previous lament concerning its decay in iii. 24. 59, *periura fides consortem socium fallit.*

21 ff. One of Augustus's most cherished purposes was the elevation of social morality; *cf.* iii. 6. Yet the reforms indicated in this stanza represent pious hopes rather than actual achievements.

22. mos et lex: *cf.* iii. 24. 35, *quid leges sine moribus vanae proficiunt?* Under *lex* Horace refers to the legislation of 18 B.C., known as the *lex Iulia de adulteriis.* **edomuit**: *has thoroughly overcome.*

23. simili: *i.e.* like the lawful husband of the mother; *cf.* Catullus's exquisite lines, 61. 217 ff.: —

'Sit suo similis patri
Manlio et facile insciis
Noscitetur ab omnibus
Et pudicitiam suae
Matris indicet ore.'

24. comes: emphatically placed at the end of the clause and verse; punishment for wrong-doing is instant.

25. Parthum: the Roman standards captured by the Parthians from Crassus at Carrhae (53 B.C.) had been returned to the Romans in 20 B.C., seven years before the time of this ode. **gelidum Scythen**: *cf.* iii. 8. 23. The Scythians are thus characterized since they dwelt in the distant North, the home of the wintry blasts; *cf.* iii. 10. 3.

26. Germania horrida: *Germany rough (with woods)*; *cf.* Tacitus, *Germania*, 5, *silvis horrida.*

27. incolumi Caesare: with *paveat*. **ferae Iberiae**: probably alluding to the successive uprisings of the Cantabri, to the savage Concani, who delighted in drinking horses' blood, *etc.*

28. curet: *i.e.* feels concern.

29. condit: *disposes, passes.*

30. viduas ad arbores: *to the waiting trees*, such as elms, poplars, *etc.*; *cf. Epodes*, 2. 9, *adulta vitium propagine altas maritat populos*, and, on the other hand, ii. 15. 4, *platanusque caelebs*, with note. **ducit**: *trains.*

31. alteris mensis: the dessert, ordinarily called *mensae secundae*. Between the main meal and the dessert it was customary to make offerings to the house gods, or Lares.

32. te adhibet deum: after the return of Augustus from Egypt in 29, the senate ordained that offerings should be made to him not only at public banquets, but also at private meals.

33. prosequitur: lit. *attends*, and so *honors*. **mero defuso pateris**: *i.e.* in sacrifice.

34. Laribus: compendiary for *numine Larum*; *cf.* i. 1. 23, *lituo tubae permixtus sonitus.*

35. Graecia: for *Graeci.*

36. memor: *i.e.* calling them to mind by sacrifices in their honor.

37. o utinam: for the hiatus, see on i. 1. 2, *o et*. **ferias**: Augustus's reign of peace and prosperity is conceived as one long holiday.

39. sicci, uvidi: *when our lips are dry, when flushed with wine.*

ODE VI.

1. magnae vindicem linguae: Niobe, proud of her twelve children, had boasted herself superior to Latona, who had only two. In punishment of this arrogance, Apollo and Diana had slain all of Niobe's offspring with their arrows, and had turned the mother into stone; *vindicem* is predicate accusative; *magnae linguae* is the equivalent of *magniloquentiae.*

2. Tityos raptor: see on iii. 4. 77.

3. sensit: with the same force as *sensere*, in iv. 4. 25. **prope victor**: *when almost victorious*, *viz.* as a result of Hector's death.

4. Phthius: the Myrmidons, Achilles's followers, dwelt in Phthiotis, a district of Thessaly. **Achilles**: said to have been slain by an arrow shot by Paris, but directed by Apollo.

6. filius Thetidis, *etc.*: the appositive shares the adversative force of the *quamvis* clause, — *although he was the son of sea-born Thetis and made Troy tremble, etc.*

8. cuspide: with *quateret* only.

13. non: the negative goes with both *inclusus* and *falleret*, *i.e. he* would not have hidden, nor would he have stooped to such deceit. **inclusus**: with reflexive force. **equo**: *sc.* the wooden horse. **Minervae**: dative with *mentito*.

14. sacra mentito: the Greeks pretended that the horse was an offering for their safe return; Virg. *Aen.* ii. 17. **mentito, feriatos**: both participles here denote contemporary, not prior, action; *cf.* i. 7. 24, *adfatus*. **male feriatos**: *keeping ill-timed holiday*. The allusion is to the festal celebrations in which the Trojans indulged when, thinking the Greeks had returned home, they drew the wooden horse into the city; *cf.* Virg. *Aen.* ii. 248 ff.

15. choreis: with *laetam*.

16. falleret; **ureret** (19): imperfect for pluperfect; the action is brought back to the present for greater vividness; *falleret* here means, *would (not) have stealthily entered*, lit. *would (not) have deceived*.

17. palam: the emphasis of the clause rests upon this word, which is strongly contrasted with *falleret*. **captis gravis**: *cruel to his captives*.

18. nescios fari: *lisping*.

19. latentem: *sc. puerum*, *i.e.* the child as yet unborn.

21. tuis: emphatic. **gratae**: *winsome*.

22. divom: genitive plural.

23. rebus: *fortunes*. **potiore ductos alite muros**: *walls built under better auspices*, *i.e.* better than the walls of Troy, which, being built by fraud (iii. 3. 21 ff.), were doomed to destruction. For the ablative of attendant circumstance in *potiore alite*, *cf.* i. 15. 5, *mala avi*.

25. argutae: *melodious*. **Thaliae**: see on iii. 4. 2, *Calliope*.

26. Xantho: a river of Lycia; on its banks was Patara, one of the chief seats of Apollo's worship.

27. Dauniae Camenae: for *meae Musae;* Venusia, Horace's birthplace, was in Apulia, poetically called *Daunia*.

28. levis Agyieu: *beardless Agyieus; Agyieus*, as an epithet of Apollo, primarily designated the god who sends his light into the narrow streets or lanes. The word is derived from the Greek ἀγυιά, 'lane.' In the Latin transcription, *yi* is diphthongal, representing υι of the Greek Ἀγυιεύς; the combination is to be pronounced like *ui* in *huic*, *cui*; *levis* (literally *smooth*, and so *beardless*) is applied to Apollo as being always young.

29. spiritum: as in ii. 16. 38, *spiritum Graiae tenuem Camenae.* **Phoebus, Phoebus**: *cf.* ii. 17. 10, for the repetition.

31. virginum primae puerique: the boys and maidens who sang the *Carmen Saeculare.* See *Carm. Saec.*, 'Occasion of the Hymn,' p. 158.

33. Deliae deae: Diana. **tutela**: *i.e.* objects of care. The word is in apposition with *primae* and *pueri.* **fugacis**: for the force, see on ii. 13. 40, *timidos lyncas.*

34. cohibentis: with *deae.*

35. Lesbium pedem: *i.e.* the Sapphic and Adonic metre, in which the *Carmen Saeculare* was composed.

36. pollicis ictum: *the beat of my finger.*

37. rite: *duly*, with proper ceremony.

38. crescentem face: of the waxing moon.

39. prosperam frugum: '*ripener of crops*' (Bryce); for the genitive, see Introd. § 37. *a.* **celerem volvere**: Introd. § 41. *c*; *cf.* i. 15. 18, *celerem sequi.* **pronos**: *i.e.* swiftly passing.

41. iam: with *nupta.* **dis amicum**: *dear to the gods*; for this force of *amicus*, *cf.* i. 26. 1, *Musis amicus.*

42. saeculo: see *Carm. Saec.*, 'Occasion of the Hymn,' p. 158. **luces** = *dies*; the celebration of the secular games lasted three days and three nights.

43. reddidi: *rendered*, *i.e.* performed. **docilis modorum**: *trained in the measures*; Introd. § 37. *a.*

44. vatis: for the force of the word, see on i. 1. 35.

ODE VII.

1. gramina campis arboribusque comae: chiastic arrangement.

2. comae: *foliage*, by a common figure; *cf.* i. 21. 5.

3. mutat terra vices: *Earth is going through her changes*; *vices* is accusative of 'result produced.' **decrescentia**: the emphasis of the clause rests on this word. Horace means, 'the rivers are *now* subsiding in their channels as they flow past their banks'; hitherto, swollen by the melting of the winter snow upon the mountains, they had overflowed their banks; *cf.* the picture in iv. 12. 3, *nec fluvii strepunt hiberna nive turgidi.*

5. Gratia cum geminis sororibus: see on iii. 21. 22.

7. immortalia ne speres: the clause is object of *monet; immortalia* is here equivalent to *immortalitatem*, *i.e.* immortal life here on earth.

9. ff. Note the variety with which the advent of the different seasons is described. **zephyris**: *i.e.* under their influence.

10. simul = *simul atque.*

12. iners: *i.e.* unproductive; *cf.* the similar force of *piger* in i. 22. 17, *pigris campis.*

13. damna caelestia: *their losses in the sky.* **celeres lunae**: *the swiftly changing moons.*

14. nos: as contrasted with *lunae.*

15. Tullus dives: the special significance of *dives* as applied to *Tullus* is obscure. Many scholars regard it as corrupt.

17. an: *whether;* for this use of *an*, *cf.* ii. 4. 13, *nescias an.* **hodiernae summae**: *to to-day's sum*, *i.e.* to the number of days that thou now countest.

19. amico animo: *to thy own soul* or *self; amicus* here seems an imitation of the Greek φίλος, lit. 'dear,' but often used as a possessive pronoun.

20. dederīs, occiderīs (21): the quantity of the *i* is unusual. In the perfect subjunctive the *i* of the 2d singular was originally long; hence the occasional reminiscence of the *i* would occasion us no surprise in subjunctive forms. But *dederis* and *occideris* are here future perfects, in which the *i* of the termination was historically short. We can only say that the future perfect here (as occasionally elsewhere) follows the analogy of the perfect subjunctive.

21. splēndida arbitria: *his imposing verdict; arbitria* for *iudicia* (poetic plural). **Minos**: traditionally represented as a judge of shades in the lower world.

23. Torquāte: apparently the same person who is addressed in *Epist.* i. 5, where, as here, allusion is made to his eminence as an orator. **genus**: the Manlii Torquati were a famous family, and the Torquatus here mentioned may have belonged to the Manlian *gens.*

25. Diana: the virgin goddess would naturally favor the chaste Hippolytus. **pudicum Hippolytum**: his refusal of the advances of his step-mother, Phaedra, wife of Theseus, cost him his death. According to one account, he was restored to life by Aesculapius. Horace, following the more ancient tradition, represents him as permanently confined to the underworld.

26. liberat: *release.*

27. Lethaea vincula = *vincula mortis.* **caro Pirithoo**: the friendship of Theseus and Pirithous was proverbial. For Pirithous's crime, see on iii. 4. 79, where, as here, Horace follows the tradition that Pirithous's imprisonment in the lower world was perpetual. Another account represents Pirithous as released by Hercules. *Pirithoo* is dative of reference.

ODE VIII.

1. Donarem: apodosis of the contrary-to-fact condition contained in *divite me* (line 5), which is equivalent to *si essem dives.* **pateras, aera, tripodas**: an apparent reminiscence of a passage in Pindar's *Isthmian Odes*, i. 18, where bowls, bronze vessels, and tripods are enumerated as prizes in the Greek games; the *paterae* were made of gold or other precious metals; the tripods usually of bronze. **commodus**: *willingly, generously.*

2. Censorine: C. Marcius Censorinus, consul in 8 B.C.

4. neque pessuma: *nor the meanest;* litotes for 'the choicest.'

5. ferres: *shouldst thou receive.* **divite me scilicet artium**: *that is, of course (scilicet), if I were rich in works of art;* for the genitive with *divite*, see Introd. § 37. *a.*

6. Parrhasius, Scopas: Parrhasius (flourished 400 B.C.) was the most famous painter of his time. In his contest with Zeuxis, "the picture of Zeuxis represented a bunch of grapes, so naturally painted that the birds flew at the picture to eat the fruit; upon which the artist, confident in this proof of his success, called upon his rival no longer to delay to draw aside the curtain and show his picture; but the picture of Parrhasius was the curtain itself, which Zeuxis had mistaken for real drapery. On discovering his error, Zeuxis yielded the palm to Parrhasius, saying that he himself had deceived birds, but Parrhasius an artist" (Smith's *Classical Dictionary*). Scopas, of Paros (flourished 395–350 B.C.), was a distinguished sculptor. Among his best-known works was the group representing the destruction of Niobe's children. **protulit**: *produced.*

7. hic: Scopas. **saxo** = *marmore.* **ille**: Parrhasius.

8. ponere: *to execute.*

9. haec vis: *this store, viz.* of treasures.

10. res: *estate.* **est egens** = *eget.*

11. gaudes carminibus, carmina possumus, *etc.*: effective chiasmus, designed to emphasize the notion contained in *carminibus.*

12. pretium dicere muneri: *to tell the value of the gift*, *i.e.* to set forth the transcendent glory of the poet's gift; *muneri* is dative of reference.

13. incisa, *etc.*: *i.e.* marble tablets engraved with inscriptions commemorating famous achievements. **publicis**: *i.e.* added by the state at public expense.

15. celeres fugae Hannibalis: *Hannibal's swift flight*, after Zama; the plural is poetic.

16. reiectae: *i.e.* hurled back upon his own head.

17. non incendia, *etc.*: either the text is here corrupt or Horace has blundered, for the poet represents the destruction of Carthage as consummated by the Scipio who won the name *Africanus* from his defeat of the Carthaginians at Zama in 202 B.C. It was the younger Scipio that destroyed Carthage. Most probably the verse is an interpolation, as Horace can hardly be supposed to have been ignorant of the common facts of Roman history. **impiae**: in view of the traditional *perfidia* of the Carthaginians.

18. eius: with *laudes*.

20. Calabrae Pierides: *i.e.* the *Annals* of Ennius, here referred to as inspired by the Calabrian muses, since Ennius's birthplace was Rudiae in Calabria. The *Annals* was an historical poem dealing with the history of Rome from the earliest times to Ennius's own day. The work naturally glorified the achievements of the elder Scipio, with whom Ennius lived on terms of intimate friendship.

21. chartae: *i.e.* poets in their writings. **sileant**: here transitive; as object, understand *id*, antecedent of *quod*.

22. tuleris: conclusion of the condition, — *would you receive.* **foret, obstaret**: *foret* refers to the present, *obstaret* to the past. **Iliae Mavortisque puer**: Romulus; *Mavors*, for *Mars*, is poetical.

25. ereptum Stygiis fluctibus: *i.e.* rescued from oblivion in the same sense as iv. 2. 23, *nigro invidet Orco.* **Aeacum**: son of Jupiter and grandfather of Achilles. He was king of Aegina and was famed for his justice and goodness.

26. virtus: *i.e.* endowment. **potentium**: *gifted.*

27. divitibus insulis: here apparently in the sense of the 'Isles of the Blest,' the abode of heroes after death.

28. Musa: the emphasis of the sentence rests upon this word; 'tis the Muse, and the Muse only, that lends immortal glory.

29. sic: *viz.* as a result of the poet's song.

31. clarum sidus: in apposition with *Tyndaridae.* For the Tyndaridae (Castor and Pollux) as the patron deities of mariners, see on i. 3. 2.

33. ornatus: *decking;* with middle force and denoting contemporary, not prior, action; *cf.* i. 7. 24, *adfatus.* The line seems a gratuitous and even embarrassing addition; many editors reject it as an interpolation, modelled upon iii. 25. 20.

34. Liber: Bacchus, a mortal raised to the gods for his services to humanity; iii. 3. 13.

As printed, this ode has thirty-four lines. In the other odes of Horace the number of lines is some multiple of 4. Probably in this ode, as written by Horace, the number of lines was also a multiple of 4. Inasmuch as verse 17 is a palpable interpolation, and verse 33 almost as certainly so, it seems most natural to assume that the ode consisted originally of 32 lines.

ODE IX.

1. Ne credas: a clause of purpose, introducing the reason for the statements made in lines 5 ff.

2. longe sonantem: *i.e.* its roar is heard afar. **natus ad Aufidum**: at Venusia: Introd. § 1; *cf.* iii. 30. 10.

3. non . . . artis: litotes for 'in new forms of verse.' The reference is to the new lyric metres of Aeolic origin which Horace made current; cf. iii. 30. 13.

4. socianda chordis: *to be wedded to the lyre; cf.* ii. 12. 4, *aptari citharae modis.* The implication that the ode is written for singing to musical accompaniment is probably a traditional fiction of poets. Greek lyric poetry was composed primarily for musical performance; but there is nothing to indicate that this was true of Horace's lyric verse. *Chordis* is ablative of association; Introd. § 38. *a.*

5. si = *etsi*, as often when following a negative statement. **priores sedes**: *i.e.* the place of honor, lit. *the first seats*, a figure drawn from the theatre. **Maeonius**: *i.e.* Lydian; see on i. 6. 2.

6. Homerus: note that the real comparison is not between individuals, but between two types of poetry, the epic and the lyric. **latent**: *are unknown.* **Pindaricae**: on Pindar as a lyric poet, see iv. 2. 1.

7. Ceae: *i.e.* of Simonides of Ceos (an island of the Cyclades); he flourished about 500 B.C., and was especially successful as a writer of elegies and epigrams. **Alcaei minaces**: the allusion is to Alcaeus's energetic invectives against Pittacus and Myrsilus (or Myrtilus), tyrants of Mitylene.

8. Stesichori graves Camenae: Stesichorus, of Himera in Sicily, flourished about 600 B.C.; he was successful in the treatment of lofty themes.

9. lusit Anacreon: *ludere* is used to refer to the light, sportive lyrics of Anacreon (550 B.C.), the chief themes of which were love and wine.

11. vivont: for the spelling, see Introd. § 34. **calores**: *passion.*

12. Aeoliae puellae: Sappho; see on ii. 13. 24; *puellae* is genitive.

13. arsit: *became inflamed;* from *ardesco* (not *ardeo*). **adulteri**: *a paramour.*

14. crinis: this and the following accusatives are the object of *mirata.* **aurum vestibus illitum**: *gold-bespangled raiment,* lit. *gold spread upon his raiment.*

15. regalis cultus: *regal splendor.*

17. primusve, *etc.*: *i.e.* the first to gain fame as an archer. The negative of line 13 extends also to this sentence. On Teucer, see i. 7. 21, note. **Cydonio**: *Cretan;* from *Cydonia,* a Cretan city. The Cretans were famous archers; hence 'Cretan darts,' 'Cretan bows,' *etc.*; *cf.* i. 15. 17, *calami spicula Cnosii.*

18. non semel Ilios, *etc.*: *i.e.* 'other Troys have been besieged and captured.'

20. Idomeneus: a Cretan, and one of the bravest leaders on the side of the Greeks. **Sthenelus**: the charioteer of Diomedes.

21. dicenda: *deserving of celebration.*

22. acer Deiphobus: one of the most valiant of the Trojan warriors. He married Helen after the death of Paris.

24. primus: emphasized by its position at the end of the verse.

26. inlacrimabiles: *i.e.* unwept and unsung.

27. urgentur: *are overwhelmed.* **longa nocte**: *sc. mortis.*

28. sacro: *cf.* iii. 1. 3, *sacerdos Musarum.*

29. paulum sepultae, *etc.*: the emphasis rests upon *sepultae,* — *in the tomb, hidden worth differs but little from cowardice;* for the dative with *distat, cf. Sat.* i. 4. 48, *differt sermoni.*

30. non . . . silebo: *i.e.* 'I will not leave you unmentioned and unhonored'; for *silere* with the accusative, *cf.* i. 12. 21.

31. chartis: *i.e.* in my poems.

32. labores: *achievements.*

33. Lolli: Marcus Lollius, consul in 21 B.C. In 16 B.C., while governor of Germany, he suffered a disastrous defeat at the hands of the Sygambri and their allies. Lollius stood high in the favor of Augustus, but the Roman historians describe him as avaricious, treacherous, and hypocritical. There is no reason, however, to doubt the sincerity of Horace's praise. Possibly Lollius had not yet developed the evil qualities mentioned; possibly they were unknown to the poet. **carpere**, *i.e.* to belittle. **lividas**: *envious.*

35. rerum prudens: *versed in affairs.* **que . . . et**: correlative.

36. dubiis: here in the sense of *adversis.* **rectus**: *well poised.* We may have here some allusion to Lollius's steadfastness at the time of his defeat by the Sygambri.

37. vindex fraudis: *i.e.* of dishonesty on the part of his subordinates.

38. ducentis ad se cuncta: *that draws all to itself.* **pecuniae**: *from money*, *i.e.* love of money, greed; for the genitive with *abstinens*, *cf.* iii. 27. 69.

39. consul: in apposition with *animus* (line 35) by a somewhat bold metaphor. **non unius anni**: *i.e.* a consul for all time, ever to be honored.

40. sed quotiens: in strong antithesis to *non unius anni*, — *not for one year but as long as* (lit. *as often as*).

41. iudex: *in its capacity as judge; iudex* is in apposition with *is* understood, referring to *animus.* **praetulit, reiecit, explicuit**: an asyndetic series.

42. alto voltu: *with lofty gaze*, *i.e.* with glance of lofty disdain. **dona**: *bribes.* **nocentium**: *the guilty.*

43. obstantis catervas: the opposing hosts of evil.

44. explicuit arma: *has carried its arms*, *viz.* of honesty and justice.

46. recte: with *vocaveris.* **occupat**: *i.e.* wins, deserves.

48. uti, pati: the infinitive with *callere* is poetical.

51. non ille: *the one that is not* (*afraid*).

52. timidus perire: *cf.* iii. 19. 2, *Codrus non timidus mori.*

ODE X.

1. Veneris muneribus: *i.e.* beauty of face and figure.

2. insperata: *unexpectedly.* **pluma**: *i.e.* the downy beard that shall take away thy blooming cheeks. **superbiae**: dative.

3. quae . . . involitant: boys wore the hair long. **deciderint**: *i.e.* shall be shorn.

4. nunc et: for the postponement of *et*, see on i. 2. 5. **prior**: *lovelier*.

5. mutatus verterit: lit. *changed shall turn;* a redundant expression. **Ligurine**: mentioned also in iv. 1. 33. **verterit**: here intransitive, as not infrequently.

6. speculo: ablative of means. **alterum**: *altered*, in predicate construction.

7. mens: *i.e.* spirit of compliance. **puero**: *sc. mihi* (dative of possession).

8. his animis: *i.e.* my present repentant spirit.

ODE XI.

2. Albani: *sc. vini.* The Alban was one of the better wines.

3. nectendis coronis: *for weaving garlands.*

4. vis: *abundance, store*, as in iv. 8. 9.

5. qua: with *fulges.* **crinis religata**: *sc. in nodum; religata* is used as middle; *crinis* is direct object. **fulges**: *i.e.* 'thou art wont to look so resplendent.'

6. ridet argento: *sparkles with silver*, *i.e.* with silver vessels.

7. verbenis: see on i. 19. 14. They are designated as *castae*, since dedicated to religious purposes.

8. spargier: archaic and poetical for *spargi.* Horace does not elsewhere in the *Odes* use such infinitive forms.

10. pueris puellae: the attendant slaves.

11. sordidum: *sooty.* **flammae**: on the hearth. **trepidant**: of the dancing motion of the flames.

12. vertice: *in wreaths;* with *rotantes.*

14. agendae: *i.e.* to be celebrated.

15. mensem Veneris, Aprilem: April is called 'the month of Venus,' since she was believed in that month to have sprung from the sea. **marinae**: *sea-born*, as in iii. 26. 5.

16. findit = *dividit.*

18. proprio = *meo.*

19. luce: for *die.* **adfluentis**: the years are thought of as flowing onward like a stream.

20. ordinat: *i.e.* counts.

21. occupavit: *i.e.* has already won.

22. non tuae sortis: *i.e.* above thy station; *sortis* is genitive of quality with *iuvenem*, which is in apposition with *Telephum.*

23. grata: with *compede*, as in i. 33. 14; oxymoron.

25 ff. Illustrations of the disaster that follows too lofty aspirations.

25. ambustus Phaethon: *i.e.* the destruction of Phaethon, who was burned by driving the chariot of Phoebus too near the sun. **avaras**: here in the sense of *avidas*, — *too eager, too lofty.*

26. grave: *i.e.* significant, one to be heeded.

27. gravatus Bellerophontem: *i.e.* having refused to bear him. After slaying the Chimaera with the assistance of Pegasus, Bellerophon endeavored to fly to heaven upon his back, but Pegasus threw off his rider, who fell to the earth.

29. ut sequare et vites: the substantive *ut*-clauses depend upon the notion of warning contained in *exemplum praebet.* **te digna**: *what befits thee.* **ultra quam licet**, *etc.*: *by thinking it wrong to hope for more than is lawful.*

31. disparem: *one ill-suited to thee.*

33. alia calebo femina: for the ablative, *cf.* i. 4. 19, *quo tepebunt.*

34. condisce: *i.e.* learn with care. **amanda** = *amabili.*

35. quos reddas: *to sing*, lit. *to render*, as in iv. 6. 43. The subjunctive is one of purpose. **atrae curae**: referring to her regrets for Telephus.

ODE XII.

1. mare temperant: *i.e.* the mild spring breezes smooth the surface of the sea, ruffled by the boisterous blasts of winter.

2. impellunt: strictly applicable only to the ships, but here applied to the sails. **lintea**: *sc. vela, sails.* **animae Thraciae**: breezes from the North; *animae* is in apposition with *comites.* For the conception of a wind as the companion of a season, *cf.* i. 25. 19, *hiemis sodali Euro.*

5 ff. The advent of the swallow is described in terms of the Procne legend. According to the commoner account, Procne, daughter of Pandīon, king of Attica, had married Tereus, king of Thrace, and by him became the mother of Itys. Tereus then dismissed Procne and married her sister Philomela. In revenge Procne killed Itys and served up the flesh of the child to his father. She then fled with Philomela. Tereus followed them, whereupon Procne was changed into a swallow, Philomela into a nightingale.

6. **infelix avis** : the swallow. **Cecropiae** : for *Atticae* ; Cecrops was the first king of Attica.

7. **aeternum opprobrium** : connected by *et* to *infelix*. **quod** : in the sense of *propterea quod*. **male** : *i.e.* too savagely, *viz.* in sacrificing her own son.

8. **regum libidines** : generalizing plurals.

9. **dicunt** : here for *canunt*, *play*, as in iii. 4. 1, *dic age tibia*.

10. **fistula** : the pipe of Pan.

11. **cui pecus**, *etc.* : Pan (the Roman Faunus) was the patron deity of the Arcadian shepherd folk ; see i. 17. 2. **nigri colles** : the reference is to the dark evergreen trees that covered the Arcadian mountains ; *cf.* i. 21. 7, *nigris Erymanthi silvis*.

13. **adduxere . . . tempora** : *the season has brought thirst* ; in Italy, even the early spring is warm. **Vergili** : not the poet Virgil, but, as the context seems to show, some merchant. Nothing definite is known about him.

14. **pressum Calibus** = *Calenum* ; see on i. 20. 9. **Liberum** : for *vinum*.

15. **iuvenum nobilium** : who the noble patrons were, is not known.

17. **parvos onyx** : some tiny receptacle made of onyx.

18. **Sulpiciis horreis** : a public storehouse on the Aventine, which later came into the possession of the Emperor Sulpicius Galba. The scholiast Porphyrio (shortly after 200 A.D.) remarks : *hodieque Galbae horrea vino et oleo et similibus aliis referta sunt.* On *Sulpiciis* for *Sulpicianis*, *cf.* iv. 5. 1, *Romulae* (for *Romuleae*) *gentis*.

19. **donare, eluere** : Introd. § 41. *c*. **largus** : *rich in promise.* **amara curarum** : *the bitterness of care* ; for this use of the neuter plural, see on ii. 1. 23, *cuncta terrarum*.

20. **eluere** : *to drown*, as *lavere* in iii. 12. 2.

22. **merce** : *viz.* the nard. **non ego**, *etc.* : *I'm not the man*, *etc.*

23. **immunem** : *i.e.* without contributing thy share. **tingere** : '*to steep*' (Page).

24. **plena** : *well-stocked*.

26. **nigrorum ignium** : *viz.* of the funeral pyre. Death and all its associations are characterized by the poets as black ; *cf.* ii. 3. 16. **dum licet** : with *misce*.

27. **consiliis** : *i.e.* plans for amassing wealth by trade ; the case is ablative (Introd. § 38. *a*).

28. **desipere** : *i.e.* to cast serious thoughts aside. **in loco** : *at the fitting time*.

ODE XIII.

1. **Audivere di, di audivere**: *the gods have heard, aye heard they have;* for the repetition (here combined with chiasmus), *cf.* ii. 17. 10, *ibimus, ibimus.* **mea vota**: apparently a reference to the sentiments of iii. 10, where Lyce is represented as refusing to reciprocate the poet's devotion. In the present passage, the implication is that he had prayed that Lyce might be punished for her cruelty by growing old while still longing to seem as beautiful as in youth.

4. **ludis**: *i.e.* as though still a young girl; *cf.* iii. 15. 4, *desine inter ludere virgines.* **bibis impudens**: such indulgence might befit a younger person, but in Lyce it is out of place.

5. **cantu tremulo**: the maudlin singing of a drunken person; *cantu* is ablative of means with *sollicitas.*

6. **lentum**: *the sluggard.* **sollicitas**: conative, — *try to rouse.*

7. **Chiae**: here a proper name, like Lesbia, Delia, *etc.*; originally 'maid of Chios.'

8. **excubat**: *keeps watch;* the word is nicely chosen in view of the technical meaning ('stand guard') which it inevitably suggests. The implication is that the god goes to sleep in Lyce's presence.

9. **importunus**: *disdainfully.* **transvolat**: the god is winged. **aridas quercus**: figurative for faded women. So in i. 25. 19, Lydia is likened to *aridae frondes.*

12. **capitis nives**: gray hair.

13. **Coae purpurae**: the purple silks made at the island of Cos, much worn by the Roman *demi-monde.*

14. **cari lapides**: *precious stones.* **semel**: *once for all.*

15. **notis fastis**: *in the public records; fastis* is ablative, dependent upon both *condita* and *inclusit; notis* suggests that the records, which are open to all, bear clear testimony to Lyce's age. **condita inclusit**: *has laid away and locked up.*

17. **Venus**: here for *venustas*, 'graceful beauty.'

18. **illius, illius**: *of her, of her, I ask;* note the short penult; for the repetition, *cf.* line 1 above.

20. **surpuerat**: for *surripuerat;* the form is colloquial.

21. **felix**: *viz.* on account of my tributes to thy charms. **post Cinaram**: *i.e.* after her death; for Cinara, see on iv. 1. 3 ff. **notaque et artium**, *etc.*: *a well-known beauty and of winning ways; que . . . et* are correlative.

24. **servatura**: the future participle here denotes purpose; on its

free use in Horace, see on ii. 3. 4. **parem**: *to equal;* in predicate relation to *Lycen.*

25. **cornicis vetulae temporibus**: for the proverbial longevity of the raven, *cf.* iii. 17. 13, *annosa cornix*, with note.

28. **dilapsam in cineres facem**: the comparison is intended to suggest that Lyce is no longer a torch to fire the heart of youth; her flame has burnt out.

ODE XIV.

1. **patrum, Quiritium**: *i.e. senatus populusque Romanus.*

2. **plenis honorum muneribus**: *with full meed of honors; honorum* is appositional genitive.

3. **in aevom** = *in omne aevom, for ever;* a pleonastic modifier of *aeternet.*

4. **titulos**: *inscriptions.* **memores fastus**: *commemorative records;* for the force of *memores*, see on iii. 17. 4; note that for poetic effect Horace here uses the rare form *fastūs* (fourth declension); ordinarily the word is of the second declension.

5. **aeternet**: deliberative subjunctive. **habitabilis**: here, *inhabited.*

6. **oras**: *regions.*

7. **quem**: prolepsis. **legis expertes Latinae**: *free (as yet) from Roman rule.*

8. **Vindelici**: see iv. 4. **didicere**: *cf.* iv. 4. 25, *sensere.*

9. **Marte**: for *bello*, as often. **tuo**: the emphatic word, — *thine were the troops.*

10. **Genaunos, Breunos**: they dwelt in the valley of the Inn in the Tyrol.

11. **velocis**: *i.e.* swift in their movements of attack and retreat. **arces**: *strongholds.*

12. **Alpibus tremendis**: awe-inspiring with their glaciers and towering peaks.

13. **deiecit**: *i.e.* hurled down from their heights. **plus vice simplici**: *i.e.* with a vengeance that more than made amends for the previous devastation wrought by these barbarians; *plus* here does not influence the construction.

14. **maior Neronum**: Tiberius, who was four years older than his brother Drusus; *cf.* iv. 4. 28.

15. **immanis Raetos**: for the Raeti, see on iv. 4, 'Occasion of the

Poem.' Strabo tells us that, whenever they captured a town, they slaughtered all the male inhabitants, even to the children.

17. spectandus quantis fatigaret, *etc.: a wonder to behold for the havoc with which he overcame, etc.; fatigaret* is subjunctive of indirect question. The ordinary caesura of the verse is neglected, as in i. 37. 14; Introd. § 43.

18. devota morti pectora liberae: *their hearts sacrificed to the death of freemen;* this observation is intended to heighten Tiberius's glory by indicating the obstacles with which he had to cope.

21. exercet: *lashes.* **Auster**: 'the boisterous master of the Adriatic'; iii. 3. 5; i. 3. 14 f. **Pleiadum choro,** *etc.*: the reference is to the autumn setting of the Pleiades, which was attended by storms.

24. per ignes: *i.e.* through the fierce tumult of the fight.

25. tauriformis Aufidus: rivers were often represented as bulls, a conception doubtless drawn from the roaring stream.

26. Dauni: a mythical king of Apulia. **praefluit**: for *praeterfluit*, as in iv. 3. 10.

29. Claudius: Tiberius (Claudius Nero).

30. ferrata: *i.e.* with iron weapons, or defended by iron mail.

32. stravit humum: *i.e.* with the slain. **sine clade**: *viz.* to his own troops.

33. te, te, tuos: emphatic repetition; the reference is to Augustus; *tuos* is here used in the sense of *propitios.*

34. quo die = *eo die, quo, viz.* August 29, 30 B.C.

36. vacuam aulam: Antony and Cleopatra had withdrawn from the palace to the Mausoleum, where they committed suicide.

37. lustro tertio: *i.e.* fifteen years later.

38. reddidit = *rursus dedit.*

39. peractis imperiis: the 'orders executed' are those given to Drusus and Tiberius by Augustus. The case is dative.

40. adrogavit: *i.e.* has won.

41. Cantaber: the Cantabrians had long been a menace to Rome, and though temporarily subdued had risen in repeated revolts. They were finally subjugated by Agrippa in 19 B.C.

42. Medus: for *Parthus*, as often. A compact of friendship between Rome and Parthia had been entered into in 20 B.C., by which the Parthian king, Phraates, restored the Roman standards captured from Crassus at the disaster of Carrhae in 53 B.C. **Indus, profugus Scythes**: Suetonius (*Aug.* 21) tells us that Augustus made treaties of friendship with the Indians and Scythians. On *profugus Scythes*, *cf.* iii. 24. 9.

43. tutela praesens: *mighty guardian; tutela*, properly abstract, is here used concretely; *praesens* as in i. 35. 2.

44. dominae: *cf.* iv. 3. 13, *Romae principis urbium.*

46. Nilus, Hister, Tigris: note the artistic change from the names of peoples to the streams near whose banks the people dwelt. The Nile suggests the Aethiopians, who, after previous hostilities against the Romans, in 20 B.C. sent ambassadors to sue for peace. The Hister suggests the refractory Dacians; the Tigris the Armenians, subjugated by Tiberius in 20 B.C.

47. beluosus Oceanus: the waters about Britain were fabled to breed monsters unknown in other seas. In representing the British Ocean as heeding Augustus's mandates, Horace probably refers to the embassy sent to Rome by certain British kings, — at what time is uncertain.

48. obstrepit: *roars around;* lit. *roars at.*

49. non paventis funera Galliae: the firm faith of the Gauls in the immortality of the soul and in happiness after death enabled them to face destruction with resolution; *Galliae* is genitive. For the poetic plural in *funera*, *cf.* i. 8. 15.

50. durae Hiberiae: *cf.* iv. 5. 27, *ferae Hiberiae;* as the Cantabrians have already been alluded to above, Horace is here probably thinking of other wild tribes of the Spanish peninsula. **audit**: *obeys.*

51. caede gaudentes Sygambri: see on iv. 2. 34.

52. compositis armis: '*with weapons laid to rest*' (Page).

ODE XV.

1. proelia: *i.e.* of Augustus's martial achievements. **loqui** = *canere*, as iv. 2. 45.

2. lyra: with *increpuit*, — 'rebuked me by striking his lyre.' The same god gives the warning who had endowed him with the gift of song; see iv. 6. 29, *mihi Phoebus artem carminis dedit.*

3. ne darem: (*bidding me*) *not to spread;* a substantive clause, depending upon the idea of ordering involved in *increpuit.* **parva Tyrrhenum**, *etc.*: 'my tiny sails of lyric song on the vast sea of Augustus's glory.'

4. tua Caesar, aetas, *etc.*: forbidden to sing of martial deeds, the poet proceeds to rehearse Augustus's triumphs in the field of peace.

5. **fruges . . . uberes**: agriculture had been well-nigh ruined by the protracted civil wars.

6. Note the impressive polysyndeton (*et . . . et . . . et, etc.*) continued till line 16. **signa**, *etc.*: a poet's exaggeration of the facts, for which see on iv. 14. 42. **nostro Iovi**: note the emphatic position of *nostro*, — *our* temples, as opposed to those of the Parthians. *Iovi* (= *templo Iovis*) is used generically for Rome; the standards were actually deposited in the temple of Mars.

7. **superbis**: *splendid.*

8. **postibus**: dative of separation with *derepta.* **vacuom duellis**: *free from wars;* prolepsis. On the form of *vacuom*, see Introd. § 34. For the form of *duellis*, see on iii. 5. 38.

9. **Ianum Quirini clausit**: the temple or arcade of Janus was closed when no wars were in progress. Till the reign of Augustus this had happened only twice in Roman history. Instead of *Ianus Quirini*, we elsewhere find *Ianus Quirinus.* Horace here seems to use *Ianum* to indicate the temple, *Quirini* to designate the god. **ordinem**: object of *evaganti.*

10. **frena licentiae iniecit**: *put a curb on license;* for the conditions complained of, see especially iii. 6 and iii. 24.

12. **veteres artis**: the old virtues that had made Rome great, *frugalitas, fortitudo, iustitia, temperantia, patientia, fides, castitas.* See especially Book iii., Odes 1–6.

13. **Latinum nomen, Italae vires, fama imperi**: the three stages in the extension of Roman dominion.

14. **imperi**: with both *fama* and *maiestas.*

15. **ortus**: a striking instance of the poetic plural.

17. **custode rerum**: *cf.* iii. 14. 15, *tenente Caesare terras.*

19. **ira**: *sc. bellica.*

21. **qui Danuvium bibunt**: the recently defeated Vindelici and other Alpine tribes referred to in iv. 2; iv. 14. *Danuvius* is the name of the upper Danube. For this means of indicating a nationality, *cf.* ii. 20. 20, *Rhodani potor.*

22. **edicta Iulia**: the conditions of peace and alliance which Augustus (whose adoptive gentile name was Julius) had imposed upon foreign nations. **Getae**: see on iii. 24. 11.

23. **Seres**: see on i. 12. 56. **infidi Persae**: *cf. Epist.* ii. 1. 112, *Parthis mendacior.*

24. Tanain prope orti: the Scythians; see on iv. 14. 42; note the anastrophe of the dissyllabic preposition.

25. profestis lucibus: *on working days; lux* for *dies*, as frequently.

28. rite: *in due form.* **adprecati**: first used by Horace, and not again found till Apuleius, two centuries later.

29. virtute functos: 'who had wrought deeds of valor' ('*the heroic dead*,' Page). **more patrum**: with *canemus*. Cicero, in *Tusc. Disp.* i. 2, alludes to the custom here mentioned.

30. Lydis remixto, *etc.*: *with song mingled with the music of Lydian pipes; tibiis* is ablative (Introd. § 38. *a*). Plato mentions the Lydian style of music as soft and adapted to banquets.

31. Troiam, Anchisen, progeniem Veneris: the source and founders of the Roman race; under *progeniem Veneris*, we are to understand not only Aeneas, but his illustrious descendants, Julius and Augustus.

CARMEN SAECULARE.

1. silvarum potens: so Venus, in *Odes*, i. 3. 1, is called *diva potens Cypri.* On Diana as goddess of woods and groves, *cf. Odes*, iii. 22. 1, *montium custos nemorumque;* Catullus, 34. 9, *domina silvarum virentium.*

2. decus: in apposition with both *Phoebe* and *Diana.*

3. semper: with both *colendi* and *culti.*

5. quo: with *dicere.* **Sibyllini versus**: see 'Occasion of the Hymn.'

6. lectas, castos: grammatically *lectas* limits *virgines*, and *castos* limits *pueros*, yet logically both adjectives belong to each substantive.

7. septem placuere colles: in that the sanctuaries of the gods appear on the hills.

9. alme Sol: frequently identified with Apollo.

10. promis: *usher in.* **et idem**: *and yet the same.*

13. rite: *duly.* **aperire**: dependent on *lenis; cf. Odes*, i. 24. 17, (of Mercury) *non lenis precibus fata recludere.*

14. lenis: the imperative force extends also to *lenis*, — *be gentle, etc.* **Ilithyia**: a Greek goddess (Εἰλείθυια) who presided over the birth of children; she is here identified with Diana; *cf.* iii. 22. 2. As the name was unfamiliar to Roman ears, Horace adds two simple

Roman designations, *Lucīna*, properly an epithet of Juno in the capacity of helper in child-birth, and *Genitalis*, newly coined by the poet. In *Ilithyia*, *yi* is diphthongal, with the sound of Greek υι; *cf. Odes*, iv. 6. 28, *Agyieu*.

17. producas: *rear, train up*, as in *Odes*, ii. 13. 3. **patrum decreta**, *etc.*: Horace alludes to the *lex Iulia de maritandis ordinibus*, proclaimed by Augustus in 18 B.C. (the year before the saecular celebration), by virtue of the tribunician power with which he had been invested. The measure is here spoken of as the *patrum decreta*, — probably because Augustus had issued the edict after consulting with the Senate and receiving the sanction of that body. This edict was intended not only to increase the number of marriages, but also to encourage the birth of children by promising certain honors and immunities to fathers of large families, while on the other hand certain penalties were imposed upon the unmarried and upon childless married people.

18. super iugandis feminis: *i.e.* concerning the encouragement of marriage.

19. prolis novae feraci: *i.e.* that give promise of being fruitful in new offspring; the genitive with *ferax*, as in *Odes*, iv. 4. 58.

20. lege marita: lit. *the married law*; but here apparently in the sense of *marriage rites*.

21. certus undenos, *etc.*: *that the fixed circuit of ten times eleven years may bring again, etc.* For the late postponement of *ut*, *cf. Odes*, iv. 2. 21, *iuvenemve*.

22. cantus referatque ludos: for *cantus ludosque referat*; see on *Odes*, i. 30. 6.

23. ter . . . frequentis: *i.e.* thronged for three days and nights, the period set for the celebration.

25. veraces cecinisse: *truthful in your past predictions*; *cf. Odes*, ii. 16. 39, *Parca non mendax*. The perfect tense here has its full force.

26. quod semel dictum, *etc.*: *as has been once ordained, and so may the fixed course of events maintain it*; *quod* serves both as subject of *dictum est* and as object of *servet*, — to our feeling a somewhat awkward construction.

27. iam peractis: *sc. bonis fatis*; the reference is to the *saeculum* just closed.

29. fertilis frugum: *rich in crops*; for the genitive, see Introd. § 36. *a*; *fertilis* is in predicative relation to *tellus*, — *may the earth be rich and bless Ceres, etc.*

31. fetus: *the crops.* **aquae**: *the rains.* **salubres, Iovis**: with both *aquae* and *aurae.*

33. condito: *sc. in pharetra.* **telo**: *viz.* the arrow.

37. Roma si vestrum, *etc.*: the context clearly implies that Rome *is* the work of the gods. Hence the passage virtually means, 'in the name of your own work and our Trojan origin.' Special emphasis rests on *vestrum* and *Iliae.*

38. litus Etruscum, *i.e.* the coast of the Mare Tuscum, on which Aeneas and his followers landed.

39. pars: *the remnant;* in apposition with *turmae.* The reference is to the Trojans who accompanied Aeneas after the fall of Troy.

41. sine fraude: *without harm;* for this meaning of *fraus,* see on ii. 19. 19.

42. castus: used apparently in the same sense as the Virgilian *pius.*

43. munivit iter: *viam munire* is the technical expression for building or paving a road; so here *munivit iter* has nearly the force of our 'paved a way,' in its figurative sense. **daturus plura relictis**: destined to give his followers larger things (Rome) than they had left behind (Troy).

45. di: the gods in general.

47. Romulae genti: *Romulae* for *Romuleae,* as in *Odes,* iv. 5. 1. **rem**: *prosperity.* **prolemque**: a hypermetric verse, appropriate in view of the fulness of blessings here entreated.

49. quae vos veneratur: *what he prays of you; veneror* here takes two accusatives. **bobus albis**: *i.e.* in connection with the sacrifice of white steers.

50. clarus sanguis: Augustus. On *sanguis* 'descendant,' *cf.* iii. 27. 65.

51. bellante prior, *etc.*: the wish in *impetret* extends also to *bellante prior,* — 'may he prove superior to the foe that disputes his power, just as he is ever generous to the fallen'; *cf.* Virg. *Aen.* vi. 853, *parcere subiectis et debellare superbos.*

53. mari terraque: with *potentis.* **manus**: *sc. Romanorum.*

54. Medus: see on *Odes,* iv. 14. 42. **Albanas**: a poetic variation for *Romanas,* since the Romans were sprung from Alba.

55. Scythae responsa petunt, Indi: see on *Odes,* iv. 14. 42. **superbi**: with *Scythae.*

61. augur, *etc.*: we have here the four phases under which Apollo was commonly conceived: (1) as augur; (2) as archer, 'the far darter'; (3) as the god of music and leader of the Muses; (4) as the god of healing.

63. fessos: for *aegros*.

65. Palatinas aras: at which the present hymn is being sung. **videt aequos**: *gazes upon with favor.*

66. rem Romanam: *the Roman state.* **felix**: with *Latium.*

67. alterum in lustrum meliusque semper aevom: *to lustra ever new, and ages ever better; semper* is to be taken with both phrases.

69. quaeque: *and Diana who; Diana* is joint subject (with *Apollo*) of *proroget.* **Aventinum tenet Algidumque**: Diana had long had a famous temple on the Aventine, founded by Servius Tullius; she was also worshipped on Mt. Algidus (in Latium, southeast of Rome).

70. quindecim virorum: ordinarily one word; the separation is poetical. For the *quindecimviri*, see 'Occasion of the Hymn.'

71. puerorum: including both sexes.

73. haec: *viz.* what we have entreated. **sentire**: *purpose;* the infinitive depends upon *spem*, which here takes the construction of *spero.*

75. doctus: *viz.* by Horace, the author of the hymn; *cf. Odes*, iv. 6. 43, *docilis modorum vatis Horati.* **Phoebi et Dianae**: dependent upon *laudes.*

EPODES.

EPODE I.

1. Liburnis: see on i. 37. 30. **inter alta propugnacula**: *viz.* of Antony's Egyptian ships, which were constructed with high towers.

4. tuo: *sc. periculo.*

5. quid nos: *sc. facturi sumus.* **quibus te si superstite**, *etc. to whom life is sweet if (I have it) with thee alive.* The ellipsis with *si* seems somewhat harsh.

7. utrumne: redundant for *utrum.* **iussi**: *sc. a te.*

9. hunc laborem: *sc. militiae.* **laturi**: *sc. sumus.* **decet qua**: for *qua decet.*

10. non molles: litotes for *fortes.*

12. inhospitalem Caucasum: *cf.* i. 22. 6.

13. occidentis . . . sinum: *the remotest corner of the West.*

15. roges: *would you ask?* The question is virtually equivalent to a protasis, *si roges, — should you ask.* **tuom**: *sc. laborem;* for the form, see Introd. § 34. **quid iuvem**: *what help I should lend;* potential subjunctive in indirect question.

16. firmus parum: referring to the poet's health, which was not robust.

17. comes: *as comrade;* with conditional force, — 'if I am with thee.'

18. qui maior, *etc.*: *maior* has predicative force; *habet = occupat,* — *lays hold with greater power on those who are absent* (*from the friends they love*).

19. adsidens avis: *a brooding* (*mother*) *bird.* **implumibus pullis**: *for her unfledged nestlings;* dative of interest with *timet.*

21. relictis: *if left behind;* with *pullis.* **non ut adsit,** *etc.*: *non latura* stands in adversative relation to *timet*, and *ut adsit* in turn stands in adversative relation to *non latura*, — *though not likely to lend more help despite her presence* (lit. *though she be present*).

22. praesentibus: superfluous repetition of the idea contained in *ut adsit.*

23. militabitur: *sc. a me.*

24. tuae spem gratiae: according to Kiessling, not 'hope of thy favor,' but 'hope of giving thee pleasure.'

25. non ut iuvencis inligata, *etc.*: 'not that more straining oxen may be yoked to my ploughs'; lit. *not that my ploughs may strain, fastened to more oxen.*

27. pecusve . . . pascuis: *or that my flock may seek Lucanian pastures for Calabrian.* Only rich men would be able to send their flocks away from Calabria to the cooler Lucania in the sultry season; on the heat of Calabria, see *Odes*, i. 31. 5, *aestuosae Calabriae.* On the force of *mutare*, see note on *Odes*, i. 17. 2; *pascuis* is ablative of association; Introd. § 38. *a.* **ante sidus fervidum**: *i.e.* before the heat of the blazing dog-star.

29. neque ut superni, *etc.*: 'nor that I may possess a villa of shining marble near lofty Tusculum.' Tusculum, high up in the Latin hills, was a favorite summer resort in Horace's day. **Tusculi Circaea moenia**: Tusculum, according to legend, was founded by Telegonus, son of Circe and Ulysses.

30. tangat: *i.e.* be near; the villas were on the hillside just below Tusculum itself.

31. satis . . . ditavit: an allusion to the Sabine farm given to Horace by Maecenas in 33 B.C., two years before the date of this epode.

32. haud paravero: *I'll not lay up (riches).* The future-perfect is but a stronger future.

33. quod premam: *to bury.* **avarus**: with the subject of *premam.* **ut Chremes**: Chremes (a character borrowed from Attic Comedy) is typical for a miser.

34. discinctus: *dissolute, reckless; ut* is to be understood with *nepos.*

EPODE II.

1. procul: here used as a preposition, governing the ablative *negotiis.*

2. ut prisca gens: apparently a reference to the Golden Age.

3. exercet: *works, tills.* **suis**: like *paterna, suis* points out that the man is tilling his own estate; he is not merely a tenant farmer.

4. solutus omni faenore: *i.e.* freed from the many worries of money lending. The speaker (Alfius) naturally thinks of the hardships of his own vocation.

5. excitatur: *sc. ex somno.* **miles**: *as a soldier.*

6. horret: *shudders at;* here used transitively.

7. superba . . . limina: an allusion to the morning *salutatio* paid by *clientes* to their *patronus.*

9. ergo: *i.e.* since he is exempt from the various annoyances just enumerated. **adulta propagine . . . populos**: the training of the vine on the poplar is here spoken of as wedding the poplar with the vine; see note on *Odes,* iv. 5. 30. The ablative is one of association; Introd. § 38. *a.*

11. reducta valle: *sequestered valley.* **mugientium**: *sc. boum; cf.* the use of *latrantes* for *canes; balantes* for *oves, etc.*

13. inutilisque, *etc.*: the poet passes to the mention of fruit trees and their care.

14. feliciores: *i.e.* more fruitful.

16. infirmas: *defenceless.*

17. decorum: *crowned.*

18. Autumnus: here personified. **agris**: *in the fields.*

19. ut: exclamatory, — *how!* **gaudet decerpens**: *i.e. delights to pluck,* a Greek form of expression.

20. certantem purpurae: *vying with the purple;* another Grecism; *cf.* ii. 6. 15, *viridi certat Venafro;* Introd. § 36. *c.*

21. qua muneretur te: *with which to honor thee; i.e.* in order that he may honor thee with them. Logically *qua* refers to *pira* as well as to *uvam*. The first fruits were regularly offered to the gods. **Priāpe**: the god of gardens and vineyards. **pater**: a common epithet of all deities.

24. tenaci: *i.e.* thick; lit. *that holds (together)*.

25. altis ripis: *i.e.* between their high banks. **interim**: as he lies there.

26. queruntur: *warble*.

27. fontes obstrepunt: *i.e.* the fountains with their plashing waters vie with the music of the warbling birds.

28. somnos levis: *soft slumbers*, as in *Odes*, ii. 16. 15. **quod invitet**: relative clause of result, — 'a sound so sweet that it lulls to slumber.'

29. tonantis: merely a standing epithet of the god, and so without special significance here. **annus hibernus** = *hiems*; *cf. Odes*, iii. 23. 8, *pomifero anno*, 'autumn.'

31. trudit: a stronger *agit*. **multa cane**: poetic for *multis canibus*; *cf. Odes*, i. 15. 6, *multo milite*.

32. obstantis: *i.e.* placed in their path.

33. levi: *smooth, polished*. **rara retia**: *wide-meshed nets*; *i.e.* as compared with the nets used by fishermen.

34. dolos: in apposition with *retia*.

35. pavidumque leporem: note the fine suiting of the metre to the sense of the line. The anapaest (*pavidum*) followed by the tribrach (*-que lepo-*) suggests the quick darting of the frightened hare; a second anapaest in *laqueo* helps to maintain the movement of the verse. **advenam gruem**: *i.e.* the migratory crane, which came to Italy from the North in the winter season, and was highly esteemed as a table delicacy; *advenam* has adjective force; *cf. Odes*, i. 1. 1, *atavis regibus*.

37. quas amor curas habet: incorporation of the antecedent in the relative clause. **habet**: *i.e.* involves, occasions.

38. haec inter: for the anastrophe, *cf.* iii. 3. 11.

39. in partem: *i.e.* performing her share. **iuvet**: *i.e.* help tend.

41. Sabina qualis: for the Sabine mother as the type of housewifely virtues, see *Odes*, iii. 6. 37 ff. **perusta solibus**: *sun-burnt*.

42. pernicis Apuli: for the industry of the Apulians, *cf. Odes*, iii. 16. 26.

43. sacrum: the hearth is called sacred as being the centre of family worship and the place near which the statues of the gods were often set up. **vetustis**: *i.e.* well seasoned. **extruat, siccet, adparet**: continuing the protasis begun in *quodsi iuvet.*

44. sub adventum: *against the coming, i.e.* in anticipation of his return.

45. textis cratibus: a sheep-fold made of wicker work.

47. dulci: grammatically with *dolio*, logically with *vina.*

48. inemptas: *i.e.* simple.

49. Lucrina conchylia: the oysters of the Lucrine Lake near Naples were highly prized. **iuverint**: *sc. magis; iuverint* introduces the apodosis of the conditional sentence begun in line 39.

50. magisve: *sc. iuverint.* **rhombus, scari**: *turbot, scar;* both fish were highly prized.

51. siquos, *etc.*: *if winter, thundering on the eastern waves, should turn any to our coasts, i.e.* if winter's storms should divert any of these fish from the eastern Mediterranean to Italian waters; on *intonata*, here with active force, *cf. cenatus* 'having dined'; *pransus*, 'having lunched,' *etc.*

53. Afra avis, attagen Ionicus: evidently special delicacies.

55. pinguissimis: the epithet is transferred from the fruit to the branches.

58. malvae salubres: the wholesome mallows are mentioned also in *Odes*, i. 31. 16, *leves malvae.*

59. Terminalibus: this festival fell on the 23d of February.

61. ut: exclamatory, as above, line 19.

65. postos: *ranged (around)*; by syncope for *positos; cf.* Virg. *Aen.* i. 249, *compostus pace quiescit.*

66. renidentis: *i.e.* sparkling in the firelight.

67. locutus: *sc. est.*

68. iam iam futurus: *on the very point of becoming.*

69. redegit: *called in.* **Idibus, Kalendis**: the regular points in the month for financial settlements.

70. ponere: *to put it out, viz.* at interest. On *quaero* with the infinitive, *cf. Odes*, i. 37. 22, *perire quaerens.* Note the effect of the asyndeton in intensifying the surprise reserved for this closing line.

EPODE III.

1. Parentis senile guttur fregerit: *strangle an aged parent; cf. Odes*, ii. 13. 5, *sui parentis fregisse cervicem.* In the present passage, *fregerit* is future perfect. **olim siquis**: *if ever any man.*

2. senile: grammatically with *guttur*, but logically with *parentis*.

3. edit: archaic subjunctive form for *edat*, from *edo*, 'eat.'

4. O dura messorum ilia: *Oh, the tough stomachs of harvesters*, *i.e.* to be able to eat garlic with impunity, as was their wont; *ilia* is used for *ventres*; similarly *praecordiis* in the following line.

5. veneni: with *quid*.

6. viperinus cruor: regarded as a potent poison; *cf. Odes*, i. 8. 9.

7. incoctus me fefellit: *i.e.* 'has it been brewed with these herbs without my knowing it?' For the Grecism, *cf. Odes*, iii. 16. 32, *fallit sorte beatior*. **an malas Canidia tractavit dapes**: *or did Canidia prepare the poisonous dish?* Canidia was a notorious sorceress of the day; see *Epodes* 5 and 17.

9. ut: *when*. **Argonautas . . . candidum**: *i.e.* fair beyond all the other Argonauts.

10. ducem: *viz.* Jason.

11. ignota . . . iuga: *i.e.* as he set out to put upon the fire-breathing bulls the yoke to which they were strangers. The yoking of these monsters was one of the tasks imposed by Aeetes upon Jason when he sought to recover the Golden Fleece. By Medea's magic powers, as the legend ran, he was enabled to accomplish the feat.

12. hoc: *viz.* garlic, to serve as antidote against the furious bulls.

13. hoc: the almost immediate repetition of the word and its position at the beginning of the verse lend special emphasis, — *in this were steeped the gifts with which she* (Medea) *punished her rival*. The reference is to the cloak and diadem presented by Medea to Creusa (or Glauce), daughter of the Corinthian king, Creon. The gifts burst into flame and consumed Creusa. *Paelicem* is literally *mistress*; Jason had deserted Medea for Creusa.

14. serpente alite: *i.e.* on her chariot of dragons; the singular is here collective.

15. siderum vapor: *i.e.* the heat of the dog-star, whose influence was supposed to affect the temperature. **insedit**: *brood over*.

16. siticulosae Apuliae: *cf. Odes*, iii. 30. 11, *pauper aquae Daunus*.

17. nec munus . . . aestuosius: *nor did the gift burn hotter into the shoulders of manful Hercules*. The allusion is to the gift of the poisoned tunic sent to Hercules by Deianira, when the hero fell in love with Iole; the garment proved his death; *efficacis* refers to Hercules's famous labors; *aestuosius* is used predicatively.

19. siquid concupiveris: *i.e.* 'if you ever do any such thing again.'

21. puella: *sweetheart.* **opponat, cubet**: optative subjunctives; *precor* is parenthetical.

EPODE IV.

1. sortito: *i.e.* by nature's decree. **obtigit**: *sc. discordia.*

2. discordia est: *sc. tanta.*

3. Hibericis funibus: excellent ropes were made of the Spanish *spartum*, a kind of broom. **peruste**: *scarred;* the man had been a refractory slave and had been visited with the customary slave punishments. **latus, crura**: synecdochical (Greek) accusatives.

4. dura: with *compede.*

5. licet ambules: *although you strut about.*

6. genus: *i.e.* thy origin.

7. Sacram Viam: the route of triumphal processions, and a favorite promenade. It passed along the base of the Palatine Hill and through the Forum. **metiente**: *i.e.* traversing the entire length of the street.

8. bis . . . toga: the size is evidently unusually large, and marks the man's effort to ape the extreme of fashion; *bis trium ulnarum* (about three yards) refers to the width of the toga before being draped about the person.

9. ut vertat, *etc.*: *how righteous indignation spreads over people's faces as they pass by; vertat* is best taken in its literal sense of 'change,' 'alter'; *huc et huc* is poetical for *huc et illuc; euntium* is for *praetereuntium*, — the simple verb for the compound, as frequently in poetry.

11. 'sectus,' *etc.*: '*scourged*,' the indignant utterances of those passing by. The reference is to the time when the upstart was still a slave and had committed offences that incurred the punishment here mentioned. **flagellis triumviralibus**: the *triumviri capitales* were a board of magistrates, who, in addition to the maintenance of public order, took cognizance of petty offences committed by slaves.

12. praeconis ad fastidium: 'till the beadle was tired'; the *praeco* was charged with securing execution of the penalties imposed by the *triumviri.* Punishment was administered by the *tortor*, while the *praeco* continued to call out the nature of the offence. The slave's violations of the law had been so flagrant or so frequent that the beadle had finally become exhausted.

13. arat: *i.e.* owns. **Falerni fundi**: valuable land, as producing the famous Falernian wine.

14. Appiam: *sc. Viam.* The Appian Way led south from the city; hence it was the natural thoroughfare to the man's Falernian estate. **terit**: *i.e.* travels.

15. sedilibus in primis: at the theatre. **magnus eques**: sarcastic, —*as though a great knight.*

16. Othone contempto: in 67 B.C., L. Roscius Otho, a tribune for the year, secured the passage of a law providing that the first fourteen rows of the theatre should be reserved for those of equestrian rank. The upstart is presumably not really an *eques*, but his enormous wealth, vastly in excess of the equestrian census of 400,000 sesterces (about $20,000), makes him thrust himself into the front rows of the theatre, in lofty scorn of Otho's law.

17. quid attinet: *of what use is it?* **tot ora**, *etc.*: *for so many heavy ships with (brazen) beaks to be led against the pirates*, lit. *so many beaked prows of ships of heavy weight.*

19. latrones atque servilem manum: alluding to the free-booters and runaway slaves armed by Sextus Pompeius and used to man the fleet with which for a time he defied Octavian.

20. hoc, hoc tribuno militum: *i.e.* there is no hope of success with such leaders; for the emphatic repetition in *hoc, hoc*, *cf. Odes*, ii. 17. 10, *ibimus, ibimus.*

EPODE V.

1. At: an abrupt introduction, according with the terror of the boy who speaks. **o deorum**, *etc.*: *i.e.* 'in the name of all the gods in heaven.'

3. fert: *means.* **omnium**: the four hags, Canidia, Sagana, Veia, Folia.

4. voltus: *sc. ferunt.*

5. te: Canidia, leader of the women. **si vocata**, *etc.*: *i.e.* 'if thou hast ever had offspring.'

6. Lucīna: an epithet of Juno in her capacity as the patron goddess of child-birth. **veris**: see 17. 50.

7. per hoc . . . decus: the purple border of the *toga praetexta*, the dress of boys. **inane**: as failing to afford the protection due a helpless youth.

8. improbaturum: *sure to show his disapproval*, a milder word instead of *puniturum*, evidently intended to soften the hearts of his tormentors. On Horace's free use of the future participle, see on *Odes*, ii. 3. 4.

9. **noverca** : the type of cruelty.

11. **ut haec**, *etc.* : *as the boy halted, having uttered these plaints with quivering lip; haec* is the accusative of result produced with *questus*, which agrees with *puer.*

12. **insignibus** : *i.e.* his toga and *bulla*, the locket worn at the throat of children as an amulet to protect them from the 'evil eye' and other malign influences.

13. **impube corpus** : in apposition with *puer.* **quale posset mollire** : *such as might soften;* clause of characteristic.

14. **Thracum** : *i.e.* barbarians.

15. **Canidia** : her real name is said to have been *Gratidia;* for such disguises in names, see note on *Odes*, ii. 12. 13, *Licymniae.* **implicata**, *etc.* : *i.e.* like a Fury ; the participle is used as a middle; hence the direct objects, *crinis* and *caput.*

16. **incomptum** : *dishevelled.*

17. **caprificos, cupressus** : *i.e.* bits of wood from these trees. The nouns are subjects of *aduri.* Note that *cupressus*, usually of the second declension, is here declined according to the fourth; *cf.* the similar use of *myrtus* in *Odes*, ii. 15. 6.

18. **funebris** : see on ii. 14. 23.

19. **uncta** : to be taken with both *ova* and *plumam.*

20. **strigis** : the owl was a bird of evil omen ; *strigis* limits *ova* as well as *plumam.*

21. **Iolcos** : a Thessalian city, mentioned as the source of poisonous herbs, since the Thessalian women were famed as sorceresses. **Hiberia** : the Pontic Hiberia in Asia Minor is meant.

23. **ossa** : bones from a human body.

24. **Colchicis** = *magicis*, such as Medea of Colchis, the most famous of mythical sorceresses, was wont to use in her incantations.

25. **expedita Sagana** : *Sagana* (another of the witches) *girt high*, for freedom of movement.

26. **Avernalis aquas** : water from ill-omened Avernus, the noisome lake near Cumae, regarded as the entrance to the lower world. The water was thought to possess magic power.

29. **abacta nulla**, *etc.* : *Veia* (another of the witches), *held back by no sense of guilt.*

30. **ligonibus** : poetic plural.

32. quo posset, *etc.*: *in order that buried there the boy, etc.*; *quo* is really the relative adverb ('whither'), referring to *humum*.

33. longo die bis terque: *twice or thrice in the course of the weary day*; the words limit *mutatae*. The sight of fresh viands would naturally intensify the sufferings of the boy.

34. inemori: this verb is found only here. **spectaculo**: dative.

35. cum promineret ore: *protruding with his face*; a circumstantial *cum*-clause, equivalent to a present participle. **quantum exstant**, *etc.*: *i.e.* only as much as the bodies of swimmers are raised above the surface of the water.

38. amoris poculum: *a love-charm*.

39. interminato: *forbidden*; for the passive use of perfect passive participles of deponent verbs, *cf. Odes*, i. 1. 25, *detestata*. **cum semel** = *simul ac*.

40. intabuissent: oblique form, after a secondary tense, of an original future perfect indicative (*cum intabuerint*).

42. Foliam: the fourth of the witches.

43. otiosa Neapolis: *gossiping Naples*. Naples, according to the scholiast, was Canidia's home, and so took a natural interest in her doings and those of her associates.

45. excantata: with both *sidera* and *lunam*. **voce Thessala**: see on line 21.

47. inresectum pollicem: *i.e.* a thumb whose nail was uncut.

48. rodens: a mark of frantic rage.

49. aut quid tacuit: *or rather what did she leave unsaid?* *i.e.* to what abominable utterances did she not give vent? **rebus meis**: *to my deeds*.

51. Diana: *i.e.* Luna. **quae silentium regis**: *cf.* Virg. *Aen.* ii. 255, *tacitae per amica silentia Lunae*.

53. adeste: *be propitious to me*. **hostilis domos**: *i.e.* the homes that resist Canidia's power, particularly that of Varus (the *senem* of line 57).

55. formidulosis: *i.e.* inspiring dread.

57. senem adulterum: *the old rake*; the Varus of line 73; *cf Odes*, i. 1. 1, *atavis regibus*. **quod omnes rideant**: *a sight for all to laugh at*; relative clause of purpose.

58. latrent: *bark at and drive* as suppliant to Canidia's presence. The word is here transitive and governs *senem*. **Suburanae canes**: the Subura, to be thought of as Canidia's home, was a disreputable quarter of Rome lying between the Esquiline, Viminal, and Quirinal.

59. nardo perunctum: Varus had been anointed with the magic perfume by Canidia, in order that the dogs might set upon him and drive him to her.

60. laborarint: *have wrought, have prepared.*

61. quid accidit: the charm refuses to work. **dira**: *i.e.* potent. **barbarae**: Medea's home was Colchis. **minus** = *non.*

62. venena: *philters; venenum* originally meant 'love-charm,' 'philter,' from *Venes-*, root of *Venus*, 'love.' The primitive form **venes-num* regularly became *venēnum* by compensatory lengthening; B. *App.* § 89. The meaning 'poison,' therefore, is a secondary signification of the word.

63 ff. For the myth see on *Epode* 3, 13 f.

63. superbam: in winning Jason's affections from Medea.

65. tabo: here for *veneno.*

69. indormit unctis, *etc.*: *he sleeps on perfumed couch, forgetful of all mistresses* (Canidia included); *omnium* is emphasized by its position; *oblivione* is ablative of attendant circumstance.

71. solutus: *i.e.* freed from my influence. **veneficae scientioris carmine**: *by the charm of some cleverer enchantress.*

73. non usitatis . . . recurres: *i.e.* 'I'll brew a stronger charm and bring thee back to me.' The stronger charm, apparently, is to be made from the marrow and liver of the unfortunate boy.

74. O multa, *etc.*: *O creature doomed bitterly to weep, viz.* for thy resistance to my spells.

75. nec vocata mens tua, *etc.*: 'and by no Marsian spells shall thy devotion come back to me.' Canidia, as she goes on to say, will use some stronger spell than those employed by Marsian witches. On *Marsis* for *Marsicis, cf. Odes,* i. 1. 28, *Marsus aper.*

77. infundam tibi: *I'll mix for thee.*

78. fastidienti: *i.e.* scorning me and my spells.

79. mari: ablative of comparison with *inferius.*

80. tellure porrecta super: *with the earth spread out above it* (the sea).

81. quam non . . . flagres: *than thou fail to be consumed with love for me; meo* here is equivalent to an objective genitive.

82. atris ignibus: *smoky flames.*

83. sub haec: *thereat; sub* may mean either 'just before' or 'just after.' **ut ante**: see lines 1–10, above.

84. lenire: historical infinitive, with conative force, — *did not strive to soothe.* **impias**: *the wicked hags.*

85. unde: *with what words.*

86. Thyesteas preces: *i.e.* such curses as Thyestes had hurled at Atreus, who had slain Thyestes's sons and served their flesh to their father at a banquet. This curse was familiar to the Romans of Horace's day in Ennius's tragedy of *Thyestes.*

87. venena maga, *etc.*: *your magic spells have not the power to alter right and wrong, nor to avert human retribution; maga* is for *magica; convertere* is used zeugmatically; with *vicem* it is equivalent to *avertere.* On *vicem* in this sense, *cf. Odes,* i. 28(2). 12, *vicesque superbae.*

89. diris: *with curses.* **dira detestatio**: *my awful execration.*

91. quin: *nay more.* **perire iussus**: *doomed to die.*

92. Furor: *as a fury.*

93. umbra: *as a ghost;* to be taken with the subject of *petam.*

94. deorum Manium: the shades of the departed were regularly styled *di Manes.*

96. pavore: *i.e.* by the terror I inspire.

97. vicatim: *from street to street.* **hinc et hinc**: *from this side and that;* poetic for *hinc et illinc; cf.* 4. 9, *huc et huc euntium.*

98. anus: in apposition with *vos.*

99. post: adverb.

100. Esquilinae alites: *i.e.* the carrion birds that haunt the Esquiline cemetery, a sort of potter's field outside the walls; for the hiatus (or possibly only semi-hiatus), *cf. Odes,* i. 28(2). 4, *capiti inhumato.*

101. heu mihi superstites: *i.e.* 'I, alas, shall not live to behold the sight.'

102. effugerit: the future perfect emphasizes the certainty of consummation.

EPODE VI.

The identity of the person against whom this epode is directed, is uncertain.

1. hospites: *strangers,* who can have done no harm to thee. **canis**: *like a dog.*

2. ignavos: nominative with *canis;* Introd. § 34. **lupos**: figurative for 'equal foes.'

3. quin: *why not?* **huc** = *in me.*

4. me remorsurum: 'me, who will retort with bites.'

5. qualis, *etc.*: *like a Molossian hound or tawny Laconian;* with *Molossus* and *Laco, canis* is to be understood. The like ellipsis is common in modern languages; *cf.* our *Newfoundland*, *St. Bernard*, *etc.*

6. amica vis pastoribus: *sturdy friends of shepherds*, lit. *strength friendly to shepherds.* In *Georgics*, iii. 404 ff., Virgil speaks of Molossian and Spartan hounds as faithful watch-dogs.

7. aure sublata: the pricked up ears mark the keen pursuit.

8. quaecumque praecedet fera: *i.e.* whatever creature I pursue.

9. tu: emphatic. **cum complesti . . . odoraris**: the *cum*-clause is explicative, indicating the logical identity of the two statements, — 'thy howl simply means that thou hast sniffed the smell of food.' Divested of the figure, the passage means that the man is attempting blackmail.

11. in malos: with *tollo.*

13. qualis . . . gener: the allusion is to the poet Archilochus of Paros (700 B.C.). Lycambes had promised Archilochus his daughter Neobūle in marriage, but broke his pledge, whereupon the poet by his bitter invectives drove both Lycambes and Neobule to suicide. *Lycambae* is dative of agency; *gener* is used prospectively.

14. acer hostis Bupalo: Bupalus was a Greek sculptor belonging to the latter half of the sixth century B.C. He is said to have made a bust of his contemporary, the ugly-featured poet Hippōnax, of Ephesus. In revenge for this, Hipponax is reported to have lashed the sculptor in satiric verses; *Bupalo* is governed by *hostis*, which is here equivalent to *inimicus.*

15. atro: *venomous.*

16. inultus: here with active force, — *without revenge.* **flebo**: equivalent to a deliberative subjunctive, — *am I to burst into tears?*

EPODE VII.

1. Quo, quo: for the repetition, *cf. Odes*, ii. 17. 10, *ibimus, ibimus*, with note.

2. aptantur: *i.e.* being fitted again to the hand. **conditi**: *that have (once) been sheathed.*

3. campis . . . super: anastrophe. **Neptuno**: for *mari*, as often.

4. Latini: more poetical than *Romani*; *cf. Odes*, ii. 1. 29.

5. non, *etc.*: *i.e. non fusus est sanguis, etc.* **ut . . . ureret**: *i.e.* with no such patriotic purpose as in the earlier days.

7. intactus: *i.e.* as yet untouched, unsubdued. **ut descende-**

ret: the Sacra Via (see on 4. 7) fell considerably as it approached the Forum, after which it rose sharply at the Capitoline Hill, where it led up to the Capitolium, the temple of Jupiter.

8. **Via**: ablative of the way by which.

9. **secundum vota**: *in accordance with the prayers.* **Parthorum**: see on *Odes*, i. 2. 22. **sua dextera**: *by its own right hand.*

12. **numquam . . . feris**: *never savage except against beasts of another kind.*

13. **furor, an vis acrior, an culpa**: *madness, or some cruel spell, or guilt?*

17. **sic est**: the poet answers his own question; *sic* looks forward. **acerba fata**: the same idea as in *vis acrior* above.

18. **scelus . . . necis**: *i.e.* punishment for the crime of a brother's murder; *necis* is appositional genitive.

19. **ut**: *ever since;* for this force of *ut, cf. Odes*, iv. 4. 42.

20. **sacer nepotibus**: *a curse on posterity; nepotibus* depends loosely upon *sacer.*

EPODE IX.

1. **repostum Caecubum**: on the Caecuban wine, see *Odes*, i. 20. 9, note. For the syncope in *repostum, cf. Epodes*, 2. 65, *postos.*

2. **victore laetus Caesare**: *rejoicing at Caesar's victory.*

3. **sub alta domo**: the reference is to Maecenas's lofty palace on the Esquiline; *cf. Odes*, iii. 29. 10. On the special force of *sub*, see *Odes*, i. 5. 3, *sub antro.* **sic Iovi gratum**: *i.e.* Jove approves the celebration of the victory he had vouchsafed.

4. **beate**: *happy, i.e.* rejoicing at the victory.

5. **sonante, etc.**: *to the strains of the lyre mingled with those of the flute; mixtum tibiis* is compendiary for *mixtum tibiarum carmine; cf. Odes*, i. 1. 23, *lituo tubae permixtus sonitus; tibiis* is ablative of association; Introd. § 38. *a.*

6. **hac . . . barbarum**: *i.e. lyra Dorium carmen sonante, tibiis barbarum (carmen sonantibus); barbarum* is equivalent to *Phrygium.* The Doric mood was appropriate to martial songs; the Phrygian was common at festive gatherings; *cf. Odes*, iii. 19. 18.

7. **ut nuper**: *just as recently; nuper* is always a flexible word, and here refers to the events of five years previous (36 B.C.), when Sextus Pompeius was defeated at Naulochus and driven from the sea by Agrippa. **actus freto**: *driven from the sea; actus* for *abactus.* **Neptunius dux**: a sarcastic reference to Pompey's claim that he was

the son of Neptune, — a claim put forth as the result of his earlier naval successes.

10. servis: dependent upon both *detraxerat* (as dative of separation) and *amicus*. **perfidis**: *viz.* to their masters.

11 ff. In touching upon the disgraceful conduct of Antonius's followers in submitting to the behests of a foreign queen, — Cleopatra, — Horace's purpose is to bring out in stronger relief the glory of the recent victory; the past shame, urges the poet, is now partially redeemed.

11. Romanus emancipatus feminae, *etc.*: *Romanus* (with *miles*) is emphatic, and *emancipatus feminae* even more so, — *the Roman* (the type of manly freedom) *bears stakes and arms,* AT THE BEHEST OF A WOMAN (Cleopatra); the bearing of stakes and weapons was in itself no indignity, being the ordinary duty of the Roman soldier; *emancipare* is strictly used of transferring the title of property; where the object is a person, it means 'to sell into slavery.' So here, lit. *enslaved to a woman.* **posteri negabitis**: *i.e.* such a thing will be incredible to future ages.

13. vallum: the *valli* were used in making a temporary barricade. **spadonibus**: the attendants in the courts of oriental countries were regularly eunuchs. For the Roman contempt of this class, *cf. Odes*, i. 37. 9, *contaminato cum grege turpium morbo virorum.*

14. servire potest: *can bring itself to obey.* **rugosis**: physical decay is rapid among eunuchs.

15. turpe conopium: the *conopium* is simply a rational device for protection from the attacks of gnats and similar insects; but it is an oriental contrivance with an oriental name, and so evokes the scorn of the poet, carried away as he is by his spirit of national feeling.

17. ad hoc: *at sight of this.* **frementis verterunt**, *etc.*: two thousand Galatians (*Galli*), under the command of Amyntias and Dejotarus, had fought for a time in the army of Antonius, but deserted to Octavian before the battle of Actium. Note the ĕ of *verterunt,* — not an arbitrary shortening, but a reminiscence of the original quantity; *cf. ridēt, Odes*, ii. 6. 14.

18. canentes Caesarem: *i.e.* shouting his name; *cf.* Virg. *Aen.* vii. 698, *regem canebant.*

19. hostiliumque navium, *etc.*: 'the ships of the enemy (Antony and Cleopatra), when summoned to draw off to the left and retreat, hid in the harbor,' *i.e.* when Cleopatra gave the signal for retreat many of her own ships refused to follow; *citae* is here the participle, from *cieo.*

21. Io Triumphe: *cf. Odes*, iv. 2. 49 f. **moraris . . . boves**: *i.e.* 'do you delay to bring forth the golden chariot and the victims for celebrating the victory?' The chariot, richly decorated with gold and ivory, is that in which the *triumphator* rides to the temple of Jupiter on the Capitoline, where the priests sacrifice the *intactas boves*, which had formed part of the triumphal procession.

22. currus: the poetic plural, as in i. 15. 12. **intactas**: *viz.* by the yoke. Sacrificial victims must be unsullied by earthly uses.

23. Iugurthino bello . . . ducem: Marius. **parem**: *i.e.* equal to Octavian.

25. Africanum: understand *parem ducem*, in predicate relation. The younger Scipio is referred to. **cui super**, *etc.*: *whose valor sealed the doom of Carthage.*

27. terra marique victus: the statement is incorrect. Though defeated in the naval engagement, Antonius still had nineteen legions of soldiers and some twenty-two thousand cavalry at his disposal. For several days after Antony's flight, these troops awaited his return, and then surrendered to Octavian. **hostis**: Antonius. **punico . . . sagum**: *has changed the scarlet cloak for one of sombre hue* (lit. *one of mourning*); scarlet was the color of the cloak of the commanding general. On *mutare*, 'take in exchange,' see *Odes*, i. 17. 2; *punico* is for the usual *puniceo*.

29. centum . . . urbibus: the Homeric ἑκατόμπολιν Κρήτην; *cf. Odes*, iii. 27. 33, *centum potentem oppidis Creten.* **Cretam**: object of *petit.*

30. ventis iturus non suis: *destined to fare with unpropitious winds;* on the general principle that his star is waning and whatever he does will be fraught with disaster. On the free use of the future participle, *cf. Odes*, ii. 3. 4. Just as *suus* often has the special meaning of 'favorable,' so here *non suis* means 'adverse.'

32. incerto: *i.e.* he sails aimlessly; the epithet is transferred from Antony to the sea.

33 ff. Horace imagines himself already at the celebration of the victory.

33. capaciores: *i.e.* larger than usual. **scyphos**: large beakers with two handles. **puer**: the attendant slave.

35. quod . . . coerceat: *to stay my rising qualms.* Horace speaks as though on ship and afraid of sea-sickness, for which the dry Caecuban is represented as a preventive. By *nauseam*, he figuratively means his disgust at Antony's escape.

37. curam . . . rerum: *anxious fear for Caesar's fortunes.* Antony and Cleopatra, though put to flight, were still masters of powerful resources. It was not till a year later that they were finally vanquished, and Horace was able to burst out into his jubilant *nunc est bibendum* of *Odes*, i. 37.

38. Lyaeo = *vino*: see on *Odes*, i. 7. 22. **solvere**: *to banish.*

EPODE X.

1. Mala alite: *under evil auspices*; ablative of attendant circumstance; *cf. Odes*, i. 15. 5, *mala ducis avi domum.* **soluta**: *setting sail.*

2. olentem: *filthy.*

3. ut verberes: jussive subjunctive, introduced by *ut* instead of *utinam*, as repeatedly in early Latin; *memento* is a parenthetic addition. **latus**: *sc. navis.*

4. Auster, *etc.*: all the storm-winds are invoked to do their worst, — Auster, Eurus, Aquilo, and Notus (line 20).

5. niger Eurus: transferred from the black clouds that Eurus gathers to Eurus himself; *cf. Odes*, i. 5. 6, *aspera nigris aequora ventis.*

7. quantus frangit: *with all the might with which it breaks.*

9. nec appareat: with the frequent occurrence of *nec* in optative and volitive expressions, *cf. Odes*, i. 9. 15, *nec sperne.*

10. qua . . . cadit: for the storms supposed to accompany Orion's setting, *cf. Odes*, i. 28 (2). 1, *devexi Orionis*; on *tristis*, *i.e.* bringing gloomy weather, *cf. Odes*, i. 3. 14, *tristis Hyadas.*

12. Graia: logically with *victorum.*

13. cum Pallas, *etc.*: Pallas, in consequence of the judgment of Paris, had hitherto been angry against the Trojans. But at the sack of Troy, Ajax, the son of Oïleus, had ravished Cassandra in Pallas's temple. Hence the goddess now turned her wrath upon the Greeks as they were returning home from Troy. For her vengeance upon Ajax in particular, see the vivid passage in Virgil, *Aen.* i. 39 f., *Pallasne exurere classem Argivom, etc.*

14. impiam: as bearing the impious Ajax.

17. illa: *viz.* that into which you are wont to break on such occasions.

18. preces et: for *et preces*; *Odes*, i. 2. 5.

19. Ionius sinus: the sea off the western coast of Greece. **udo**: *i.e.* rainy.

21. opima praeda porrecta: in apposition with the subject of *iuveris*.

22. mergos iuveris: *you delight the gulls, viz.* by furnishing them a rich feast.

24. Tempestatibus: *the gods of the storm.* The *Tempestates* often appear as divinities in Latin literature. The sacrifices offered to them are ordinarily made for the purpose of averting bad weather. Here the promised victim is vowed under unique conditions.

EPODE XI.

4. in pueris . . . urere: *to inflame me with passion for boys or maids; urere* depends upon *expetit*.

5. hic tertius, *etc.*: lit. *this third December is shaking the leaves, i.e.* 'the third winter is now shaking,' *etc.*

6. Inachia furere: for the ablative, *cf. Odes*, i. 4. 19, *quo virgines tepebunt*. **silvis**: *from the woods;* dative.

7. me: dependent upon *pudet;* the irregular word-order is well suited to the sudden whirl of memory with which the past returns.

8. fabula: *i.e.* the talk of the town. **conviviorum paenitet**: *i.e.* 'it pains me to recall the gatherings.'

9. quis: ablative plural. **amantem arguit**: *convicted the lover, viz.* me. **languor**: *my listlessness.*

11. contrane, *etc.*: *to think that a poor man's blameless heart can avail naught against gold; i.e.* the poor suitor cannot compete with a richer rival. *Valere* is the exclamatory infinitive; *ne* in such expressions is best taken, with Warren, as the intensive particle, the shortened enclitic form of the asseverative *nē*. **lucrum** = *aurum*.

13. simul calentis, *etc.*: *as soon as the god had warmed me with the quickening wine and brought my secrets from their hiding-place; calentis* depends upon the genitive idea involved in *mea* to be understood with *arcana*. The god is called *inverecundus*, as banishing all sense of shame in those who indulge too freely in his gifts Note that *simul* (= *simul ac*) is here followed by the pluperfect of iterative action.

15. quodsi, *etc.*: *but if righteous indignation should boil up in my heart; libera bilis* like *liberrima indignatio* in 4. 10; *praecordiis* is ablative.

16. ut . . . fomenta: *so as to scatter to the winds the thankless remedies that nowise ease my grievous wound;* the *fomenta* are the hopes the lover indulges or the vain consolations of his friends.

18. desinet . . . pudor: (*false*) *modesty removed shall cease to vie with my unequal rivals; i e.* 'I will cast aside false shame and cease to vie'; we should expect *desinat*, parallel with the protasis (*inaestuet*); *desinet* is more vivid. By *imparibus*, are meant rivals superior in wealth but inferior in mind and heart. For the dative, *cf. Odes*, ii. 6. 15, *viridi certat baca Venafro.*

19. ubi . . . laudaveram: 'whenever I had uttered these praise-worthy sentiments'; iterative, hence the pluperfect tense; *cf. simul promorat* above. **severus**: *with stern resolve*, *i.e.* for the time being. **te palam**: *in thy presence;* anastrophe.

20. iussus: *sc. a te.* **incerto**: *irresolute*, uncertain whether to return home or to visit his mistress.

21. non amicos postis: *unfriendly doors;* so styled as refusing admittance; for the picture of the lover excluded by his cruel mistress, *cf. Odes*, iii. 10. 2 ff.

23. gloriantis: with *Lycisci.* **quamlibet mulierculam**: *i.e.* even the fairest.

25. unde = *a quo.*

26. libera consilia: *the frank counsels.*

28. teretis: *slender.* **longam renodantis comam**: like the Spartan maidens; see *Odes*, ii. 11. 23.

EPODE XIII.

1. contraxit: *viz.* by covering the heaven with clouds.

2. deducunt Iovem: Jove was conceived as himself descending in the storm. **siluae**: here trisyllabic, as in *Odes*, i. 23. 3.

3. Threicio Aquilone: the poets set the home of the north wind in Thrace; for the hiatus (or semi-hiatus), *cf.* 5. 100, *Esquilinae alites.* **rapiamus occasionem de die**: *let us snatch opportunity* (*of enjoyment*) *from the day.* The day is conceived as offering the opportunity to Horace and his friends.

5. obducta solvatur fronte senectus: *let seriousness* (lit. *old age*) *be banished from the clouded brow.*

6. tu: the *arbiter bibendi*, or master of ceremonies; see on *Odes*, ii. 7. 25. **Torquato consule meo**: the Torquatus who was consul in 65 B.C., the year of Horace's birth. **move**: *bring down*, as in *Odes*, iii. 21. 6, (*testa*) *moveri digna bono die.*

7. cetera: *i.e.* all else except the pleasure of the passing hour. **mitte loqui**: a poetic periphrasis for a prohibition, as *Odes*, i. 38. 3, *mitte sectari.* **haec**: present cares and troubles. **benigna vice**: *with kindly change.*

8. reducet in sedem: *i.e.* shall bring to a happy ending. **Achaemenio**: Persian; see on *Odes*, iii. 1. 44.

9. perfundi: *to anoint oneself*; with middle force. **fide Cyllenea**: *i.e.* the lyre invented by Mercury, who was born on Mt. Cyllene, in Arcadia; *cf. Odes*, i. 10. 6; *fide* for *fidibus* is poetical.

11. nobilis Centaurus: Chiron, the teacher of a number of young heroes, among them Achilles. **grandi alumno**: *his tall foster-child*, *viz.* Achilles, who, as a hero, was of heroic stature. **cecinit**: here, as often, of prophetic utterance.

13. manet: *awaits.* **Assaraci tellus**: Troy; Assaracus was one of the Trojan kings.

14. findunt: *i.e.* flow through. **lubricus et**: for *et lubricus.*

15. reditum rupere: *have cut off thy return.* **certo subtemine**: *by fixed decree; subtemen* is properly the 'woof,' or the part woven into the warp of cloth.

16. mater caerula: the sea-nymph Thetis is called 'blue' from the color of the sea; see on *Odes*, i. 17. 20, *vitream Circen.*

17. illic: *viz.* at Troy.

18. alloquiis: here, *consolations.*

This epode exhibits Horace's first treatment of a theme with which he subsequently deals repeatedly in the *Odes.*

EPODE XIV.

1. imis sensibus: *over my inmost senses; sensibus* is dative of reference.

2. oblivionem: *viz.* of the promised poems; see below, line 7.

3. Lethaeos: *i.e.* such slumbers as are inspired by the waters of Lethe's stream. **ut si traxerim**: *as though I had drained;* for the postponement of *ut si*, see on *Odes*, i. 2. 5.

4. arente fauce: *i.e.* eagerly; the singular *fauce* is poetical.

5. candide: *noble.* **occidis saepe rogando**: *cf. Odes*, ii. 17. 1, *cur me querellis exanimas tuis?*

6. deus, deus: here the god of love, Cupid.

7. iambos: the reference is to the Book of *Epodes;* Introd. § 8.

8. ad umbilicum adducere: *to bring to completion.* In Horace's day, works of literature were written on long rolls of papyrus or parchment, the last page of which was at the extreme right-hand edge of the roll. To this outer edge was attached a wooden rod, about which the entire manuscript was then rolled. To the end of the rod was fastened a projecting knob, the *umbilicus* ('navel,' 'boss'). Thus, 'to bring to the knob' became equivalent to 'to bring to an end.'

9. **Samio Bathyllo**: some youth of whom Anacreon was enamoured. Anacreon spent some time at the court of Polycrates, king of Samos; for the ablative with *ardere*, *cf. Odes*, ii. 4. 7.

11. **flevit amorem**: 'sang of his love in plaintive strains.'

12. **non elaboratum ad pedem**: *in simple verse.*

13. **ureris ipse miser**: *i.e.* 'you yourself are a victim of the tender passion, and so can understand my distraction.' **non pulchrior ignis . . . Ilion**: 'if no fairer beauty kindled Troy (than kindles thee),' *i.e.* 'if even Helen was not fairer than thy present love.'

15. **gaude sorte tua**: implying that Maecenas's lot is happier than Horace's. **nec uno contenta**: Phryne has other lovers.

EPODE XV.

3. **numen laesura**: one offends the majesty of the gods by false swearing.

4. **in verba iurabas mea**: *iurare in verba* is to take oath according to a prescribed formula. So here Neaera is represented as plighting troth according to the form suggested by Horace at the time, and explained in lines 7–10.

5. **artius atque**: *more closely than.* **hedera adstringitur ilex**: *cf. Odes*, i. 36. 20, where likewise the clinging ivy is used as a symbol of fond devotion.

6. **adhaerens**: *sc. mihi.*

7. **dum**: *as long as.* **lupus**: *sc. esset infestus.* **Orīon**: for the supposed influence of Orion in bringing stormy weather, *cf. Odes*, i. 28 (2). 1.

8. **turbaret**: the secondary sequence is owing to the imperfect *iurabas.*

9. **intonsos . . . capillos**: Apollo was conceived as perpetually young; *cf.* i. 21. 2.

11. **virtute**: *manhood, manly resentment.*

12. **siquid viri**: *any manhood;* lit. *anything of the man.* **in Flacco** = *in Horatio.*

13. **potiori**: *to be a more favored rival;* as in iii. 9. 2, *nec quisquam potior.*

14. et: *but.* **parem** : *i.e.* a mate suited to him, one who will requite his love with faithful devotion.

15. nec . . . formae: 'nor, once offended, will his stern resolve yield to the charms of thy beauty'; *offensi* depends upon *eius*, to be understood with *constantia*.

16. si . . . dolor: 'if my resentment really rises'; the hypothetical statement seems to suggest that reconciliation is still possible.

17. et tu: the rival. **felicior**: as being *potior* (line 13).

19. sis dives licebit: *though thou be rich;* in prose we should have *licet*.

20. tibique Pactōlus fluat: *i.e.* 'and shouldst thou have the treasures of Midas,' whose fabulous wealth is said to have come from the golden sands of the Lydian river Pactōlus.

21. nec . . . arcana: *i.e.* 'and though thou knowest the inner mysteries of philosophy.' **renati**: Pythagoras owed his existence to his reincarnation.; see *Odes*, i. 28 (1). 10, *Panthoiden.*

22. Nirea: the fairest of all the Greeks that came to Troy; *cf.* iii. 20. 15.

23. translatos . . . amores: *i.e.* 'Neaera will prove faithless to thee as she has to me.' **alio**: adverb; *to another quarter.*

24. ast: archaic for *at.* **vicissim**: *i.e.* as thou laughest now in scorn at me. **risero**: the future perfect emphasizes the certainty of consummation; *cf.* 5. 102, *effugerit.*

EPODE XVI.

1. Altera aetas: *a second generation*, just as a previous one had been sacrificed in the civil dissensions between Marius and Sulla and their partisans.

3. quam: its antecedent is *eam*, to be supplied in thought as the object of *perdemus* in line 9. **finitimi Marsi**: alluding to the Social, or Marsian, War of 91–88 B.C.

4. Porsenae: who endeavored to secure the restoration of the Tarquins.

5. aemula virtus Capuae: after the disaster of Cannae, in 216 B.C., Capua had aspired to the supremacy of Italy, but was soon reduced to a Roman praefecture (211 B.C.). **Spartacus acer**: leader of the servile insurrection of 73–71 B.C.; see on *Odes*, iii. 14. 19.

6. novis rebus infidelis Allobrox: *the Allobroges faithless in* *time of revolution*, alluding to the collusion of the Allobroges with the Catilinarian conspirators. See Cicero's third speech against Catiline. The Allobroges at the time had long been subjects of Rome.

7. **nec fera**, *etc.*: *nor savage Germany with its blue-eyed hosts;* the reference is to the invasion of Roman territory by the Cimbrians and Teutons. These were overwhelmingly defeated by Marius and Catulus in 102 and 101 B.C.; *pube* is ablative of quality.

8. **parentibus abominatus**: *parentibus* is dative of agency; *abominatus* is used passively; *cf. Odes*, i. 1. 25, *detestata.*

9. **impia . . . aetas**: *we, an impious generation of accursed blood, i.e.* of accursed origin; *cf.* 7. 18, *scelus fraternae necis.*

11. **cineres insistet**: *insisto* is here used transitively, as occasionally in the poets. **urbem**: *i.e.* the ground on which the city stands.

12. **verberabit**: *shall trample.*

13. **quae ossa**: incorporation of the antecedent in the relative clause. **carent**, *etc.*: *i.e.* are in the tomb, and so protected from sun and wind. Porphyrio tells us that according to Varro the tomb of Romulus was behind the Rostra, in the Forum, or Comitium. The ordinary account represents Romulus as ascending to heaven.

14. **insolens**: *in wanton sport.*

15. **quod expediat**: a potential characterizing clause, — *a course that would be wise.* The antecedent of *quod* is *id*, to be understood in apposition with *carere laboribus.* **communiter**: virtually equivalent to a substantive, *omnes* or *universi.*

16. **malis laboribus**: our present woes. **carere quaeritis**: for the infinitive, *cf. Odes*, i. 37. 22, *perire quaerens.*

17. **sit**: jussive. **hac**: explained by the following *ire.* **sententia**: *resolve.* **Phocaeorum**: forced by the elder Cyrus to abandon Phocaea, its inhabitants registered a vow not to return till a mass of iron which they threw into the sea should rise to the surface.

18. **exsecrata**: *having cursed.*

21. **quocumque**: *i.e.* anything will be better than to remain here.

22. **protervos**: *cf. Odes*, i. 26. 2, *protervis ventis;* for the form, see Introd. § 34.

23. **sic placet, suadere**: like *sententia*, above in line 17, these are technical terms of legislative procedure, and as such lend impressiveness to the poet's utterance. **habet**: here in the sense of *potest;* Greek ἔχω is similarly used. **secunda alite**: *under happy auspices;* see on 10. 1, *mala alite.*

25. iuremus in haec: *sc. verba;* see on 15. 4, *in verba iurabas mea.* **simul imis**, *etc.*: *i.e.* let it not be lawful to return till Nature's laws are reversed; *simul* for *simul atque*, as often.

26. ne sit nefas: *i.e.* 'be it lawful.'

27. domum dare lintea: *spread our sails for home.*

28. Matina cacumina: Mt. Matīnus was a spur of Mt. Gargānus on the eastern coast of Apulia.

30. nova . . . libidine: *unite monsters in unnatural desire.*

31. iuvet ut = *ut iuvet*, — *so that tigers delight.*

32. adulteretur, *etc.*: *and the dove mates with the hawk*, its inveterate foe; *miluo* is ablative of association; Introd. § 38. *a.* For the trisyllabic form, *cf.* 13. 3, *siluae.* The word is regularly *milvos.*

33. credula: prolepsis.

34. levis hircus: *the smooth goat;* prolepsis. Horace means, 'when the shaggy goat shall lose his hair and become smooth like the fish of the sea.'

35. haec exsecrata: *i.e.* having made these solemn pledges sealed by curses.

37. aut: *or at least.* **indocili grege**: the common herd that knows no better and can learn no better. **mollis et exspes**: *sc. pars.*

39. vos: adversative asyndeton, — *but ye*, *i.e.* the *melior pars.* **tollite**: *away with!*

40. Etrusca praeter, *etc.*: *i.e.* 'and speed away from Italy.'

41. Oceanus circumvagus: the Homeric conception of Oceanus as a stream surrounding the circular disk of the earth.

42. arva, beata arva: *the fields, the joyous fields.* **divites insulas**: according to the mythical conception, the Happy Isles were the abode of heroes after death. Subsequently they were conceived as an idyllic land situated in the general vicinity of the Canary or the Madeira Islands.

46. suam . . . arborem: *and the ripe fig graces its native tree;* the emphasis rests upon *suam.* Ordinarily the fig required grafting and careful attention to insure a proper harvest. **pulla**: lit. *dark*, the color of the fig when ripe.

48. levis crepante, *etc.*: the repetition of the *l*-sound secures a happy suiting of the sound to the sense in this line.

50. tenta: *distended.* **amicus**: *i.e.* willingly, unbidden.

51. vespertinus: *at evening-tide.*

52. intumescit alta viperis: *swells high with vipers;* what is a peculiarity of the viper, is here attributed to the ground on which the viper lies.

53. ut : *how.*

54. arva radat : *lays waste the cornfields,* as often happened in Italy.

56. utrumque temperante : *governing both* (*extremes*), heat and rain.

57. non huc, *etc.* : *i.e.* the Happy Isles to which Horace calls his countrymen are as yet uncontaminated by the vices of human kind. **Argoo remige pinus** : *i.e.* no Argo with its crew; *pinus* is for *navis,* as often in the poets.

58. neque impudica Colchis : *nor shameless Colchian* (*sorceress*); *i.e.* no Medea; *cf.* 5. 24.

59. Sidonii : *Phoenician;* the Phoenicians were the most daring seamen of all antiquity, and so are cited as typical of maritime enterprise. **cornua** : lit. *yard-ends;* and so by metonymy for vessels.

60. laboriosa : transferred from *Ulixei* to *cohors; cf. Odes,* i. 15. 33, *iracunda classis Achillei,* 'the fleet of the wrathful Achilles.' **Ulixei** : for the form of the genitive, *cf. Odes,* i. 6. 7.

61. nullius astri aestuosa impotentia : *no star's blazing fury.* Phases of the weather were regularly attributed to the influence of the stars; *cf. Odes,* i. 28 (2). 1; iii. 1. 27. Note the shortening of the *i* in *nullius.* For the force of *impotentia, cf. Odes,* iii. 30. 3, *impotens.*

64. ut : *ever since;* so also in 7. 19, *ut fluxit.*

65. quorum secunda fuga : *a happy escape from which, viz.* from the present hardened generations.

66. vate me : *by my prophecy; vates* is here used in the sense of 'prophet'; the construction is ablative absolute. **datur** : *is offered.*

EPODE XVII.

1. Iam iam : *at length.* **do manus** : *I surrender.*

2. Proserpinae, Dianae : the divinities of the lower world were supposed to preside over magic rites.

3. non movenda numina : *the inviolable majesty.*

4. libros carminum, *etc.* : *books of incantations that can unfix the stars and call them down from heaven.*

6. Canidia : see *Epode* 5, 'Occasion of the Poem.' **parce** : *cease!* **vocibus sacris** : *thy magic spells.*

7. citum . . . turbinem : *turbo* is the magic wheel, whose revolution wrought the charm; reversing its movement was supposed to break the spell of the incantation. **citum**: participle of *cieo*, as in 9. 20; lit. *set in motion*, and so, *revolving*. **solve, solve**: the word is not exact, and betrays the agitation of the speaker, who, in his desire for release from torment, begs Canidia to release the wheel; *volve* would have been the correct word. For the repetition, *cf. Odes*, ii. 17. 10, *ibimus, ibimus*.

8. movit, *etc.*: reasons why Canidia should heed his prayer: 'Others have granted mercy; so mayst thou.' The *nepos Nereius* is Achilles, son of Thetis, Nereus's daughter. Telephus, king of the Mysians, wounded by Achilles, had been told by the oracle of Apollo that he could be healed only by the rust of Achilles's spear. He thereupon appealed to Achilles for succor, and the hero granted his request.

11. unxere, *etc.*: Horace says that the Ilian matrons anointed Hector's body after the king (Priam) had fallen at Achilles's feet, — a somewhat involved and obscure way of saying that Achilles, at Priam's entreaty, gave up Hector's dead body, thus enabling the Ilian matrons to anoint it preparatory to burning it on the funeral pyre. **addictum**: *given up to*.

12. homicidam Hectorem: a not especially felicitous rendering of the Homeric Ἕκτορα ἀνδροφόνον, 'the man-slayer Hector'; *homicida* means 'murderer.'

14. heu: with *rex procidit ad pedes Achillei*. **Achillei, Ulixei** (16): for the form of the genitive, see on *Odes*, i. 6. 7.

15 ff. Ulysses's comrades were changed back from swine to human forms by Circe, *i.e.* Circe relented and consented to restore Ulysses's men to human shapes. **saetosa,** *etc.*: *bristling with hardened skins*; *saetosa* limits *membra*. **exuere**: perfect indicative.

16. laboriosi: with *Ulixei*.

17. sonus = *vox*.

18. notus honor: *i.e.* their wonted dignity of feature.

20. amata nautis, *etc.*: *beloved of sailors and pedlers*; the mock compliment is full of scorn.

21. iuventas: *sc. mea*. **verecundus**: here in the sense of *rosy*.

22. ossa pelle, *etc.*: *i.e.* 'my bones are covered with a shrunken yellow skin.'

23. tuis: emphatic; the poet pretends to concede Canidia's sovereign power. **est**: *has become*. **odoribus**: *i.e.* her magic compounds.

24. ab labore me reclinat: *relieves me from torment*.

25. urget: *presses on the heels of.* **neque est**: *nor is it possible;* like the Greek οὐκ ἔστιν.

26. levare . . . praecordia: '*by taking breath to ease my sore-strained lungs*' (Bryce).

27. negatum: *etc.: I am forced to admit what I once denied.*

28. Sabella carmina: the Sabellian (Sabine) women were currently regarded as adepts in witchcraft. **increpare, dissilire**: in apposition with *negatum*.

29. Marsa nenia: *by Marsian incantation;* witchcraft flourished also among the *Marsi*, *cf.* 5. 76, *Marsis vocibus*, where also *Marsus* for *Marsicus*, as here.

31. atro delibutus, *etc.:* see note on 3. 17.

32. nec Sicana, *etc.: nor the live Sicilian flame in blazing Aetna.*

33. donec cinis . . . ferar: *i.e.* 'till I become dry ashes and be borne by the winds'; *ferar* is in the subjunctive, owing to the notion of expectancy involved in the *donec*-clause.

34. iniuriosis: as scattering the ashes and so preventing their interment.

35. cales, *etc.:* '*you're always heated up, a very factory of magic drugs*' (Bryce); *venenis* is ablative of means; on *Colchicis* = *magicis*, see on 5. 24.

36. quae finis: *finis* is here feminine, as in *Odes*, ii. 18. 30, *fine destinata.* **stipendium** = *poena.*

39. mendaci lyra: he wishes Canidia to understand *mendaci* as referring to his former utterances; in reality he uses the word with reference to his promised praises of her worth.

40. sonari = *laudari.*

41. perambulabis, *etc.: i.e.* 'I will represent thee as deified and as changed into a golden constellation.'

42. infamis: *reviled.* **vicem**: *on account of.*

44. adempta . . . lumina: the poet Stesichorus (630–555 B.C.) had reflected upon Helen's character in his verses. Castor and Pollux, in revenge for this insult to their sister's memory, were said to have stricken the poet with blindness. Later, moved by his recantation, they restored his sight — another illustration of clemency, like those above; even the gods, urges Horace, are not unrelenting.

46 f. The poet, with mock sincerity, pretends to be recanting former aspersions cast upon Canidia's lineage and practices, but the mock recantation is really but an effective repetition of the former charges. **O nec paternis obsoleta sordibus** : *O thou not stained by thy father's mean estate.*

47. nec in sepulcris, *etc.* : *and that art not a hag clever to scatter, etc.* **in sepulcris pauperum** : *among the graves of the poor.* The reference is to the graves in the Esquiline burial-ground, where the poor were interred, and where Canidia was in the habit of practising her incantations ; see on 5. 100, and *cf. Sat.* i. 8.

48. novendiales dissipare pulveres: *to scatter funeral ashes, i.e.* ashes that she had stolen from the graves of the dead.

49. hospitale: *kindly.*

50. tuosque venter Pactumeius: *and Pactumeius is a child of thine;* the emphasis rests upon *tuos*, as it does also upon *tuo* in *tuo cruore.* Horace implies that he had previously denied Canidia's maternity of the child ; he now recants.

52. utcumque fortis, *etc.*: *whenever you bound forth a lusty young mother.* The description suggests that Canidia recovers too quickly from childbed to warrant the belief that she has really been confined.

53. quid obseratis, *etc.*: Canidia speaks.

54. non saxa, *etc.*: Horace's way of putting the thought obscures the logical perspective. He means: 'Not deafer to the cries of helpless sailors are the cliffs that Neptune beats, than I to thine.'

56. inultus ut, *etc.*: *thou unpunished to have divulged and ridiculed the Cotytian rites!* a so-called 'repudiating question,' *i.e.* a question whose form implies that the speaker emphatically repudiates its content. It is a further development of the deliberative. The Cotytian rites were celebrated in honor of a Thracian goddess named Cotytto. Women only were admitted to the ceremonial. Canidia here implies that Horace had secretly attended the celebration of the rites, and had then spread the account among his friends.

57. sacrum liberi Cupidinis: *the festival of unbridled love;* in apposition with *Cotytia.* The *Cotytia* were extremely licentious.

58. Esquilini pontifex venefici: *director of the Esquiline witchcraft.* Canidia taunts him with assuming power to regulate the practice of witchcraft, just as the *pontifex* regulated matters of religion.

60. quid proderit: *i.e.* 'if I cannot punish thee.' **ditasse . . anus**: *i.e.* to have paid them for the secret of their arts. The Paelignians, like the neighboring Marsians, were adepts in sorcery.

61. velocius: *i.e.* working swiftly, —*potent.* It does not mean 'fatal,' but simply 'effective.' **toxicum** : *potion.*

62. sed tardiora, *etc.*: *i.e.* 'thou shalt long for death.'

63. in hoc: *for this purpose*; explained by the *ut*-clause.

64. novis usque laboribus: *for torments ever fresh*; dative of purpose. **ut suppetas**: *that thou mayst be ready.*

65. optat quietem, *etc.*: *desires respite from his perpetual longing for the bounteous feast.* Canidia introduces a series of examples of men subjected to torment for their misdeeds, in order to intimate to Horace that his own sufferings will be like theirs. **Pelopis infidi**: he had hurled into the sea Myrtilus, the charioteer by whose help he had won the chariot race and secured the hand of Hippodamīa, the daughter of Oenomaus, king of Elis.

67. obligatus aliti: see on *Odes*, ii. 13. 37.

68. supremo: poetic for *summo.* **Sisyphus**: see on *Odes*, ii. 14. 20.

69. vetant leges Iovis: *i.e.* they forbid the impious to escape the penalty of their sins.

70. modo . . . modo: *now . . . now.*

71. ense Norico: *cf. Odes*, i. 16. 9 and note.

72. vincla: *the noose.*

73. fastidiosa tristis aegrimonia: '*sad with loathing weariness*' (Page).

74. umeris: *sc. tuis.* **eques**: *as a rider.*

75. meae insolentiae: *to my unexampled might.* Nothing can withstand her magic power.

76. an quae, *etc.*: *or am I, who, etc.* The antecedent of *quae* is the subject of *plorem* in line 81. **movere cereas imagines possim**: *am able to influence wax images.* In *Sat.* i. 8, Canidia is represented as practising her arts on waxen images representing the persons whom she aimed to influence.

77. ut ipse nosti curiosus: in *Sat.* i. 8, Horace describes certain of Canidia's incantations. Hence Canidia characterizes him as *curiosus*, *a prying meddler.*

79. crematos excitare mortuos: *i.e.* to call up the shades of those who have died and whose bodies have been burned.

80. desideri . . . pocula: *i.e.* to mix love-potions; *cf.* 5. 38, *amoris poculum.*

81. plorem artis, *etc.*: *must I lament the failure of my craft, ineffective in the case of thee (alone)? Exitus*, literally 'outcome,' is a so-called *vox media.* It may mean either a good outcome ('success') or a bad outcome ('failure'). It has the latter meaning here.